EAGLE PASS

by

Stephen T. Gerdel

Eagle Pass

Book Two
The Oak Mountain Trilogy
By Stephen T. Gerdel

Published by Watershed Inc.
524 Olympus
Cedar Hill, TX 75104
www.watershedarts.com

Edited by Beth Swoboda

Cover design by Katy Tapley

ISBN 978-0-9814541 2-2

EAGLE PASS

BOOK TWO

The Oak Mountain Trilogy

by

Stephen T. Gerdel

List of Main Characters

Yolanda Vasquez	Hotel maid who discovered assassin's body
Baktir Jussein	Leader of invasion army in Dallas
Mike Trapper	Special agent to the president
Elli Trapper	Mike Trapper's wife
Preston Marshall	Husband of President Harriet Marshall
President Al Makin	Vice-president for Harriet Marshall
Aaron Stevens	Commanding officer at Little Rock OCT
Keith Dillon	Office of Counter Terrorism technician
Barry Goldstein	White House security technician
Steve Granger	Marine captain and best friend to Mike Trapper
Samantha Long	State department weapons expert and negotiator
Alvaro Herrera	Leader of invasion army in Los Angeles
Gene Westrup	Brigadier general, Camp Pendleton, CA
Rachel Jones	CIA officer turned terrorist aka Mother
John Michaels	Sergeant major of security at Camp Pendleton
Bill Jenkins	Lieutenant colonel in Marine reserves
Beatrice Vasquez	Yolanda Vasquez's mother
Alex Hodson	FBI, Washington D.C.
Ray Jergins	Department of Justice, Washington D.C.
Jim Parker	Lieutenant sniper, Dallas Marine reserve unit
Perry Hitchens	Sheriff in Cleveland County, TX
Robert Hitchens	Sheriff Perry Hitchens's son
Rick Johnston	Secret Service agent Washington, D.C.
George Raker	Secret Service agent Washington, D.C.
Angela Crain	Department of Homeland Security
Bill Ketcham	Secret Service, Surveillance and Intelligence
Lt. Mark Strattmann	Officer at Main Gate, Camp Pendleton, CA
Jalal Uddin bin Kahmir al-Ahmad	Egyptian ambassador
Travis Temple	Lifelong friend of Sheriff Perry Hitchens
Ilo Campbell	Owner of Denney's Lounge and Restraunt
Yusef	Lead assassin at Grey Horse Farm
Bob Meeks	Corporal with Dallas Marine reserve unit
Donald Stewart	Retired director of Secret Service

This book is dedicated
To my best friend
And beloved wife,

Jan

who with remarkable
patience endured my
long nights,
re-writes,
and
at the end of it all
still loved me.

chapter 1

Eagle Pass, TX, US/Mexico Border, Wednesday 9:30 AM CST

The two border guards sat quietly in their small station, watching the beginnings of the coverage of the presidential funeral in Washington DC. It was distant to them, something that happened back East and had virtually no effect on their daily routine.

The day, filled by the news of the funeral, would pre-empt the baseball game they had looked forward to watching. As a result of the funeral, border crossings from Mexico had been few, with only two of the five lanes open.

The quiet day left them with the feeling of a holiday that still required them to work. It was almost a holiday. The two guards shared it as their private joke.

Another private joke they shared was the reason they imagined for two massive snowplows on the Mexico side. Everyone knew they were not expecting snow, at least in the measure those behemoths were equipped to move. Jokes regarding their purpose ranged from sand storms to effectively dealing with the regulatory border bull from Washington. What was not noticed that morning was the ancient military tank placed between the two snowplows, with its 50 mm cannon aimed directly at the guard stations. One of the two guards saw the odd shape between the now familiar plow blades. Just as he thought to mention it, the barrel exploded directly at him. In less than a second, before there was time to figure it out, the guard station disintegrated with the force of the explosion.

Immediately the giant snowplows moved forward. If traffic had been heavy like most other mornings, every car and truck would have been shoved to the side. The two massive plows quickly made a path through the debris from the guard station.

Behind the giant plows, three-thousand Mexican militants, accompanied by eight-hundred Mid-Eastern militiamen, streamed into south Texas. The scene was repeated at every border crossing from Laredo to Tijuana. The invasion had begun.

Dallas Police Department, 8500 Stemons Freeway, Dallas, TX 9:40 AM CST

Yolanda Vasquez sat down at the desk of Sergeant Peter Ricketts and began reading the official statement. It was the account she gave of the discovery of the body at the Radisson Hotel early Monday morning. Her hands shook as she held the pages. Her mouth was dry and she wanted to leave.

Yolanda had begun her tasks as a maid at the hotel when she discovered a body. It was believed to be the body of the man who assassinated the president of the United States Sunday afternoon. He was lying face-down in a pool of blood. Even after forty-eight hours she could not remove the image from her mind.

The door to the squad room burst open. Automatic gunfire ripped the walls, desks, and occupants. Yolanda spun around too fast and toppled her chair. She crashed to the floor. Still holding the papers, she quickly slid from the chair and hid under the desk.

Sergeant Ricketts ran from the file room, reaching for his handgun. Before his weapon was fully drawn, a single slug struck him in the forehead. He fell forward and crashed to the floor right in front of Yolanda, his eyes staring blankly.

Yolanda buried her face in her hands praying the whole thing would stop. But the bullets flew and the bloodshed continued. The return fire was slight by comparison.

After ten minutes of the hellish outburst, the mayhem stopped. Yolanda stayed motionless under the desk. She sobbed silently, attempting to pull herself together while trying to decide her next move. She stuffed the papers into her purse as quietly as she could.

In the distance she heard voices. Men's voices. The men were speaking Spanish. Her mind raced as the voices grew louder. She knew they would find her.

The thought of capture terrified her. Yolanda began to sob out loud. She could not make it stop. Suddenly two men with large automatic weapons peered under the desk.

"Please! Please! Don't shoot me!" Yolanda cried in Spanish. "Please don't kill me!"

The two men reached under the desk and dragged her out.

"What are you doing there?" one demanded. "Why are you here?"

"It was a speeding ticket. That is all!" Yolanda lied. "They said I was speeding! I was not! I tried to tell them, but they would not listen!"

"Do you expect me to believe that?" one man roared at her.

"Please! That is why I came here. I was not speeding! I only want to go home! Please!" Yolanda was shaking in terror. Now the tears were streaming down her face.

"We are going to kill you like the rest of the gringo pigs! You are their whore! You deserve to die for serving them!" The second man raised his gun and pointed it directly at her face.

"No! Please!" Yolanda cried. "Please don't kill me!"

"Ramirez!" A third voice came from behind her. It was the voice of Baktir Hussein, the unit's self-appointed colonel and unquestioned leader. "Can't you see, you idiot? This woman is not in a uniform! Do you see a weapon on her? What kind of an animal are you?"

The grip the two men held on Yolanda's arms relaxed. They let her go. Their anger melted into brutish confusion. The men stepped away from her.

Colonel Baktir Hussein was a killer. He was raised Muslim but abandoned his faith years ago. Spilled blood was no longer the horror it once was. Good Muslims detest the sight of blood. Baktir had learned to relish the sight, especially the blood of Americans.

Colonel Hussein entered the room. "Don't you two know how gringos torment your women? Remember? We are not here to kill your sisters and brothers or mothers and fathers."

He looked around at the eleven officers, both men and women, who lay dead at their workstations. His eyes sparkled with delight. Death was a justified end for these infidels. But he lamented that these found death so quickly.

His eyes locked on Yolanda. The sparkle vanished from his eyes and chilled to a hard gaze of hate.

"I can see she is not a gringo." He walked to Yolanda and gently stroked her cheek with his hand. She trembled at his touch.

"You are not a gringo, are you?" He could have crushed the life out of her with his bare hands. Through his stare he caressed her soft skin gently as he leered with a sick, twisted smile.

"No, sir, I am not even here legally," she replied softly turning her eyes to the floor.

"See, my brothers? Save your wrath for the gringos. Think of the fat, pasty white women just waiting for your anger to visit them." He smiled at his twisted thoughts. The other two men smiled and laughed.

When he turned to Yolanda his smile vanished.

"Now, get out of here while I am in a good humor!"

She quickly moved past the men and ran for the front door.

Sheriff's Office, Lubbock County, TX – 9:33 AM CST

The doors to the sheriff's main office at the courthouse burst open. Within seconds twenty-eight well-armed men ran through them, shooting everyone they found.

The seven deputies just completing their night shifts were finishing their reports at their desks, their side-arms holstered. They never had a chance. Four more officers were preparing to answer a domestic call. Hearing the shots, they ran toward the main office with weapons drawn. Automatic weapon fire cut them down.

The leader of the assault quickly rummaged through the slain sheriff's desk and found the names and addresses of the men and women not scheduled for work that morning. They would be pursued in their homes and properly dealt with. Three-man teams were dispatched to eliminate them and any family members they found.

Twenty-eight men, well trained in combat, became an assault force that matched the existing roster man for man. The weaponry was the overwhelming factor. Uzis, shotguns, fully and semi-automatic rifles were considered minimal issue.

For years, the agents of Zetas, employed by the drug cartels and fanatical groups opposing American influence in Central and South America, had been smuggled across the porous US border. The agents established themselves in communities throughout the Southwest.

As illegal aliens, no one bothered them because they would do the work that most American high school kids would no longer do. The "Mexicans," identified only because of their darker skin color, were known as hard workers who did an excellent job for a minimal wage.

In fact, many of the nearly twelve million within the U.S. borders were hard working, sincere people. But in their midst lived the agents of many loosely affiliated gangs: La Raza; Tres Puntos; Los Toros; Vagos; Sombras, and many others. The two main alliances, La Gran Raza and La Gran Familia, joined in a common purpose under the leadership of La Orden.

Funding was made possible by La eMe and Mara Salvatrucha, Mexican and Salvadorian mafia groups, joined with Al Qaeda in their world-wide quest. Now more than two-hundred and twenty thousand strong in the States, they were well armed and trained for a purpose.

That purpose began today. The day of the funeral for the president of the United States of America, slain three days earlier by their fellow warrior, was the call to arms. The failure to contaminate the Eastern Seaboard with radiation from the Oak Mountain power plant was a disappointment, but it did not break their resolve.

The border between Mexico and the United States was eliminated in a matter of minutes, as was every law enforcement officer in Southern California, Nevada, Arizona, New Mexico and Southwest Texas. The task at hand was to subdue the arrogant protests of the local whites, enlist the oppressed black and brown populations, and kill anyone who stood against them.

The greedy Americans had taken too much. It was time for payback.

Grey Horse Farm, New Salisbury, Kentucky – 10:35 AM EST

Mike and Elli sat on the porch. The children had attacked and tackled Mike after he jumped from the helicopter that brought him from the White House. By now their interests had returned to taking a ride on Granddad's pony. The laughter and squeals of delight echoed from the far side of the barn as the party raged on.

Elli pulled close to Mike's side. The quiet morning took her back to her childhood, and the mornings of adventure she and her sister shared. She was delighted to see her children find the same excitement.

Mike was tense. She could tell by the tightness of his muscles, his speech, that he was distracted by the events of the night before. She was not surprised. She wanted him to have the time he needed to unload and then relax.

Elli knew he would pour out the details of his night of terror. She had learned through the years the details would come when he was ready. For now, she was happy he was with her. They were together and nothing could happen to disrupt this amazing morning.

"Are you two gonna sit there and cuddle all morning, or can I get some help with these peas?" Elli's mom had chores to be done. The day was pressing on, and there was no use wasting it.

"Well?" Mom said.

"Do you have any idea how long it's been since I have snapped peas?" Mike said with a huge smile on his face.

"Since God made dirt?" Elli asked.

"Actually, it was shortly after that," Mike kidded. They both jumped up from the swing and went to the table Elli's mom kept on the porch for such tasks. Spring days were incomplete without garden work of some kind. Great painters labored to capture such scenes. Happy family faces enjoying the pursuit of life, unaware of what life was about to bring upon them.

chapter 2

Sumas BC, US/Canada Border, Wednesday, 7:30 AM PST

The guard walked casually to the red Toyota that pulled under the canopy at the crossing station. No hurry. Everyone in line could wait. There were only three cars. The family in the van would get wherever they were going in plenty of time. The four coeds in the Jeep behind them were probably up to no good anyway.

The alarm had jarred him awake at five a.m. He hated that alarm. He hated waking up alone. Still, he made his way to work by six with too little sleep, and too much on his mind.

The border guard pulled a clean information sheet from the back of the case and clipped it to the writing surface. The man in the car was smiling at him. The border guard was glad to have a friendly customer.

"Welcome to the United States. Are you traveling today for business or pleasure?" he asked. *Why the hell are you smiling with that cheesy grin, you slime ball?* he thought.

The driver of the car calmly raised his sunglasses and said, "Welcome to hell!"

The detonation of three satchel charges on the backseat of the Toyota decimated every living thing within a hundred feet. A single satchel charge carried 20 pounds of explosives. It was commonly used to level an entire house in Iraq creating a pressure wave traveling 26,400 feet per second, the same speed required by the space shuttle to obtain orbit.

In that split second the Toyota and the border guard were incinerated. The family in the mini-van was blown to pieces. The Jeep filled with coeds was thrown back thirty feet landing on its top crushing the occupants.

The sound of large diesel engines roared from the back of the line of rubble. The twisted and broken vehicles mounded against each other and slid to the side of the road. The giant snowplows moved through the rubble with ease.

Teams of heavily armed men followed the plows, hundreds of them. The men had arrived the day before inside several semi-trailers that had parked with other trailers waiting to be shipped into the United States. They had waited patiently inside the trailers. Timing was very important to the mission ahead.

Their mission was the same as those in the south: search, kill and destroy. They had trained for over two years in the remote regions of the Northwest Territory, and assembled quietly at the news of the assassination in St. Louis.

The advance teams had crossed the border Monday morning and gathered the cells of warriors scattered throughout the region. Many were born in the States and raised in preparation for jihad. Others had immigrated through Mexico during the past several years, gradually working their way north to their assigned territory.

Finally, the call had come, one that had been long awaited. Their time had not been wasted. The training they had received was world class. Their weapons were powerful, large caliber, and fully automatic.

The advance teams hit the local police and sheriff departments at the same time the border stations exploded. The planning, as in the south, was one officer to one warrior. The difference was that all the warriors were on the move while only a portion of the officers were on duty. The officers were quickly eliminated. Off-duty officers were then hunted and killed.

The trucks, filled with armed men pursued a demanding time-table, as they sped through the border crossing. Sumas has been chosen as a crossing point over White Rock twenty-two miles to the west due to the larger rail yard and the smaller border complex. Large semis were inconspicuous among the containers waiting to be loaded.

Once across the border, dozens of semis roared along Highway 9 and East Badger Road. It was a twelve-mile trip to meet the advance teams that crossed through White Rock only twenty minutes before. The advance teams set up road blocks by simply shooting anyone who happened by. The way was clear for the advancing convoy.

After the turn south onto Guide Meridian road, it was another twelve miles to Interstate 5. From there, it was a straight shot to Seattle and their primary target. Local police and state troopers were meeting the same end as those along the southern border. The elimination of law enforcement was nearly complete in Bellingham, and well underway in Everett before the convoy got to the Interstate.

Jihad did not require mercy. Jihad is justice for the non-Muslim, and the duty of every true follower. It is Allah's will. Quick and final justice.

The Capitol, Washington DC – 10:45 AM EST

The coffin bearing the body of President Harriet Marshall was carried reverently down the Capitol steps by a six-man military honor guard. At the top step the Marine band began to play "Hail to the Chief." No other sound was heard. Thousands stood in silence as the honor guard completed their drill flawlessly

The caisson drawn by six white horses with three riders waited at the bottom of the Capitol steps. The honor guard gently placed the coffin in the caisson and stepped back smartly.

Preston Marshall and his two children stood silently waiting for the procession to begin. President Al Makin stood with Preston, along with members of Congress, and foreign dignitaries. The only sounds were the soft commands of the honor guard and the shuffling of the horses' hooves on the pavement.

At the silent command of Army Major General William B. Evans the procession began. Major General Evans escorted Preston Marshall and the two children to their position following the caisson. The route was just over a mile and a half down Pennsylvania Avenue, across 14th Street NW, and then to the church on 16th Street NW.

St. John's Episcopal Church is known as the Church of the Presidents, since every president had attended services at one time or another as a tradition of sorts. But for the Marshall family, it had become a very specific and deliberate tradition. They had made St. John's their church home.

The street along the route was lined with tens of thousands of mourners. Most stood silently. Many wept. The sense of loss was palpable. In spite of the clear blue sky and bright sun, the mood was one of intense sorrow. Sorrow only made bearable by the strength shown by Preston Marshall.

Preston stood to his full height, shoulders squared and his back straight. His son stood on his right and held his hand. His daughter, who reminded Preston so much of her mother, firmly grasped his left. The family had been through a great deal together, and today would be no different. The day unwanted and unexpected, but as always, they would endure it together.

Dallas PD, 8500 Stemons Freeway, Dallas TX – 9:50 AM CST

Yolanda ran from the police station in terror. The scene of mayhem and death would not leave her mind, the sound of automatic gun fire rang in her ears. Her hands shook as she fumbled with the keys to unlock her car.

"Go in the lock!" she said out loud. "Go in!"

Panic held her in its grip. Everything was spinning. She could not believe what she had seen and heard. She could not erase it from her thoughts.

Finally, the key slipped into the lock on the door handle. Yolanda threw the door open and fell into the front seat of her car. Her hands were shaking. She wasn't sure she could drive. She just knew she had to get away from there. The engine roared to life, and the tires squealed as she raced from the curb.

"What just happened? What was that?" Yolanda yelled as she rubbed her face realizing tears were running down her cheeks. "That was insane! They killed them!" She held her hand tightly over her mouth trying to control the sobs that racked her body.

Slowly, her thoughts began to clear. She knew she would need to leave. She could not afford a chance encounter with those men. Not after what she had seen. The next time they saw her, they would kill her. She was certain of that.

"I've got to get Mama and go. Where can we go? Where?" She fanned herself with her hand. She no longer tried to stop the tears. She wanted to scream. She wanted to run.

The plan that dropped into her mind surprised her. It was very clear. In one instant, she saw it all.

Yolanda gripped the steering wheel with both hands, her knuckles were white. Her teeth were set, and her dark eyes burned with a fire of determination. She was going to run. She would run hard and fast out of this town. There was no time to waste. She had to go. Now!

Office of Counter Terrorism, Little Rock, AR – 9:55 AM CST

Colonel Aaron Stevens walked down the hall to his office at OCT, still tired from three days of intense investigative work. His team had done an amazing job. They had a couple of lucky breaks that enabled them to prevent the explosion of the nuclear reactors at Oak Mountain, but the loss was still great.

Sixty Marines and the crews of the three helicopters gave their lives in the attempt to stop the terrorists. However, the enemy had received advance warning of their approach, and those three choppers never stood a chance. Betrayal had come from the highest levels of the government. One could only guess who the traitor in the White House might be.

Aaron's five hours of sleep was enough. He dreamed about the investigation and the details they had sorted. He woke feeling he hadn't stopped reviewing and analyzing information, even in his sleep. But he had slept. He was ready.

Folders and papers from the last three days swamped his desk. Today he needed to complete his report then get everything scanned and e-mailed to Washington. The prospect of shuffling paper for the next ten hours was something of a relief.

"Colonel Stevens?" He hadn't even sat down.

It was Keith Dillon his surveillance team leader. The look on his face was too familiar. A look Aaron was not pleased to see.

"What is it, Keith?"

"Sir, we aren't sure," Keith began. "It seems that virtually every DHS First Response unit in the southwest has gone off-line. We didn't receive any log-ins or alert statuses. It's like they're all turned off."

Since September 11th great measures had been taken to improve communications across the country between local, state, and federal law enforcement. The simplest and most effective was the requirement that every office of law enforcement log-in to a DHS website at specified times. It was low profile, not really secret, but intentionally kept from becoming public information.

With a completed log-in, the server at OCT would register that department. Without a log-in, an alert status was registered, other departments were notified and required to investigate. If conditions were normal, a simple acknowledgement of someone present was sufficient.

But to have no one log-in was unusual. The lack of response from hundreds of departments was cause for concern.

"Have you talked with the guys in DC about the computer virus they've been fighting?" Aaron was hoping for the simple fix. He already knew Keith would have suspected the spread of the infection.

"I did that first," Keith replied. "I called Barry Goldstein's office and they told me they had been able to confine the virus to the northeast quadrant. I think the better part of New England and most of the Atlantic seaboard is off-line for a while. They've never seen such an aggressive virus."

"Yeah, let's hope we don't see it again, ever!" Aaron's thoughts were rapidly reviewing what protocols might need implementation. "Did you call anyone?"

"Not yet. This thing is just a few minutes old. I mean, we're what, ten to fifteen minutes past sign-in?" Log-in times varied every day.

"Right," Aaron replied, checking his copy of the schedule. "Check Wichita, Oklahoma City, and Dallas, and see what you get. Surely someone out there can help us."

Keith nodded and walked briskly from Aaron's office. Aaron turned to his desk and the piles of loose leaf and folders that would consume his day. He sighed and dug in, hoping a day of boring paperwork was before him.

Crescent Beach, VA - 11:00 AM EST

Steve Granger wasn't sure if he was awake or dreaming. His left calf ached. The drugs helped, but they didn't completely remove the discomfort. However, the other comfort he was receiving almost nullified the effects of the gunshot wound.

The soft breeze from the beach gently brushed the morning with a hint of honeysuckle. The smell of the ocean would mix in and suddenly overwhelm the fragrance of the small blossoms. Then, there was Sam.

He could smell her skin. He could feel the warmth of her body, and the softness of her touch. No one ever touched him like that. He was convinced her fingers were magic. Where ever she touched him, she soothed him. She *was* magic.

Samantha Long sat in the wicker swing with Steve's head cradled in her lap. She stroked his forehead, and toyed with his wavy hair. Neither of them spoke. For now, words were set aside. Their words had caused them both much pain in days past.

Sam and Steve had spent more time in the past three years either arguing or living apart, than they enjoyed together. The last several hours were different. There was a fresh sense the two might find common ground. Maybe, just maybe, there was hope.

The night before, at Oak Mountain Nuclear Power Plant, Sam watched Steve bravely charge, without hesitation, into a fight against terrorists. When he was shot and she saw him fall to the ground, her heart stopped. In that split second, in a moment's time, Sam feared the loss of the one man she loved.

Her immediate reflex was to draw down on the shooter, and with a single shot to his head, drop him from twenty-five yards. *Nobody does that and gets away with it!* she thought.

Since that moment they remained together. They spoke just the right number of words. They admitted to each other where they stood, and where they knew they were wrong. It is written that "love covers a multitude of sins." In that time, Sam and Steve discovered a new and personal meaning of those words.

chapter 3

LAPD, Los Angeles, CA - 8:05 AM PST

The assault was the same, the effect decisive. The result was many dead and dying police men and women. To the assailants, it was a matter of war, where mercy had no place. The only objective was victory. They had talked and negotiated for a long time, and it gained them nothing. Gringos, infidels, names meant nothing. The killers would subjugate or eliminate all of them.

"Are all of them out of there yet?" Alvaro Herrera entered the police station after the shooting stopped. His advance team of four hundred and thirty three took control of two separate police stations, killing everyone inside, and hunting down every off-duty officer attached to the departments.

"*Si,* Colonel Herrera. They are just taking the last ones out now." *The last ones* were the bodies of the police killed in the onslaught. The wounded were kept in one of the offices for interrogation and execution. If there was no information to be gathered from a survivor, they were shot.

"Good. I need someone to clean this office out for me. I will operate from here." Colonel Herrera was a strong commander and tolerated no slack from his men. If he was not obeyed, his wrath was immediate and final. During training, he had killed several men who exhibited the American trait of talking back. None of it was tolerated.

Immediately, five young warriors entered the office to carry out his command. Since he didn't read English, all the papers were discarded and the desk swept clean. The telephones were returned to their proper positions and chairs set upright.

In the corner of the office, the television silently displayed the events in Washington. The procession moved slowly through the streets lined with thousands of mourning Americans. Alvaro sneered.

"Those fools!" he said and spat at the screen. "They act like they are mourning for their woman president. They have not begun to understand what it is to mourn." He hated gringos. He watched the bodies as they were carried from the station. It gave him renewed pride in his Mexican heritage. His father, his grandfather, and for many generations before, his family had lived with insults from the pasty, white gringos.

Some gringo was always the boss, and treated Mexican workers like animals. Gringos showed no respect. Even those who bothered to learn the language spoke Spanish poorly and sounded stupid.

Colonel Herrera slowly walked behind the desk and sat in the chair freshly cleaned of the blood spilled by its former occupant. The five soldiers quickly finished cleaning and left the office. He leaned back in the chair watching the scenes in Washington.

"Is there anything else I may do for you, *Senor?*" The question was timid, and if taken wrong, could lead to a harsh punishment. But leaving it unasked was a much greater error.

"Make coffee. Strong coffee," was the gruff reply. Colonel Alvaro Herrera had work to do. It was time to call his fellow officers and learn of their success. And for that, he would need coffee.

St. John's Episcopal Church, Washington DC – 11:15 AM EST

The pace of the funeral entourage was on schedule but painfully slow. The TV anchors talked softly about the fallen president, her family, the nation, and how the country had come together. There was nothing of substance, or what might be called news in what they said. They were simply filling the time between events.

Occasionally, some explanation was required for those unfamiliar with Washington, such as interesting tidbits of what the caisson was passing. They made comments about historical events that had taken place in one building or another. Cameos of celebrities were scattered among the bystanders. This day would be noted in history as one of the darkest for the nation. It was quiet, solemn, and a little boring.

The procession halted in front of St. John's. The military pall bearers moved into place with precision. The casket was reverently removed from the caisson, and then carried with great ceremony into the church. The Marshall family followed the casket into the church that was filled to capacity straining the capabilities of the security teams.

Harriet and her husband had decided months before, shortly after she had secured the nomination. Quietly and privately, they had gone over the details. Details and decisions they hoped would forever rest undisturbed and unused.

The guests who walked with the family of the president followed them into the building to their reserved seats. No one spoke a word. Some nodded and smiled slightly to a familiar face or fellow politician. The only sounds were the shuffling of hundreds of feet moving down the aisle, the creaking of the pews as mourners seated themselves, and the organ playing Bach.

Finally, the last person was seated, and the organ fell silent. The Rev. Gerald Welsby, senior pastor, quietly rose from his seat and walked to the pulpit. The Marshall family attended services as regularly as possible for a president. They counted Rev. Welsby as a friend. The pastor's face was pale and solemn. He gazed over the congregation and began reading the 23rd Psalm.

Crescent Beach, VA - 11:20 AM EST

"Are you awake?" Sam's voice broke into Steve Granger's semi-conscience dream.

"Not sure. Are you real or part of my dream?" He smiled and kissed her. "Did you make coffee already?" Steve propped himself up on his elbows, and squinted at the sunlight breaking though the half drawn shade. "Are you gonna force me to drink that stuff?"

Sam smiled as she sat on the bed beside him. She knew he loved coffee, especially her coffee.

"Nope. This is mine. You'll have to get up and get your own if you want any." She couldn't help herself as she began to laugh.

Steve reached for her arm, nearly spilling the steamy cup.

"Hey! Wait a minute! This is for you, really!" Sam managed to get the coffee cup onto the nightstand beside the bed before Steve wrestled her into his arms. This was right. This was the way it was supposed to be.

"I wanted to ask you something," Steve began through a broad grin. "When did it change for you? I mean, when did *this* make sense?"

Sam looked down. That moment of change was both shocking and difficult for her to address. She sat up straight and looked directly into his eyes.

"When you got hit." Tears welled up in her eyes. She didn't attempt to stop them. "All the time you were in Iraq that was the one thing I couldn't bear to think might happen to you. I did all this positive thinking crap, you know, Steve's fine, he'll be alright, he's got to come home safe and unhurt. Then, you did."

Sam sniffed, grabbed a tissue, and blew her nose. She turned back to him and shrugged her shoulders.

"You came home just fine. You looked great. I could hardly believe it when you walked in." Sam was working hard to not blubber.

Steve reached out and gently touched her cheek.

"And all of a sudden, the very thing I dreaded the whole time you were in Iraq happened right before my eyes!"

"Honey, nothing bad happened. I'm fine." Steve said.

"And when that bastard shot you, I don't know, I couldn't believe it, I couldn't let that just go by! I thought, no! It was all in slow motion. I drew up my pistol, and it was like I could see the bullet hit him before I pulled the trigger! It was the strangest thing."

Sam looked at Steve. He was smiling. "Do you know what I mean? I mean, how did that happen?"

"I *do* know what you mean. I've seen it many times," Steve replied sitting cross-legged on the bed.

"So, that's not weird?" Sam asked.

"No, baby." He pulled her into his arms. "I mean, well, shooting somebody with a handgun at twenty-five yards and dropping them with a single shot is a little weird, but not the rest." He turned her face to his.

"Really?" Now Sam was getting a little blubbery. But this time it was okay. There was no pretense, no more walls. This time, blubbering was fine.

Sam buried her face into Steve's shoulder and sobbed. It was cleansing for her and she didn't hold back. He held her. Minutes passed without measure.

Finally, Sam sat up and looked at Steve through tear-reddened eyes. She knew she looked a mess, but she didn't care.

"Okay, what about you? When did it change for you?" Sam sniffled.

"I have to admit, it was at that very same moment. When you scolded me for getting shot, and then shot the other guy instead of me, I knew we had a fighting chance." Steve smiled and they both broke into laughter.

Sam pulled herself close to Steve and clung to him. "This is right. This is what I've always dreamed about. I could stay right here with you and never need another thing. This is enough."

Their moment, this special quiet moment, was interrupted by two cell phones ringing simultaneously on the kitchen table.

Grey Horse Farm, New Salisbury, Kentucky – 11:25 AM EST

Mike had hopped from the helicopter nearly an hour ago. The nightmare of the battle at Oak Mountain Nuclear Power Plant had left him exhausted. The loss of life was the greatest he had experienced in any of his commands. And, that loss had been inflicted by only a few. But he felt the real fear of how many more seeking to do harm might arise.

Mike was satisfied and frustrated that those causing the damage were all dead. He was satisfied from a point of simple vendetta and frustrated because he felt he would never learn who sent them.

Mike put the previous night out of his mind. The sight of his children running to him across the field worked its magic. Buried in their loving tackle, he felt a thankfulness that was new and deep. Then, there was Elli.

Mike had loved her from the first smile. It was one of those things he just knew. That's her. She's the one. Issue settled. He set his heart and mind at that first smile to win her, and he had done exactly that.

Although she was hesitant at first, Elli had grown to love this strong and patient man. In him she saw the strength she had always loved in her father and the gentleness of her mother's eyes. She had marveled at the combination, wondering that what seemed so opposite in her parents was so well suited in him.

The green beans were snapped and Elli's mom left to begin creating an amazing lunch. Mike and Elli learned that food was at its best when her mom did the cooking.

Elli settled at the base of the giant oak tree on the west side of the house. While the kids played on the rope swing and climbed the wooden fence by the barn, Mike dozed quietly with his head in Elli's lap. She smiled, stroking his head and twirling his hair in her fingers.

"Are you going to sleep?"

"Hadn't decided yet," Mike replied resting his head on her lap. "You gonna make me?"

"You need sleep, but nope. I'm not going to force it. Just wanted to know if you were still with us."

"No other place I'd rather be."

"Not even dreamland?"

"Elli, I'm already there. Don't need sleep for that." Mike grinned and Elli bent down and kissed him.

"Mom will have lunch ready in a few minutes. I didn't want you to be so groggy you wouldn't enjoy it. I don't want a short nap that could leave you cranky."

"How could you possibly imagine I wouldn't enjoy your mom's cooking?" Mike gasped in feigned offense.

"Such a thought never crossed my mind," Elli replied through a warm smile.

The phone in Mike's pocket began to buzz. At first it seemed out of place. *Why would anyone call me now?* He sat up from Elli's lap.

"This is Mike Trapper." Elli and Mike exchanged a glance noticing the change in his voice. It was his business voice. It was the way he talked at work, not his resting, glad-to-be-home voice. The change surprised both of them.

"Hey, Mike. This is Aaron Stevens." Mike had never received a social call from Colonel Aaron Stevens. And Aaron's tone of voice carried a sense of foreboding.

"What's up, Aaron?"

"I'm afraid this thing may not be over yet. Do you have a minute?" Aaron asked.

No, Mike thought, *I don't have any minutes for anything!*

"What do you mean?" he asked instead.

"Mike, we haven't received passive DHS log-ins from hundreds of police and sheriff departments all across the Southwest. It's like no one showed up for work or something."

"It's the 'or something' that bothers me," Mike said. "How late are the missing log-ins?" He was familiar with the system. The Department of Homeland Security alert protocol was the first project he had joined when he arrived in Washington.

Up to this point the system had worked perfectly. Only two events were recorded since start-up. One was caused by a hurricane, the second by a distraught and slightly inebriated, disgruntled deputy. Every other pre-determined log-in provided notice that each department was operational.

On this morning, the third day after the assassination of the president, the day after a terrorist attempt to explode a nuclear power plant, the day of the presidential funeral, the system showed something was different in the southwestern United States.

"Mike, the log-in was scheduled for 11 a.m. eastern. They're twenty minutes late." Aaron's tone was as sobering as it had been since Sunday. Mike sensed Aaron's tension. They both knew without saying that the attempt at Oak Mountain was only a part of some greater plan.

"Have you talked to Barry at the White House?"

"No, Mike, they're still trying to stop that virus from yesterday. Have you been online this morning?" Aaron asked.

"Are you kidding? I've been here for less than an hour. I haven't had time for any of that."

"Well, you can't. The internet is shut down because of the virus. Both Boston and Washington are off the main grid. Chicago is blocking everything, trying to contain the virus. St. Louis and Atlanta are doing the same. Everything in between is simply down."

"The whole East Coast?" Mike asked. He was staring at Elli as he talked. Her expression told him she didn't like what she was hearing.

"The East Coast and everything as far west as Atlanta, St. Louis and Chicago," Aaron replied. "We have satellite communications, but nothing up the backbone."

Mike's thoughts began running wild with speculation. Losing a president was bad enough, but to be faced with a nationwide breakdown in communications was unthinkable.

"Mike, I feel like we're still running behind something we haven't even identified."

"And something that wasn't finished last night." Mike's assessment was grim. In the back of his mind he envisioned commandos storming the barn fifty feet away. Whatever was happening, it was widespread, well organized, and completely unexpected.

chapter 4

11th Street Hub Office, Seattle, WA – 8:25 AM PST

It took eleven shots. The small crew working the morning shift in the hub office was eliminated quickly, and the banks of servers shut down. The objective was not to destroy the facility, simply to control it. Then remove those maintaining it, cut off communications, and wait for the full operation to be concluded.

"Eduardo! Come in here and fix this thing!" Eduardo was the only man on the team with any technical training. There was one man on every team. He received training at one of the many small technical schools in the Midwest like the others. It was all paid for with government grant dollars for alien residents of the United States, legal or not.

"What is it?" Eduardo asked entering the room.

"This fat pig fell against the computer and knocked it over. Is it broken?"

"Help me move him," Eduardo said.

The two lifted the body of the large technician off the equipment, and dropped it in the center of the room. There were other men to carry out the bodies. They would be around soon enough.

Eduardo gently set the cases of the hard drives upright, and ran some brief systems checks. It was then he noticed the blood on his fingers. The shot to the back of the technician's head had left splatters on the keyboard. He did not like that.

"Bring me a rag!" he shouted. "Can't you kill these gringos a little more neatly?"

"Give a compadre a little education, and he bosses everybody around. *Si, senor!* I will hurry and get you a very special rag so your fingers won't be sticky."

The sarcasm was not lost on Eduardo. He had endured a great deal of ribbing for having learned something useful. But responding with a wise-crack wasn't the answer. He just wanted a clean rag.

St. John's Cathedral, Washington DC, 11:30 AM EST

Reverend Welsby's sermon focused on the richness of the Marshall family. His stories about President Marshall as a young mother devoted to numerous causes filled the minds of everyone in the room with memories of days past. There were chuckles and smiles, and the frequent daubing of a tear-filled eye. The love the Marshall family had shared for too short a time embraced the hearts of everyone in the room.

Preston Marshall sat tall in the pew. His heart was broken, but he would be a tower of strength for his kids. They were no longer children. They had watched their mom work her way up the political ladder, winning the confidence of hundreds of professional politicians and millions of voters. Her ascent in politics had been amazing to them as children, and winning the presidency was nothing short of a miracle. They loved their mom and marveled at the supporters who had swirled around her. She was their hero.

Reverend Welsby closed his soliloquy with the story of the family's outing into the great northwest that ended with a bear raiding their camp while they slept. In the morning the family awoke to a campsite void of food. Everything outside was virtually destroyed, but everyone was safe. They quickly left the scene for breakfast at McDonalds and never camped again. It was a story the family had laughed about ever since.

The crowd stood amid soft chuckles and warm grins. The organ swelled and the choir sang Harriet's favorite hymn, "How Great Thou Art."

After the song, the family quietly filed to a private room, and the congregation began to exit the front of the church. Most were quiet and reflective, but all felt the relief to let Harriet Marshall rest in the peace she had earned.

Camp Pendleton, CA – 8:35 AM PST

Brigadier General Gene Westrup studied the alert he had received. It made no sense to him. The automatic e-mail was generated in the Office of Counter Terrorism in Little Rock, Arkansas. Alerts were sent to every first response unit and military training base in the country. Lackland AFB, Fort Riley, Fort Leonard Wood, Fort Bragg, along with thirty-six other military training centers received the same message. Nothing actionable, but the alarm had been rung.

What the hell is this all about? Brigadier General Westrup wondered. Experience is the greatest asset to a professional Marine, and this alert was outside his. After commanding Task Force Pegasus in Iraq supporting 1 Marine Expeditionary Force and the 2nd FSSG Forward in support of Operation Iraqi Freedom II MEF, Camp Pendleton was a quiet relief. He had seen a lot, but this alert made little sense to him.

Why would half the southwest not log-on, and all on the same day? he thought.

He was aware of the passive notification system established by the Department of Homeland Security, and he had been on the sidelines during its installation. He had been briefed in detail about the system's operational capabilities and purposes, but nothing like this had happened before.

Stemmons Blvd. PD, Dallas TX – 10:40 PM CST

Baktir Hussein, colonel and commander of the murderous teams that had eliminated hundreds of police officers and employees, was not pleased. The pace of cleaning up the station and removing the bodies was much too slow.

The Spanish-speaking members of the team were tasked with the removal. Dozens of blood soaked bodies were stacked in the alley behind the station. Baktir wanted them away from the station and disposed. He didn't care how it was done or where they were taken. He wanted them gone!

"Why is this mess not cleaned up?" Colonel Hussein raged at the troops. The men cowered at his booming voice. That enraged him all the more.

"Do not stop! You! You! And you! Get over here and clean this room! Or I will shoot you myself!" He pulled his pistol and aimed at the three terrified soldiers. The young men were frozen in fear by his rage.

"Aarrugh!" Baktir roared. "Just do it!"

Baktir charged from the room. *I swear I will kill all of them!* There was a timeline in his mind. Time was moving too fast with too little done. He tore his way through the destroyed station. Grabbing a map, he went to the steps at the front of the building.

A group of men who did not speak Spanish waited for him. They had not carried bodies from the station. They did not carry bodies. They carried guns. He spoke to them in Arabic.

"You will each collect twenty men who can shoot. Collect the vehicles you need, gather extra weapons and come back here in one hour! I will tell you what to do." Colonel Hussein's icy stare pierced each man.

The White House, Washington DC – 11:43 AM EST

Barry Goldstein hadn't slept in nearly two days. The run-up to the assault at Oak Mountain Nuclear Power Plant had kept him busy, but the insertion of a very aggressive and destructive virus by

Rachel Jones left him nearly overwhelmed. The new systems in the White House were compromised, as was much of the eastern seaboard. But the old systems, the slower ones, weren't "smart" enough to keep up with the virus. It had simply flown past them leaving them unaffected.

But it hadn't left Barry unaffected. He was exhausted. His eyes burned from the inside with fatigue. Through his efforts and the cooperation of several hundred others scattered around the east and mid-west, the virus was nearly contained. Now, they had to kill it.

Barry's phone rang on his desk. "Goldstein. It had better be good. I don't have time for it." His greeting was terse, and left room for only the most important communications.

"Barry, this is Brigadier General Gene Westrup at Camp Pendleton. And everything I say is good."

"General Gene! Hell of a day you picked for a visit." In fact, General Gene, as he was known to the family, had married Barry's aunt, and was always full of exciting tales of a military nature from his deployments around the world. Those stories made General Gene the favorite uncle of all the Goldstein kids. And since Barry was a favored nephew, General Gene was just fine.

"Not a social visit, Barry. I need intel updates. What's happening with the law enforcement log-on delays? I understand you sit at the very core of our nation's nerve center, and I figure if anything was happening, you should know.'

"Sorry, General, but you've got me there." He spoke as he typed code he hoped would be effective in restoring the vital systems at the White House. "I haven't seen anything about delays on the DHS system. We've been fighting this virus since yesterday." Barry quickly filled his uncle in on the events in the White House while the military operation was underway at Oak Mountain.

"So if the internet is down all the way out to St. Louis," General Gene began, "you wouldn't know about the late log-ins farther west, would you?"

That fact struck Barry hard. *These bastards have cut the country in half!* he thought. That worried crease in his forehead suddenly deepened.

"Barry," the general began slowly, "we received an alert from Little Rock about half an hour ago that hundreds of the passive log-ins across the southwest simply didn't happen. It's like nobody showed up for work. If Washington hasn't heard about this, we may have a problem brewing."

Barry stopped and sat back in his chair. His mind had been chasing code at lightning speed for more hours than he could remember. Now one rational thought put it all together.

"Wait! Uncle Gene, are you telling me you think Washington is cut off from everything west of the Mississippi, and something is going on all across the southwest?"

"Right on point, sonny." General Westrup paused. Then he spoke slowly. "Do you have any reference of late log-ins anywhere?"

"No, sir, none." If Barry didn't know, no one in DC knew. They were all at the funeral.

"General, sir," Barry's tone moved from serious to grave. "You need to call Colonel Aaron Stevens at the Little Rock OCT. Talk to him. I need to call the president."

Grey Horse Farm, New Salisbury, Kentucky – 11:45 AM EST

Mike's cell phone buzzed in his pocket. Elli heard it. Actually, she felt it more than heard. Mike was leaning against the giant oak on the west side of her parents' house and she was laying in the grass with her head on his lap. The vibration of the phone jolted her from a light slumber, causing her to sit up abruptly.

"Trapper," Mike spoke crisply into the phone. Elli knew it wasn't going to be anything either of them wanted to hear.

"Mike, sorry, but you're going to need to come in on this." It was Colonel Aaron Stevens again in Little Rock OCT. "President Makin is bringing the entire team back to DC. That's all I can say. A chopper will be there in an hour or so. Sorry, man."

Mike was sorry, too. He knew Elli would not be happy about it. He sheepishly turned to her after closing his phone.

"I have to go back." It was all he could say. He didn't know what was happening or why he needed to be there, but his brief hours-long holiday was over.

"Okay. When?" Elli's gaze was steady.

"The chopper will be here in an hour or so."

"It's serious then, right?" Elli asked.

Mike's phone buzzed again. He looked at her, and then pulled the phone from his pocket.

"Trapper."

"Mike, good. This is President Makin. Did I catch you at a bad time?" Mike's training and respect for the Office brought him bolt upright.

"No, sir! I mean, I wasn't expecting that you'd call, Mr. President. What can I do for you?"

"Mike, they've called you about returning to the White House, correct?" the president asked.

"Yes, sir. Just now."

"Good. I've slipped away from the funeral for President Marshall for a briefing, and I knew immediately I needed you back here. We aren't sure what's going on, but I know I can trust you, and I need you."

"Yes, Mr. President." Mike didn't want to be in Washington at all. Grey Horse Farm was just fine. This was where he wanted to be.

"The chopper left a few minutes ago." Mike heard the president expel a long breath. "Mike, I really appreciate this. Thank you."

"Yes, sir. I'll be ready." The phone went dead.

Elli was already on her feet pulling Mike by the arm. He stood for a moment asking what was going on with his expression. Elli held his hand firmly and marched to the house.

Inside, she poked her head into the kitchen and said something Mike couldn't decipher. Then she pulled him down the hall, up the stairs, and into their room.

It was one of those things Mike had never figured out. Once the door closed, Elli's clothes seemed to simply melt off her body. She pushed him hard, and he fell backward onto their bed.

As she removed his clothes, she paused. He was still a little dazed. Elli kissed him.

"If you're leaving here to serve the president of the United States," she said with great determination, "you're gonna leave here feeling like a man!"

And suddenly, he did.

chapter 5

Highway 7 & I-70, Kansas City, MO – 10:50 AM CST

Rachel Jones pulled into a parking stall in front of the BP station. She had managed to get far from Washington unnoticed. Or so she hoped. She was tired, frightened, and still mad as hell.

Rachel Jones had served quietly for nearly seventeen years in the Central Intelligence Agency, applying herself with excellence. She was brilliant, and her superiors made note of her hard work and service. Over the years, she was promoted for her devotion and dedication to the job. She hadn't married, made little contact with her family, and remained totally committed to her duties.

At least, to what appeared to be her duties. She had worked for the CIA, but the real job, the one stowed in her heart, was not for her country. It was a much deeper passion that had driven her all those years. It wasn't patriotism, or love of country. Nor was it a heart-felt pride to serve. What drove her was revenge.

She walked into the BP, wearing the sun glasses and the scarf she wore when she left DC. She felt rumpled and dirty. She wanted a warm bath. She was also running low on cash.

The store was empty except for one clerk behind the counter. The morning coffee rush had been over for an hour, and the lunch crowd wouldn't show up for another thirty minutes.

Why would anyone eat food from a place like this? she thought. She calmly checked some items in the aisle, and picked up a few things she needed. The disposable cell phone with pre-paid minutes was a great find.

She approached the counter with a smile on her face while she raised her purse to the counter.

"Good morning, ma'am. Did you find everything you—"

His sentence was cut short by three blasts from the .45 automatic Rachel pulled from her purse and fired into his chest. The clerk was slammed against the racks of cigarettes behind the counter, and crashed to the floor.

"Almost," was her only response. Rachel walked behind the counter and emptied the cash register. To her surprise the safe was open. She smiled, bent over to check the contents, and helped herself. *This has been a very worthwhile stop*, she thought with a grin.

Rachel walked into the tiny office behind the counter and found the surveillance recording machine. She pushed the eject button and removed the disc. She slipped the disc into her purse. It would find a new home some forty miles away in a grassy ditch west of Olathe.

On her way out of the store she paused. She had a soft spot for sweets, especially pastries. She emptied the contents of the Krispy Kreme cabinet into a bag, grabbed two large bottles of water, and calmly left the store.

Outside, the gas lanes were empty. Rachel marveled at how easy she found it to begin her 'life of crime.'

"Life of crime!" she said out loud. Then she laughed.

As she pulled from the BP parking lot, she opened the disposable cell phone and dialed the number that was reserved for this day, for this very moment. This call had been planned from near the beginning. She knew it, kept it hidden in her memory, held it secret for all these years. To her, this was an historic moment.

She held the phone to her ear, imagining the surprise of the person who was reaching for the phone at the other end. This contact was the one they had dreaded for as long as she had kept the number in her memory. It was, indeed, historic.

"Hello?" a soft voice said from the other end.

"Hello. This is Mother."

Grey Horse Farm, New Salisbury, Kentucky – 12:05 PM EST

Mike heard a buzzing that sounded too familiar. Elli lay softly across his shoulder running her hand up his abdomen. They both knew their time together was short, but this brief encounter would not soon be forgotten.

"I gotta get my phone."

"What?" Elli asked as she raised her head from his chest.

"My phone. I have to answer it." Mike slowly lifted himself as Elli rolled to her side. He glanced toward her. Her eyes were closed. She was astonishing.

Mike's phone buzzed again. It snapped him from his attention on Elli. He searched for his jeans mixed with the blankets and her clothes on the floor by the bed. Finally, he found it.

"This is Mike Trapper."

"Took long enough!" It was Aaron Stevens at the OCT in Little Rock.

"Your timing is remarkable. What's happening?" Mike was coming around. He scratched his head and rubbed his face.

"Listen, Mike. We have a huge break on this. How soon will you be in DC?"

"Uh, the chopper should be here, I don't know, maybe thirty minutes. Then it's about an hour or so back. Why?"

"Well, it's something I need to show you. In the situation room beneath the White House they have a device you need to see."

"Okay, but can't you just tell me?" Mike asked reaching for his jeans.

"Not this. Not on the phone. You gotta see it," Aaron replied. "I'll have them get on it so everything is ready the minute you arrive."

"That's fine, Aaron. But it'll be a while."

"Mike, this is big." Aaron hung up from his end.

Mike was reaching for his clothes when he felt a hand moving up his back. The warmth of her touch was too much. He turned back to the woman he loved and moved smoothly into her embrace.

The chopper won't get here that quick, he thought.

Mainside, Camp Pendleton, CA – 9:10 AM PST

General Westrup picked up his desk phone and dialed a fellow Marine he had known for decades. He leaned back in his chair, still trying to frame his thoughts into a coherent sentence. The last three days had raised a number of alarms in his mind, and he didn't want to lose track. He was feeling suspicious and didn't like the uncertainty that accompanied it.

The phone rang three times.

"Sergeant Major Michaels." John Michaels' deep rich voice would fill any room at a level for normal conversation. When he laughed, he boomed. When he made a point, the words were driven like nails.

"Sergeant major, this is General Westrup. Do you have a minute?"

"Absolutely, general, what can I do for you, sir?"

To soldiers with a history, a greeting given with rank denotes respect, even among friends. Gene Westrup and John Michaels held deep respect for each other since Viet Nam. They were on the last helicopter to leave the roof of the Pittman Apartment building on Gia Long Street in the evacuation of Saigon on April 29, 1975.

The two young Marines had been sent to evacuate the CIA Director and his remaining staff. The dramatic event was captured by a Dutch journalist, and later incorrectly identified as the evacuation of the U.S. Embassy. By the time they left, the embassy had been emptied, and was only minutes from being looted and destroyed. Their chopper was the last one out of Saigon.

"John, I've got something that's just twitchin' around in the back of my mind. I can't seem to make it settle." General Westrup told his friend of the alert he had received from the Department of Homeland Security. They discussed the events of the last few days, and the enormity of the task to coordinate it all.

"Gene, have you really thought about this, or are you just havin' a fit caused by Marge's chili?" John chuckled softly into the receiver.

"Well, I gotta admit, that chili has been barkin' at me since about three a.m." They both laughed.

"Listen, I know you. From the tone of your voice I know you aren't calling me to talk about chili. What's up?"

"No, it's more than chili." Gene grew silent. "I don't want to make a big stir, but what if you called a general drill, put all these brave young soldiers on priority alert, just like we were bein' attacked by the whole damn Red Chinese Army."

"I don't suppose you want me to tell them we *are* expecting the Red Chinese Army, do you?" He paused. "I'm sorry, Gene. It's just early and I haven't even got through my mail yet."

"I understand, I understand." Gene wasn't flustered. There was just one particular, very sober and disquieting thought he couldn't let go. "You're fine, John. I understand. But I'm serious about this."

"So, you're thinking a drill scenario on the order of mass invasion, right?" John asked.

"Something along that line. For the next six hours, let's zip this base up as tight as it can get. Then we'll get everybody up to priority alert, serve them lunch in the field, and call it a day."

Gene leaned back in his chair and swung toward the large window in his office looking out over Mainside, the heartbeat of Camp Pendleton. "How's that sound to you, John?"

"We haven't had a drill like that in months, general. Sounds like we're due. I'll crank it up immediately."

"Thank you, sergeant major. Oh, by the way, I'll be in your office in fifteen minutes. Is the coffee hot?"

"Indeed it is. And by the time you get here, it will be fresh, too." As always, there was a smile in John's voice as it boomed into General Gene Westrup's ear. The general grinned. John's master sergeant made the best coffee in California. Gene afforded himself the treat of a surprise visit at least twice a week.

The alert hit the Camp in mere moments, and nearly 60,000 Marines and Sailors scrambled to their assignments. The MPs closed the gates, and began turning back traffic. Twenty-two thousand citizen employees continued their tasks at their stations with a mild measure of alarm. After all, it was just a drill.

On the tarmac, the crew of an AmTrans 4097 AWAC was completing flight prep to return to McGuire Airbase in New Jersey. At that very moment, a request was in route to the 305th Air Mobility Wing of the US Air Force and the 21st Expeditionary Mobility Task Force, asking permission for the aircraft to remain in the area to participate in the drill.

A half-dozen well-armed AH-1Z Super Cobra Attack helicopters were airborne in moments, followed by their slower, big brother S-70 Battle Hawks. Thirty-five thousand recruits-in-training found themselves deployed alongside veterans of battles in Fallujah, Al Anwar Providence, and a dozen other places they had heard about on the news.

Amid the turmoil of a major alert, one Hummer moved calmly through the mayhem. Its principal passenger looked out at the young soldiers with pride, and a sense of wonder. It was his unsettled thought that brought this all to action. The precision of it all was a marvel to behold.

And by now, he thought, *the coffee should be fresh, and hot.*

Crescent Beach, VA – 12:10 PM ES

Steve and Sam stood on the deck overlooking the beach and the ocean. The sea never stopped. They both watched with reserved foreboding as the waves crashed on the sand. It never stopped. There was always something prepared to crash down like a giant wave. Neither spoke, but both knew what the other was thinking.

Another wave was coming in. The storm of the previous three days had crashed on them as it had on the nation with unmeasured force. But just because the storm passed, didn't mean the waves would stop. They felt a difference this time. They could stand together. They would strengthen each other. Regardless of the ferocity of the storm or the wave, they would endure it.

Over the crashing of the waves on the beach, Steve and Sam heard the thumping of rotors as the helicopter approached. The quiet they shared in the past few hours could be re-discovered. They chose to remember that quietness. They would find it again.

Steve reached and touched Sam's hand. She turned to him. Their eyes met; she smiled softly and looked down at the sand at their feet.

"Hey," Steve said, causing her to look back at him.

"What?" Sam asked through a warm and inviting smile.

"Are you ready for this?"

"The chopper?" Sam asked and giggled.

"No," Steve smiled. "The rest of it. Us from here on."

Sam looked at Steve with new understanding, a new appreciation for what they shared. Her smile was radiant.

"Yes, as long as you're around." She kissed him.

The sound of the wind and waves was swept away by the pounding roar of the chopper as it settled on the sandy beach near the house. Sand flew in the air and stung their faces as they raced to board.

I-635 and Highway 75, Dallas, TX – 11:15 AM CST

Eleven men stood at the side of the busy interstate. Parking on the side of this interstate exchange was near suicide, but the risk of being overheard or seen anywhere else could mean certain death. The five trucks were parked in such a manner that someone driving might assume a tangle of bumpers and fenders requiring the exchange of insurance information. It happened every day on I-635.

A shorter man in jeans and a plaid shirt was speaking emphatically and emotionally to the others around him. There were no smiles. Every face was grim.

"I'm telling you, they shot every single cop in the place. Male, female, didn't matter. They killed 'em all!"

"Damn. You afraid they saw you or somethin'?"

"Not afraid of bein' seen. I just know what I saw!" the shorter man said.

"Bill, it's the same over on Fifteenth Street. Every cop in the place was shot, and dumped out back."

Bill Jenkins had been the chief of police in Dallas for fourteen years back in the late 80's and through the 90's. He was still a lieutenant colonel in the Marine Reserves as a weekend warrior. He was just a weekend warrior with a history, and an attitude.

"Call the other guys in your units," Bill began as he adjusted his hat. "Have them check around on how wide-spread this thing is. Let's get as many together as we can, and meet at the Training Center up in Frisco. Don't nobody do anything stupid. Tell everyone to keep it cool and be there by one o'clock."

Bill looked at the men with him. They represented veterans from every minor scrape and major conflict from Viet Nam, to Grenada, to Desert Storm. They were older, and a bit softer. A couple of the guys were downright pudgy. But in their hearts, they were Marines. That didn't change.

"One o'clock, then." A quick nod confirmed it. They would be there, and they would be ready.

LAPD, Los Angeles, CA - 9:25 AM PST

Colonel Alvaro Herrera sipped strong black coffee from a San Francisco 49'ers mug. The 49'ers had been his team since he was a boy. He was pleased to find the mug at the station. It was one of a dozen that had not been shattered to pieces in the assault.

"Colonel Herrera!" his young assistant shouted as he threw open the door. "They are charging the station!"

"What? Who is charging the station?" the colonel said as he stood and rounded the corner of his desk. "What are you talking about?"

"The gangs! They are attacking us!" The young man was clearly terrified. His face was pallid and clammy with sweat.

Colonel Herrera grabbed his rifle and pistol, and pushed his way into the hall past the young man. He heard the angry voices jeering threats against the army he had led into the city. His army had come from every direction with explosive speed and removed all law enforcement, just as planned. Their first objectives were met across the city in a matter of minutes. The colonel was confident they would handle this skirmish with similar skill.

He kicked open the front doors of the station. They were already damaged and his brutal kick against them served only to remove the doors from their hinges. He also captured everyone's attention.

Nearly one hundred faces spun in his direction. Every face was angry.

"Who do you think you are?" Herrera yelled in Spanish. He leveled his weapon and slowly panned the group. Another three dozen rifles immediately appeared through every opening on the front side of the building. "I am Colonel Alvaro Herrera, commander of the Los Angeles regiment of the Liberation Army of Baja California."

He did not care to kill Latino gang members. He brought the Yemini sharp-shooters for that. They would kill any non-Muslim without hesitation. It only took a word, and it would be done. Two dozen of the rifles aimed at the mob were held by the Yemini fighters. They were eager to serve.

"Why are you here, and who is you leader?" Colonel Herrera demanded.

A large, well-muscled man in his late twenties slowly moved toward the colonel. Herrera measured him as he approached. He would not allow anyone to threaten or challenge his position. Then, the young man spoke.

"We are the Latin Family. We own this territory you have invaded. You will tell me why you have come here to my town and caused all this trouble."

"I will tell you nothing," Colonel Herrera spat back at him. "If you do not know what is going on here, you are stupid, too stupid to be Latino."

"We have owned this town for thirty years." The young man raised his voice. "We took it from the blacks who chased out all the white people. We have business here and you are making things difficult for me."

"Ooo, you have business," Herrera mocked him and laughed coarsely. The men in the windows chuckled. Their weapons remained ready.

The smile melted off his face as he turned back to the strongly built young man. He had made his mind up.

"You will listen to me, you and all your business." Herrera sneered as he waved his pistol at the angry mob. "For nearly one hundred years we have been looking for this day. For thirty-five years we have been training, buying weapons, establishing base camps, and bringing fighters into this country.

"You were all in diapers and being burped by your mothers when preparations were finalized, rehearsed, and kept secret for this day." Herrera's voice echoed through the morning air.

"You have no say in this," he continued. "You have made no contribution to this effort. You have not helped in any manner!"

"We are the Latin Family and you will—"

One shot from Colonel Herrera's pistol dropped the young man to the pavement. He didn't move again.

Colonel Herrera looked out over the mob. They were instantly timid, confused, angry, frightened, and shocked. Cut off the head and the mob has no will or understanding. His decision was final.

"The rest of you may join him if you wish." There was no kindness in his words. His eyes burned with unspeakable cruelty as he glared into the faces before him.

"You may also go to your homes and be the women you have been trained to be." Herrera swaggered across the steps of the station. He knew these men hated him. That was exactly what he wanted. Herrera knew he could turn their hatred against an enemy, any enemy.

"If you want to fight for your families, your women, your ancestors, then come and join us." Herrera nearly spit out the words. "If not, we will shoot you, and you can die in your own blood and piss."

Colonel Herrera turned his back and strode into the building. Slowly and singly, the men in the mob laid their weapons down. The Latino soldiers moved into their ranks searching them for more weapons before leading them off to be re-trained and equipped to serve the colonel.

The twenty-four Yemeni riflemen held their positions. Each was disappointed there was no one to kill with so many deserving candidates. But there would be more. There would be many more.

chapter 6

Plano, TX – 11:45 AM CST

A few miles west of the meeting on the interstate, things had moved beyond a planned resistance. Armed citizens had gathered and were aware of the shootings in the police stations. No television networks were needed to spread the news of the brutal attacks. Cell phones, text messages, and CB radios were doing the job.

Groups of men in the neighborhoods along both sides of the Dallas North Tollway began gathering women and children into the homes near the center of the developments. Deer hunting rifles, shotguns, collector-vintage AK-47s, and anything that would chamber a round were brought from closets and gun-racks to kitchen tables for quick cleaning and inspection.

Armed men stood at the entrances of subdivisions, partially blocking the street with their pickups or the family minivan. Everyone was tense, and the news was sketchy. But it was becoming very clear that something was going on, and it wasn't being done the way things were supposed to be done in Texas.

Little had been heard from anyone in the south metropolitan area. One call from a fellow church member living in Duncanville relayed a frantic tale of neighborhoods being overrun by thousands of angry blacks and Mexicans. White families attempting to make a run for it were gunned down. The phone call ended suddenly with the sounds of pandemonium and shouting, followed by shots and silence. Whether it was one home invasion or a riot, no one could tell. But the imaginations of the general populace were running toward the worst of possible outcomes.

George Richards, cradling his Marlin 336 in his arms, leaned against the side of his Dodge Caravan. It wasn't a new rifle, but it was the best gun he had ever shot. It never failed him. He always got his limit of whitetail deer. But today wasn't about hunting deer, and as far as he knew, there were no limits.

A silver Camry swung toward the entrance where George and his neighbor Phil stood. They both knew the car and the driver.

"Hey, Bill. What's goin' on?" George asked taking a step forward.

"I just met with the guys from Guard and Reserve units across the north end of town," Bill said through his open window. He slipped the lever to park. "We're gonna be gatherin' at the Training Center up in Frisco in about an hour." Bill Jenkin's words brought a good deal of comfort. Somebody was doing something about whatever it was that was going on.

"Should we be gettin' our families outta here?" Phil looked around as if expecting an imminent attack. "Isn't there some way to find out if things is goin' bad?"

"You boys are doin' everything we need to do for now. We don't need to go lookin' for trouble just yet. If trouble comes our way, we're ready, at least." Bill smiled as confident a smile as he could muster. "Just keep your heads up and your eyes open."

"Yes, sir," came the staggered response from the two guards.

Bill waved his hand and drove into the subdivision. Dozens of times in his life, men had looked to Bill for confidence and a solution. Bill Jenkins was never lacking in confidence. The solution never seemed far away. But in just about every circumstance he could remember, he was able to measure what he was up against. This time he wasn't sure. He wasn't afraid of what they might be facing; he just didn't know what it was.

Grey Horse Farm, New Salisbury, Kentucky – 12:50 PM EST

Mike was coming slowly down the stairs buttoning his shirt. Elli's mom stood in the kitchen doorway with a smile on her face. Mike could feel the flush rising in his.

"Oh, you kids!" she chuckled, and Mike felt his face go beet red. *Damn!* he thought. But he smiled, walked up to his mother-in-law and gave her a hug.

"You raised a wonderful woman, Mom." Mike loved Elli's parents as much as his own. Their love and support for Mike and Elli had been a great help over the years, and a deep bond of appreciation had grown between the four of them.

"She's a fire-brand, like her daddy. He's the romantic one, you know," she said with a broadening smile.

"Yep," Mike replied. No, he didn't know. But now he did, and he blushed even more.

Thunderous clatter rose behind him as Elli flew down the stairs. She never came downstairs slowly or quietly. She leaped from the fourth step, and slammed into Mike's back grabbing his neck, and wrapping her legs around his waist.

"Giddy-up there, horsy!" she yelled.

Mike quickly regained his balance and laughed at her playfulness. He loved it. The kids had seen their mommy tackle daddy many times. It was part of her routine that brought a life of never-ending surprise.

"Are you hungry?" Elli's mom asked through laughter.

"Hungry as a bear!" Elli blurted out before Mike could speak.

"I meant Mike!" Elli's mom said waving a swat at her daughter.

As they walked into the kitchen, the house began to shake; the roar that filled the house nearly deafened them. Mike rushed onto the porch.

"Oh, my lord!" Elli thought she heard him say through the din.

A huge blue and white helicopter was settling onto the lawn much closer than the one that brought Mike home just a few hours ago. Closer and bigger. Much bigger.

The side hatch opened, and in a man white shirt and tie and black suit stepped onto the lawn while the props spun ferociously overhead. He walked briskly toward the house.

"Elli," Mike said turning to his stunned wife, "it's Marine One. That's the president's personal chopper!"

Elli didn't know whether to laugh, or cry. She chose to stand there with her mouth open.

The VH-71 "Kestrel" had been selected to replace the aging fleet of VH-3D "Nighthawks" that had ferried presidents and vice presidents since the mid-1990s. The advanced avionics, weaponry and near 200 mph air-speed encouraged the replacement. The speed was also the reason the helicopter arrived earlier than expected. Mike was glad it had not come five minutes earlier.

He felt a tugging on his sleeve. He turned to see Elli's mom pushing a brown paper bag toward him. *Lunch on the fly,* he thought, *literally.*

To Mike, the bag contained a treasure, one he would not pass-up. He took the bag, hugged his mother-in-law, then held, and kissed his wife. He would have rather stayed right there forever. He loved the smell of her hair, the scent of her skin, and her warmth. He didn't want to let go.

"Agent Trapper?" The man from the helicopter was yelling to be heard over the roar of the props.

"Yes, I'm Mike Trapper." Mike extended his hand.

"The president of the United States requests that you accompany us to the White House, where he is waiting for you." He then stepped aside, ushering Mike toward the chopper.

Mike took two steps when he saw the small band of rough-riders standing motionless by the fence. Each face plainly showed they didn't understand why another helicopter was at Granddad's house.

"Just a minute," Mike said to the man from the helicopter. He jogged toward his children.

"Daddy, are you gonna leave?" Five-year-old Sara slouched and stuck out her lower lip. She looked crushed. Mike felt crushed with her.

"I know, guys, I just got here. I'm sorry, but something very big has happened, and the president has asked me to help."

"The president? You mean the real president?" Robbie asked as only a six-year-old could.

"That's right, Robbie. That's the president's helicopter. He sent it so I could get back to Washington real fast."

"We're gonna miss you again, daddy!" echoed around him in a muddled chorus and he was smothered by eight tiny arms.

"I miss you already!" Mike answered and hugged his children. "I gotta go. I'll be back as soon as I can, okay?"

"Okay," came from each child with a kiss for their daddy. Mike forced himself away from their grasp, and waved to them as he crossed the lawn to the waiting chopper. Midway he was grabbed by Elli.

"Me last, me last!" she chortled. Mike laughed, and kissed her once more. Then he hopped on-board the president's helicopter, clutching mom's brisket sandwich in its paper bag.

Stemmons Blvd. PD, Dallas TX – 11:55 AM CST

Just over three-hundred men stood in front of the station. They were heavily armed, and most were from the Middle East. Every one of them had spent the morning killing, tracking down and killing more men and women attached to the police departments across northwest Dallas.

Colonel Baktir Hussein exited the building to address them. In the last hour, most of the bodies had been removed from the area, but his mood had not brightened. The scowl on his face was carved from years of hardship. He counted it an honor to be part of jihad.

"I have prepared maps for each team of men," Baktir began. "Your leaders have them. You will follow their instructions as you did this morning. The operation is the same. You have trained for this day for many months, even years. Do not withhold your revenge. There is no mercy for these people. Complete your tasks quickly and return here. Our enemy does not know you are coming. Now, go! May Allah be with you!"

He didn't mean the part about Allah. He no longer cared about Allah. But he knew the others did, and the words would strengthen them. They were trained to kill infidels. It would be pleasing to Allah, they believed.

"Allahu akbar!" rumbled from three hundred voices. The men moved quickly to the cars and trucks. There was work to do.

Cascade Parks Apartments, Mesquite, TX – 12:05 PM CST

"Mama!" Yolanda yelled as she entered the apartment. "Mama! Come quickly! Where are you?"

Beatrice Vasquez had grown old early in life. She had worked two jobs, six and seven days a week since their arrival in the States years ago. She came to East Dallas when Yolanda was only a toddler. It had been a continuous battle, constantly moving to find a better home for her little girl, forever on the hunt for a better job for herself. She never found time to take a break from the demands of life long enough to become an American citizen.

"What are you yelling?" Bea had been asleep for only an hour, and waking abruptly left her feeling hungover. "Please, no yelling! What is it? What is it?"

"Oh, Mama!" Yolanda was still on the edge of panic. She held herself together until she saw her mom. Then the tears began to flow.

"Mama! It was terrible! All the shooting! And the officers, the men and women! They killed all of them!"

The sight of her normally cheerful daughter so distraught frightened Bea. She grabbed Yolanda and held her in her arms.

"It's okay, baby! Shhhh! It will be all right! Quiet now!" Bea stroked her hair to calm her, but with little success.

Finally, the tears subsided and Yolanda was able to relate the terrible events she had witnessed in the police station, and fearing for her life, managing to escape. They were terrible men. They were evil. Something awful was underway.

"Mama, we need to leave! We need to get out of this place. Right now! We have to go!" Yolanda pleaded and cried.

"We will, sweetheart. We can have some lunch, and get you calmed down a bit. Then we can take a drive and figure this out." Bea's motherly touch could almost always soothe and quiet her little girl. This time, however, she was not making any headway.

Suddenly, Yolanda sat straight upright and squared herself with her mother. The panic was gone. Tears were still streaming down her cheeks, but there was firm resolve and absolute clarity in her eyes. She cleared her throat.

"No, Mama. You need to hear me. I love you. But right now, we *must* leave."

The two women stared into each other's eyes in silence. An understanding that can only pass between mother and daughter gripped them both. There was no question. It was time to leave.

"Yes," Bea nodded. "Yes, we must. I understand."

"Mama, I'm going to throw some clothes together. You make us some food we can travel with. We have no time to spare. Very quickly, now."

The two women held each other for one more moment. Neither knew what lay ahead of them for today or tomorrow. But right now, they needed to go.

Arlington Cemetery, Washington DC - 1:15 PM EST

The procession from St. John's Cathedral was slow and reverent. The streets of Washington DC were lined with thousands of families, working men and women, politicians and government employees. Every American ethnicity, profession, trade, and craft was represented by the crowd. And every one of them mourned the loss of a friend.

The grave site was across the shallow valley from the Eternal Flame at the grave of President John Kennedy. Behind the site, only a few yards to the east, stood the Tomb of the Unknown Soldier.

The crowd that accompanied President Marshall to her final resting place stood surrounded by the graves of those who had given their lives in service to the nation.

The fallen president was laid to rest amid a sea of thousands of white crosses marking the ultimate of personal sacrifice. To those standing, they were placing a hero among heroes. It was fitting.

The bagpiper played *Amazing Grace*, and the US Marines Men's Chorus sang the *Battle Hymn of the Republic*. Emotions ran to the depths of one's soul. Brave men, veterans of ferocious battles, some lame and broken by war, stood at attention as tears filled their eyes.

Preston Marshall stood with his daughter and son beside the casket bearing his wife's remains. He gazed over the thousands who came to share these final moments. He knew he would never be able to thank so many for the love and the respect shown to his wife. There would be time to reflect and share stories with his children, but not now.

This time was for a nation shrouded in grief. He had watched his wife bear the weight of the presidency. Now he was experiencing the strength, support, and embrace of a powerful nation. That embrace held him upright. And he was thankful.

I-35 and Highway 50, Emporia, KS – 12:25 PM CST

Rachel Jones came to a dead stop on what was normally a busy interstate. It was a parking lot. Rachel got out of the car and looked ahead.

A good mile down the road she could see flashing lights. She couldn't tell if it was Kansas State Troopers or Emporia Police. She didn't care. She had no use for either of them. They were in her way.

She walked across to the inside lane by the median and peered ahead. Cars and trucks were crossing the median and heading toward her. *Good*, she thought. *Get them out of my way!*

She hurried back to her car as traffic began to move. The progress was maddening. She inched forward.

Finally, she pulled beside a state trooper.

"Officer! What is going on here? I need to get to Oklahoma City, and I need this highway to get there!" she demanded placing her hands on her hips.

"Sorry, ma'am. But not on this roadway, and not for at least a couple of hours," the trooper replied. "The road's blocked by a serious accident five or six miles southwest of here. We're rerouting traffic down Highway 50."

"That takes me out of my way! I don't want to go that way!" Rachel said taking a step toward the officer. She almost slipped and said, *Do you know who you are talking to?* but she caught herself.

Rachel Jones, Washington CIA Chief and now traitor, changed her tone. She flushed a little, realizing how close her anger had taken her to revealing her identity. She sighed and smiled back at the trooper.

"I'm sorry. It's been a long day and here it is just noon." Rachel laughed, resurrecting her bubbly nature. She hoped it would work.

"There are lots of folks upset today. And it seems they all gotta get somewhere on this road. Ma'am, if you'll just follow those folks goin' to the right, I'd appreciate it." His tone was polite and he smiled.

"Thank you, officer. I'm sure I'll get there sooner or later, maybe a little later." She smiled and laughed again. "Bye, bye."

Rachel pulled slowly toward the off ramp to Highway 50 west. Her mood changed immediately. She was angry again.

chapter 7

The Southwest United States – 10:30 AM PST

Many men and women had contributed their ideas over the years. The outline and construction of the mission had been designed in great detail. Several trial runs had been made around the world. Those tests provided vital information for training purposes. Much of the useable information had been gathered from TV news footage on American networks. Tactics used by this enemy were developed from details at press conferences where the press pushed a congressman to leak a tiny bit of information. Eventually, all the tiny bits added up.

Mumbai, India had been a target for terrorists' attacks for nearly twenty years. Many procedures and tactics were employed. They ranged from single attacks to the explosion of several bombs across the city in 2006 that killed 209 civilians, and wounded another seven hundred.

But the greatest test of a surprise assault on a large metropolitan area came in late 2008. Twenty warriors were selected and trained for three years for the operation. The objective was to assault several public locations in South Mumbai—a train station, hospital, a café, a cinema, community building and a handful of large hotels.

After entering the city at night in small fishing boats, the terrorists broke into small teams. The owners of the boats were killed and dumped, and their entrance was undetected.

Within forty-eight hours, hundreds were dead or wounded. The police and the NSG neutralized every effort, except the attack on the Taj Mahal Palace & Tower Hotel. The standoff continued another full day until the remaining attackers were killed or captured.

The attack was considered a success. Twenty had gone in, nine died, one was captured. Ten returned to their base without the Indian government knowing they were ever in Mumbai. After the attack, the mission planners decided that law enforcement posed the greatest challenge to their plans. In future assaults the police would be neutralized first.

And so the assault on the southwest United States required hundreds of thousands of terrorists to first defeat those protecting the American communities. Within a matter of minutes the extermination was executed with remarkable accuracy.

In a very brief time, while the nation mourned their fallen president, the borders of the country were changed.

The White House – 1:35 PM EST

Mike Trapper was jogging up the steps to the West Wing of the White House. He felt an urgency that energized him. The files he read during the flight awakened him. He knew there wasn't much time, and a great deal needed to be unraveled.

Alex Hodson of the FBI and Ray Jergins from the Department of Justice met him as he entered the building and fell into step on either side of him.

"Mike, we need to take you downstairs on this one," Alex began. "Who in the world would ever imagine the assassination of a president would be used as a distraction. Damn! These guys are bad," he muttered.

Mike had heard rumors of the lower levels in the White House, but he'd never gone below the third basement level. How many levels actually existed was classified and beyond his clearance level. He had the feeling he was entering a new realm that few would ever hear about, much less see.

"Mike, we didn't see the preparations being made over the last few days, and they've sorta taken us by surprise. Not that we can't handle it; we just didn't catch it in time."

"Well, Ray, are you going to tell me what this is all about?" Mike asked.

Ray looked at Alex for a second, then to Mike.

"No. I think you need to see it for yourself."

The elevator whirred and dropped at a speed near freefall. The roast beef sandwich Mike ate on the flight lifted a bit in his gut, just enough to heighten the sensation of falling.

The stop was smooth but heavy, making the men feel more than their normal weight. The door opened onto a huge room. The entire wall directly across from the elevator door was a huge video screen. Mike guessed it to be at least twenty feet across and twelve feet high. The screen displayed a satellite view of North America from several hundred miles in space.

"Mike, you can only be here for a few minutes," Ray began as he pushed a couple of desk chairs out of the way. "What we are going to show you can be performed for a short time and only at certain times. The power drain for the equipment in this room can cause serious brown-outs all along the coast on a normal business day. Since today is a holiday of sorts, it probably won't be noticed."

"The first image you will see is one obtained last Sunday morning," Alex added. "Mort, will you bring up IOWTR-4739.6." He turned back to Mike. "A few years back, the government commissioned a project at Louisiana State University to make detailed topographical maps of the earth. LSU jumped at the opportunity.

"We gave them the limited use of a specific satellite for their study. The technology went beyond simple map making, however.

Through some enhancements, the students learned they could overlay other sophisticated technologies.

"From those discoveries we learned, for example, how to find a cell phone of a missing person. In 2001 the FCC required the activation of Phase II of the Enhanced 911 program called the Automatic Location Identification, or ALI. Back then, the technology was required to place the location of a single cell phone within 100 meters of its actual spot. It's the same technology that parents can use to track their kid's cell phone that caused so much concern a few years ago.

"Did you know these things emit signals even when they're turned off? When the New York Times spilled the beans on that one, the insurgents in Iraq began removing the batteries so they couldn't be tracked."

Mike had heard all that before, but it had never bothered him, until now.

"Anyway, we're way beyond all that," Alex continued. "These kids are smart. Not only did they develop the algorithms to identify a single cell phone ping, thus giving a very precise location, they learned how to turn them all on at once, and see virtually every cell phone in the country."

At that moment, the men turned to the large screen. Millions of specks of light began to flicker across the image of the United States. Metropolitan areas were simply ablaze in a white mass created by the locations of hundreds of thousands of private phones. Rural areas were more speckled as the population was scattered.

Mike's eyes were drawn to eastern Kentucky. He wondered if one of the small flickers was made by Elli's cell phone. He felt a little unnerved by what he was seeing.

"Okay. I get it. That's a lot of cell phones. What's next?" Mike asked, shifting his weight a bit.

"About a year ago, one of the LSU students wrote an algorithm that identified cell phones by the nation of origin. It was a creative use of the national identifier number used in overseas calls. Every nation has a number. The US is "1*", China is "86", Sweden "46." They all have numbers. The phones licensed in those countries carry the same codes internally."

Mike was confident this would get somewhere soon, but he felt it had better do so soon. He was just a little agitated.

"I'll get to the point. Here are all the cell phones in the States that have batteries in them that are charged. The battery dies, we lose the ping. This image was captured Sunday morning, like I said. Mort, bring up 4739.7." He turned to Mike, "And we can do this country by country."

Suddenly the screen lit up with millions more points of light, but rather than white they were light orange.

"This is the same scan and time frame as the previous image, but with cell phones licensed in Mexico added," Alex clarified.

The highest concentration of the orange lights were scattered throughout Mexico. There were hundreds across the southwest United States as well.

"The next image was made Monday morning. Mort, bring up 4739.8." Alex looked at the huge screen. The orange pixels along the northern Mexican border increased dramatically.

"And then 4739.9."

A chill ran through Mike as he watched the US/Mexico border become sharply outlined by millions of the tiny orange lights. The entire border from the Gulf to the Pacific was perfectly defined by a definite orange line.

"That was yesterday," Ray added. "It's the same on the Canadian border in the east and along the west coast. Even the orange pixels in the States are gathered together. See, here. They were scattered, but now there is one pretty good size dot. Over here, too."

Ray's hand pointed out clusters of orange dots across the southwestern states. Mike was suddenly aware that his mouth was hanging open in amazement.

"Mort, can you add in 98, 966, and 20?" Turning to Mike he said, "Those are the codes for Iran, Saudi Arabia and Egypt." The orange line along the border was intensified with the addition of three more colors, each color representing the code for its country of origin.

"Mike, while we were hunting all over St. Louis and Dallas looking for an assassin, these guys were gathering along the nation's borders."

Mike was speechless. Alex turned to Mort and the other technicians in the room.

"We're gonna bring it live!" he spoke with a loud voice, causing everyone to turn to their work stations.

"This is where we drain the power-swamp," Ray said almost in a whisper.

Somewhere in another room Mike heard the deepening hum of a huge power drag. It reminded him of an approaching B-29 that seemed to come up behind them and stop somewhere overhead with a deep, throbbing hum. The hairs on the back of his neck stood up.

The screen in front of them surged to a new definition. The line along the border vanished. The southwest United States was flooded with orange, including flecks of red, dark green, and purple.

"What the . . ." Mike couldn't speak. He was astonished to see most of Texas, New Mexico, Arizona and California flooded with color.

"Okay," Alex began taking a step toward the screen, "this is what's happening right now. This is why the passive DHS system didn't work."

Mike looked at Alex with horror in his eyes. He couldn't believe what he was seeing.

"Mike," Alex said, "we've been invaded."

LAPD, Los Angeles, CA - 10:40 AM PST

Colonel Alvaro Herrera felt he had accomplished a great deal in a short time. The detailed planning had helped. The execution was perfect. Ahead lay the challenge of governing. That would begin in two days. Today, order must be established.

The last four of his lieutenants walked into the conference room with stern looks on their faces. The LA police were well trained in street combat and had proved difficult to conquer. The lieutenants had lost many men in battles with police. Today the police had been beaten. They were all dead.

"Welcome to all of you," the colonel began. These were his brothers. Alvaro Herrera felt closer to this group of men than any other in his lifetime. Their valor and battle skills made him very proud.

"You have made this a day of great celebration for our grandchildren. They will dance in the streets in the years to come because of your bravery today." The colonel looked at his lieutenants. The fatigue of battle shrouded the face of every man. Though only a few hours had passed since breaching the borders, the fighting had been intense.

"We are ready to begin the second phase of our conquest and we must move quickly. We have indicated on these maps the location of Reserve and National Guard stations across the area. You will lead your teams and secure those facilities."

The colonel led them through the details of the plan, giving attention to every matter, asking his lieutenants questions to test their complete understanding of the operation. When he was confident they knew their mission, he stood erect at the end of the conference room table.

"Do you have any questions?" He looked around the room.

"Sir, if I may?" one young man asked.

"Of course, please," Herrera replied.

"Sir, we had an encounter with civilians," the lieutenant said.

Colonel Herrera looked at him with surprise. "Did you kill them?"

"No, sir, they posed no threat to us," the lieutenant began sheepishly. "They seemed happy to see us. We were not expecting such a welcome. They brought us flowers and sang songs. They were very strange."

"Oh, I know what you mean," the colonel replied. "Don't worry about those people. They are annoying and stupid. You may kill any of them if they bother you. They are of no use to us. Am I clear?"

"Yes, colonel!" softly echoed from the men in the room.

"Good. Feed yourselves and your men. Then, finish your work." The colonel left the room.

chapter 8

I-35 & GW Bush Expressway, Dallas TX – 12:40 PM CST

Yolanda Vasquez and her mother packed in record time, at least for them. Yolanda's mother Bea always accused her of being the slowest packer. She was the slowest at getting anything started or completed of all the children in her family.

Of course, Yolanda defended herself saying that she was very particular about what she would wear and how she would look for whomever they were going to visit. But it was always an excuse. Yolanda had a hard time making decisions. Today that was not a problem. Clothes of every color and pattern had been thrown into her largest bag, then the bag thrown in the trunk of the car.

Traffic was lighter than she expected. Lunch time was always busy, even in their neighborhood in Mesquite. The mid-day meal was a good excuse to celebrate. At least in the Vasquez family, mealtime was a time of celebration. It was the same with many of the families who had come to the States from their village.

As she drove, Yolanda was lost in her thoughts of childhood. Life was simple in Cabo San Lucas. But when the large hotels came and brought high paying jobs life was different. Not everyone could get a job in the hotels. Her mother was one of the lucky ones. She spent many hours working in their home doing laundry, cleaning and preparing meals for those who worked at the hotels.

When a pickup truck, filled with very angry looking men cut her off, she was slammed back to reality. The truck swerved into her lane, nearly clipping her right front fender. She held her tongue and stifled the urge to honk at these idiots.

"Honk at them!" her mother yelled. "How can they be so rude! I'll show them a thing or two! Where is my phone? I'll call the police!"

Bea Vasquez began angrily rummaging through her handbag. She wanted to pull out a pistol, but she knew the problem of an illegal Mexican grandmother carrying a gun. There was no good outcome if she were caught. Still, she wanted to.

"Mama! No!" Yolanda shouted back at her. "Mama, those look like the men I told you about! Not the same ones, but, look, see how angry they are? Look at their eyes."

Bea went white. In her moment of anger she hadn't seen the eyes of the men in the truck. They glared at her with an unspoken warning. Yes. They would shoot her right there on the spot. Then they would have a good laugh and go on their way.

"No, Mama! You can't!" Yolanda reached over and touched her mother's arm. Bea was barely aware of her touch. Two of the men looked directly at her as they passed. She knew the threat in their look. She'd seen that look before.

"Yes, yes, baby. I know," Bea said without looking at Yolanda. Her eyes were fixed on the pickup. She had nearly forgotten. She had been barely older than Yolanda when she last saw that hate. It was the same look on the face of the man who killed her husband when Yolanda was a baby. She had forgotten, but she knew the look.

Mainside, Camp Pendleton, CA – 10:45 AM PST

The dust seemed to be settling a little. Brigadier General Gene Westrup and Sergeant Major John Michaels stood at the window sipping just about the best coffee in the northern hemisphere. An alert of this massive scale was unusual. It was just as unusual as the niggling thought that would not leave the back of the general's mind.

"John, let's get a sit rep and see what's up," Gene said softly to his friend.

"Your wish is my command, buddy." John Michaels picked up his desk phone and quietly repeated the general's request. The phone was returned to the cradle.

"It'll take a couple of minutes. The boys are just now set up and beginning to collect reports. I would imagine everyone is enjoying a break in their routine on such a beautiful day." He smiled as he spoke. The desk phone rang.

"Michaels," he snapped into the receiver.

"Sergeant major, this is Lieutenant Evans in Ops. You called for a sit rep?"

"Yes, lieutenant. What do you have for me?" John Michaels looked into the distance with a fixed expression. He grunted, then listened some more. Then he grunted again.

General Gene was curious. He couldn't read his friend's face well enough to make a determination. And all the grunting was getting on his nerves. Finally, John spoke to the lieutenant.

"Thank you, lieutenant. Keep your ears and eyes open, and let me know immediately if anything changes." John grunted once more, paused, and replaced the phone.

"What the hell is going on?" Gene was amused and irritated at the same time.

"Well, sir, everything's pretty quiet. The deployment is at one hundred percent. There is no activity on the perimeter." John looked at Gene without amusement.

"Gene, the AWAC we borrowed is picking up a lot of chatter. And it's not our guys they've been listening to." He paused and stared directly at Gene.

"So? Come on John. What is it?" Gene was normally a patient man, but the general was coming out in him.

"Gene, the chatter is military sounding and mostly in Spanish."

"Mostly?"

"Yeah," he paused and faced him. "The rest is Arabic."

National Guard Armory, Frisco, TX - 1:05 PM CST

The voices were muffled, but the buzz of conversation was constant. Although there were only forty-five men and women assigned to this transportation unit, more than two hundred were crammed into the meeting hall. To call it a meeting hall was a stretch. It was simply the largest room in the building.

Several of the guardsmen and women had come from other units on the south and west sides of the Dallas metropolitan area. Many of them had witnessed attacks on police stations that left them stunned by the brutality and swiftness of its execution. All of them, and most of the others, then quietly packed up their families and prepared to send them out of town to other family members or friends. The talk among those gathered in the small clusters around the room was grave.

Lieutenant Colonel Bill Jenkins was the highest ranking officer in the room. As he stood to his full height and cleared his throat, the room hushed.

"Ladies and gentlemen," he looked at those around him. "Soldiers." A chill ran through every person in the room. "I don't need to remind you that our first mission, regardless of past deployments, rescue missions, or meals-on-wheels programs . . ."

A soft, nervous laughter filtered through the crowd.

"Our first mission," he continued, "is to protect the homeland from all enemies, both foreign and domestic. Each one of you swore your life to that sacred oath. We aren't here representing a political party or any specific viewpoint, save one. And that one is liberty.

"That one particular idea we treasure has been challenged this morning. We have no idea how many have been killed or injured. Communication has been sketchy, but from what we have gathered, this assault is widespread and well planned.

"While the nation mourns our fallen president, it seems several hundred of the guests in our country, legal and otherwise, have taken up arms against us. I don't know who they are, what they want, or where they came from. All we know is that we have evidence of tremendous violence unleashed against law enforcement in and around this city. Mark, would you share with us what you saw this morning?"

Bill turned to a young man in his mid-twenties. Mark stood and faced the crowd.

"I'm supposed to start a new job with Fed-Ex on Monday, and I needed to provide my fingerprints for their records. Since it was close, I went to the police department over on Stemmons. I walked around the corner to the main entrance just in time to see a hundred heavily armed men crash through the doors and open fire on everyone inside."

As Mark relayed his experience, the room was completely silent. Many of these men and women had encountered surprise attacks in Iraq and Afghanistan. Some of the older warriors still suffered from nightmares from what they saw and endured in Viet Nam and Cambodia. Only a few of those in the room had never seen combat.

"After all the shooting," Mark concluded, "I saw one Mexican lady run out of the building to her car."

Four other men told their stories; one from Midlothian in the south, two from Irving, and one from Garland in the east. The stories were all the same: swift and brutal assaults on law enforcement, leaving no survivors.

As the last witness completed his account, the silence was crushing. A military assault on the United States hadn't happened since Pearl Harbor.

Bill Jenkins stood again to address the group. "Ladies and gentlemen, we have standing orders to stop this if at all possible. But for us to all go home, put on our uniforms and reassemble at our normal unit locations like a drill weekend is just about the dumbest thing we could do. So, we're not going to do that.

"We have our communication network we use for natural disasters. It's limited in range, but we all know how we can relay information from one group to the next. Until we hear from Washington, we can't know the scope of this."

The colonel continued to detail a plan of surveillance and initial response for the various units. It would be up to the men and women in the room to contact the others attached to their units, set meeting times, and begin to organize countermeasures to the attack.

The armory was unlocked and weapons unpacked and made ready. Both pistols and automatic weapons were laid out with hundreds of clips containing seventy rounds each. Some of the weapons were of older designs considered to be out of date, but every one of them was clean, well-oiled, and ready to fire.

The unit assignments were finished, responsibilities agreed upon, timetables coordinated, and teams assigned to complete the alert. There were nods of agreement from all around, and men carrying arms left the meeting room.

The blast that met them at the main door killed sixteen guardsmen immediately. The walls of the hallway exploded and splintered under the hail of bullets. The stunned group of soldiers, back-peddling madly into the meeting room, shouted at each other over the roar of the gunfire.

The deployment was swift. Guardsmen ran in crouched positions into the second floor classrooms overlooking the parking lot. Fifty more headed to the back exit of the building as magazines were slapped into place and rounds chambered.

Within seconds the second floor erupted with heavy fire, surprising the gang of twenty or so that had launched the surprise barrage into the front of the building. Fifteen seconds later, fifty Guardsmen with automatic weapons opened fire from both flanks in a thunderous roar.

The soldiers on both flanks moved into the open and continued firing into the three pickup trucks that brought the assailants to the armory. Although the assailants had initially gained the element of surprise, the gang was quickly mastered and eliminated by superior training and experience.

The firing ceased as suddenly as it began. Silence rang in the ears of those approaching the still bodies of their attackers. The dead men were carefully checked. First, to make sure they were dead. Second, to make certain there were no grenades hidden beneath a dead body.

In the entrance hall of the building, friends knelt over their own dead and dying, tending their wounds with both sobs and prayers. The violence of the attack left even the most battle-hardened soldier shaken.

Bill Jenkins stood in the doorway of the armory surrounded by the bodies of his fallen comrades. A chill gripped his spine.

This is war!

Roosevelt Room, White House – 2:15 PM EST

Mike walked into the Roosevelt Room to the chair he had left just over a dozen hours before. To be back in the same room with a new problem felt almost surreal. All that had occurred in this room just yesterday seemed like a more distant past. Nothing was fitting into a frame of normal time.

The demonstration on the large screen, in the highest security level in the White House 'basement', opened Mike's eyes to the advanced level of technology available to him and the team he was determined to reassemble. But that same demonstration unnerved him.

Alex Hodson was with Mike and noticed his unease. It wasn't the first time he had seen the reaction on someone unfamiliar with the government's ability to monitor its citizenry. He watched Mike for several seconds before speaking.

"Are you doing okay?" Alex hated to see someone freak out over technology. He had seen some visitors become overwhelmed and actually faint.

"Sure," Mike replied. "Why do you ask?" Mike was doing his best to cover the reaction he suspected was clearly visible.

"Well, you're white as a sheet."

"Yeah, I have to admit that was some experience down there," Mike said. "You think those kinds of things exist, but . . . it's just different when you actually encounter one."

"I know what you mean." He was intentionally not telling Mike about the things he had seen that made him feel exactly the same way.

"I mean to actually look at every cell phone—" Mike was interrupted by the door swinging open and an aide entering.

"Mr. Trapper?"

"Yes."

"Sir, there's a call for you from Brigadier General Westrup at Camp Pendleton. Line three." The aide nodded toward the phone blinking on the conference table.

"Thank you." Mike reached for the phone. "Hello, general, this is Mike Trapper."

"Mike, good to hear your voice," General Gene began. They had spoken only twice since Operation Iraqi Freedom. Gene Westrup commanded the force that Mike had been attached to. He was honored to award Mike his first Purple Heart, and later the Silver Star in theater. To him, Mike was one of hundreds of heroes in his commands. He liked Mike, and was proud to know him.

"Same here, general." General Gene, as he was known by friends and family, was a top notch commander, a very intelligent man and a leader with true compassion for his troops.

"Mike, I have a very interesting situation here and I need some help making sense out of it." The general described the report he received from OCT in Little Rock that morning, the strange feeling creeping around in the back of his mind, the priority alert he had called at Pendleton, and the intel they were gathering from the AWAC circling above the camp.

Mike sighed and began detailing the events he witnessed in the last few minutes. He made eye contact with Alex waiting to see if he was going too far with his description. Alex made no indication of any concern. He knew the seriousness of the matter. He also knew General Westrup's security clearance.

"From the look of things," Mike continued, "much of our southern border with Mexico has been compromised. I would probably conclude that 'niggling thought' you described as being almost clairvoyant. You did the right thing."

General Gene could finally put it together. He didn't like it. But likes and dislikes had very little to do with what decades of training prepared him for. He knew the weight of command, and he bore it well.

"Mike, can you give me any intel on what we might be looking at?" the general asked.

"Just a minute, sir." Mike placed his hand over the mouthpiece of the phone and looked at Alex.

"Alex, can that thing downstairs take a look at Pendleton?"

"Today, in this circumstance, most certainly." Alex stood and left the room.

"General, sir, we are going to provide you to-the-minute intel very shortly. Does your AWAC have infrared or AG visual capabilities?" Mike asked.

"Not to my knowledge, Mike. We were using it for some communication drills for some of the recruits. It was supposed to go back east today, but I requested an extended stay. Why do you ask?"

"Sir, you can probably hear a lot of chatter, but I think we will be able to let you see where that chatter is coming from. It shouldn't take but a couple of minutes—"

Alex's return interrupted Mike in mid-sentence.

"Got it!" Alex grabbed the remote and clicked it at the 42" LCD screen on the far wall.

The image loaded quickly. It clearly showed the perimeter of the camp. Literally thousands of white dots were scattered across the map in the camp.

But north along I-5 in both the north and southbound lanes they saw a huge mass of orange with flecks of red, dark green and purple. And to the south another mass of colored dots that virtually covered the town of Oceanside; most were orange, but the other three colors were included.

"Uh, general, sir," Mike began. "You might have a problem."

chapter 9

Oklahoma Information Center, I-35 North of Red River
1:30 PM CST

Yolanda Vasquez wasn't as tired as she was frightened. The drive through the north part of Dallas and even as far north as Denton were particularly unnerving. After the near run-in with the men in the pickup, Yolanda noticed more and more trucks loaded with angry men, most of them carrying weapons.

She drove very fast, afraid to stop. Past Denton and Sanger the trucks were fewer on the road, but several were parked on the exit ramps leaving I-35. The first exit that was not "guarded" by a truckload of men was the information center just north of the Red River and the Oklahoma/Texas state line.

Yolanda pulled into the parking lot and stopped under the only shade available. In another five years the tree would be large enough to actually make shade, but this little bit would have to do.

She pulled the wrinkled papers from her purse. It was the police record of the body at the hotel she had been reviewing when all hell broke loose at the police station. Not that it mattered now. Everyone with any authority in the department was dead. Yolanda forced her thoughts to remember why she even stopped at the police station.

Oh yes, the president! she thought as she flipped through the pages. She recognized the information on the papers as the story she had told the police after finding the body of the man in the hotel room. The nightmare was coming into focus.

On the last page were names and phone numbers of other people, but she didn't know any of them. She wondered if what had happened in the Dallas Police Station had happened everywhere.

Her eyes fell on one name and phone number with an area code she hoped was far enough away. Certainly this madness hadn't reached that far. Yolanda rummaged through her purse for her cell phone and began punching the numbers. She held the phone to her ear and waited.

"Trapper," a voice snapped at the other end.

"Hello?" She spoke timidly into the mouthpiece. "Hello?"

"Hello," the voice said firmly. "This is Mike Trapper. Who is this?"

"Yes, hello," Yolanda said nervously into the phone. "Mr. Trapper? Is that what you said?"

"Yes, I am Mike Trapper. Who are you?"

"Yes, Mr. Trapper, I am Yolanda Vasquez. I am calling you from someplace in Oklahoma. Your number was on a paper at the Dallas Police Department."

"Okay, why do you have this number, and what can I do for you? I'm sorry, but I am very busy right now, and—"

"Mr. Trapper, please, I am very frightened. I was in the police station in Dallas this morning when a terrible thing happened." Suddenly the events of the day caught up with Yolanda. She began talking in Spanish and crying at the same time. Everything rushed out with sobs and totally incoherent speech.

* * * * *

Mike stood up listening intently to the woman crying and screaming at him over the phone. The hair stood up on the back of his neck. "What did you say about the dead man at the hotel!"

"I was the one who found him. It was horrible, but that's—"

"Wait! Please," he yelled into the phone. "Hold on. Slow down just a bit!" Alex Hodson looked up from the new intel they received from Camp Pendleton.

Mike was flapping his hand and looking at Alex with wild eyes. Alex looked back at him bewildered and shrugged his shoulders. "What?" he mouthed.

"Please, ma'am. Hold on! What was your name again?" Mike heard the sobs dwindle to sniffs and coughs. Then she told him her name.

"Yolanda Vasquez," he repeated. Alex stood up abruptly. He knew immediately she was the woman who had found the assassin's body in the Radisson Hotel the morning after the president was killed. Alex began waving at Mike.

"Put it on speaker! Put it on speaker!" he said frantically but softly to Mike.

"Okay, Ms. Vasquez, slow down just a bit. I'm at the White House with some other people who need to hear what you are trying to tell me. Are you okay?"

Mike hit the button for speaker on his phone and Yolanda's voice burst into the Roosevelt Room at the White House.

"Where are you? Did you say the White House, the one in Washington DC?"

"Yes, ma'am, we're in the White House. Now, where are you?"

Mike heard her take a deep breath. She began her story. She started with the morning she found the body, and then how she had gone to the police station this morning to confirm her statement with the officer who filed the report.

She wept as she related the gun battle in the police station and how she barely escaped with her life. She told of the drive out of Dallas and the hundreds of pickup trucks loaded with men carrying guns.

Mike was nearly in shock himself. He was speaking to the woman who discovered the assassin's body, and getting an eye-witness account of the massacre in Dallas. Both Mike and Alex were madly scratching notes.

"And when I didn't see a truck here I pulled off to rest for a minute. That's when I found your number." Yolanda felt drained. Had one been available, she could have crawled into bed and slept for hours.

"Ms. Vasquez, may I call you Yolanda?" Mike asked.

"Of course."

"Yolanda, where are you going? I mean, you left Dallas to go somewhere. Where are you headed today?"

"We have family in Wichita and we just had to get away. I don't know, there are so many others still in Dallas. But I just had to get mama and me away from there. It was so terrible—"

"All right, Ms. Vasquez, Yolanda, are you able to drive on to Wichita?"

"Yes. Yes, I think so. I feel better now." Yolanda sniffed and wiped tears from her eyes. "Thank you for listening to me. I felt like I was going insane."

"You're welcome, and you're not crazy. If you feel you can make the drive, please start your car and head to Wichita. What are you driving?"

Yolanda described her car and gave him the plate number.

"I'm going to have someone meet up with you and get you safely to your destination, is that all right?" Mike asked.

"Yes," she replied. "That would be very good."

"Yolanda, after I get confirmation that they're coming, I'll try to call and tell you where they'll meet you. Would that be all right?"

"Yes. I would like that." Yolanda was still sniffling and wiping her tears.

"Good. Thank you for calling. You get right back on the road to Wichita, okay?"

"Yes, I will, Mr. Trapper," Yolanda said with great relief in her voice.

"Okay. We'll talk soon. Bye."

"Bye," was the soft reply on the other end. They hung up.

Mike slumped back into his chair and stared at Alex. Both men sat in amazement. She was an eye witness to the rampage in Dallas.

She was their first contact with someone who had been on the scene. She was the only one from that scene who came out alive.

Mike picked up the phone and began dialing the number of an old friend. Someone he knew he could trust.

Stemmons Blvd. PD, Dallas TX – 1:35 PM CST

"Colonel Hussein!" Baktir Hussein surprised himself by yelling as he answered the phone. "What is it? I'm busy."

"Uh, colonel, sir," the pause was long enough to really irritate the colonel.

"What!" he bellowed.

"Sir, we've run into some problems, sir." The timidity in the caller's voice was almost more than Baktir Hussein could bear. He knew there would be resistance. That's why all his men had many guns. Resistance was to be dealt with harshly.

Baktir was also aware that he and his men were operating on very little sleep, and everyone was on edge. He quieted himself and decided to answer softly. He cleared his throat.

"And what, if I may ask, might I do for you to ease your difficulty?" he replied sarcastically.

"Sir, we are being shot at, and we cannot find where it is coming from." The voice on the phone was fearful and clearly under great stress. "We were reviewing the map to our objective when two of our men were hit. They died instantly. We ducked behind the truck, believing it a safe place, but two more were shot as we hid."

"So, you would like me to come up there and ask them to stop shooting at you?" Colonel Hussein rubbed his temples. *Why am I surrounded by imbeciles*? "How many of your men have weapons?"

"Sir, we all have weapons, even extra ones, especially now with four dead."

"Here is what you must do," Baktir began. "Are you listening to me?"

"Yes, colonel, I am listening."

"On the count of three you all jump up and fire your weapons in every direction. That will scare them away. Do you understand?" Baktir held little confidence that the soldier did actually understand.

"Yes, sir. We will do that."

Before Baktir could answer he heard the thud of the impact of a bullet through the receiver. He knew the sound. The man he was talking to was dead.

Faint voices on the other end of the line began yelling at each other in Spanish. He understood some of it. But it was obvious to him that his team was pinned down and being systematically eliminated. There were more shots. Two, then three in rapid succession. Then it was quiet.

"Hello? Are you there?" Baktir ventured a question on the chance some of the men had found cover. "Hello? Is anybody there? Hello!"

Suddenly he heard a voice. It wasn't in Spanish.

"Yes, whoever you are, you sick son-of-a-bitch. We're here. We're gonna clean up your garbage, and then we're coming to get you!" The call ended with the sound of crushing plastic.

Baktir sat up abruptly and held his phone away from him. *How did they get there so quickly? How could that be? How could they know?*

Slowly, he placed his phone on the desk.

"We must have an answer for this," he said out loud. He looked out the window and realized for the first time the Americans could already be mounting a serious resistance. *This is too early. This has come back at us too soon!*

The Roosevelt Room, White House – 2:40 PM EST

Mike hung up the phone. For a moment he stood leaning on the table with his shoulders hunched, his head hanging. He'd never seen anything on this scale. He had fought battles and skirmishes in small villages in Iraq. He'd commanded several hundred troops in operations, some lasting days. But he had never faced a conflict that encompassed logistics or manpower on this scale.

"Alex," he said turning to his FBI counterpart. "Are you feeling the same thing about this that I am? Am I going nuts, or is this as huge as it looks?" Mike looked befuddled. He could deal with several dozen well-trained troops. This was far beyond that.

"Mike," Alex began haltingly, "if my estimation of this is correct, you're gonna find yourself coordinating dozens of generals who command thousands of soldiers before this is over."

"Do you know when the president will be back? We need to call in the joint chiefs. What do you think?"

"I think so, at the very least." Alex paused and leaned toward him. "Mike, we should get the governors in on this as soon as possible."

"Funny you should say that."

The doors to the Roosevelt Room swung open and Samantha Long flew into the room. Her attire was far too casual for the White House, and Mike immediately assumed she again had been hastily summoned from some well-deserved R&R, as he was. Immediately behind her was Captain Steven Granger. He was equally casual, and wearing bandages for the wounds he'd received in the gunfight at Oak Mountain the day before.

"Sam! Steve! How'd you get—I mean, what are you doing here?"

Mike smiled and went to greet them. Both Sam and Steve had performed key roles in the assault on the nuclear reactor. Their combination of military discipline and expertise in munitions and explosives proved essential in stopping the attack.

"They came for me," Sam began, "because I was here yesterday, and . . . we were together, and—"

"And I wasn't gonna let her go without me!" Steve chimed in with a broad smile.

"You were together . . ." Mike looked at Sam. What happened next made Mike's jaw drop to the floor. Sam blushed. Mike grinned and laughed. "You two were together, and you both came out *alive*?"

"Hey, we got some things settled," Steve said, rising to Sam's defense. Still, Sam blushed like a school girl. She had stifled a smile, but Mike could see a sparkle in her eyes that he knew well from his many homecomings with Elli. It was unmistakably a girl thing.

"Well, I'll be . . ." Mike sat on the corner of the conference table and smiled. In fact, he couldn't stop smiling. Then he snickered. He felt like he was in seventh grade and caught his best friend holding hands with a girl.

"All right. Cut it out." Sam pulled herself together. She hadn't expected as casual a reception upon entering the Roosevelt Room. When she saw Mike and Alex alone in the room, she relaxed. She was relieved there wasn't a huge crowd poring over piles of data in the room.

"Listen, guys," Sam continued, raising her hands. "They brought us back here for some very good reason. Now, what the hell is going on?"

Her ability to rebound and turn on her hard, outer shell astounded Mike. He knew she was on point and there was much to explain, and still more to uncover. Mike and Alex backed up to the simultaneous breaches of the country's northern and southern borders early that morning, and began to fill her in.

North Texas – 1:45 PM CST

Nearly an hour had passed since the shoot-out at the armory in Frisco. After some very hasty discussion, plans were made and action was taken. The adrenal rush that every soldier experiences after combat was pumping through the veins of every man and woman who left the armory.

Weekend warriors, as they were called for decades, hurried to their homes, gathered families and friends, loaded their vehicles with minimal clothing and provisions and headed north.

Their ability to travel the main interstate routes was the priority. After contacting guardsmen and reservists with conference calls on cell phones, they discovered that most law enforcement and military reserve units south of Dallas/Fort Worth were compromised or eliminated. Efforts to contact authorities and commanding officers failed on both private and military communications. They were probably dead.

Reserve and Guard units to the north were less affected. Some had experienced no attacks whatsoever. General opinion held that the bulk of whoever or whatever created the gun battle in the Frisco armory, was heading toward them from the south. Any effort to resist or combat the assaulting force in the midst of it made little sense. A line needed to be drawn. And that line would be drawn somewhere to the north.

Men and women with military experience were congregating all across northern Oklahoma into western Kansas and southeast Colorado. To the east, guard units in Fort Smith and Little Rock experienced similar attacks. There, the assaulting forces were smaller and quickly defeated.

Had the terrorists been paying attention, they could have noticed the preparation and exodus of family cars, trucks, motor homes, passenger buses and school buses heading north from Dallas on I-35 and Highway 75. They might have questioned the heavy traffic northbound from Wichita Falls and Lawton on Interstate 44, or even on smaller roads like Highway 54 running through Guymon and Liberal. It could have been noticed, but it wasn't.

Mainside, Camp Pendleton, CA – 11:50 AM PST

General Gene Westrup was now able to identify that niggling thought that would not go away: instinct. It was military bred instinct. The confirmation from Mike Trapper at the White House brought the answer. A large mob was gathering at the Main Gate of Camp Pendleton.

General Westrup's concern was for his men at that gate and the hundreds of Marines working and training at Del Mar some five miles to the south and San Onofre to the west.

Two hundred armed troops were dispatched to each location from Camp Margarita and Camp Talega. The forces were instructed to establish a perimeter several hundred yards from the gate should there be an advance by the mobs on the other side.

The deployment was nearly complete, and the niggling in the general's brain converted itself to combat mode. He pulled out all the stops. No one had seen a mob like this one assembled outside a military base in the history of the United States. One had to wonder, *what are they thinking?* What is the purpose of a brutish mob even attempting to threaten or to make a stand against the best equipped and most accomplished military force in the world?

General Westrup picked up the phone on the desk in front of him and dialed.

"Trapper."

"Mike, this is General Westrup. I wanted to let you know we're at full deployment and see if you have a better grasp of the big picture than we do."

"Sir, we're beginning to get an idea, but it's developing very rapidly. We're making a list of people to contact. If you're buttoned up there, hold your positions until we have a better overview than we do now." Mike wanted to sound a bit more confident, but he knew he didn't.

"Mike," the General began, "I know I'm in charge of just a small part of this, and may be jumping rank a bit, but has anyone met with the governors about activating the guards and reserves?"

The thought struck Mike hard. Every governor was attending the presidential funeral. Most of them would not be aware of what was happening over the last few days or especially the last few hours. The news networks hadn't picked up anything. DHS was barely up to speed. Mike suddenly realized he might know more about the events of the morning than anyone. That is, except for those who had planned the attack.

"Mike?" General Westrup broke into his thoughts.

"Yes, sir, general, I—I'm sorry," Mike stammered. "It just occurred to me that very few people know anything about this. No, sir, the president has not met with or spoken to the governors about the invasion. You're right. He needs to do so immediately." Mike's thoughts were moving quickly and his words weren't keeping up with his thinking.

"Convenient for them, these bastards whoever they are, convenient there's a big funeral in DC today, isn't it? Mike, do you think it's all tied together?" General Gene had finally voiced it. The words were spoken. Was it really one huge plot?

Mike paused. There was too much information. The events were too widespread to be coincidence. This wasn't just a very bad day in Washington.

"Sir, I'm not sure at this point what we're facing, but general, I think you may be right. Somehow it's a little too convenient."

chapter 10

I-35 and 13th Street, Wichita, KS – 2:05 PM CST

The old Derby refinery had been shut down years earlier. It's rusting hulk was a reminder of a nearly dead industry from a time when America produced its own oil. Rachel Jones stood beside her car and sneered at the old plant.

"A fitting symbol of your pompous vanity! Dead." She spoke out loud even though there was no one to hear her. They were close enough. And soon, they would from hear her. Soon they would all hear from her. She laughed under her breath, but the shadowed smile quickly left her lips.

The corners of her mouth turned down as hate found its grip. *Soon enough*, she thought, *soon enough.*

There were more miles to cover before she reached her destination. And she wanted to get there before dark.

National Guard Armory, Frisco, TX – 2:15 PM CST

Bill Jenkins was nervous. The surprise attack at the armory had forced them to make changes in their plans. What began as a plan for resistance had become one of reorganization and retreat. They had decided to head north out of Dallas as a mass force. They had heard of other units in Oklahoma banding together. They could join them and better coordinate their efforts.

"Sir, we think y'all need to get outta here. I think the others are on the road." Jim Parker was a young veteran with two tours in Iraq under his belt. He had been part of the surge in Iraq that had turned the tide. Jim Parker specialized in intelligence and counter espionage ops.

"I suppose you're right." Bill didn't want him to be right. He didn't want the whole mess. "I guess we better play the hand we've been dealt and look for the opportunities that might lie ahead."

Bill kicked the dust with the toe of his boot. He didn't like to quit. He didn't like to cut and run. But he knew it was the best thing to do this time.

"You boys gonna be all right?" He asked the question knowing the answer.

"Major, sir," Jim leveled his gaze at his commanding officer, "we were all dropped a hundred miles from our home base with a gun, a map and the mission to create havoc right in the home town of some real nasty folks. We did that. We didn't get caught. And we came home safe. Sir, this is our home. It's my turn to be the real nasty guy."

Bill Jenkins looked into his eyes. It was then he realized he was glad Jim and his team were on his side.

"Okay, Jim." Major Jenkins grasped the hand of the young warrior. "Keep in touch."

Jim Parker and ten other young Marines stood to the side of the parking lot as the vehicles started their engines and began to depart. The people leaving would meet up with vehicles from a half dozen locations across the north side of Dallas. Then they would head north to Oklahoma.

"Boys!" Jim called out as the last vehicle left. "We'll probably have some company pretty soon. We need to talk it through."

The small army of eleven went through the shattered doors of the Armory and down the hall where their friends had died. They had plans to prepare.

Arlington National Cemetery, Washington DC – 3:15 PM EST

The sound of a lone bugle playing *Taps* echoed across the 624 acres of gentle rolling hills, as it had thousands of times since May of 1864. Originally a part of the family farm of General Robert E. Lee, the land was dedicated for the burial of soldiers. The turmoil of the Civil War and distrust of that time had healed on these grounds that had become the final resting place for fallen warriors. Its most recent addition being the remains of a much loved president, Harriet Marshall, now laid to rest.

As the bugle played, birds flew their erratic patterns pursuing their daily survival. Tree branches swayed in the gentle breeze that brushed by, stirring the short-cropped grass. But all else stood motionless and silent in the final moments of the commemoration of the passing of a president. The last note of the bugle was carried off in the breeze. A nation stood in silence.

In the distance, an indiscernible command was called, followed by the sound of soldiers coming to attention. The orders of the drill sounded the final retreat of pomp and ceremony. The crowds of political and common people turned back toward their normal lives that had been violently interrupted.

Preston Marshall and his children lingered at the grave. He knew he would never be able to thank all the men and women who honored his wife with such majesty. Though they were all performing assigned tasks, the simple jobs performed by many thousands made it significant.

He had lost his best friend. Now he faced dealing with the memories he treasured, and remaining strong for the two young lives at his side. Together they were more than a family. They had always been a team. Together they were unbeatable, unflinching, undaunted. And he knew, somehow, even with Mom out of the picture, the team would live on.

Standing there, Preston Marshall turned toward the White House in the distance and softly said, "Now, go get those bastards!"

Los Angeles, CA – 12:25 PM PST

The police in the greater Los Angeles metropolitan area made valiant stands before their defeat. They were not as quick nor as skilled with their weapons as their opponents. Many fought ferociously to their deaths. The vicious brutality of the mid-eastern invaders bested them in the end.

Colonel Alvaro Herrera sat in the passenger seat of the Humvee he selected from the station's parking garage. There were many cars from which to choose, but he liked power. He took the biggest and meanest looking vehicle he could find.

The citizens of South Los Angeles welcomed the invaders as an army of liberation. Neighborhoods broke into celebration and many joined to help in looting. One hundred years of waiting was long enough. Now it was time to re-unite their American home to their homeland, Mexico.

The colonel's Humvee drove into the plaza of the South Towne Mall and was greeted by ten thousand cheering men and women. It was from here the door-to-door reclaiming of land and property was to begin.

Colonel Herrera climbed out of the massive vehicle and pulled himself to the roof. He stood with his arms raised in victory as the crowd cheered and danced before him. He felt like a returning king surrounded by adoring subjects.

Slowly the crowd calmed and quieted as the colonel waited to speak.

"My dear Latin-Americanos, welcome to the first day of the Great Liberation!" he yelled over the crowd.

Again ten thousand voices erupted in celebration. Colonel Herrera let them go. He was delighted by their enthusiasm. Eventually they quieted themselves, awaiting his next sentence.

"We have come here today to break the bonds that have enslaved you!" The cheering exploded and the party raged on.

"You have suffered for many years under the hand of Gringo masters," he continued after several minutes. "They have grown wealthy and fat on the backs of Latino workers for too many years."

What Colonel Alvaro Herrera actually said was of little importance. Everyone in the crowd knew it was their day of liberation. The suspense was building. The excitement was more than could be contained. With every declaration the people became more engaged in the idea of conquest. They were ready to take back from their white masters what had been taken from them: their pride, dignity, respect, and wealth.

"And now it is time for you to take this land into your hands!" Herrera almost believed his own words. "I say to you, GO! Make yourselves the masters! Reclaim your properties and position and take the land!"

The cheering throng of thousands ran to their cars. Permission was given. Now they would claim their reward. This time, it wasn't going to be simple lootings of merchants and warehouses. This time they would claim new homes, new cars, new lives and great wealth. This time they had the guns to make it happen.

Interstate 35, Central Oklahoma – 2:35 PM CST

Yolanda and her mother drove further into Oklahoma. There were no more trucks loaded with angry men. Every overpass brought renewed tension to Yolanda, followed by great relief when no trucks appeared. She felt she was leaving a nightmare behind, even though her emotions continued to rise and fall. The constant emotional swing was wearing her out.

"Mama, do you want to listen to some music?" Yolanda asked her snoozing mother.

"What? You want to listen to music? I want to sleep. You listen. Don't bother me."

Yolanda smiled. Her mother's dry humor always made her smile. Even as a child she enjoyed Mama's teasing and jokes. Their life together was fun. They made it that way. Yolanda turned on the radio and found a station playing her favorite music.

The band was from Mexico and very popular among the young people of south Dallas. She sang along with her favorite songs and danced in her seat as she drove. All the while, Bea acted like she was asleep, totally oblivious of the music. With her eyes closed, she smiled as her lovely daughter enjoyed herself.

As they crested a hill, the sight before them made Yolanda catch her breath. "Mama . . ."

The interstate ahead was blocked by police cars with their lights flashing. The southbound lane was also blocked. Nothing was going through. Yolanda had given no thought to the light traffic on the southbound side of the highway. Her fear of a truck parked on an overpass had been her only concern.

This particular overpass was packed with trucks of every description. Yolanda gasped when she realized the men standing beside those trucks carried rifles. The traffic was slowing down but moving through the police cars rather quickly. As Yolanda approached, six armed men stepped out to stop her.

Yolanda brought the car to a complete stop. She rolled down the window before she realized the music was blasting inside the car. She fumbled, reaching for the radio. More than a dozen rifles were raised and aimed directly at her.

"Oh, mama . . ." Her voice trembled.

"It's okay sweetheart. Show them your hands." Both Yolanda and Bea slowly raised their open hands and looked down the barrels of too many guns.

"We need ya to step out of the car, ma'am. Just take it easy." The man speaking to her seemed just as nervous as Yolanda felt.

"What is happening? Who are all these people?" Yolanda was terrified.

"Nothin' to worry about. Just need for you good folks to step out of the car." His voice was polite, but the revolver he held was too close for Yolanda to find any comfort in his words.

"That's the one, ain't it?" someone yelled from overhead.

"The license plate checks out. It's the one, sure is."

"I'm opening the door. Do you see my hand is opening the door?" Yolanda slowly reached to the latch and gently pulled on it. The door popped and the man pulled it fully open. Yolanda's mother was helped out of the car, all the while she kept her hands raised. A nervous smile remained on her face.

"Please, ma'am. Would you get out of the car and step over here?" the man asked Yolanda. Everyone moved slowly. Every eye stayed fixed on Yolanda and Beatrice Vasquez.

Out of nowhere a Jeep Cherokee with a sheriff's emblem on the door roared up and slid to a stop in the gravel. A large man in his early fifties hopped out. He was wearing a brown shirt with a star pinned on his chest.

"Hold on there! What's all this? Everybody stand down!" His booming voice provoked an immediate response. The rifles were quickly drawn back and pointed skyward.

"You're here already," he continued as he strolled toward Yolanda and her mother. "Made pretty good time. Sorry, are you Ms. Vasquez? Yolanda Vasquez?"

"Yes, I'm Yolanda Vasquez. Am I in trouble?" Yolanda pushed her hair back from her face. Her hand shook.

"No, no trouble at all. Ma'am, I am so sorry for all this. My name is Perry Hitchins. Lot of these folks call me sheriff in these parts, but please, call me Perry." He grinned at her around a thin cigar.

"We got the word you were comin' this way, but you arrived before I was able to explain to the boys here. I'm afraid they thought you might be some kind or criminal." He smiled a smoky smile. Yolanda was still shaking from facing a dozen rifles. "I was told by Mike Trapper that I would meet someone—"

"And that someone is me, Ms. Vasquez," he interrupted. As he tipped his hat he said, "At your service at a very difficult time for all of us. I am so sorry. This must have been very frightening for you."

"Thank you, Mr. Sheriff," Bea said, wiping the perspiration from her brow.

"Good ole Mike." Perry relit his cigar. "He's a good trooper. You know Mike somehow?"

"No, not really." Yolanda briefly told the story of her experience that morning in the Dallas police station and of their trip up I-35.

"You and your mother are the first ones out, you know. Well, the first folks with first-hand experience, anyway. Gotta bunch headed this way that are pretty heavily armed."

"You mean the men I saw this morning are coming this way?" A new fear began to rise in Yolanda.

"No, not the *hombres*. Not the bad guys. Our guys. National Guard and Reserve folks." He puffed heavily on the little cigar.

"Do they know about all the men along the road? They all have guns," Bea spoke softly to Sheriff Perry.

"We didn't know until just now. They probably won't know until they see them or we give them a call. John, you wanna give Colonel Jenkins a call and tell 'em what they're headed into?"

Someone Yolanda presumed was named John nodded and walked away from the immediate circle. She looked back at Sheriff Perry. He was on his phone again.

As he spoke, he grinned hugely and took off his sunglasses. Yolanda saw the bright, sparkling eyes that the glasses hid. She thought he was a very kind looking man. She smiled at him, and then she blushed. She almost felt like she was flirting and had embarrassed herself

"Ladies, we're gonna get you right on up to Wichita, to your friends, or wherever you want to go. That okay?" He looked at Yolanda expecting a response.

"Yes, yes Mr. Sheriff, I mean, Perry." She blushed again. Now she was angry with herself.

"That's good!" The Sheriff called over his shoulder with a very loud voice. "Robert!"

An answer came from a few feet farther back.

"Robert, come on over here."

A younger man walked up beside Sheriff Perry. Yolanda nearly gasped. *They could be brothers! They look so much alike!*

"Ms. Yolanda Vasquez," he said to Yolanda, and to her mother, "Mrs. Vasquez, this is my son, Robert P. Hitchens III. There's no other man I would entrust your safety to more than my son."

Pleasantries and greetings were exchanged. Yolanda was totally taken by this handsome young man. She realized she was staring and quickly redirected her eyes. She knew she should say something but she refused to stammer. Nothing witty came to mind.

"H—hello," was all she could force out. He tipped his hat.

Her mother took her by her arm as the young Mr. Hutchins began to lead them to his vehicle for the remainder of their trip. Their belongings had been transferred for them. Yolanda didn't have a single thought about her most valuable possession, her old car. Her thoughts were no longer captivated by fear. A new sensation pulsed through her body, and it was one she liked.

chapter 11

As the white SUV headed north, the men and women at the overpass gathered around Sheriff Perry Hitchens to learn what they were facing. John walked to the center of the group closing his cell phone. His blue eyes looked out from under his cowboy hat with a sternness that relayed what he had learned on the phone.

"What did the colonel have for us, son?" Sheriff Perry asked

"Well, Sheriff, nobody's fired at them yet. They got a lot of hard looks, but nobody tried to stop them or nothin'." John wasn't used to speaking to large groups, but he had known most of these men and women since he was a boy.

"He said there are a lot of Mexicans with a lot of guns all over the place. Most of the Dallas families are in the front. Some are with the main group. But they're all comin' this way and should be here soon."

"How far out are they, John?"

"About an hour, sir." John kicked the rocks with the toe of his boot.

"That puts them just into Carter County." The sheriff paused. "Anybody hear anything from Ardmore?" Everyone was silent. "How about Davis? Anybody call back?" Again there was silence. Perry Hitchens knew the several attempts to contact both towns meant the evil they had escaped was nearby.

The sheriff, his son Robert, and two of his deputies had left early that morning to hunt quail. They arrived at their hunting spot before daylight, while the world slept. They were ready at first light. It was a good morning to hunt.

Their return to town shortly after 9:30 a.m. brought them face to face with a band of killers who had murdered two secretaries and three deputies on duty. In moments, the seven terrorists learned the deadly impact of birdshot at point-blank range.

"Scrubbs," Perry said, "why don't you and Bob head on down to that lookout point south of Paul's Valley. Take the 150-binoculars and radio back what you see. Boys, be very careful, ya hear?"

Perry turned to the rest of the brave men and women volunteers and began dispersing them around the immediate area. He kept the groups small and mobile, but well equipped for any contingency.

The sheriff stood on the overpass looking south. He was gravely concerned for many friends who lived a few miles down the interstate. No one had been able to contact them. He was also concerned about what was coming from Dallas. The morning had brought too much death. Too much terror. There was nothing normal about it. Perry opened his cell phone and began to dial.

Roosevelt Room, White House – 3:45 PM EST

Mike briefed Steve and Sam with the information collected to that point. Several teams in the White House lower levels were working to contact military stations, guard and reserve units across the country. Communications were still limited.

The Internet was broken into several localized blocks, and not functional as the world-wide communication tool it was the day before. Cell phone usage was spotty because many services depended on internet transfer stations. Several of them were shut down. In other parts of the southwest, far northwest, and northeast, even buried phone cables had been cut.

Mike turned to Alex Hodson.

"Alex, how frequently can we get updates on the ALI maps from Mort downstairs?" he asked.

"If we keep the data print to a localized area, I think we can update every fifteen minutes or so. We can't just bring up the whole country very often."

"Great. Would you ask Mort to give us a picture of the area around and south of Norman, Oklahoma?" Mike looked at Alex, then back to Steve and Sam.

"I can ask," Alex replied. "Do you have any other places in mind?"

"I don't know yet. We've made some contacts across the southwest, but not many. If we could see where the foreign groups are going, we might be able to head them off."

"I'll check with Barry and see how they're coming with containing the virus and what he can do for us."

"Good," Mike responded. "Then we need to talk with Aaron Stevens at OCT in Little Rock, and get a current stream of intel up and running as soon as we can."

"Mike, the State Department has some tools that might be helpful," Sam said stepping forward. "But I'll have to go discuss it with the director. I'll be back in half an hour." She took a quick look at Steve.

"Excellent, Sam," Mike nodded. "Steve, I need you here with me to coordinate the contacts we make with the guard and reserve units."

"That's fine, I'll stay." He and Sam exchanged glances. Sam grinned slightly and pushed her way out of the room.

The phone in Mike's pocket began to buzz.

"Trapper," he snapped.

"Mike, Perry Hitchens out here in God's country."

"Perry! So, I guess you got my message."

"That I did. And I want you to know I sent Ms. Vasquez and her mother on to Wichita with my son, Robert," Perry said.

"Great. Man, I haven't seen Robert since the end of my first tour in Iraq," Mike replied. "What's it been, five years?"

"Almost six," Perry said. "Time is slippin' by, boy. Only gets worse." The sheriff and Mike chuckled. Then he added, "Mike, do you have any news for me?"

"Not at the moment, Perry. We may have intel that will give us the position of anything headed your way. I just don't have it in my hands yet."

"Is it gonna take an act of Congress and a box of my mother's chocolate chip cookies, to get this information?" Perry smiled. "Do you remember the guys' response to that box from my mom when we were in Iraqi? The smell of homemade cookies caused a minor insurrection."

"That's one day I'll never forget!" Mike laughed into the phone. "I still want to meet your mom and get that recipe for Elli."

"Sorry, but her location is top secret."

"Okay, I think I'll have the intel in a few minutes. You just have to understand we're busting through some new and difficult territory in all this. I haven't even briefed the president yet."

"That's fine, Mike. I understand. You do what you need to do. "I just want you to know if we have a serious situation here in Norman, I might need some help. Catch my drift?"

"I do. I'll get back to you as soon as I get anything pertinent in my hands. Promise."

"Thanks, Mike," Perry replied. "Talk to you soon."

Mike closed his phone and turned to Steve.

"Steve, we need to find out where the foreign groups are congregating. Then contact groups of guardsmen and reserves to slow their progress. Anything new?"

"The guys downstairs made contact with a half dozen groups in Texas, Oklahoma, Kansas, Colorado, and then of course, Pendleton," Steve said. "But that's it so far."

At that moment, the door flew open and a Marine entered.

"Mr. Trapper, the governors are convening in the second-floor Reception Area, and are ready for you to brief them."

Mike looked at the Marine and then at Steve.

"Captain," Mike said, "I haven't briefed the president yet."

"Yes, sir. The president will meet you there any moment. He's on his way to the White House."

"Okay. I guess we're good to go." Mike shrugged and began gathering his notes. His mind was spinning, not knowing what to include or what to leave out.

"Mike."

Mike stopped and looked at Steve.

"Mike, they're just a bunch of men and women who have no clue what's going on. Give them the information you shared with Sam and me. They need to hear it. The president needs to have his say in this. Hopefully, they'll understand we're beginning to get a handle on things, and then let us do our jobs." Steve looked at Mike with such a simple, expectant look on his face, Mike had to agree.

"You're right," Mike answered, slipping his papers into a folder. "They just need to be brought up to speed."

Mike nodded to Steve and smiled. Then he bounded out of the room and up the stairs to the Reception Area.

Stemmons Blvd. PD, Dallas TX – 3:05 PM CST

"Colonel Hussein. We are here as you commanded." The young man's eyes were ablaze with excitement. "We are honored to be part of the great reclaiming of Texas and Baja California for Mexico. My great-great grandfather fought against Sam Houston at the Alamo. We are answering the call of generations to reunite our family's lands to Mexico."

Colonel Baktir Hussein looked up from his desk. He had commanded the taking of the police station on Stemmons Boulevard early that morning. Its central location was perfect to monitor and execute missions throughout the Dallas/Fort Worth area. He was pleased with the progress and eager to hear the results from units dispatched earlier.

"Thank you, gentlemen," Colonel Hussein said, surprising every man in the room. No one had ever addressed them as "gentlemen."

"We have taken great strides in this first day of the conquest," the colonel continued. "Your rapid and decisive action eliminated the Gringo authority that oppressed our people and held our land for over one-hundred years. Your fathers and mothers are cheering your efforts in the streets of your hometowns across Mexico."

Colonel Hussein smiled as he looked at the group of young "soldiers" in their mismatched uniforms. He was hoping they took his smile as one reflecting his pride in them. He hoped they would overcome their exhaustion and not become weary of killing the Gringos. There were many more to kill.

"I need information on the missions we dispatched earlier today," Hussein continued. "Have we heard back from the teams sent to the National Guard and Reserve Training Centers?"

"Yes, Colonel Hussein!" The young soldier on the far side of the room spoke loudly. "Sir, all of the units have returned with great success. There is only one we have not heard from."

"And which one is that?" Colonel Baktir Hussein's tone was less buoyant than only moments before.

The young soldier stood at attention. His eyes darted from side to side. He didn't want to be the bearer of bad news. Not to this guy.

"Sir," he began timidly, "I believe it was one that went to a town north of Dallas."

"You believe . . ." Colonel Hussein's voice dropped nearly an octave. His glare was not reflecting pride.

"Sir," the soldier began again, "*Si*, we have not heard from the team that went to Frisco."

"And who has been sent to see what happened to the fine warriors I sent to Frisco?" Colonel Hussein's voice was turning to a very disturbing growl.

"Sir, I—I don't know that anyone has gone to find the team." The young soldier who had spoken so boldly only moments before now stood terrified and virtually by himself, quaking.

"Then, I am sending *you!*" boomed Colonel Hussein at the trembling soldier. He was furious that there was not a report of total victory.

"*Si*, colonel. I will gather a team to go with—"

"No! I said *you* will go find out for me! Do you understand? *You* will go." Baktir's rage was not satisfied by the deaths of a few dozen Americans. He had fought in Iraq and been captured. He survived the time in prison at Guantanamo Bay, and with deception and patience, won his release.

Now, in the homeland of his most hated enemy, his rage exploded at a moment's notice. The colonel's glare should have caused the young soldier's clothing to burst into flame. The soldier would have preferred such a definitive end.

"Now, get out of here!" he screamed at the young soldier. His voice was deafening.

The young man, trembling in fear, marched out of the building. He climbed into the cab of an old Ford truck and turned the key. As the engine roared to life, he began to sob.

chapter 12

Sam walked briskly into the room and opened her mouth to speak. She stopped. Steven Granger was sitting on the edge of the conference table talking to the president of the United States.

"I guess the greeting, 'hey babe!' wouldn't be appropriate, would it?" Sam smiled a winning smile and continued, "Good afternoon, Mr. President."

"Good afternoon, Samantha." The president smiled and extended his hand to her. The president's involvement over the last few days had warmed relations with many in the State Department. A new closeness with him had also been realized by those working on the Oak Mountain project.

Vice President Makin's ascent to the presidency had come to pass with the assassination of his predecessor, Harriet Marshall. President Makin had been an unlikely choice for the second seat on the ticket, and his lack of experience, coupled with being little known in Washington made him questionable from many quarters. He had to prove himself.

"No, I don't suppose Mrs. Makin would appreciate you greeting me in that manner, at all," the president said smiling. Steve stood and walked to meet Sam.

"We've actually just started mending some fences of our own, Mr. President. We still have a lot to do." He looked at Sam. Steve finally felt life could make sense.

"Have you heard anything from Mike?" Sam asked walking to the table and sat on the edge taking Steve's place.

"He's meeting with the governors upstairs right now. Steve and I were about to go up and sit in. Want to join us?" President Makin asked.

"I'd be honored," Sam replied.

The threesome left the Roosevelt Room and climbed the stairs to the Reception Area on the Second Floor. They could hear Mike's voice echoing in the stairway.

". . . would be the best we could hope for at the moment. Until all communications are reestablished, we're at a disadvantage." Mike looked up and saw President Makin, Sam, and Steve entering the room.

"Mr. President!" Mike exclaimed.

The governors turned to see him, and many began applauding. Others joined in haltingly, and finally all stood, honoring the office regardless of their opinions or affiliation.

President Makin walked to the front of the room acknowledging the applause and greeting many of the governors along the way.

"Gentlemen, and ladies," he said, smiling and partially bowing to the women governors in the room. "Thank you for your warm greeting on a day that otherwise holds great uncertainty. I'm sure Mr. Trapper has provided you with information that is new to you. So, if I may, I'd like to join this meeting as an observer. Mike, would you continue?"

"Thank you, Mr. President. Based on the information I've shared with you, I need to ask for your cooperation. We'll be working with the joint chiefs to unravel what has happened, and stop any further advance. Yes?" Mike motioned to the governor of Texas.

"Mike, from what I hear, you believe my state, along with maybe a dozen others, could be in a state of war with some unknown invading army. Is that about it?"

"I know that sounds simplistic and incomplete, but, yes." Mike replied. "With the joint chiefs, and the approval of the president, we'll convene a call-up of the National Guard, Army, Naval, and Marine reserves as well as any vets that are on re-call status. But we aren't to that point this afternoon."

"Just how long might we be waiting for such a call, young man?" the governor of Alabama asked.

"At any moment, Mr. Governor." was Mike's response. "Ladies and gentlemen, we're gathering intel right now to convey to law enforcement and reserve officers who are banding together across the central parts of the country. Our processes for gathering intelligence are severely hampered, but we're doing everything we can. When the decision is made, may we count on your support and cooperation?"

"Excuse me, Mike." The governor of Vermont stood to speak. "There are some of us that are not convinced a military response is yet warranted. Aren't you willing to admit that your reaction to a supposed threat may be a bit over the top?"

"With all due respect, Mr. Governor," Mike began, "this morning thousands of Americans died at the hands of an army of unknown origin. We have eye witness accounts to back that up. The attackers are brutal and well organized. The fronts of attack include the entire border with Mexico, the border between the state of Washington and British Columbia in the west, and the tiny border of Vermont and Quebec in the east. Sir, honestly, I don't know that you have a state to go home to tonight."

Mike's words hung in the air. The governor from Vermont stood motionless, staring blankly at Mike. Very slowly he sank back into his chair.

"At this point," Mike continued, "I'm asking for your cooperation in dealing with a large scale invasion. You will be kept informed along with your congressmen and women as we learn more. Can we count on your states' resources to help?"

Around the room the leaders of their respective states stood and voiced a positive response, including the governor of Vermont.

Mike motioned to the president who stood and took the floor.

"Ladies and gentlemen, we don't know what we are facing. It is strange we've gathered to lay to rest President Marshall, only to be challenged with another, even greater threat."

The president stopped and looked at Mike, Steve, and Sam. Then he turned to address the governors again.

"What you don't know, and couldn't know, is that these three people, Mike Trapper, Steve Granger, and Samantha Long, were the principle leaders in the investigation of President Marshall's assassination.

They were also part of the strike force that thwarted an attempt to explode a large bomb in a nuclear reactor only a few miles from Washington DC in just the last twenty-four hours."

The governors were dumbstruck and silent. The president continued. "We have been piecing it together all morning, and suspect the intent was to set off the explosion only hours before the president's funeral, casting radioactive material across the DC area. The assassination appears to be the calling together of this invading 'army,' or whatever one might call it. The exploding of the power plant was intended to distract our attention, and enable this invasion.

"We assume those who planned the assassination and the assault on the Oak Mountain Nuclear Power Station hoped that thousands of American citizens, most members of Congress, and the governors of many of our states would be outdoors this morning and exposed to high levels of radiation unaware. You and I were targets of this heinous plot.

"These are not unrelated incidents. It appears to be a well-planned incursion, an organized effort to divide and cripple this nation. The intent also seems to be the retaking of much of the southwest United States back to Mexico. Perhaps they feel they were robbed of their homeland by the early American settlers, and have taken these actions to re-annex the southwest.

"Ladies and gentlemen, I have recalled this team of patriots to continue to pursue this investigation, and what has escalated to war. As commander in chief, I will, of course, direct the military to respond to protect our homeland. But this team has a network of professionals between many departments of our government up and running. I will be working with them and depending very heavily on their discoveries with my decisions. They have many leads to follow. Perhaps they'll discover more persons inside our government who have aided this attack.

"Yes, there have been some identified as conspirators in launching this plan. I am sad to report that my own closest advisor, Ronald Wallis, was complicit in this plan. It is early on, and I would advise you to keep this information very close, and share it with very few. We don't know where these events will take us as a nation. But we must stand together if, when this is all over, we are to have a nation."

The president stepped back and motioned to Mike.

"Mike, we have a meeting to convene in the Roosevelt Room." To the governors he said, "We will keep you informed through your senior senator's office, and make our contacts with you there. Thank you for coming."

The president turned and ushered Mike, Steve, and Sam out of the room and down the stairs. Behind them applause, applied with a definite tinge of astonishment, filled the room.

Arlington, VA – 4:25 PM EST

The cell phone buzzed on the coffee table in the small apartment. The lone inhabitant of the apartment hurriedly shuffled through the clutter in the room to answer it.

"Junaid," he spoke softly into the mouthpiece.

"Shining star has followed the western sun." The voice on the other end of the phone was not known to the one answering the call. Only the code was expected.

"Very well," he replied. "Keep yourself warm." He closed the cell phone and looked around the room. *There is more to be done here. There is more*, he thought. And as he considered his opportunities, a smile spread across his face.

National Guard Armory, Frisco, TX - 3:26 PM CST

The old Ford pickup drove slowly down the street to the National Guard Armory. Its driver cowered behind the steering wheel, barely visible. He down shifted as the truck slowed. The truck bucked and whined as he let the clutch in.

The young man, sent by his commander to investigate, was trapped. He knew if he disobeyed Colonel Hussein he would be shot. He feared if he found the missing team dead, he would find the same fate.

Inwardly, he cursed himself for speaking so boldly. He had been a fool to be so brash. He should have stood quietly. Why did he think he could impress the colonel?

He could see the three trucks that carried his fellow warriors to the National Guard Armory. The trucks were to be empty. *Where is everyone?*

Slowly, he drove to the side of the parked trucks. He gasped when he saw they were riddled with holes. *Bullet holes!* The windows were broken. Everything was shot up.

"Where is everyone?" he said aloud as he came to a stop.

"We're right here, little buddy," a voice said softly over his left shoulder.

The young man turned to his left only to meet the barrel of a very large rifle that was shoved against his nose. The Americans had come up behind the truck as he pulled into the parking lot. The young driver was so intent on the destroyed vehicles that he hadn't noticed them. And the fact there was no rearview mirror on the old Ford didn't helped.

"So, where are you comin' from, little buddy?" another voice asked as a second rifle entered the passenger side window. "You lookin' for your friends?"

The young driver felt all the blood rush from his face. His hands trembled and his mouth was suddenly dry. He tried to talk but there was no breath in his lungs. Then, he wet himself.

Mainside, Camp Pendleton, CA – 1:28 PM PST

Brigadier General Gene Westrup poured a third cup of coffee. There hadn't been time for lunch, and the hot coffee muted his hunger. As good as it was, the coffee would not unwind the knot in his forehead. It wasn't a headache. It was very intense focus.

"John, what's our deployment?"

"Sir," John began, "we have full battalion strength at every gate. The choppers are providing observations and prepared to engage if necessary."

"Do you think these boys are ready to shoot another man?" The question had rested in each man's thoughts.

"General, I know your concern with these young men, but were we ready in Saigon?" John asked.

"It's a grave matter to train one man to kill another. It's a much deeper issue to give the command to pull the trigger. We've both killed men. And, no, we weren't ready. The experience of actual combat is something you can't teach a man. No one is ever truly ready."

"You're right," John replied. "Let's go through it again. I want to discuss the super-toys, too."

Super-toys are the weapons the military doesn't have. They are the science of black ops and commando magic. Very few know they exist and what their capabilities might be. But extreme circumstances call for special measures. The proper tool for the job was very important. Both men wanted the right one.

Roosevelt Room, White House – 4:30 PM EST

Mike, Steve, Sam, and the president of the United States entered the Roosevelt Room and were greeted by one very anxious page and a number of familiar faces. Of the team that had pursued leads for the raid on Oak Mountain there was Rick Johnston, Secret Service; Angela Crain, DHS; Ray Jergins, Justice; and Alex Hodson of the FBI.

Also in the room were Bill Ketcham, Director of Surveillance and Intelligence for Secret Service, and Barry Goldstein of White House Communications. Missing, not surprisingly, was Rachel Jones, whose whereabouts was unknown. Everyone wanted to find her and talk with her. Rachel had been on the investigating team when her role in the assassination plan was discovered. In the confusion, she fled and disappeared.

Greetings were exchanged briefly and the team resumed their places around the table.

"Mike," Sam interjected as soon as she could, "I checked with the State Department and we've been given exclusive rights on a proprietary communications satellite."

Steve looked at Sam with surprise.

"Are you saying State has its own satellite?" He was astonished.

"Well, yes. The kind of thing we need in emergencies." Sam smiled.

"What are the parameters and specs we need to know?" Mike asked. With most other communications reduced in capability, a working method of communication was pure gold.

"It's really a simple procedure," she replied. "Any dish can utilize it. The trick is to know the location, and then to pass muster and download the software. We control that and can make any exceptions we need."

A young page quietly entered the room and interrupted.

"Excuse me, Mr. Trapper?" The page had waited but was obviously eager to leave this particular room. "Sir, I have this file for you."

"Thanks." Mike said as he took the file. The contents were two Advanced Location Identification printouts, or ALI maps of south Norman, Oklahoma focusing on the exit at mile marker 104. As Mike had seen on the huge screen deep in the bowels of the White House, thousands of dots were scattered across the area. The majority were white specks that Mike remembered were representations of cell phones originating inside the United States. Overlaid with the dots were lines representing street and highways as one would find on any online mapping service.

In the upper right hand corner of the first picture was the date and time stamp of when the ALI mapping was completed. He noted the date on the first page was two days ago at four in the afternoon. Then, he moved to the second ALI map.

The lines and dots were much the same, but there was a concentration of white dots in a diagonal line southwest of the city limits of Norman. Farther south and to the east, Mike saw another distinct grouping of white dots, followed by hundreds of orange dots, all tracing the path of northbound Interstate 35.

The shock on Mike's face was seen by everyone. He turned to Alex.

"Alex, update everyone as much as you can on these ALI maps. I need to make a phone call."

He tossed the maps to Alex and stepped into the hallway.

Stemmons Blvd. PD, Dallas TX – 3:32 PM CST

Colonel Baktir Hussein was restless. Not all of the teams he had dispatched were returning with the reports he wanted. Some came back empty handed. One team was eliminated before arriving at their destination. No one seemed to be doing what he had commanded. Then there was the team he sent to Frisco and the young man he had sent to find them.

"Has anyone heard from that moron I sent to check on the Frisco team?" he yelled at the top of his voice.

His aide immediately stepped into the doorway.

"Nothing, sir. Shall I call him for you?" the aide asked.

"That would be very nice of you," Baktir replied with dripping sarcasm. He snarled and shook his head. *Imbeciles!* he thought. *They make my life miserable.*

The aide dialed the number and waited. It rang. The aide's eyes shifted from the floor to the colonel, the trees outside the window and back to the colonel. As the phone continued to ring he became more agitated and fearful.

"Sir, there is no answer," the aide said fully aware that the wrong response could mean his death.

"Give me that phone!" Colonel Hussein's eyes burned with anger. He grabbed the phone from the aide and held it to his ear. He would force someone to answer by his rage alone. Suddenly, there was an answer.

"*Si?*" He didn't recognize the voice, but it didn't matter.

"Where the hell are you?" the colonel yelled. "Why haven't you called in? What did you find in Frisco, you maggot?"

"And good mornin' to you too, whoever the hell you are." The voice was decidedly American. The colonel gasped and went white.

"Hey, an' we've got your little buddy right here." The voice was smooth and mocking. "As a matter of fact, he's been singing like a blue jay all about you and your little army. Just so ya know, when we're through with this little rat, we're gonna waste him, cause we don't take no prisoners. Besides, he smells like piss and we don't really like him very much."

"You listen to me, you—" the colonel bellowed.

"No! *You* listen to me!" the voice replied. "We know *where* you are. We know *who* you are. We know *what* you plan to do and *when* you plan to do it. We're comin' for you, you fat, rat-bastard!"

The call was again ended with the sound of crushing plastic.

The colonel was speechless. The call surprised him. He had to change the plans he had made.

"Colonel!" his aide said interrupting his thoughts. "Sir, we just heard from the spotters north of the city. He said there are hundreds of cars and trucks driving very fast out of the city!"

The colonel paused. The man on the phone said they were coming to get him. He would give them a surprise and not be here. *Ah ha! That will throw a wrinkle in their plan!*

"Assemble all the teams immediately! We'll go after the band of cowards that flee our mighty forces!" The gleam was back in his eye. He would escape the threat of the man on the phone and eliminate several hundred who tried to run.

He leaped from his desk and ran to the front of the building where the teams were beginning to gather.

Interstate 35, Exit 104, Norman, Oklahoma – 3:35 PM CST

The phone clipped to the hip of Sheriff Perry Hitchens began to jingle with one of the dumbest ringtones his daughter could have downloaded. She did it as a joke. He groaned every time it played, vowing someday he would change it.

"Sheriff Hitchens," he spoke into the phone.

"Perry, this is Mike Trapper in DC."

"Whatcha got for me, son."

"There is a caravan of several hundred that we believe to be Americans. It looks like they are about an hour and thirty minutes from your location, depending on how fast they're actually moving."

"Do you know how many vehicles are involved?" the sheriff asked.

"Well, a lot. But Perry, I don't know how to explain this to you. We were counting pings from cell phones, not vehicles."

"You were counting what?"

Mike quickly explained the locator system and how phones were identified nationally. Perry filtered the information before replying.

"So, I've got a bunch of white dots comin' at me? Are they friendly and do they have guns?"

"Perry, we *know* they have cell phones. What they are carrying I can't tell you."

"Mike, we're gonna keep an eye out for 'em." Perry walked toward a cluster of his men. His greatest fear was the likelihood of a real battle, right in the heart of his homeland. "Is there any help you can give me, Mike?"

"At this point, that's all I've got. But you need to be ready. I can only say get everybody you can, and God speed." Mike felt weak and ineffective.

"Mike, I'm surrounded by good men and women who have been in the fight. We'll get more. Don't you worry, son. We'll take

care of these folks and be ready for anything the day might bring."
Perry clipped the phone back onto his hip and addressed his small
army.

"Okay, listen up!" he yelled to the group. "We've got a ton of
folks runnin' out of Dallas. I want all of you to get on your phones
right now and call every able-bodied man or woman who might give
a rip to lend a hand. And tell 'em to get their butts out here."

Then he turned to John and spoke softly.

"John, call Travis down at the armory in Goldsby, and see what
they have that still works. Have someone get a hold of the boys I
sent to Paul's Valley and tell them to get back here. I'm gonna' have
a little talk with a few friends of mine."

Sheriff Perry Hitchens knew he had some time to prepare. He
also knew he had a lot of good friends to help him.

chapter 13

Oval Office, White House – 4:35 PM EST

While the team was briefed on the events of the day, Mike was ushered into the Oval Office by President Makin. Mike was surprised when the president invited him in, but since they hadn't talked, he was relieved to have some time with him. Besides that, the president was the commander-in-chief and Mike knew he was going to need some heavy-duty help.

"Take a seat, Mike," the president began. "First, I want to apologize for bringing you back so abruptly from your family. I know you've been working non-stop since the assassination Sunday afternoon. I appreciate all you have done, even revealing that my most trusted friend was a traitor."

"Sir, there is no need for that. It is my sworn duty to protect and defend," Mike responded.

"I fully understand that. I am surrounded by men and women who bear that same devotion to this country. I will thank you officially and publicly when this is over. This is not as 'Mr. President.' Mike, I want to thank you as a man, just one guy to another. Thank you, Mike, for your loyalty and service. It's not just a matter of duty or words. I need great people to help me bear this immense responsibility."

"Thank you, Mr. President." Mike could find no more words. His respect for this man, who had been thrust into the presidency, was elevated to a new level. Maybe it was just because he was sitting in the Oval Office alone with the president. But inside, he knew it was more than that.

"Now," President Makin began, "you need to know what we learned early this morning that initiated my calling you back here. And I need to know what you saw on those ALI maps."

The president told Mike of the calls the OCT team in Little Rock had intercepted, and the threat assessment the country faced with the breakdown of the communication systems. Then, Mike relayed the ALI maps information, and the report of citizens making a stand in Oklahoma, as well as the information he'd received from Camp Pendleton. It was all current information and happening while they spoke.

"Okay, Mike," the president concluded. "You have a roomful of people waiting for your return, and there is certainly enough to be working on. You need to know, Mike, that Preston Marshall, the president's husband, told me you were a man I could count on. I want you to know that I plan on doing just that."

Mike stopped in the open doorway of the Oval Office. Thinking again of the friends he had gained in Preston and Harriet Marshall brought a flood of memories to his mind.

"Sir, thank you very much, Mr. President," Mike said and he pulled the door closed behind him.

Main Gate, Camp Pendleton, CA – 1:40 PM PST

The crowd had continued to grow throughout the late morning. The young guards standing at the Main Gate were nervous. The crowd stayed back at least one-hundred yards from the entrance into the military camp. They were on all sides.

Directly to the west, the northbound lane of the San Diego Freeway was blocked. Trucks and cars loaded with un-uniformed, armed men and women crossed the median and parked on the highway itself. The grassy area directly adjacent to the main gate was turned into a parking lot with hundreds of vehicles.

The mob paced back and forth, seeming to wait for some sort of signal to move ahead.

To the south and east, the scene was the same. Hundreds of parked cars blocked Harbor Drive and filled the grassy area behind the apartment buildings to the east. And still, cars and trucks loaded with civilians poured into the area. To the north, vehicles were coming directly across the Freeway onto the grass just south of Wire Mountain Road.

The Marines at the Main Gate were accustomed to dealing with the public in a courteous manner. Today the gates were closed. All the men believed it was just a drill. But as the crowd grew, it didn't look like a *normal* drill. They were outnumbered five or six-thousand to one. It was a guess because no one could begin to count.

The phone rang at Main Gate.

"Sir! Corporal Owens, Main Gate, Sir!"

"Take a deep breath corporal. This is Sergeant Major Michaels, Mainside." John Michaels knew these young men were terrified with no idea what was going on.

"Corporal," he continued, "how many Marines are at the Gate right now?"

"Sir! Twenty-six Marines stand at-the-ready manning the Gate, sir!" the corporal replied.

"Stand your ground, Marine," John said calmly into the phone. "This is a different circumstance, and we are going to handle it differently. Do you understand, corporal?"

"Sir! Yes sir!"

"Give me to your officer in command," the Sergeant Major requested.

"Sir! Yes sir!"

"Sir, Lieutenant Strattmann speaking."

John Michaels introduced himself and told him about the plan. He explained that atrocities were committed across the southwest and in other parts of the country. There was no desire to cause further casualties. They designed a plan to deal with a crowd, or as in this case, a large mob bent on less than honorable outcomes.

"Do you have any questions, lieutenant?" the Sergeant Major asked as he concluded his explanation.

"No sir. We'll prepare immediately, sir." Lieutenant Strattmann hung up the phone and turned to the roomful of Marines.

"Start every Humvee we have at the Gate, and put a driver in each vehicle at-the-ready. Assign every man a seat in a vehicle and await my command." The Marines scrambled out the doors and took positions beside the vehicles at the Gate.

Vandegrift Boulevard was the only way out for the Marines at the Gate. As they watched nervously, the crowd continued to grow. The mob was thousands deep on every side. From time to time defiant shouts would stir the throng to life. And the life in the horde was angry.

Interstate 35, North of Oklahoma City, OK – 3:45 PM CST

The GPS had been true for the entire trip, but the coordinates didn't make any sense to her. Rachel Jones knew enough to read maps and understand longitude and latitude quite well, but why she was sent to the outskirts of the main city was beyond reason.

Rachel prided herself in knowing. She knew a lot. As a student she would read all that was assigned, plus everything else she could find related to the subject. She always made sure she would know more than anyone else. She had succeeded. Her scholastic work brought her great rewards, known and unknown.

To have directions to a particular location with no idea why she was going there, made her uneasy. But she was more than uneasy, much more.

"There has to be some mistake," she said aloud to herself. "This is just nuts!"

She made the phone call as she left Wichita. She knew her contact would be waiting, probably knowing the next step. They would know why these coordinates were so important. Not knowing was what made her angry.

Oklahoma is dull, she thought. *Why would anyone want to live here? There can't be much nightlife.* She sneered. *This has got to be the flattest, dullest, dustiest, and dumbest place on earth!*

Rachel Jones reveled in contempt. She knew she was smarter than most people. Well, actually, smarter than anyone she had ever met. And she wasn't bad looking. Her fiery red hair made her stand out. It wasn't a hint of red. Her hair was *red.*

Flaming red! Flaming, raging, fires of Hell red! She laughed again, loudly. She was feeling good. This was going to be a great day!

Then she saw it. That had to be it.

Oh, sweet Jesus, this has got to be the place, she mused gleefully. She grinned and laughed. She could hardly believe her eyes.

"This is perfect! Who could have picked a better place than this?" Rachel Jones was beside herself. It was too hilarious. There was no more fitting place in all of the Americas to bring the legend to life.

And there it was, right in front of her, only a few miles away. The symbol of all she hated. To her it was the source of all trouble, calamity, hatred, scorn, lies, trickery, deceit and wickedness in the world. There it stood. Silent and ready for its destined point in history, a sentinel of the plains.

It gleamed brightly in the sun. It seemed to stand hundreds of feet above all its surroundings. But there it was: her goal.

The Cross.

The Cross had been standing at the side of Interstate 35 for more than forty years as a community expression of Christian faith. In recent years, residents of Edmond with differing persuasions sought to have it removed, claiming it was in conflict with their personal convictions. The battle was fought in the courts and finally returned to the public for a vote. The vote came back in favor of keeping the monument, but required discontinuing public funding. So far, private citizens had taken up the cause and the funding.

But today it was a symbol with a destiny in history. She was here now. Today would change the world.

LAPD, Los Angeles, CA - 1:50 PM PST

Colonel Alvaro Herrera enjoyed watching the crowds loot the surrounding stores and neighborhoods. This was a delightful side of mayhem to his thinking. He enjoyed watching the scales of moral and cultural balance shift as a result of his efforts.

The shift had come. And it came with brutality. He wasn't interested in the details. The stories would always be embellished. The amount of courage needed to kill a fearful and unsuspecting person was always greater than actually required. But it gave life flare. A little bravado and exaggeration was tolerable.

The phone on his desk rang.

"Colonel Herrera!"

"Sir, this is Benito Delavega. Everything is ready."

"Excellent," Herrera replied. "Go on the hour, just as we planned."

"*Si*, Colonel, on the hour." The phone clicked as he hung up.

Here we go. This is the big one! the colonel thought to himself. *This is one I've been waiting a long time to see.*

And on the hour, it would begin.

Oval Office, White House – 4:55 PM EST

"Mr. President," the intercom on his desk announced.

"Yes, Sharon," President Makin responded to his secretary.

"The Ambassador of Egypt is here to extend his personal greetings," was her reply.

"Please, send him in," the president answered.

Al Makin stood and walked to the front of the Resolute Desk. It was protocol for presidents to greet foreign dignitaries standing in front of the Desk, the seat of power and authority of the United States. The president stood facing his guests, symbolically "backed" by the nation, rather than as a man hiding behind that great authority.

The door opened and the aide announced, "The ambassador of Egypt, the honorable Jalal Uddin bin Kahmir al-Ahmad." The man entered wearing traditional clothing, as did many African ambassadors, preferring their national dress to the modern western business suit. The man's clothes were the finest available, and would rival those worn by kings in years past.

The ambassador slowly entering the Oval Office was frail, and to the president's consideration, far too old for diplomatic service. His skin was leathery and deeply wrinkled. He walked with a cane, slightly hunched, making him look even smaller. His eyes met the eyes of the president.

Al Makin looked closely at this man. There was something familiar, something he recognized about him. It was faint and distant, but there was something.

"Greetings to you, Ambassador Uddin, and welcome to the United States of America," the president said.

"And greetings to you, Al Tijani Mahkin bin Mohammed al Kahn, Mr. President." He gripped the president's hand firmly, but the smile on his lips did not translate to his eyes.

"What? I'm sorry, but . . . what did you call me?" President Makin was flabbergasted. "What did you say?" he asked again.

The two men sat slowly on the couch in front of the Desk. The president was too shocked to speak. He hadn't heard those words since childhood, and only from his grandfather.

The old man smiled, yet his eyes were dead and lifeless. He turned and peered directly into Al Makin's eyes and began to speak.

"You have forgotten, my son. Your years of emersion in this wicked and evil life has dulled your senses, and muted the duty of obligation to your family. You, Al Tijani Mahkin bin Mohammed al Kahn, are the one. One, from many thousands Allah has selected for His holy purpose, blessed be his name."

President Makin was pierced. His memory of his family and grandfather, his early years and training on the family compound in

West Virginia, the mysterious arrivals and departures of many people he never saw again. It was flooding back to him in waves of nostalgia and fear.

"Your grandfather," the old man continued, "was my mentor, your, father my closest friend. You, Al Tijani Mahkin bin Mohammed al Kahn, were trained from your youth for this day, for this time in history. You have been taught and prepared for the role you must now assume.

"Do you remember the words of your grandfather? Do you remember the stories he told you while you sat upon his knee?"

Al Makin's mind was flooded with childhood memories and tales of ancient Persian myths, and gods and kings; the old stories of *Hubal*, the man-god of the ancient eastern world; the predecessor of the fabled *Alilah*, the god revealed fully as Allah by the Prophet Mohammed. The stories he had heard of *Alilat*, the Morning Star, and her sisters *Uzza*, the all-powerful, and *Manat* who held fate, and the thread of life in her hands.

"Do you remember, Al Tijani Mahkin bin Mohammed al Kahn? Do you remember the prophecies of the one called to rule, the *Eagle of the West*, the child of *Alilat* to bring the Truth to the world? Do you remember, Al Tijani Mahkin?" The old man leaned forward looking deeply into the eyes of the president of the United States.

The president felt dizzy. The memories were there. They were real, and it shocked him. How could he have forgotten those stories? They were childhood tales, weren't they? What did they mean, if anything? Why was this so sudden and disturbing? Al Makin felt weak and confused.

"You remember, Al Tijani," the old man said in a deep, gravelly voice.

"I—I do remember . . . but the stories . . . the stories, they were children's stories, they were just fables . . ." the president stammered.

"You have remembered, Al Tijani. You have remembered," the old man said, this time without smiling. "Listen to me!" It was not a request from a diplomatic ambassador.

"Al Tijani Makhin bin Mohammed al Khan, you are the One, selected from thousands brought to this land for Allah's holy purpose. You will honor the memory of your grandfather. You will bring honor to Islam. You will stand, as it has been planned from the beginning of time, as the leader of this evil land, to bring truth to the heart of every man, woman and child."

The old man's eyes were wild as they bore into the president's eyes. His words fell on Al Makin like heavy weights pressing against him.

"The ancients looked to this day. You, Al Tijani Mahkin bin Mohammed al Kahn, have been placed here by their will, and you will not refuse this command!"

The old man stood in front of President Makin, speaking in a voice much too strong for so frail a man. Al Makin felt weak and unable to respond as memories and stories told to him by his grandfather flooded his thinking. Suddenly, everything went black.

Jalal Uddin immediately moved to the door and called for help.

"The president has fainted!" he cried into the outer office.

The Oval Office was instantly filled with medical staff, aides, and secretaries. The noise made by the medical staff alerted Mike and the team across the hall in the Roosevelt Room.

Mike opened the door to see the frenzy in the Oval Office. He ran to the president who was sitting on the couch, his head buried in his hands.

"Mike, Mike, oh, I'm glad you're here," the president said upon seeing him.

Mike looked to the doctor attending the president. The doctor was methodically checking his vital signs, asking questions to check his coherency, searching for any clues indicating something more serious than the stress of the day.

Finally, the doctor sat back. The flurry and shuffling of the mob surrounding the president quickly subsided.

"Mr. President, I think you're going to be just fine," the doctor said smiling. "You must cut back your schedule a bit for a few days. Too much on your plate, Mr. President."

"Thanks, Bill," the president said to the doctor. Then to everyone in the room, "Okay, back to work. I'm fine. Thank you for your concern. Thank you for your prompt assistance. Please, I'm feeling fine."

Many who had rushed to aid the president moved quickly out of the room. Mike looked around and saw he was alone with the president, his secretary Sharon, and Dr. Bill of the White House medical staff.

"Quite a scare there, Mr. President," Mike said sitting beside the still slightly shaken man on the couch.

"Where is the ambassador? Mr. Uddin? Sharon, did you see him leave? Did he say anything?" the president asked.

"Oh, no, sir. I didn't notice him," Sharon responded absently looking around the room. She walked to the door and peered down the hall.

"Well, I'm done here," Dr. Bill said. "Mr. President, if you feel anything unusual, you call me immediately, do you understand?"

"Why, Bill, are you giving an order to the president of the United States?" President Makin asked, letting everyone know his sense of humor was intact.

"Yes, sir, I am," the doctor responded without hesitation.

"You've got it," the president smiled.

Sharon and the doctor left the room, and Mike stood to leave as well.

"No, wait!" the president said, grabbing Mike's arm.

"Yes, what is it Mr. President?" Mike asked.

"That was a very unusual meeting," the president began. "I just don't remember much about it. Mike, I got so dizzy and everything was a blur. I can't tell you what happened."

"Mr. President, we can review the tapes if you like. You know we have digital video and audio of everything that happens in this room. Even right now, we're being recorded."

"We need to do that, Mike," he said. "Listen, do you know anything about this Jalal Uddin?"

"Jalal Uddin? Are you sure his name was Jalal Uddin?" Mike's face clouded and he stepped close to the president.

The president called his secretary into the office, and she was able to confirm the name was indeed Jalal Uddin, the ambassador from Egypt.

"Mike, what do you know about him?" the president asked.

"Mr. President, Jalal Uddin was one of the names in the day-timer owned by Renee Broussard that was found by the police in Singapore. It was in that day-timer we learned the information that led us to Oak Mountain." Mike was measuring the seriousness of his words as he spoke them.

"Mr. President, you may have just held an interview with the man who is behind all of this."

chapter 14

Main Gate, Camp Pendleton, CA – 2:00 PM PST

The crowd continued to grow. The Marines at the Gate stood by their Humvees, ready to mount. The taunts grew louder. The horde was emboldened, feeding on its own energy. The situation was deteriorating.

Suddenly, dozens of Humvees roared down Vandegrift Boulevard and fanned out into the area, forming a line between the Marines at the Main Gate and the sea of angry people surrounding it. The roar of the motors was deafening. The dust thrown into the air by the Humvees blinded the crowd.

Slowly, the dust cleared and the mass was hushed. Between the Main Gate and the crowd stood a full light battalion of Marines with nearly four-hundred and fifty M-16A2s aimed at the mob. A hush fell like a blanket. The silence was stirred only by gusts of wind.

Time seemed to stand still. Each side waited for the next move. Within seconds the sound of departing Humvees could be heard, yet no one on the line moved. The guards at the Gate were relieved of duty, they headed up Vandegrift toward Mainside. Still, on the line, not a single Marine moved.

The standoff held. At a silent command, the most distant squads of Marines quickly loaded into their Humvees and returned up the road. One by one they peeled off the line until the last Humvee roared back up Vandegrift Boulevard.

For one very long moment the multitude was silent. In the distance, a single voice stirred the mob. The crowd that stood in silence before the Marines, once again found its voice. The jeering mob and revving of motors sprang to life.

Then, as if on cue, the entire throng began running up Vandegrift after the Marines. Thousands on foot and hundreds in cars and pickups stampeded across the grassy field toward the Main Gate of Camp Pendleton. They charged blindly ahead, many unable to see because of the dust stirred up before them.

The rabble swarmed the guardhouse at the Gate. They smashed the windows, tore through the building, and demolished everything in their path. The destruction was like a swarm of locusts. Moving past the Gate, they headed toward the Camp Library, bent on trashing every building along their way.

The "retreat" the mob pursued was only a ruse. The Marines hadn't gone far. Only six-tenths of a mile from the destroyed guardhouse stood the light battalion. The Humvees were drawn in a line flanking a single Striker armored troop carrier.

The Striker sat ten yards in front of the line of Marines. The Marines stood watching silently with their weapons slung over their shoulders.

The crowd paused for only a moment when they saw the Marines. Then, convinced of the worthiness of their cause, and the force and might of their huge mob, they stormed toward the Marines' position.

Those in the raging mass ran as fast as they could across the rough terrain. The yells were deafening. Many carried weapons held over their heads. They knew they would have the opportunity to kill this small band of infidels soon enough.

The mob shouted insults as they ran, calling the Marines "baby killers," "murderers," "torturers" and any names of infamy they could imagine. They poured out the rage stored up from years of inflamed rhetoric about secret torture camps, Guantanamo, and Abu Ghraib. It was time to repay the brutish Marines for their many crimes.

The lieutenant picked up his mike and spoke.

"General, sir, they are charging our position." His voice was calm.

"Thank you, lieutenant." General Westrup had called it right. "At your command, lieutenant."

"Thank you, sir." The lieutenant put down the mike.

Atop the Striker, two rather large rectangular frames swiftly popped upright. The acoustic phased array (APA) had been designed nearly ten years previously for crowd control. The principle was simple: create a sonic blast strong enough to render the attacker senseless. It was non-lethal, and very effective.

The weapon had never been used within the borders of the United States. Civil Rights activists had protested the use of the acoustic phased array saying it was a deterrent to the right of assembly. In this situation the Marines held a different position on the APA. This time it was needed.

The soldiers had allowed the crowd the right to assemble. They had given them opportunity to voice their opinions, even though it came from an angry mob. The Marines had allowed them to peacefully make their point and go home. But the multitude made the wrong choice and elected to charge a U.S. Military Base maintained and protected by the United States Marines.

The horde ran madly toward the much smaller group of Marines standing across Vandegrift Boulevard spreading forty yards on either side. The cloud of dust raised by the charging mob was reminiscent of battle scenes from *Braveheart,* just before the armies crashed together in hand-to-hand combat.

And then it happened.

One sudden blast from the APA devices on the Striker slammed into the angry multitude. Those on foot were knocked flat on their backs into unconsciousness. Those in vehicles were stunned and knocked senseless as the windshields of their cars and trucks exploded in their faces. Even the dust from their frantic assault was knocked from the air.

To a man, the raging mob lay silent and motionless on the grassy field.

Roosevelt Room, White House – 5:05 PM EST

The phone in Mike's pocket buzzed.

"Trapper."

"Hi, it's me." Elli's voice flowed softly in Mike's ear. It always happened. Those words had soothed Mike's heart even after the horror of battle and brought everything into focus. Mike instinctively embraced the tenderness in Elli's voice and allowed it to entirely take his thoughts.

"Are you busy?" Elli asked naively.

"Always," Mike smiled at Elli's understatement. "How's everyone down on the farm?"

"Well, there is no problem keeping them here." Mike could hear the smile in Elli's voice. "The kids have kept dad busy all day riding the tractor, wading in the creek, you know, all that non-city activity kids love."

"Sounds like fun!" Mike laughed and smiled at the thought of Elli's dad wading barefoot in the creek. "Did they wear out the pony yet?"

"Oh, that was hours ago!" She laughed. "I wish you could have seen the antics of your children. Mom and I could barely catch our breath. Jackson and Sara were hilarious. We shot some video you can see when you come home."

"Hope that won't be long," Mike said, again reckoning the uncertainty of this assignment. "Hon, it's just more of the same. We thought we had figured it out and buttoned up last night. We didn't know it was just getting started."

"You mean the stuff out west?" Elli asked.

"How do you know about what's happening in the west?" Mike asked. He stood and rubbed the back of his neck as he walked away from the conference table.

"It was on the news. Is there something I know that you don't?"

"You saw something on TV?"

"Fox had some guy on a sat-cam in LA, and all thunder was breaking loose," Elli explained.

"No kidding." Mike hadn't seen the footage, but it would serve as proof that something massive was occurring. "Listen, I have to review some video with the president. Lotta stuff goin' on. Okay?"

"As always," Elli answered. "You know I love you."

"Yes, I do," Mike said smiling into the phone. "But, I love you more."

"No, you don't. I love you more!"

"No, I love you more."

"Bye."

"Bye." Mike was smiling as he turned to those around the table.

Stemmons Blvd. PD, Dallas TX – 4:10 PM CST

Lieutenant Jim Parker and ten other Marines made their way south from the armory in the same old Ford truck the terrified Mexican soldier drove to Frisco earlier. They wore older clothes and baseball caps. Their weapons lay unseen in the bed of the pickup.

The parking lot of the police station on Stemmons Blvd. was nearly empty. Two trucks and a van were the only remaining vehicles. The old Ford pulled slowly and with considerable strain into a parking stall.

As they climbed from the truck the men talked and laughed softly. They appeared to be a group of friends returning to headquarters for further assignment. Their weapons were carried casually as they strolled toward the station door.

Looking carefully, one might have noticed the longer barrels on the rifles. Even the pistols seemed larger. But the silencers were not noticed.

The small band walked down the hallway. Two men lounged in the first office.

"Hey, *amigo!*" Lieutenant Parker called to the men.

They looked up and smiled. Thump! Thump! Two rounds from Jim's .45 automatic slammed the men against the wall behind them.

The next office was empty. The third was the largest and obviously belonged to a ranking officer. They heard voices coming from the break room further back in the building.

The lieutenant motioned four men to move to the far side of the squad room and advance from that side. They all moved forward.

The voices in the break room grew louder as the team approached. Suddenly, a man stepped into the hallway. He was confused by what he saw.

He stood motionless for a moment. The sight of a half-dozen men slightly crouched and creeping down the hall toward him didn't make sense.

He cocked his head slightly to one side and brought his hand up as if to ask something of those coming toward him. A single shot from a silenced M-16 ended his question.

The voices in the room fell quiet. The Marines in the hall slowly sank to a kneeling position. The four on the far side continued their advance.

Three men sprang from the break room, spraying bullets wildly into the hall. Every round flew harmlessly over the heads of the kneeling soldiers.

Within a second, the Marines' return fire blew the assailants to pieces. Others remained in the break room.

Someone in the break room was in charge and giving commands. Lieutenant Parker motioned the four Marines advancing on the other side of the squad room to step into the side offices to conceal themselves.

Quietly, three insurgents exited the far side of the break room unaware of the four Marines hiding in the side offices.

Lieutenant Parker motioned his men into the side offices immediately to their left. Silently, the Marines slid out of sight.

It happened exactly as expected. The three men on the far side charged across the squad room as two more leaped from the break room into the hall. They yelled angrily as they charged.

When they met at the corner of the hall and the squad room, they stopped. For a split second they fell silent. The men didn't know where their attackers had gone.

On cue, eleven Marines stood and fired a short burst from each weapon. The five invaders fell to the floor.

Jim Parker and the Marines made a sweep through the rest of the building. No one else was there. They placed the bodies in a storage room and locked the door. The lights were turned off in all the offices and the outside doors shut and bolted. The Marines left the building empty and dark. There was more work for them to do elsewhere.

Exit 104, Interstate 35, Norman OK – 4:20 PM CST

Sheriff Hitchens and his band of citizen volunteers manned the blockade for any traffic coming from the south. Nothing would get through. And for the last twenty minutes, no one had tried. They searched the last passenger cars and cleared them to continue north. After that, it was very quiet.

The men on the overpass moved their vehicles onto the roadway below. The sheriff's cars blocked the lanes on both sides of the underpass with their flashing lights on full. No one heading their direction could possibly miss the blockade.

The only other exit available to any northbound traffic was the Goldsby exit, three miles to the south. Exit 104 was easily seen from that distance, and the sheriff was confident the oncoming ragtag fleet of armed invaders would pass the Goldsby exit.

Still, a little assurance was warranted.

During the Eisenhower administration the national and army guards began a remarkable growth spurt. With thousands of veterans returning from World War II, and later from Korea, the federal government wanted a method of maintaining their training investment in thousands of soldiers.

Goldsby was one of thousands of smaller towns across the country awarded an army reserve unit. The fanfare it brought to the small town was tremendous. Sitting on the outskirts of the city of Norman, Oklahoma made the small town an unlikely candidate. But the three-mile stretch of perfectly straight interstate made it strategic.

The World War II mindset held that an invasion of the continental United States would be accomplished using methods similar to those the Allied forces used when Germany was invaded. The first targets were expected to be industry, military installations and airfields.

To prevent the total loss of air superiority, Eisenhower designed the national interstate system that gave most major cities a straight stretch of road that could be used as a runway for aircraft. These stretches of highway would provide landing strips should an invasion destroy the adjacent airfields.

The straight stretch southwest of Norman, next to the David Jay Perry Airport, and twenty miles south of Oklahoma City, established it as a vital interest. Thus the Goldsby Army Reserve was born. And with the designation, four M26 Pershing Tanks were assigned to the unit. The old Pershing Tanks had been retired several years back and replaced with 1990's model Abrams tanks. The units had been used for training at Fort Leonard Wood in Missouri for the first Iraqi conflict.

The obvious reason was to provide aggressive, mobile defensive armor in the event of a ground war in Oklahoma. Of course, that invasion never came; until today.

Travis Temple, colonel in command of the Goldsby Army Reserve armory, grew up with Perry Hitchens and the two remained friends. Today that friendship made the call to stand against a threat to their homes and way of life. Colonel Temple made plans long ago for such an occasion.

Two of the Abrams tanks were placed in the ditches of the frontage road on either side of the interstate. They were nestled low behind the roadway and out of view from the four-lane highway below. One barrel pointed down the northbound exit ramp; another pointed down the southbound ramp, entering the interstate. A third was parked in the middle of the road to downtown Goldsby to block any attempted diversion in that direction.

The fourth Abrams tank was roaring up State Highway 74, the road that crossed the overpass where the Sheriff and his small army waited. It was a short trip even for the aging tank.

Once he arrived, Travis drove the monster tank down the embankment on the north side of the overpass and parked facing south, directly into the northbound lane.

Throughout the afternoon word spread across the county, all over Norman and into the southern neighborhoods of Oklahoma City. The ranks of the volunteers grew to over seven hundred well-armed veterans. Vets from Vietnam, both Iraqi conflicts, the Granada invasion and Afghanistan, streamed to the group preparing for a showdown on the Oklahoma prairie.

"Tiger Three, this is Tiger Six," Travis said into the mike. "Do you copy?"

"Affirmative, Tiger Six. We're set," the reply scratched through his headset.

Travis confirmed the position of the other two Abrams tanks and popped out of the main hatch looking for Sheriff Hitchens.

"We're good to go, sheriff!" he yelled to Perry Hitchens standing on the overpass.

Perry looked through binoculars down both sides of the interstate. From his vantage point he could see two or three hundred well-armed, serious vets, heavily camouflaged, lining each side of the roadway. He was ready. He just didn't know what was coming.

Life Church parking lot, Edmond, OK – 4:20 PM CST

Rachel Jones exited I-35 on the Second Street ramp, crossed over the interstate, and turned into the church parking lot, all the while staring at the huge cross at the front of the church complex. It rose 163 feet above the Oklahoma prairie and represented everything Rachel hated.

She checked her GPS just to make sure. It read 35°39'N and 97°35'W. This was the spot. The coordinates matched her instructions exactly.

A silent rage fomented deep inside Rachel, leaving her nothing on which to vent. It was more than tension, more than anger. For her entire life she had been subjugated to other people and their ideas of what she should be. Her parents, her teachers, the people at the church where she grew up. No one ever asked her. They all told her what she should do.

No one asked her!

What I think and want is important! she thought. *I have a brain! I have a will! Don't you tell me what I should do! Don't tell me!*

She looked at herself in the rearview mirror and saw the anger. She knew that rage and it empowered her. It was that rage that pushed her mother down the basement stairs. It was that rage that tried to kill her older brother with an axe. She knew it. She knew it well.

Now it's time for someone else to meet you! she snarled at her reflection. *Now it's time for someone else!*

1742 N. Waco, Wichita, KS – 4:35 PM CST

The white SUV rumbled up the old brick street that had once been smooth. Over the years, the roots of the large trees along the curbs had grown, pushing up some of the bricks slightly into rolling mounds. Wichita was one of the early "cow towns" of the 1800s that served as a trail-end for the cattle drives of the great Old West.

The railroad made it possible. The original plan called for the small town of Valley Center, north of Wichita, to be the rail-head. But the "pistols and payoffs politics" of the Old West had its influence, and Wichita won the designation.

The change of the original plan brought business and industry to the city, and with it growth. Valley Center remained a quiet, small town for over a hundred years and remains so today.

But Wichita grew into a bustling metropolis, annexing and encompassing smaller towns and villages in its expansion. With development came gangs and drugs, and their degrading influence on the established mid-western values of the city.

The north side of the city was home to hundreds of Mexican and Central American families who had entered the States legally, worked hard all their lives, and established a responsible Latino community. They were proud of their heritage and the contributions they made.

But the gangs caused serious problems for and in the Latino community. Divisions rose and lines were drawn. Bad feelings grew between families, as well as nationalities, and the solution didn't seem near.

Robert Hitchens pulled to the curb. The driveway to the home of Yolanda's relatives was narrow, and he didn't want to accidentally drive over the high curb.

"Mama," Yolanda said looking at her mother, "do you think Uncle Ernesto will be upset that we didn't call first?"

"No, baby," Bea replied. "I bounced him around when he was only a *bambino*. He knows how to respect his big sister."

Although Bea's five-foot-three-inch stature didn't qualify her as big, her birth-order and age was all the authority she needed. To her, family was more important than anything. The order of birth was a foundational element of the Latino family she belonged to and was greatly respected.

The threesome approached the house and rang the doorbell. They heard rustling in the house as someone made their way to the door. The door swung open to reveal a short, stout man in dirty jeans and a plaid shirt. The shirt tail hung loosely at his waist separated by a modestly round belly.

Not expecting visitors, he stood there looking for a split second.

"Bea! Yolanda! Oh my goodness! What are you doing here?" His exuberance slipped into Spanish, hugging and pulling the two women into the house. Over his shoulder, he called into the house, and a woman wearing an apron emerged from the kitchen.

Now the noise and conversation had four simultaneous participants. They talked rapidly over each other's words, smiling and laughing. They were joined by two teenaged children from upstairs and the volume ratcheted up another notch.

Just inside the doorway, a tall, handsome, very non-Latino young man stood with a sheepish grin on his face. Yolanda suddenly realized Robert Hitchens, their escort and deliverer, was standing awkwardly alone.

"Robert! Robert, come here!" she called to him from the midst of the throng. "Uncle Ernesto, Aunt Juanita, this is our friend Mr. Robert Hitchens, who drove us here from Norman, Oklahoma."

"All the way from Norman?" Ernesto asked. "You have come a long way. Please come and sit down. Mama . . ." The conversation was again lost in a rapid peal of Spanish. Orders were given, plates were set, chairs shuffled from all over the house, and dinner was brought to the dining room table.

Yolanda made sure she sat beside the tall young man from Oklahoma. She would translate the conversation when it lapsed into Spanish. They all laughed and ate the feast Juanita had been preparing for the last two hours. It was time for celebration. It was dinner.

Yolanda removed herself entirely from the memories of the day. There would be time for telling the reasons for their sudden arrival. The discussion would continue late into the night.

For now, Yolanda felt safe at his side, as well as a new hope in life. And Robert sat quietly, right beside her.

chapter 15

Main Gate, Camp Pendleton, CA – 2:35 PM PST

The Marines who guarded the Gate and the light battalion that came to their aid began to work through the unconscious mob that challenged them. They started at the back edge of the horde with those who were least affected by the acoustic phased array. As expected, they were the first to begin recovering.

Another four hundred Marines were en route to the Main Gate area. They would begin processing those along the front perimeter, providing medical aid where needed, making identification of those involved, and placing into custody certain parties of interest.

Lieutenant Mark Strattmann had watched the crowd warily from inside the guard station at the Gate all morning and into the afternoon. He evacuated at the right time, and none of those in his command had been injured.

"Corporal, are you finding identification on these people?" the lieutenant asked as he approached a pickup truck.

"Sir, so far none of them have anything," the corporal replied. "The guys in all six of the trucks here have no ID at all, sir."

"Sergeant," Lieutenant Strattmann called over his shoulder. "Process everyone without ID for detention until we know who they are."

And so it began. Those without ID were immediately arrested and placed into custody with the Military Police. Those with identification were detained and questioned. Some were released and sent on their way with throbbing heads resulting from the acoustic concussion. Those who were suffering ill effects of disorientation or nausea, often caused by the APA, were treated by the Marine medical staff, questioned and released.

The majority of the fifteen thousand people were simply swept up in the energy of a revolution. They responded with mob mentality to the urgings of those in charge. Most were even apologizing for their behavior as they left. The Marines collected their names and addresses and told them they would be in contact.

Then, there were the others. They had no identification. They were responding with only blank stares to the questions asked them. Believing they would be shielded from any response from the Marines, they hid at the back of the mob. They were wrong.

Those men were photographed, fingerprinted, and placed in individual cells. There were one hundred and seventeen identified as non-Latino participants and suspected to be the ringleaders. The process of identification, both civil and criminal, would do the rest. Within hours the Marines would know who these men were and where they came from.

Lieutenant Strattmann looked back at the Main Gate guardhouse. A crew was already clearing the debris and beginning to repair the damage.

Exit 104, I-35, Norman, OK – 4:40 PM CST

Sheriff Perry Hitchens stood on the overpass just west of the David Jay Perry Airport, watching for the approaching armada of vehicles.

Perry was proud of the men and women who answered the call to defend their homes and families.

It had been different in Desert Storm and Desert Shield. It was someone else's country, someone else's home. It was someone else's liberty they fought for. Today it was personal. This was his home.

He was pleased with those who came, and at the same time curious that the number was limited to a few hundred. *Where's the whole damn town?* he thought. But he refused to dwell there. He felt he had the best, and that would be enough.

Sheriff Hitchens scanned the positions of his friends and neighbors. Along the east side of the interstate, three hundred were positioned in the drainage ditch some sixty yards off the roadway. To the west, another two hundred and fifty were divided in three groups behind fencerows, under trees and in ditches. Another one hundred or so waited on either side of the overpass.

With his binoculars he could see the two tanks by the overpass at the Goldsby exit. He couldn't help but snicker at the surprise he imagined those babies would bring to the band of militants.

His handheld suddenly squawked.

"Colonel Temple, this is Charlie West in Number Two. I just seen some cars comin' up the interstate."

"Okay, Charlie," Travis Temple replied. "Can you give me an ETA?"

"Sir, my range finder puts them about two miles out. They just come over the rise north of that little lake the Smiths put in last summer."

Everyone knew about the new lake. While the lake filled very little water flowed to the neighbors. Stopping the water flow for any time at all brought neighbors as close to blows as anything could. The filling occurred over the winter, and on a gradual basis that everyone had agreed on. Everybody knew about that lake.

"Thanks, Charlie. We are advised."

Roosevelt Room, White House – 5:50 PM EST

Mike adjusted the volume on the flat-screen. The screen displayed the Oval Office during the Egyptian ambassador's visit nearly an hour before. The team, along with President Al Makin, huddled at the end of the conference table to watch and listen very closely.

The screen was divided into four separate views of the meeting. The cameras in the Oval office were equipped with sensors enabling them to move and "target" anyone in the room. The four views provided every possible vantage point and detail.

On the screen, the ambassador entered the office and greeted the president. The two sat and began to talk.

Mike watched the image of the president and looked for anything unusual, a touch or indication the ambassador made physical contact with him. They touched only with their handshake.

A few seconds into the meeting, Mike noticed the president's eyes flutter. He seemed to swoon, or lose focus for a moment. A puzzled look came over the president's face. He appeared to struggle with something.

The voice of the ambassador boomed in the room.

"You have forgotten, my son. Your years of emersion in this wicked and evil life has dulled your senses and muted the duty of obligation to your family. You, Al Tijani Mahkin bin Mohammed al Kahn, are the one. One of many thousands Allah has selected for His holy purpose, blessed be his name."

Mike winced at the extended name given to the president. He noted the look on the president's face in the video. It was an expression of shock.

"You, Al Tijani Mahkin bin Mohammed al Kahn, were trained from your youth for this day, for this time in history."

The strained expression on the president's face suddenly turned to confusion and panic. He pushed against the sofa almost climbing over the back. He seemed to resist something rising from deep within him.

Mike watched closely, trying to discern the meaning of the changes he saw on the president's face. He looked different, strangely different as the ambassador spoke.

"The ancients looked to this day. You, Al Tijani Mahkin bin Mohammed al Kahn, have been placed here by their will and you will not refuse this command!"

Mike felt something brush his hip and heard a soft thud behind him.

"Mr. President!" Alex Hodson cried.

The president of the United States lay in a crumpled heap on the floor.

Life Church parking lot, Edmond, OK – 4:50 PM CST

Rachel Jones waited for over half an hour. There was one thing she absolutely could not stand: waiting. It was a pleasant afternoon. Not too hot and the breeze was slight. In her thinking, it wasn't normal for Oklahoma.

"Surely, this armpit of the west doesn't deserve nice weather like this," she grumbled silently.

Rachel fidgeted in the driver's seat of her PT Cruiser. It was comfortable enough. But she had been sitting in it for far too many hours. The waiting only added to her intemperance.

Two vehicles slowly turned off the frontage road and entered the parking lot. Rachel eyed them with contempt and wondered if her contact was such a coward that he needed backup.

Eleven young men slowly extracted themselves from the two vehicles and stood some distance from Rachel's car. They were all of mid-eastern descent. They were all handsome and strong. She could see they were afraid.

Rachel opened the door of her car and got out. She slammed the door just for the effect it might have on these timid little souls. She walked around the front of the vehicle slowly, carefully watching the small group before her. One of the young men stepped forward.

"Assalamu alaykum," he said softly. "Allah is with you today, Mother." He touched his right hand to his chest, and bowed his head slightly in respect.

"You are right to speak softly. We don't really know how well *he* hears." She nodded over her shoulder toward the gigantic white cross that stood on the corner of the church property.

The young man smiled, and then glanced at her, uncertain if she had meant it as a joke. He quickly stifled his smile and again touched his chest and bowed.

"Yes, Mother." The young man didn't want to risk a mistake or create disapproval from this woman. He believed she held great power.

"You have been sent here, on this day, to witness the beginning of Jihad in this pagan land." As she spoke, Rachel walked toward the small group of men, eyeing them carefully.

"One of you has a destiny in this place." Rachel looked sternly into their eyes, measuring their will and resolve.

"From childhood you heard the tales of *Hubal*, the great god of the ancients." Rachel continued to pace back and forth in front of the small group.

"You know the stories," she continued. "*Hubal* was the god whose wife was stolen by lesser gods because of her beauty. His wrath against them was great and he devoted himself to the eternal purpose of protecting his three daughters, and avenging the rape and murder of his wife.

"You have heard the tales of *Alilat*, the morning star, the bringer of revelation and wisdom, how she fought valiantly at the side of her sisters when the gods attacked their father *Hubal*.

"And of *Uzza*, who used her might to capture the spears and arrows of the gods. And how she turned them in flight and threw them back into the chests of their owners.

"You know about *Manat* who holds fate and the thread of life in her hands. Today you will see her hand. Today you will see the fate of this world, the power of life and death, the revenge of *Hubal the Great*, against the one god who survived *Uzza's* might, the god of the Jewish pigs and these vermin who meet here. Today you will see *Hubal's* revenge!"

Rachel's voice rose to a screeching rage. Her eyes were wild and her gestures bold. They had reason to be frightened. The stories of the ancients were nothing to be taken lightly. They believed them to be true and have great powers over the thoughts and wills of men. Even brave warriors like themselves fell and were destroyed for not honoring the mysteries of the ancients.

"And today, at this hour, *Hubal's* revenge will begin." Rachel stopped. She looked carefully at the frightened young men.

"And do you remember the prophecy?" Rachel asked with a wiry smile. "Do you remember the child of *Alilah, the Mighty*, who held all the powers of the three daughters of Hubal? How she will come with fire and blood and bring the Eagle of the West to his rightful throne? Do you remember? Today! Today, *that* you will see!" The young men were speechless watching her.

"Come! Come with me!" Rachel waved them forward with her arm and walked to the foot of the giant cross. The young men followed her haltingly, looking at each other dubiously.

"Here! Come here!" Rachel cried as she stood at the foot of the cross. "Come to me! Here is your destiny and your salvation!"

The young men drew near, not knowing if they should obey her or flee.

Suddenly, Rachel reached out and grabbed the youngest of the eleven men. In one swift motion she slit his throat, and threw him at the foot of the cross.

"The blood of a son of *Alilah* cancels the blood of the son of Jehovah!" she screamed at the top of her lungs.

The startled men stumbled and fell backward. They were stunned, astonished. *This is really happening!* Young Jamal was dying, his head nearly removed by one stroke of the mad woman's knife. They couldn't catch their breath, they couldn't see. This was madness!

"*Alilah! Alilah! Alilah!*" Rachel screamed raising her blood drenched hands over her head. "*Alilah!* Bring us victory over the rebels of heaven!"

The young men ran and stumbled to their cars. They raced out of the parking lot, filled with wild fear that neared Rachel's madness.

Mainside, Camp Pendleton, CA - 2:55 PM PST

Brigadier General Gene Westrup chomped the end of a fresh cigar. Marge, his wife of nearly four decades, didn't approve of cigars. He knew she'd make a joke of it, spray him head to toe with air freshener, give him a hug and kiss, then not speak to him for a couple of days. That was the price he would pay. Today had been a day for a cigar.

"John, what do we have from the Main Gate?" the general asked.

"Gene, the men are bringing just over one hundred men into custody for interrogation," John replied.

"Only a hundred?" Gene replied. "I'm surprised. That was one huge crowd."

"Lieutenant Strattmann said he figures these guys were the organizers, sir." John looked at his general with eyes that conveyed more than his words.

"What makes him think that?" Gene asked.

"No ID, they don't respond to questions, they were at the back of the mob, in trucks while the ones doing their work were on foot. You know, the kind of creeps that cause a bunch of trouble, but plan to sneak away in the confusion. Real dirt bags."

"When do you expect them?"

"They should be here in fifteen or twenty minutes," John held an edge in his voice. "We're going to lock them up and let them sit for a while. See if we can knock them off their game a bit."

"Get out the old thumb-screws, are ya?" the general grinned through the cigar smoke to lighten the mood a bit.

John chuckled.

"No sir. Not these days." John was well aware of the backlash against enhanced interrogation techniques used in the past. "No, we let their imagination work on them. They will go through all their training arguments, rationalizations; all their little tricks on how to beat our system. Then, we'll switch systems on them."

He smiled. This was a game. He knew he and his interrogation teams would win. The stakes were high. He had to win.

"Well," General Gene began, "I'm headed back to HQ. We still have problems at several other gates. I can keep my finger on the pulse from there."

Gene stood and looked into the eyes of his long-time friend. They shook hands and held on to each other.

"Seems like it never ends, doesn't it?" the general said.

"Never will, and you of all people know it." John's answer was correct. They both knew it. No matter how many good and wonderful people inhabited the earth, there was always a bunch of knuckle-heads who worked overtime to be bad.

"Again, you're right. Give me a call if something comes up." He headed to the door.

LAPD, Los Angeles, CA - 2:58 PM PST

Colonel Herrera loved mayhem, especially when it was inflicted on his enemies. To him it was a perverted sense of control. His well-orchestrated plan to throw the adversary into terror and confusion enabled his brutal and violent nature.

But the colonel hated incompetence. Incompetence meant failure. It revealed that someone did not execute his most excellent plan. Someone failed him. Someone would always pay for failure.

An hour passed with no word from his forces at Camp Pendleton. Thousands were dispatched to invade and overwhelm the military base and the children who presumed themselves soldiers.

Colonel Herrera knew the cowardly nature of the American soldier. He heard of them while training in Afghanistan. Attack in daylight, then run home and hide at night. Although he never saw an American, the stories of the Mujahideen fighters kept him well informed.

"What have we heard from Hassan?" the colonel yelled into the next room. The silence that followed his command instantly angered him.

"I said what have we heard from Hassan?" Herrera was on his feet and half way to the office door.

His assistant nearly ran into the colonel as he burst into his office.

"Sir, please forgive me, sir!" the assistant fumbled. "Sir, we have not heard from Hassan or anyone who accompanied him to Camp Pendleton."

The silence underscored the profound disbelief that abruptly greeted the colonel.

"What?" was his only response.

"Sir," the assistant began again, "we have heard nothing; nothing from anyone."

The assistant stepped back in fear of the colonel's reputation. He feared the colonel's wrath. Someone always paid for failure. The assistant hoped he would not pay the price for the failure of someone else.

But Colonel Herrera only removed the cigar from his mouth and stared at his assistant.

"Nothing?" he asked.

"Nothing, sir. I am sorry." The assistant felt growing discomfort standing in the colonel's gaze. Slowly, he began to back away toward the door. The colonel's eyes followed him.

"Get my car!"

The colonel strode back to his desk and grabbed his jacket. *How could so great an army not succeed? How could thousands of heroic fighters not overwhelm an army of women like the Americans?*

It was time for him to find out for himself. It was time for someone to pay for their failure. He would find them, and they would pay.

chapter 16

Roosevelt Room, White House – 6:00 PM EST

"Mr. President! Mr. President!" Mike shouted after Al Makin blacked out for a second time in one afternoon. The president came around before the physician made it into the room.

Again, the doctor checked the president's vital signs, making sure there was no evidence of heart attack or TIA. The doctor was puzzled and full of questions.

"What was going on in here? Did any of you see the president's face before he passed out?"

"Bill, there was nothing going on. We were watching the video of the president's meeting with a foreign ambassador," Mike explained.

"We were watching the screen," Alex offered. "I didn't see his face, did any of you?"

He looked around the group, and all agreed they were watching the video very closely for any act made by the ambassador toward the president.

"Why would this happen?" Sam asked. "Why would someone just collapse like that?"

"It's not uncommon for an individual suddenly subjected to stress to have a similar reaction," Dr. Bill replied.

"But I've been under stress before and never experienced anything like this," the president added.

"Yes, Mr. President. I know your history shows nothing that would indicate a propensity for fainting." The doctor stood as coiled his stethoscope. "But you have to admit, the assassination, the bomb threat, the funeral, and all this other stuff going on, it hasn't been like this before."

Everyone on the team looked at Al Makin. He shook his head and looked at the floor.

"Maybe I've found my Achilles heel; that one weakness I never realized was there," the president said.

"Wait a minute."

Everyone turned to Steve Granger whose face had brightened by a sudden revelation.

"Mike, re-cue the video. This might be something different," Steve said as he walked toward the flat-screen TV.

"Hold on there," Dr. Bill protested. "I don't think it's a good idea to experiment at this point."

"No. If I'm right, we'll know where we are. We can combat it, and find a way to fix it." Steve was smiling and looking from person to person.

Everyone looked back at him as if he wasn't quite all there.

"We saw something like this a couple of times in Iraq," Steve began. "We had Iraqi and Egyptian men behave in the most bazaar manner, mounting a vicious attack against a well-armed patrol with something like a hammer, or a hand trowel you'd use in your garden. They would come screaming down a street at us.

"At first, we shot several of them, thinking they were suicide bombers. But, none of them exploded. Finally, one day, a trooper smashed a guy in the face and knocked him out. They took him into custody and interrogated him.

"When the man woke up he didn't remember anything. We talked to the people in his neighborhood and could find no evidence of him being in contact with an insurgent group. He was a regular guy, a normal man around town."

"What was the cause of his unusual behavior?" the doctor asked.

"It took a while," Steve continued. "The big break came with the next two or three men that attacked in the same manner. We finally learned they all belonged to this ancient order of Islam. It was pretty weird. Mike, is the video ready?"

"Sure. But I don't know about this," Mike replied.

"Mr. President, I would prefer it if you were seated." The doctor ushered the president to a chair near the screen.

"Mike, turn down the sound," Steve said.

Mike looked at him with a question in his eye.

"Just mute it," Steve gently insisted.

Mike muted the sound and pushed the play button.

The video progressed through the ambassador's entrance and greeting; through the two men sitting and the series of unusual contortions on the president's face. Then the president on the video swooned and fainted. The screen went blank.

Everyone in the room looked at the president. He was fine.

"Mr. President," Steve began. "How long has it been since anyone called you by your full, given name?"

"You mean Al Tijani Mah—" the president answered.

"Yes," Steve said interrupting him.

"Never. We never spoke our full names. I don't know why, we just never did," he responded.

"I think it's the name. Sort of a trigger," Steve said.

"Are you implying the president of the United States has a Manchurian Candidate syndrome or something?" The tone in the doctor's voice suggested irritation at the suggestion.

"It just seems to be a similar phenomenon," Steve answered. "How are you feeling, Mr. President?"

"I'm fine." He looked at the doctor with a smile. "You have to admit the only difference is that I didn't hear my full name."

The doctor was at a loss for words.

"We need to find out why this 'phenomenon' exists, and who's behind it," Mike said as he leaned back in his chair.

"Who is this Jalal Uddin?" Sam asked.

"That's going to be a problem," President Makin said. "He's a diplomat. He's got immunity."

"Yes, Mr. President," said Mike. "But that doesn't mean we can't have a talk, does it?"

"Nope." The president stood at the table. "Let's go get that bastard."

I-35, Exit 104, Norman, OK – 5:05 PM CST

The caravan of cars and trucks from Dallas approached the barricade at Exit 104 and came to a stop. The passenger door on the first car opened, and a tall, elderly man stepped onto the Interstate. Bill Jenkins stood to his full height and looked across the overpass.

"Very impressive. The Abrams brings a nice touch. Who's in charge here?" he asked.

"That would be me," Sheriff Hitchens said as he introduced himself and extended his hand. "I've got a couple hundred genuine patriots here and about, and I understand you have a bunch of rat-bastards hot on your tail."

"That's what it looks like. Pleased to meet you, sheriff. I'm Colonel Bill Jenkins, sorta in charge of this mass exodus and mild hysteria." The two shook hands.

"Colonel Jenkins, as I see it, you and your people here are about the only sane thing coming out of Dallas today."

"Thank you, sheriff," Bill began as he turned and looked down the road they had traveled. "It was difficult to leave like we did. I don't take to tucking my tail and running for the hills."

"No shame in protecting the people you care about, colonel," Perry said. "Part of the job, don't you think?"

"Yes, I do," Bill replied. "We left a handful of very talented men behind to watch the home front. About eleven men fresh back from Iraq who still had some fight in them. They decided to stay. We need to keep in touch with them and get back to Dallas as soon as we are able."

"Colonel, let's hope and pray that's tomorrow morning."

Colonel Jenkins's cell phone chirped in his shirt pocket.

"Jenkins here!"

"Colonel, this is Jim Parker in Frisco." Parker was one of the eleven who stayed behind. He was trained as a sniper and more extensively in covert ops. He was a soldier skilled in stealth, who no one knew was there until his work was done, and he was gone.

"Parker, good to hear your voice," Bill Jenkins replied. "What's goin' on down there?"

"Sir, we caught one," Jim replied.

"Caught one? Why in the world are you doin' that?" The colonel was surprised they didn't shoot their captive on sight.

"Sir, he came looking for the ones we killed this afternoon," Jim said. "I wouldn't be too worried about this one. He pissed his pants when Charlie and I surprised him. We stuck our rifles right up under his nose."

"Good job, son." Colonel Jenkins knew it would not be difficult for these men to end a life. It was refreshing to learn they didn't. "Did he give up any information?"

"Sir, Mark made the comment that it was too bad we couldn't water board the little bastard, and he started singing like a canary." Parker laughed as he conveyed the tale.

The young man they caught didn't speak English. But he did know the term "water board" and he was not willing to expose himself to torture. Fortunately, most of the young soldiers who stayed behind grew up in Dallas and had learned Spanish from friends and classes in high school.

"Sir, we cleaned out their main headquarters on Stemmons. We also know where the troops are quartered, the location of the munitions supply, their communication capabilities, and where they're headed next." Jim's tone had swung the entire spectrum, from jovial to deadly serious.

"And where might that be, son?" the colonel asked.

"Well, sir, they're coming after you, sir." Jim Parker's words were exactly what Bill expected.

"Son, you be sure you keep them busy down there."

"We can do that, colonel," Jim replied.

"Be careful. Don't get yourselves caught or hurt. Understand?" Bill Jenkins could give a command in such a manner that the man receiving it felt gratitude.

"Will do, sir."

"We'll be back as soon as we can," Bill said.

"Yes, sir," was the brief reply.

The connection was broken as the colonel closed his phone.

"Perry, this is going to be a huge mess before it straightens out, isn't it?" Jenkins noted.

"That's the way it looks."

The discussion moved on to matters at hand. They reviewed the deployment of troops, and decided those who came from Dallas had good reason to join the fight. The families were sent on into Norman where they were welcomed into homes across the city.

The number of weapons deployed to the ditches and lines on either side of the interstate doubled. Not a man among them entertained a frivolous thought. They were there for a fight. And now they knew one was on the way. Today, people were going to die.

Conference of Governors, White House – 6:10 PM EST

The governors of all fifty states chose to remain at the White House in the Second Floor Reception area after hearing from the president regarding the events of the day. The room buzzed with discussion.

All the governors spoke with their senators and representatives, and those that could, with their staff members back home. The governors from Texas, Louisiana, New Mexico, Arizona, California, Nevada, Washington, New Hampshire and Vermont were unable to reach their offices. No one answered.

In a brief meeting of the Joint Chiefs it was decided to immediately activate the national guards and the reserves in an unprecedented call to arms. They would rely on the information gathered from the ALI maps and begin the pursuit of clusters of the orange dots throughout the country. Regions that were free of the orange clusters would be directed to join with other units to form the resistance, and secure a border somewhere across what was the United States of America only a few hours earlier.

In one day most party affiliations had vanished. It no longer mattered. Every man and woman in the Reception Area held concerns about their own state, their friends and families. There was no time to bicker or be political. Now was the time to make a stand and to keep the country safe from the evil seeking to destroy it.

I-35, Exit 104, Norman, OK – 5:15 PM CST

"Travis? This is Charlie, again." Charlie's voice was weaker than before. Reality was setting in.

"Yes, Charlie. What ya got for me?" Travis Temple could hear the difference in Charlie's voice. He understood it. Before battle, men often reflect on their lives. They deal with fear before the fight. The choice must be made so the battle can be fought.

"Well, it looks like a ton of vehicles headed right toward us," Charlie said. "There's a bunch of them, Travis."

"It's alright, Charlie. Remember, you're in an Abrams tank. They're in pickup trucks. We know they're coming. They don't know we're here. You've got the advantage. You're gonna be all right, Charlie."

"Oh, yes sir. Don't worry about me," Charlie replied. "It's just been a while since I killed a man."

And it had. Charlie hadn't faced combat since the last days in Viet Nam. The war was hard on him, and left a deep scar inside Charlie, a scar he'd carried for over thirty years.

"Let's hope it doesn't come to that, Charlie."

Sheriff Hitchens listened to one side of the conversation. No one could back down. No one could change their mind. This was going to happen right now.

"Okay, ladies and gentlemen, take your positions. We've got rats comin' up the road," Perry said into his radio. Everyone knew their part and was trained well enough to not jump the gun. Perry hoped those with the training would keep the younger and less experienced in line.

Now he could see the stream of cars and pickups in his binoculars. *What in the world do these people think they're gonna do?* he thought. *But, then again, they don't know we're here. They haven't thought that far ahead, yet.* Perry smiled.

The first cars of the armada passed the Goldsby exit ramp. They continued to stream north at ninety miles-per-hour. The Reservists in the three Abrams watched in silence, waiting for them to pass.

"Travis, they've cleared the exit," came over the hand-held from Charlie in Number Two.

"Rog-o." Travis knew it wasn't acceptable tank-talk, but he was a little nervous, and frankly didn't care if it was proper.

North Bound I-35, South of Norman, OK – 5:17 PM CST

Colonel Baktir Hussein and hundreds of his insurgents pursued the fleeing Americans with great haste. The size of the motorized armada grew with every sentry parked on overpasses along the way. The plan was to overtake the fleeing band of farmers and office workers, kill them and leave burning wrecks to intimidate any further escape attempts.

The fleet of cars and trucks flew north at ninety miles-per-hour with no stops. They expected to catch their prey south of Oklahoma City. There they would be joined by other killing teams to finish their task. Spurred by anger and urgency, there was little talk.

There was little talk until the lead cars came over the small rise just past the Goldsby exit. The sight of flashing lights and many vehicles caused everyone in the lead cars to sit up.

"What is that?" the driver asked.

"It would seem the cowboys have put together a posse to greet us." Colonel Hussein was amused. He smiled. Those in the car with him chuckled. "These silly American farmers and cowboys do not know who they are up against. The only things these women shoot are rabbits and squirrels."

The men laughed. They smiled at each other and checked their weapons. This was going to be fun. Killing weak old men and women, especially American men and women, was delightful to them.

They were a mile from the overpass when they began to slow down. They saw the flashing lights on the four sheriff cruisers blocking the roadway. The closer they got, the more they were able to discern it was an actual blockade.

"Look!" Baktir began. "See the cowboy standing on the overpass? Do you think he is the sheriff?" The men roared in laughter at the single man standing with his hands on his hips atop the overpass.

"We will shoot him first!" the driver chimed in with tears rolling down his cheeks.

"Yes, my friends," Colonel Hussein said, beaming a bright smile, "today in the Old West we will have a real Mexican standoff!"

The mood in the car was giddy. Men in the other cars at the front of the caravan were equally entertained. The sight of the "cowboy sheriff" brought laughter from every vehicle. Unfortunately, none of them noticed the large object lingering in the shadows.

They came to a complete stop fifty yards south of the overpass.

1742 N. Waco, Wichita, KS – 5:20 PM CST

Yolanda and Robert walked haltingly to the front door. The noise of the family behind them continued seemingly unaware of their departure. It was anything but the truth. Bea and her brother Ernesto talked loudly as they carefully watched the tall young man and the lovely Yolanda. The looks between them for the better part of an hour were telling. Something was up.

Yolanda walked slowly, wanting to be away from the rest of the family, but not wanting Robert to leave. She liked his quiet demeanor. He was handsome. His smile was breathtaking. And then there were the qualities she could not put into words.

Robert was lost in a similar infatuation. Yolanda had a sparkle in her eyes that totally confounded him. He wanted nothing more than to spend as much time with her as possible and learn as much about her as he could. But he didn't want to intrude on her family.

"Are you going to drive back to Norman tonight?" Yolanda asked quietly.

"Norman?" Robert replied. "Why, no. Why would I go back there?"

"I thought you would go there to help your father." Yolanda was hopeful he might stay.

"No, he can get along just fine without me," Robert answered. "Besides, I live right here in Wichita. Not much left for me in Norman." Robert looked down at the floor and forced his hands into his jeans pockets.

"You *live* here in Wichita?" Yolanda was surprised. *Why didn't I ask that before?* She was ashamed of herself. She had been selfish and only concerned about her safety and getting her mother out of Dallas.

"Oh, I'm sorry," Robert said. "I just didn't think to tell you I lived here. I thought maybe you knew. Didn't my dad tell you I was coming home anyway?"

"No, he didn't," Yolanda said apologetically. "No, but it is fine that you are here. I'm glad you didn't come out of your way to help us." Yolanda bit her lip. That didn't come out the way she intended.

"Oh . . . well, that's no problem," Robert said. "Heck, I would have brought you here even if it was out of my way. I mean, I don't really . . ." He didn't know how to finish. He had almost blurted it out, but caught himself.

Yolanda caught it also and took encouragement from his fumbled words.

"So, do you work here in town?" she asked changing the subject knowing exactly where she wanted the conversation to go.

"Well, I do some work at the university, uh, Wichita State." Robert wanted it to be very clear he wasn't at a trade school or something worse. "I'm finishing my Masters in business."

"That sounds like difficult and interesting work." She had no idea if his studies were difficult or interesting. She found him interesting.

"Oh, I suppose it could be. But I enjoy it," Robert said leaning against the door frame.

They stood at the door, neither one knowing what to do next. Yolanda spied the porch swing.

"Mama! We're going out on the porch," she said over her shoulder and quickly led Robert out the front door.

In her haste she had grabbed Robert's hand and pulled him on to the porch. Once outside she was shocked at what she'd done. She hadn't asked him if she could take his hand. She hadn't asked him if he wanted to sit on the porch with her.

"I am sorry," Yolanda blushed. "I have been too forward. I didn't even ask if you wanted to come out here. Please, forgive me."

"Oh, no. I mean, yes, I really don't mind being here with you." That wasn't what he meant either. "No, I like talking to you. I just didn't want to take you away from your family and all. I mean, you just got here, and I'm sure you have a lot to talk about. You know, we just met and, well, I didn't want seem like I was pushing my way in, I mean, interrupting or anything."

Robert blushed. He had blathered. She knew he was embarrassed.

Yolanda put her hand on his upper arm. She wanted to comfort him and tell him it was fine. But when she touched him, the moment she felt the firmness of his arm under his shirt sleeve, she needed to pause. She swallowed hard and took a breath.

"Robert, you are not intruding. You have been a wonderful help to me and my mother." Yolanda could have dropped the words 'and my mother' and been just fine. She suddenly realized how tenderly she spoke the words. So did Robert.

He looked at her. Her eyes were deep liquid pools that drew him in. He knew he was out of his league. He had no idea what was going on. But it was fine with him. Then he caught himself.

"I'm sure you have lots of guys back in Dallas . . ." His words broke and he looked sheepishly at his feet.

"Oh, yes, there are guys everywhere in Dallas!" Yolanda said laughing it off.

"Yeah, well I'd better be . . ."

"No! None of them are worthy of even a thought," Yolanda interrupted. "No, there is no one in Dallas I have any interest in. They are either old or stupid. I cannot bear the thought of them."

Both Robert and Yolanda knew that not all men in Dallas were either old or stupid. She made her point. And he got it. He smiled with a new confidence and hope that maybe what he felt was something close to what she was feeling.

"But I'm sure there are many beautiful women at the university," Yolanda said with just enough question it demanded an answer.

"Yeah, there are a lot of very pretty girls, but they're girls. I'm not looking for a girl. They're not as grown up, well, like you are."

Yolanda could tell he wanted to kiss her. She ached to kiss him. They sat together in agony, unwilling to move lest the spell be broken.

An additional three sets of ears listened from just inside the front door. Bea, Ernesto, and his wife had slipped quietly into the living room to eavesdrop on the young couple.

In that moment, Robert touched Yolanda's cheek. She turned her face to his and they kissed. Yes, life was going to be different. Life was going to be better.

chapter 17

I-35, Exit 104, Norman, OK – 5:25 PM CST

"Perfect," Sheriff Hitchens said out loud. The armada of vehicles bringing the militants north from Dallas stopped and sprawled before him on the interstate. He stood on the bridge directly over the two northbound lanes. He wasn't ready to duck and run for cover just yet. *I'm gonna stare these bastards down*, he thought.

Everything was at a dead stop. No one exited any of the vehicles. Nothing moved. Perry opened his comm. device that gave him command of the speakers on all four cruisers. Then he spoke.

"This is Perry Hitchens, Sheriff of McClain County. You are hereby ordered to exit your vehicles, surrender your weapons, and lie face down on the ground."

As expected, there was no response. Perry waited. *Maybe they need to think it over*, he mused. A full minute passed. There was still no response.

"Again, I am Sheriff Hitchens of Cleveland County, and I am telling you to lay down your weapons and surrender."

At that command, two cruisers backed to the edge of the road and one Abrams tank slowly crawled into their space under the overpass. The barrel of the behemoth was leveled directly at the lead vehicle. There was silence.

*   *   *   *   *

Inside the lead car, Baktir Hussein saw the Abrams tank move into position with its barrel pointing directly at him. He had one choice. Strike first, or die a coward.

"Shoot the cowboy," he commanded.

*   *   *   *   *

Perry noticed some movement on the passenger side of the lead car. Then, there was the report of a rifle followed by the *zing* of the ordnance passing inches from his right ear. That sealed their fate.

The barrel of the Abrams exploded a single round into the first car. On impact, the car burst into a fireball that was thirty-feet in diameter, destroying the first seven vehicles in the pack. That was when all hell broke loose.

The cars at the back of the line reversed and turned to escape. They were met by three Abrams tanks closing in on them from the south. Number Four drove up the median between the north and south bound lanes while Numbers Two and Three churned along the shoulders on either side of the Interstate.

Three simultaneous blasts from the approaching Abrams incinerated ten vehicles at the back of the pack. No one else indicated further interest in taking on the three Abrams.

Weapons suddenly jutted out every window and over every roof, and began firing at the overpass and the Abrams tank beneath it. That was the cue everyone was waiting for.

Both sides of the Interstate and the shoulders of the overpass erupted in a hail of bullets. Only a few of the weapons were automatic. Most were hunting rifles. There were Wetherby

Magnums, Springfields, and 7mm Remingtons, all designed to drop a deer or elk from six hundred yards. The Americans systematically picked targets one at a time.

The men in the cars were receiving fire from every side. Dozens were killed in the first few minutes. The survivors found refuge between the vehicles in the center of the roadway. That left them exposed to the weapons on the overpass.

The three tanks came within range of the shootout and opened fire with their .50 caliber machine guns. They fired sparingly because the Army had allotted them only twelve-hundred rounds per tank, per year. And those were intended for practice, not actual combat. Each tank had only four rounds of ordnance for their big guns. Today's primary objective was as a deterrent to retreat.

The armada of insurgents was surrounded, but gave no sign of surrender. The four Abrams advanced their positions to within thirty yards from the surrounded cars and trucks. But even the .50 caliber shells were unable to penetrate far enough into the debris and wreckage to curtail the firefight.

"Perry? This is Travis. Do you read me?"

"Go ahead, Travis!" Perry was hunkered down behind the side rail of the overpass, trying to stay out of sight.

"We've got 'em bottled up. What do you want us to do next?"

"I want you to hold them there for a few more minutes." Perry didn't want to make any kind of assault where the lives of his friends and neighbors would be at risk.

"Okay. But you need to know we are pretty low on ammunition at the moment." Travis replied.

"I know. Space it out. Keep it steady." Perry was also uncertain how many rounds were carried by the citizens on each flank. He did know the supply was limited, but just how far away that limit was bothered him.

The firefight continued for nearly ten minutes, but it seemed like an hour. The men inside the cars were very well supplied with ammunition and fired unabated toward their unseen foes. The number of shells leaving the cluster of cars was ten times the number coming in. The difference was the accuracy of the incoming ordnance. Nearly every one found its intended target.

"Travis," the sheriff yelled into the radio. "Tell them down the line to sight-in their ankles below the vehicles. Take that shot and make the kill when they drop."

In a few minutes the strategy took full effect. Fewer and fewer of the insurgents were popping up over the hood of a vehicle and spraying automatic weapons fire into the fields.

If a hunter could sight-in a white tail deer at four hundred yards for a clean kill, they most certainly could pick out the feet of their adversaries at sixty yards. And these folks were very good at setting up their shots.

Suddenly, Perry's radio broke into chatter.

"Raptor Strike Six to Sheriff Perry Hitchens. Come in, Sheriff Hitchens. Raptor Strike Six, over."

Perry scrambled to grab his radio.

"Sheriff Hitchens here. Go ahead Raptor Strike Six, over." Perry wasn't real sure what *raptor strike* was, but he was happy to have help in deciding this matter.

"Sheriff, what's your precise location? Over."

Perry knew his handheld GPS was somewhere on his belt. Finally, he found it hanging on his left hip.

"Okay, we're on the overpass just west of David Jay Perry Airport, south of Norman. Let's see, the coordinates are 35°09'16.67"N, and 97°28'21.77"W, over."

"Affirmative, sheriff. What's your deployment? Over," the pilot asked.

"Well, we are on the overpass with about a hundred troops. We have about three hundred troops to the east along the drainage ditch about sixty yards off the roadway. To the west there's another two hundred or so fifty yards off the road. To the south, we've got three Abrams on the shoulders and in the median. Does that help? Over," Perry replied.

"That's where we thought you were. Prepare for fly-by. Raptor Strike Six, out."

Perry was sitting on the overpass with his back to the battle going on below. Within seconds the flash of an F-22A Raptor streaked overhead. The explosion of the thunderous roar of the jet engines shook the overpass.

The fighter passed overhead at just under seventy-five feet, traveling two hundred miles-per-hour. The impact of the fly-by left Perry breathless. It also stopped the automatic weapons fire from the cars parked on the interstate.

Suddenly, dozens of weapons were pitched from the now battered cars and trucks. All down the line, weapons flew to the side of the road, and men stood with their hands raised.

Perry saw the beginnings of surrender. Some of his men in the ditches began to stand and move toward them.

"Hold your positions! Do not advance! Hold your positions!" Perry yelled into his radio.

The men stopped and turned back to their hiding places, but not quickly enough. From inside the cluster of cars, several shots were fired and Perry saw two men knocked to the ground.

"Hold your positions!" Perry yelled again into the radio. *Damn!* he thought. *It's not worth losing one man to this!*

Perry opened his radio.

"Raptor Strike Six, this is Sheriff Hitchens, over."

"Sheriff, this is Raptor Strike Six. Go ahead, over."

"Raptor Strike Six, do your stuff. Over," Perry said into his radio.

"Sheriff, tell your boys to keep their heads down. Raptor Strike Six, out."

Perry grabbed his hand-held and yelled into it.

"Everybody down! Hold your positions! Stay Down!" He had no idea what to expect.

"Surrender your weapons and lie face down on the ground!" Sheriff Hitchens said into the comm. device. His words echoed from the speakers on the parked cruisers blocking the interstate. "Face down on the ground!" he repeated.

Many of those who surrendered their guns and stood with their hands in the air, moved to the side of the road and lay face down on the shoulder of the roadway. Not all did.

In trial tests, the F-22A Raptor, while flying Mach 1.5 at 50,000 feet, successfully dropped a 1,000 pound JDAM rocket on a moving target 24 miles away. The fly-by had been for effect, it wasn't necessary.

The targets were entered and three JDAMs launched from the F-22A Raptor. By this time, the fighter was fifteen miles to the east, heading north. The missiles traced a wide arch through the blue sky and turned toward the Interstate.

Perry watched their path as the missiles turned toward where he sat. He was suddenly hoping that young pilot had his numbers straight.

"Everybody off the bridge!" he yelled as he began running toward the end of the overpass. "Get off the damn bridge!"

The dozens of armed men on the bridge scrambled to the embankments at the end of the overpass just in time.

The three JDAMs slammed into the cars and trucks along the northbound lane of I-35, engulfing them and their occupants in a wall of flame. There was no more small-arms fire to be heard.

The battle on Interstate 35, or the "Stand-off at Norman" as it came to be known, was over. The forward charge of the insurgent army was stopped. Twenty-two of those who surrendered their weapons survived the blast. They were far enough down the shoulder, laying on their faces, and avoided the explosion of the missiles. A total of four hundred and thirty-seven died in the attack. None were United States citizens.

Months later it would be concluded that all but eighteen were illegal Central American immigrants. The eighteen non-Latino combatants were identified as being from Iraq, Egypt, and Syria. They were also in the country illegally.

Only two Oklahoma residents were injured in the incident. Both were shot when several of the insurgents had tossed out their weapons and surrendered. Their wounds were serious, but not life threatening.

Norman, Oklahoma had faced the challenge and won.

White House Basement, Washington DC – 6:35 PM EST

Rick Johnston and his partner George Raker were reviewing security tapes after the unusual meeting between the president and the ambassador from Egypt. The tapes followed the old man in traditional Egyptian dress as he left the Oval Office.

On the tape it was obvious. Everyone was running into the Oval Office while the old man fearlessly walked away. The video followed him down the long hallway, past the Cabinet meeting room, and into the hallway connecting the West Wing to the White House.

But the old man did not turn toward the White House. He went immediately outside to a waiting car. Rick made note of the license plate and sent it down one level to be traced and confirm the owner of the vehicle.

Once the car left the White House grounds, Rick and George knew their task would become more difficult. Washington DC, the home of the federal government, was so afraid of one administration or another, traffic cameras were few and far between. No one wanted to be the mayor of the city that placed cameras on every corner and share the blame for their improper use.

They would have to depend on good old police work. Get the facts, just the facts.

"This is Agent Rick Johnston," Rick said into his phone. "What do you have on the plates I sent down a few minutes ago?"

Private records were one thing, but diplomatic records were kept to a minimum. At times, when tensions around the world were high as they were in the 1960s, countries shared little information. In days past countries built walls and set up batteries of missiles. Today, they controlled information.

"Yes, Agent Johnston," the voice replied on the other end. "We did follow that tag number, but it isn't one that appears on the Egyptian Embassy registered list."

"What? Are you saying the ambassador of Egypt was not riding in an official embassy vehicle?"

"What I am saying is the tag number you asked me to trace is not on the Egyptian list of official embassy vehicles."

Rick rolled his eyes. He knew he would never get used to people who handled data as simple facts. He always saw the facts surrounding the data as a dynamic that made all of it relevant.

"Well, then perhaps I should ask," Rick began, trying not to sound sarcastic, "would it be too difficult to discover exactly *who* owns the vehicle with that tag number?"

"No sir, that shouldn't be difficult at all. Check back with me in a few minutes. I should have that information shortly."

Rick wanted to scream. He put the phone down and looked at George. George was grinning and shaking his head.

"Boy, you look like you could skin that desk jockey alive," he said and chuckled.

Rick's face was flushed bright red and his eyes burned with frustration. He knew he would have to get used to it. This was Washington DC, and he was dealing with the federal government.

Mainside, Camp Pendleton, CA – 3:40 PM PST

The unidentified captives from the incident at the Main Gate were led one-by-one into individual holding cells. Each one was marched past Brigadier General Eugene Westrup and a half-dozen of the tallest, well-built Marines on base.

It was the first step of the interrogation process. Each captured man, alone, was presented as a beaten foe to the conquering officer-in-charge. General Westrup's job at this point was to stare down each defeated foe. His glare was accompanied by the angry stare of the six men with him.

The message to the captives was simple: you are alone; we beat you; you have lost your cause; you cannot win; and we will dominate you even if it costs you your life. The intention was humiliation without words or personal contact.

One hundred and seventeen men were paraded past the general. One hundred and seventeen times the general expressed personal contempt and military triumph to the captors. One hundred and seventeen seeds of fear were planted before each man was isolated in a cell.

chapter 18

Roosevelt Room, White House – 6:45 PM EST

The room was full. Now the nine departments were represented by teams. The investigation had been blown wide open.

Links had been made to the ALI mapping equipment in the deep levels of the White House. The State Department communications satellite was operational and ready to provide ultra-high speed internet connections and voice communication to anywhere in the country. The room was filled with large flat screens, telephones and technically savvy people to make it work, and keep it working.

Mike sat at the helm. He communicated all he could from Norman, OK, Camp Pendleton, Little Rock and a half-dozen other points across the country. A large map of the United States hung on the west wall of the room. As points of communication were established, they were marked on the map.

The line of resistance to the invading force ran a ragged diagonal line across Louisiana from the southeast corner to the northwest, then into Texas, further north to Muskogee, and west to Oklahoma City.

Oklahoma City was in turmoil. Bands of militant invaders roamed the streets. They had attacked law enforcement facilities with alarming success. But there was resistance from citizen groups. The citizens didn't stand up and challenge the invaders. They simply shot them from rooftops and other unidentifiable locations.

The bands of thugs patrolling the streets pulled back to locations that could be defended. Any white person seen on the streets was immediately shot. The militants killed without hesitation.

The line dipped to encircle Norman, Oklahoma. Norman was a walled city. Earthen berms were constructed at strategic locations, and sentries posted throughout the city. No one was concerned about food and water. Those were in ample supply.

The greatest concern was a surprise attack, or breach of the city's perimeter. Every citizen was on alert. Every citizen was armed. All the citizens stood together.

From Norman the line moved north again and cut across northern Oklahoma into southwest Kansas. Southwest of Liberal, Kansas, the advance of the invading group was thwarted by bands of local hunters.

When a truck loaded with armed men was spotted, teams were dispatched to intercept and destroy it. The flat ground allowed fairly easy surveillance of any approach. The advance team set up immediately at the side of the road with weapons designed to kill a grizzly. Three marksmen would place two rounds each into the front end of the advancing vehicle, destroying the engine.

Six men sat one hundred yards back on each side of the highway, took aim and counted those riding in the truck's bed. Each man in the bed of the truck was a numbered target.

On the count of three, twelve rifles exterminated their targets. The strategy worked several times, even when three or four trucks came in convoy. It was always a process of counting the targets, sighting them in, and taking them out. And one day the trucks stopped coming.

On that particular day, one of the marksman hunters miscounted. Two rounds hit the fifth man in the truck bed. The sixth man was left standing.

There was discussion about correcting the mistake, but the sight of one very frightened invader running down the highway in the direction he'd come from, was too entertaining. No more trucks came toward Liberal.

The mountains of northern New Mexico proved difficult for the invaders. Many of the residents of the region were retired military. A number of them were hunters who had time and the will to stand in the way of the advancing invasion.

Albuquerque law enforcement took the full hit. But when word got out, the response from American citizens was rapid and violent. Groups of families and entire neighborhoods banded together to resist. In the end, the invading militia was too strong. Thousands of Americans fled the city to join those in the surrounding mountains.

Farther west, the cities of Tucson, Phoenix, Mesa, north to Las Vegas and all of Los Angeles fell to the violent morning assaults. In every city and town along the staggered line, resistance groups banded together to stand their ground.

Mike turned to Alex Hodson. "Anything new from LA?"

"Every channel we've attempted has gone unanswered or is disconnected," Alex replied. "We have received reports from the western states of bands of citizens fighting off the invaders."

"It looks as if the geography outside the city proper slowed them down," Steve added. "Our guys found extra protection in the mountains with trees and rocks. They had a lot to hide behind."

"The territory that we have to regain runs inland about a hundred and fifty miles and all the way up the coast from Mexico to Washington State. Right?" Mike asked.

"Oregon is overrun," Angela Crain added. "The Department of Homeland Security has confirmed the loss of all law enforcement, television and radio stations, internet services, and social service facilities."

"Social service facilities?" Alex asked. "Don't they help immigrants and the poor?"

"Of course, they do," Angela said and tossed her pen onto her note pad. "Why anyone would target those agencies is beyond me."

The bitterness in Angela's voice was evident. She had been raised by a single mom in South Carolina. She knew poverty. The social workers' tireless efforts to help her mother are what had drawn her to public service. She knew the weak and poor were being neglected and abused. Angela didn't need to think about how bad conditions might be. She knew they were bad.

"Weren't there folks out there willing to stand against them?" Sam asked. She was dumbfounded that anyone would simply step to the side and do nothing.

"I can only assume many people along the west coast didn't agree with war. For years they protested war against a tyrant was as bad as the tyrant himself," Alex said. "I don't know if there was a will to stand against a gang of thugs."

"So, except for the eastern third of the state of Washington, the eastern edge of Oregon, and the mountains of California, all the west coast is gone. Is that what you've determined?" Steve asked. "I'm just trying to grasp what happened in the last eight hours. We didn't cover that much ground in Desert Storm."

"We didn't have half the American military already in Iraq, either," Mike added. "We have to remember, several hundred thousand of these folks were here and in place, some for a very long time."

The extent of the invasion was sobering. The openness of the country's borders had enabled a foreign army to be placed inside the country. They trained quietly and banded together as a secret society with a vicious mission.

"We have some very sick people in charge of this mess on the other side," Sam added. "In any general population, five percent could be classified as criminally insane. So, besides the imported zealots, we could have five percent of twelve million people who are crazy enough to do anything they're told."

"Add a little jihad attitude to, what, six-hundred thousand whack-o's . . ." Steve's words trailed off into a thought no one ventured to entertain. Everyone knew the problem was huge. But no one had put a number to it.

Mike looked at Steve. Then he turned to Alex.

"Six-hundred thousand?" Mike was incredulous.

"Mike," Alex began, "that's just the crazies. How many more of the twelve million illegal immigrants believe in the cause and are perfectly sane?"

Camp Pendleton, CA - 3:50 PM PST

Colonel Herrera was displeased with the failure of the mob at the Main Gate. His arrival north of the Camp sent a wave of encouragement through the waiting mass of willing warriors.

"Sir, the crowd was knocked down by a sonic blast!" The lieutenant relayed the series of events from the charge and destruction of the Main Gate to the blast that silenced the horde. More extreme measures were planned for those still holding the base.

The large number that engaged the Marines and failed was only a part of the group gathered in Los Angeles. The colonel ordered every available man and woman to locations north and south of the Camp. He would show the Americans his resolve.

"It's now time to bring everyone to the front," Herrera began as he glared at his officers. "You will make our full strength and fury known. I want every soldier in place and ready. Now!"

At 4:00 p.m. the signal was given. Thousands charged and overran the Christianitas Gate west of San Onofre. They also attacked the San Onofre Gate itself and quickly killed several Marines.

Las Pulgas Gate was overrun, but the Marines at the gate were alerted to the attack and escaped. The officer in charge called for reinforcements. Their fellow Marines were already on the way.

Marines were immediately deployed down Christianitas Road from the 5th Marines, 1st Combat Engineers at Camp San Mateo. They were combat engineers, but first, they were Marines. They knew how to fight.

Initially, the Marines were willing to meet an unarmed mob with a non-lethal force to subdue it. This time weapons were drawn and blood spilled. The order from headquarters at Mainside was to pull all the stops and hold nothing back.

No more talking, no hospital care for anyone with a headache. This time the Marines were sent to kill an invading army.

Yesterday's training exercises had become today's battle. Soldiers from the 11th Marines Brigade came in full force down Las Pulgas Road. The 1st Marines headed up Basilone Road toward San Onofre. The fight wouldn't be fair, and it wasn't intended to be one. It was going to be decisive.

At the same time, armed terrorists attacked the west side of the huge base, thousands more bravely, yet foolishly, mounted assaults on the Fallbrook Gate into the Naval Weapons Air Station, and the San Luis Rey Gate south of Mainside.

While those attacking from the west were a few miles from the main Marine forces, the horde attacking from the south and east were charging into the face of the world's strongest and most effective warfare machine.

The front line was immediately drawn by the bodies of fallen insurgents. They did not advance into the Camp on the east and south sides. Faced with the full force of Marine fire power on the ground and the helicopter gunships flanking them from above, the untrained attackers never stood a chance. Still, it was one they took. It was also one they lost.

The firefight along Christianitas, San Onofre and Las Pulgas roads were not as intense or as close in proximity, but the results were the same. The Marines stopped every advance dead in its tracks and engaged in an extensive mopping up exercise until every enemy soldier was dead or captured.

The fire-fight was twenty minutes of absolute hell. Eleven Marines were killed in the five battles, and more than one hundred fifty were hurt. But the loss on the attackers' side was nearly one hundred percent. And no one felt bad about that.

Arlington, VA – 6:55 PM EST

Once again the cell phone buzzed against the top of the coffee table. The young man scrambled through the clutter of the small apartment to answer it. He knew he couldn't make the caller wait long for him to answer.

"Junaid," he spoke softly into the phone.

"You need to know of a new meeting place," the voice said. "The former venue is much too small. There will be a plane for you and your associates so you may arrive on time. The others will meet you and take you to the new meeting place."

"This is good," the young man said. "We have been waiting to learn what arrangements we should expect. Do you anticipate this to be an adversarial meeting with our customers?"

"They are like women and children," was the response. "There will be no problem. Your efforts will move the eagle's eye."

"Very well," he replied. "Keep yourself warm."

He immediately broke the cell phone into several small pieces, tossed it into the garbage can, grabbed a light jacket and left the apartment. He wouldn't be back.

White House basement – 6:58 PM EST

Rick Johnston had been waiting for nearly twenty minutes. That was enough time to find the owner of a license plate. Now he was angry.

"Take a breath, son," George Raker began. "It won't do you or anyone else any good to start yelling at folks who'd rather be at home by now."

Rick steamed. He knew George was right. He knew blowing his stack at an hourly employee, one with a security clearance, was counter-productive. Rick took a deep breath and looked at the floor. Then he looked at his older and wiser friend.

"You're right," Rick said. "But just once I'd love to—"

"And that once would be all she wrote." George looked at him with eyes that had seen it all before. "That one time would get you back on street patrol in Mayberry RFD. It's just not worth it."

George's words of wisdom were enough. Rick looked at him and smiled.

"Okay," Rick said as he picked up the phone. He punched in the numbers and waited.

"Yes, this is Agent Rick Johnston in Security," he began. "About twenty minutes ago I called in a check on a license plate. Do you have any information for me?"

"You say your name is Rick Johnston?" the person asked.

"Yes," he calmly replied.

"Just a minute." The employee put Rick on hold before he could protest. He looked at George, who had perched himself on the corner of a desk. The seconds seemed like minutes as Rick's temples began to throb.

"You say your name is Johnston?" the voice asked.

"Yes! J-O-H-N-S-T-O-N. Johnston!" Rick labored to keep his frustration in check.

"Just a minute."

Rick stood and raised his free hand over his head as he gritted his teeth. Silently, he bent over and slowly began to pound the desk in front of him.

George couldn't help himself. He began to snicker. He choked and coughed, then laughed out loud uncontrollably. The harder he tried to stop, the worse it got. Rick slowly calmed. *It's gonna be like this,* he told himself. *Get used to it.*

chapter 19

Oklahoma City, OK – 6:00 PM CST

Rachel Jones caught her breath and boldly walked away from the young man's body at the foot of the giant cross. No one even noticed. She was greatly pleased at her accomplishment. The legend was coming to life. She was the bearer of life to the legend. She was significant and intent on making a difference in the world around her.

The young men had fled the parking lot. Jamal their friend lay dead, slaughtered by the mad woman. They drove wildly through the sparse traffic. Rachel found it easy to follow them, even from four blocks behind. She found it very entertaining.

Rachel slowly drove her car into the parking lot at 701 Colcord Drive. The main offices of the Oklahoma City Police Department were the command center for the invading militia. The force of fifteen-hundred employees and police officers had been no match for the twenty-six hundred invaders.

Rachel recognized the cars the young men had driven parked in front of the building. She drove her car behind theirs, parked and walked into the building with something of a swagger. After all, she was a legend.

The two guards at the door stood and pointed their rifles at her. Their eyes were angry. They had seen much violence. As she approached she smiled at them.

"*Umm ghadan ismi! Ilahi Alilah!*" she screamed. The guards were terrified and stumbled backward against the wall of the building.

"*Umm ghadan ismi! Ilahi Alilah!*" she screamed a second time.

The words came from an ancient text that was believed to hold great power. They claimed the speaker was the one bringing the birth of a new age, and that she was the daughter of Allah. That claim would never be made by a true Muslim. To speak so boldly before Allah meant certain death.

But this woman with fire-red hair spoke the words and did not die. To the cowering guards, she was perhaps the most powerful person in all Islam.

Rachel walked with grand authority between the two guards into the building. Men on every side stepped back. They had heard her words.

She continued down the long hall into the mayor's office, or so it had been until that morning. Every eye in the room turned and looked at her. The ten young men who witnessed the brutal sacrifice of their friend Jamal stood before a large desk. As she approached, they stepped aside.

Rachel stood in the center of the room. She looked directly into the eyes of every man. Finally, she looked at the mid-eastern man sitting behind the desk. His eyes burned with rage.

You stupid fool! Why are you still sitting? Rachel thought. Slowly, she raised her hands high over her head.

"*Umm ghadan ismi! Ilahi Alilah!*" she hissed with a threatening glare. Her face was flushed with excitement. She boldly spoke as the heir of *Hubal*, daughter of *Alilat*, *Manat*, and *Uzza*. Princess of *Alilah!*

"So, you are the one who slit the throat of my only son, Jamal," the man sitting behind the desk said softly. "Is this true?"

"I am Mother, Princess of *Alilah!*" Rachel replied. Arrogance dripped from every word.

"You are an American CIA Operations Chief, and you killed my only son!" the man at the desk said firmly.

"You are counted as worthy among others. Abraham, our father, was willing to sacrifice his son. You should be brave and proud of his sacrifice!" Rachel screamed back at him.

"But Allah provided Abraham a ram and spared his son. You have slaughtered mine!" he yelled back.

In one swift motion he raised and fired his Remington .44 Magnum directly into Rachel's chest. The impact slammed her body against the wall behind her. Slowly, she sank to the floor in stunned disbelief. Life quickly melted from her body.

The men in the room stood in stunned silence.

"Get that white trash out of my sight!" the man behind the desk raged.

OCT, Little Rock, AR – 6:15 PM CST

Keith Dillon, walking into Colonel Aaron Stevens's office, looked intently at two pieces of paper in his hand. He was distracted enough by what he was reading that he bumped into the door jam and nearly lost his balance.

"Colonel," Keith began, "they're back at it."

"Who's back at what?" Aaron said without looking up. "Keith, I'm buried up to my neck in scattered fragments of bilge. Nothing connects in any manner that makes sense. And after a second long day we still have no progress. In spite of what I accomplish in an hour, I'm farther behind.

"I'm sorry, sir," Keith replied. "We've intercepted two phone calls to someone calling himself *Junaid*. It doesn't match any of the voice prints so far. Seems like someone new."

"What do you have on the call?" Aaron asked.

"Only obscure references," Keith replied. "Both calls advised the caller to *keep yourself warm*," he said referring to his papers. Keith shrugged his shoulders and continued, "Probably some code about staying hidden."

"Ya think?" Aaron wasn't impressed with the depth of analysis. The sarcasm was wasted on Keith. He'd lived with it for years working for Colonel Stevens.

"Probably," Keith replied nonchalantly. "The first call refers to someone called *Shining Star* following the *western sun*." Keith looked up at Colonel Stevens. "Like Shining Star went west, ya suppose?" he said blankly.

"Okay, I'll buy it," Aaron replied with an equally blank stare.

"The second one is different. Something about a *new meeting place*, a plane to get them there on time and that the meeting wouldn't be *adversarial* because the clients would be like *women and children*." Keith stopped and offered no analysis.

"Do you want to share an opinion or any thoughts about that call?" Aaron asked.

"Nothing more than the obvious," Keith said without expression. "You know, a new place, a plane to get there, and a very weak client or actual women and children." Again, Keith shrugged his shoulders.

"Is that it?" Aaron asked feeling just a little annoyed.

"Except for the phone numbers and their locations." Keith stood stoically silent.

"Are you having fun with this? Or are you just slowly cracking up and preparing to apply for mental leave because of the pressure?"

"No, sir, not at all." Keith suddenly looked very tired. "This is just the part of the conversation I wanted to avoid."

"All right, just tell me." Aaron had seen Keith in dozens of difficult situations and suddenly realized how hard this was for him.

"Well," Keith began, "the receiver of the calls is in an apartment in unincorporated Virginia not far from DC. The person placing the calls is in the White House."

"Oh, crap." Aaron stared at Keith for a full second. Then he grabbed his phone and began dialing.

Roosevelt Room, White House – 7:20 PM EST

Mike dialed Elli's cell number and waited. It had taken much longer than expected to coordinate the systems between departments and get everyone on line. After nearly two hours of routing and re-routing, everything was functioning.

The State Department satellite provided instant communication across the country. Guard and Reserve units were assembled and getting mobile. ALI maps were incorporated to identify the location of groups of non-nationals and assist Guard units in compromising any mission the non-nationals might pursue. The Air Force provided two dozen Global Hawk drones to identify and target suspect groups.

The Roosevelt Room was crowded with people and equipment making a constant buzz. The atmosphere was much different from the day before.

"Hello," Elli said softly.

"Hey, babe, it's me," Mike answered.

"Oh, Mike. Are you about to collapse? You sound tired," Elli said.

"I think we passed tired a couple of hours ago." Mike sighed and looked at his wrist watch. "Wow. I didn't realize it was this late. We haven't talked about dinner or anything. I didn't even know I was hungry, until now. Did you eat?"

"Yup," Elli replied with a smile Mike could hear. "Mom made a pot of mac and cheese with hotdogs in it. The kids were ravenous. They scattered food all over the table and floor. They ate and told me their adventures at the same time. I think they were oblivious to Mom and me most of the day."

"I don't need to imagine the table and floor. That happens a lot at our house." Mike was happy to hear that everything was normal with the kids.

"Daddy has them out back getting a fire started to roast marshmallows," Elli said. "I'm not worried about Robbie, but Sara and Jackson are going to be a mess." She laughed. Mike smiled.

"Okay, babe. I just wanted to make sure everything was all right," Mike paused, thinking about Elli. "And . . . I wanted to hear your voice."

"I would settle for a little more than your voice, buster," Elli said with a hint of seduction.

"That's an understatement," Mike replied. "But since that's all I can offer tonight, it will have to do."

Laughter between Mike and Elli always came easy. There was no one they would rather be with, talk to, or love than each other. Joy was an unbreakable bond between them.

Mike's phone beeped in his ear.

"Honey, I've got to take this call. Sorry. I love you."

"I love you, too." Elli's voice was gone too soon for Mike.

"Trapper," he said.

"Mike! This is Aaron."

"Hi, Aaron. What's up?"

"I don't think you are going to like this too much," Aaron said and paused.

"Hey, I don't like any of this too much. Let me have it." Nothing was going to surprise Mike at this point. He was far beyond any reasonable expectation.

"We picked up two calls today," Aaron began. "Both were placed in the DC area. The receiver was in the unincorporated county in Virginia. Mike, the person placing the calls was in the White House."

The news crashed down like a ton of bricks. *No! No! We've been through this already!* he thought.

Mike slowly lowered himself into his chair at the end of the conference table. He held his forehead in the palm of his hand, messaging his scalp. It was an unconscious reaction he had once explained helped his brain work. That was in fourth grade. It didn't help then, and it didn't help now. He did it anyway.

"Mike?" Aaron said.

"Sorry, Aaron." Mike was searching for words. "That shocks me. Didn't we just go through this?"

"Yeah, we did. We must be alert to the fact these people have compromised much of our security and infiltrated our ranks. Everywhere. We don't know who they are."

"Do we know anything about the people on the calls?" Mike felt helpless, hopeless and nearly overwhelmed. He couldn't believe it was happening again.

"Mike, we know both calls originated in the White House and we have the number that made the call."

"You have the cell number?" Mike interrupted. "Give it to me!"

He scribbled the phone number on a note pad. His hands shook. He knew how to pinpoint the location of that particular phone.

"Aaron, thanks." Mike said trying to rush him. "Is there anything else?"

"Oh there's a lot of other stuff," Aaron answered. "You just don't need to know it yet."

Mike snickered. *Dang straight! Just give me what I need.*

"Thank you, Aaron," Mike said and closed his phone. He immediately stood from his chair and walked toward Alex Hodson and Steve Granger across the room.

"Alex. This is priority. Steve, get Sam."

Mike ushered Alex out of the Roosevelt Room into the hallway. Steve and Sam were three steps behind them. They stopped outside the Oval Office for a brief discussion when the door opened. President Makin stepped into the hall.

"Mr. President," Mike said. "Sir, do you have a moment?"

chapter 20

Hollow Brook Lane, Dallas, TX – 6:25 PM CST

Everyone considered Jim Parker a very nice person. He was active in his church and community, helped with little league in the summer and basketball in the winter. He was an avid outdoorsman, proficient skier and exceptional kayaker. He was also a sniper, capable of dropping an enemy soldier from eight-hundred yards.

The poor, young soldier they captured in Frisco gave more information than they needed. Nonetheless, detailed notes guided the discussion and a plan was completed. The eleven American vets seethed with nervous excitement. They were on a genuine search-and-destroy mission in their home town. There was only one objective: kill the bad guys.

The old hotel on Hollow Brook Lane had a checkered reputation at best. Besides being dirty and poorly managed, the everyday clientele skirted the edge of respectability and the law. The insurgent mob found little hesitance in eliminating everyone in the building and establishing a barracks for troops. And to most of the invaders it was cleaner than home.

After leaving the police station on Stemmons, Parker led the team into the shrubbery at the edge of the golf course to the east. They found the perfect position to keep watch on the hotel and remain out of sight. The team waited and rehearsed their plans.

As evening approached, the eleven Marines moved south through the brush. Their objective was in view. Timing was crucial and they needed to move quickly.

Lieutenant Parker divided the group into three squads: two four-man squads and the third comprised of two other men and him. They spread across the area east of the hotel with fifty feet between each squad.

They checked their weapons and turned the radios on. Jim Parker could feel the tension. This task was not as simple as taking the police station. This was room to room, floor to floor search-and-destroy. Each man carried four 9mm pistols, six clips for each handgun, and an M16A4 with four 70-round clips. Every weapon was silenced. Every discharge designed to be lethal.

It was almost time.

White House, Washington DC – 7:30 PM EST

Mike quickly informed the group assembled in the Roosevelt Room about the two phone calls originating inside the White House. As he spoke he watched each face drop. What they all feared was coming to reality. Someone in their midst was working with the enemy.

"How are we going to catch someone right in the middle of everything?" President Makin asked. He was the most bewildered. The realization his grandfather, a man he admired and loved deeply, was part of a decades-old plot to destroy the nation, weighed heavily on him.

"I don't think this guy will fight if we approach him," Steve offered. "He's been hidden for a long time. Someone like that knows their luck will run out someday."

"I think I'd go insane from the pressure alone," Sam said.

"To my thinking, whoever it is, they're probably close to the edge anyway." Mike knew the effect of fear. He'd seen it before.

"Could we use the machine downstairs?" Sam asked. "You know the dot thing." Sam's occasional lack of technical verbal acuity left her a little flushed.

"You mean run an ALI mapping for one cell phone?" Steve asked.

"Yeah, I guess. We can do that, right?"

"We can always ask," Mike said and looked at the president.

"I don't ask," President Makin responded with a smile. "I'm the president. Mike, you come into my office. Alex, get on the phone with the guys downstairs."

"Yes sir."

Mike had a spring in his step. He followed the president into the Oval Office.

OCT, Little Rock, AR – 6:35 PM CST

Colonel Aaron Stevens looked at the transcript and the notes Keith Dillon scribbled in the margins. He circled key words: meeting place; plane; women and children; shining star; western sun.

He tried to link them in a random pattern. Then, he reversed it. He pulled up his thesaurus and tried to match meanings for each word. Again, he reversed the order. Then, he scrambled it. Nothing fit.

There has to be more here. Someone in the White House had made the coded calls. They had to have meaning.

Maybe they don't mean anything? Maybe the intent is to throw us off. But why risk a call from inside the White House if the objective was to distract us?

Morning star had to be a code name. *What is 'morning star'?* Aaron asked himself.

A quick internet search brought several possibilities. In Christian mythology Lucifer was known as the Morning Star fallen from heaven. Mid-eastern mythology identified Venus as the goddess of the morning star. Venus was also the goddess of sexual love and desired by all the gods for her great beauty.

Lucifer, the adversary, was the one angel of heaven who defied Jehovah. *Who would that be to these guys?* Aaron pulled himself back. *You're going over a cliff here that doesn't make sense.*

He reached across his desk to his intercom.

"Keith. Would you come back in here?"

Keith didn't answer. The creaking of his desk chair coming upright from a leaned position was enough for Aaron to know he was on his way.

"Whatcha need, boss?" Keith asked as he strode into Aaron's office.

Aaron led Keith through the hare-brained associations he'd made. There had to be something he wasn't seeing.

"Okay, this Lucifer guy. He rebelled against God, right?" Keith asked. "I mean, I went to Sunday school but I'm no biblical scholar."

"That's what the book says," Aaron replied.

"To *our* enemies, who would be rebelling or defying their plans?" Keith rarely showed emotion. His face was dead-panned.

"To my way of thinking, every true blooded American alive," Aaron answered.

"No, man, this is code." Keith realized he failed to address the colonel by his rank. He ignored it and pressed to his point.

"Code is for targeting. Don't ya get it? A code name identifies or locates a target." Keith stood flat footed in front of Aaron's desk.

"You mean somebody, specifically?"

"That's what I think," Keith replied. "I think this is a target on someone who is working against their plans, someone who has the power and position to bring it all to a halt."

"You think they mean their Lucifer?" Aaron asked slowly.

"Who do you think our enemies consider their greatest adversary?" Keith asked.

"I don't know."

"Think of someone who has their eye on the ball and even their finger on the trigger of some mighty force that could destroy all their work." Keith pressed. "Who would that be?"

The pieces fell into place in one instant in Aaron's mind. Mike. Elli. Women and children. A plane to take them to their new meeting place. His face blanched.

"Keith," Aaron bore into Keith's eyes. "Check every private and public charter in the DC area for a flight plan filed to eastern Kentucky. Stat!"

Keith left the office. Aaron pulled up a navigation map and began entering information as he had many times to register his own flights. He searched Eastern Kentucky for airports. Then he entered the location of Elli's parents' home.

His hands trembled. He couldn't stop.

"Oh, crap! Oh, crap! Oh, crap!" He couldn't believe his eyes.

Interstate 66, West of Washington DC – 7:40 PM EST

Rick Johnston and George Raker stared blankly into the sunset. The colors were a rare contrast to the dull, endless hours required of them. The clouds in the western sky exploded with yellows and oranges that glistened and danced against azure blue deepening into the coming darkness.

Memories, music and daydreams drew both men away from the road passing beneath. Rick was almost asleep in a soft, quiet zone of rest. He was fighting sleep.

George was warmed with the memory of the first sunset he shared with his wife, Jenny. He missed her. It had been nearly five years, but he thought of her, even thought things through with her in mind, every day. George felt she was more a part of him than he was of himself. Just that thought made him chuckle.

"What's so funny?" Rick asked.

"Nothing funny," George said through a smile. "Just . . . something." He smiled and looked out the window of the SUV. He liked Rick. Rick wouldn't press the issue. He understood that thoughts and memories were private.

"I can't believe we're headed out here again." Rick shook his head with measured disbelief. The license plate on the car that left the White House with the mysterious Egyptian ambassador was registered to the estate of Mohammed al Kahn, the president's grandfather. Questions needed answers and they had been sent to ask them.

"At least we know where we can get a hot meal," George said with a grin.

"You don't mean . . ." Rick stammered. "You aren't thinking we would stop there, are you? Are you?"

"Hey, I missed lunch! I'm a big man and need to take care of myself." George was enjoying himself.

"But you can't be serious!" Rick complained. "We nearly lost half a dozen agents to that breakfast menu. I can't believe this!"

"Oh, now, it wasn't that bad. If you'd eat more than tofu and free range your gut might be able to take real food."

"Real food!" Rick bolted upright against the restraint of his seatbelt. "You call that real food?"

"Yes. I call it real food. People have been eating it for thousands of years. It's fine. I certainly don't think much of a tofu burger." George was smiling as he watched the passing scenery.

"Yeah, but that stuff kills people! I can hardly believe what I'm hearing."

"Listen," George began, "we know this man. We've broken bread with him. He's a source. He watches who comes up and down that road. He sees everything that comes in and out of the compound. Besides, it's time to eat."

Rick didn't want to admit it, but George was right. Ilo Campbell was very observant. He was a patriot. And anyone that could manage Bernice must be respected.

"All right," Rick sighed. "We'll dine at Denney's."

The sky continued to darken as miles slipped by. Rick gritted his teeth. George's mouth watered in anticipation of a great meal. And Swoope, VA was about to be visited by the Secret Service, again.

White House Basement – 7:43 PM EST

Alex Hodson sat with Mort at his control panel. Both men spoke softly and kept their work off the huge screen that stood before them. The flat screen monitor on Mort's desk would do.

"The president signed off on this, right?" Mort was nervous about looking so close to home.

"Signed off and insisted," Alex replied. "Can you bring it in closer?"

"I can bring it down to your left earlobe if necessary," Mort snarled. He felt he was spying on the White House.

"Just do this," Alex insisted. "If it all comes back bogus, fine. If we turn something up, we have to check it out. We need to check this."

"Okay," Mort sighed with resignation. "Do you have the number?"

"Here." Alex placed a small piece of paper on the desktop.

Mort picked up the paper and adjusted his bifocals to make sure he entered the proper numbers. It was a single phone number. Mort sighed again and reached for his keyboard.

Mort's fingers flew over the keyboard in a rumble denying individual clicks between keystrokes to be heard. He paused and looked at Alex with eyes that begged the question, *Are you sure?*

"Just do it." Alex was firm. The president had ordered it.

Mort tapped the Enter key.

A single white dot appeared inside the translucent outline of the White House. The view was from overhead. The white dot did not move.

"There you go." Mort looked as if he had committed a mortal sin. "Are you happy now?"

"Can you tell what floor it's on?" Alex asked.

"Sure." Mort tapped several keys and a column of numbers appeared at the right side of the screen.

"Okay, these numbers represent the distance from the satellite." Mort was calmer. Now he was working his system and skillfully allowing it to do its magic. "The numbers at the top are smaller, and they get larger as we go down the list. Do you see?"

Mort turned and looked at Alex. Alex saw the fear in Mort's eyes.

The top number was 1189882.10675. The second number was slightly larger at 1189891.035. The twenty-four numbers increased in what appeared to be a random factor.

"I see them. What do they mean? Bigger or smaller than what?" Alex asked.

"Watch this." Mort brought the cursor up the screen and touched the line representing the White House roof. The second number in the column lit up.

"That means the guttering on the White House is one million, one hundred eighty-nine thousand, eight hundred ninety-one and thirty-five one thousandth feet from the satellite. About 225 miles up." Mort was matter-of-fact. "The satellite is in a geo-synchronous orbit and does not move, theoretically. It probably does, a little."

"That makes sense," Alex replied. "What about the dot?"

Alex was pressing to the one thing Mort wasn't eager to discover.

"Well, first we need a reference point. Not the roof." Mort looked quickly at Alex then back to the flat screen. He placed the cursor on the ground floor, by the front entrance to the White House.

The number 1189927.08625, the seventh on the list, lit up. Mort looked at Alex.

"Got it," Alex said, "Distance from the satellite."

"Yeah," Mort reply was breathy.

"I'm with ya, Mort. Let's look at the dot," Alex said reassuringly.

He moved the cursor to the dot. The eighteenth number lit up. The dot was exactly one million, one hundred eighty-nine thousand, nine hundred sixty-two and five hundred forty-five one thousandths feet from the satellite. Mort looked at Alex. There was perspiration on his upper lip.

"That's in the second basement, directly beneath the office of the assistant to the president and press secretary," Mort said. Alex knew exactly where that was. Alex knew precisely who sat there. And now he was sorry he did.

"Can you print that for me, Mort?"

North Waco Street, Wichita, KS – 6:45 PM CST

Yolanda and Robert walked slowly along the old brick sidewalk. They had known each other for a few minutes more than four hours. But nothing was ever so real to either of them as their time together.

Both lived their lives expecting to meet the right person. Suddenly and simultaneously they did. They both knew it in an instant and without question. It was as natural as breathing.

"Are you going to stay here in Wichita for a while?" Yolanda asked as they strolled.

"That's the plan, unless I hear from dad." Robert's tone clearly expressed his devotion and love for his father. "If he needs me for something, I'll have to go. Yolanda, you must understand that it's been me and him together since Mom died."

"Oh, I do, really I do." Yolanda was quick to agree. She knew the bond of a father and son couldn't be much different than the bond she shared with her mother.

"Yeah," Robert said as he stopped and faced her smiling. "I guess you and your mom have been through a lot, too."

Yolanda wasn't exactly sure what *through a lot* meant to Robert, but she assumed he was referring to something difficult. She was quick to agree.

"Yes, we have. But we have a lot of friends and family in Dallas." Just the thought of the life that had been wonderful to her brought buoyancy to her speech. "Many people from our town in Mexico came north. We all live near each other, and it almost feels like we are home again. Except here everyone has a job!"

Yolanda blushed and smiled at her joke. Robert grinned broadly as she leaned against him. She pressed her cheek against his chest, feeling that if he didn't hold her up she would surely collapse. He buried his face in her hair. The fragrance nearly made his knees buckle.

They didn't care about the cars driving by on Waco Street. They didn't care what time it was, where they would be tomorrow or what might happen an hour from now. It was the moment. It was their moment, and they embraced it fully.

chapter 21

OCT, Little Rock, AK – 6:52 PM CST

Colonel Aaron Stevens scanned flight plans and maps of eastern Kentucky. Most of the airports consisted of grass strips and single buildings. The mountainous countryside didn't lend itself to the long, flat stretches of ground needed by even small planes. Landing strips were few and far between.

"Colonel!" Keith Dillon called as he moved quickly down the hall toward Aaron's office.

"What did you find?" Aaron asked.

"About an hour ago a flight plan was registered for a single engine plane and five passengers." Keith entered the office and spread his notes over the maps on Aaron's desk.

"Okay, up here." Keith ran his finger along the map following I-295 north of Washington. "Here."

His finger stopped at Suburban Airfield that paralleled the interstate.

"The flight plan shows the plane leaving there at 8:30 this evening and heading west." Keith scanned the map knowing what he was looking for but failing to find it.

"What's the name of the field?" Aaron asked.

"Suburban," Keith replied absentmindedly.

"No! The one they're headed to!" Aaron snapped.

"Oh, yeah, right." Keith looked again at the flight plan. "It's, uh, Seller's Field near Olive Hill, Kentucky."

"Here it is. This is the one!" Aaron stabbed his finger into the map. "What's their ETA?"

"They don't seem to be in much of a hurry," Keith mused. "Shows here they plan to land just before 9:30 Eastern."

"That gives us very little time," Aaron began. "Look, that puts them fifteen miles northeast of Elli Trapper's parents' home. And driving in those hills is anything but fast. The drive will take a good thirty to forty minutes. We've got three hours. I'll call Mike."

"I'll contact Andrews and see what they recommend." Keith bolted for the door, moving more quickly than Aaron had ever seen him move.

Roosevelt Room, White House – 7:55 PM EST

Sam grabbed Steve's elbow and pulled him away from the conference table. Steve noted the rather grim look on her face and braced himself. He wasn't going to argue with her no matter what. He was going to make an effort in the relationship.

"Listen," she began. "I know we've opened a lot of areas of discussion in the last couple of days, but there's one thing we need to talk about right now."

"Sure. What's bothering you?" Steve asked.

"This whole thing here," Sam said. "I mean, right here in the White House, where it should be the safest, we've found a threat."

"It's still something we need to address. We can't just leave it alone."

"No, I know that." Sam rubbed her forehead fighting both tears and frustration. "But . . ."

Steve knew the 'but' was often a launching pad for many of their past arguments.

"But . . .?" Steve said waiting.

"Honey, I don't want you to be the first to go running into some room with guns blazing against who-knows-what odds, or what kind of gang of thugs and then getting hurt again. I mean, it's just been one day since you got shot at the nuclear plant. You're wounded! You can't go around being the big Marine every time someone causes a little trouble, you need to rest and get well. This whole thing is just—"

"Sam." Steve had to stop her. He held her by the shoulders with both hands and looked directly into her eyes.

"Sam, I'm not going to do that. Take a breath." Steve held her and could feel the tension working in her.

"It's just—"

"Sam, stop this." He drew her face up to his. "There isn't going to be a shootout in the White House. I'm not in charge of the Secret Service. They will take care of this. Please, slow your imagination down just a bit."

"But you're wounded and—"

"Sweetheart, it's no big deal. It was a flesh wound," Steve insisted. "Yeah, two inches to the left and it would have shattered my femur, but it's fine. You don't see me running up stairs, or tackling bad guys. I am slowed down. You're here. That makes me hero enough."

Sam shielded her eyes with her hand and sobbed silently. He saw the tears running down her cheeks. The stress had come back heavily on her. Steve had seen full grown men fall apart under the stress of battle, even facing the simple threat of combat.

"Hey." Steve gently lifted her chin. "What we have found is greater than all this. I'm not going to do anything stupid. There's no reason for you to get so worked up. We'll be fine."

He pulled her close and held her as her shoulders convulsed under his embrace. Steve wasn't about to let her go and didn't care who was watching this tender, personal moment.

But everyone in the room did see them. Everyone in the room knew the story of the fight at the Oak Mountain power station. They all respected the bravery and patriotism of Steve and Sam. They all saw, but continued the work before them without a pause.

I-35 and Exit 104, Norman OK – 7:00 PM CST

Sheriff Hitchens and Travis Temple stood on the overpass surveying the massive cleanup left by the missile strikes. "Damn, looks like a tornado ripped through here, just more . . . concentrated."

"They got the second load on its way to the junkyard," Travis said. "Not much to be salvaged though."

"That's the one good thing about all this, Travis. Scrap metal is still a thriving business."

The survivors were in custody, many providing extensive details regarding the attacks in Dallas. The leaders of the uprising were in the cars in front and the last cars. All had met a fiery end by the blast from an Abrams tank. Others had remained between the cars and trucks. They perished in the attack of the F-22 Viper.

The survivors realized they were outgunned, and their cause was not worth the cost. They tossed their guns and lay prone at the roadside. That choice saved their lives, and their cooperation offered a faint hope of someday resuming life outside of prison.

Sheriff Robert Hitchens was in charge. He didn't worry about the charred cars and trucks. Each vehicle was inspected and all the evidence was collected and properly labeled. The interstate was treated as a huge crime scene as officers and volunteers sifted through the rubble.

Sheriff Hitchens reviewed the transcripts of information from the survivors. The more he read, the greater his concern. Pieces were fitting together he had not expected. The twenty-two enemy survivors were painting a very clear picture of what was coming in the ensuing hours.

The sheriff's mind was racing with possibilities. One thing was certain, the evening patrols were going to be anything but routine.

He opened his phone and dialed a very familiar number. It rang once.

"Hello."

"Robert, this is Dad." The sheriff was glad to hear his son's voice.

"Hey, dad, how's it going?"

"Things are well in hand here," the sheriff began. He relayed the events of the standoff and the results of the F-22 missile strike. "So, we've been busy. How was your trip?"

"Trip was fine, Dad. I think I have some things I want to talk to you about, though."

"Really? We'll have to do that very soon." He paused as he imagined what was behind his son's words. "Son, I want you to stay in Wichita until I call you again. There are some things I want to get cleared up before you come back. Can you manage that all right?"

"Sure." Robert was in no hurry to drive back to Norman unless his dad asked him to. And that didn't seem to be likely tonight. "As long as you're okay and you don't need me for anything."

"Not at the moment," his father answered. "You get that young lady and her mother to their family?"

"Sure did. About that . . . sorta want to talk a few things over with you when we have some time."

The sheriff paused. *That's a little odd*, he thought.

"Of course. We can do just that." Suddenly the sheriff's mind was spinning in a different direction. He smiled. "We can do that real soon, son."

"Thanks, Dad. Is that it?" Robert's question made it clear he had something else to do than talk on the phone.

"No, I just wanted to check and see if you were okay." Sheriff Hitchens was smiling. "Sounds like you are."

"Pretty right fine, Dad. Pretty right fine." Robert could tell from the tone of his father's voice that he had figured it out.

"Good night, son," Sheriff Hitchens said as he closed his phone.

Hollow Brook Lane, Dallas, TX – 7:03 PM CST

The command was given at the top of the hour. Three teams of heavily armed American veterans moved from the protection of the woods behind the hotel, toward the building. Jim Parker smiled slightly, partly from nervousness, but also with pride, watching his friends, his band of brothers move silently and flawlessly in executing their approach.

The cars in the parking lot around the hotel provided cover. The broad, open spaces of the parking lot and the lights around the building gave the greatest opportunity for detection. Silently, one by one, the lights were extinguished. A single shot from a silenced M-16A extended the darkness without giving notice. Jim Parker and the Marines from the Frisco Armory made their way toward the building.

Elated that their force had moved fast and killed many, the enemy inside the hotel reveled in the success of the day. Their stories included discoveries of families hidden in attics, basements and storm shelters hoping to escape the violence. None did. The men and boys were killed on sight. Men and boys had no value for the advancing horde. The women and girls were useful, at least for a while.

The men laughed at the stories of their surprise attacks. Their hearts felt light. Finally, they were given the opportunity to pay back the disrespect and humiliation poured on them for more than a hundred years. They had been the defeated, but now they were the victors.

Each team of Marines arrived simultaneously at the building's three entrances. A team of four men entered the large glass double entry in the backside, center of the building. Two teams of three Marines entered at the far ends framed by glassed-in staircases leading to the upper floors.

At the center entrance, Jim and three Marines greeted the desk clerk. He had been forced to stay on the job for nothing more than appearance sake. He obviously wanted to leave. Jim warned him in very clear Spanish that it was time for him to go home. He did not hesitate.

On the first floor, one Marine remained at each end of the hallway leading to the rooms. Two Marines began the door-to-door search, working toward the center. The four Marines in the middle provided cover to the advancing soldiers and watched the main entrance.

The first floor was empty.

The teams moved up one floor. This time the roles were reversed. Two Marines worked from the center toward the ends, covered by the other Marines. Room 214 was the first contact.

Laughter and loud, gruff voices could be heard several doors down the hall. The methodical approach was maintained. No room would be left unsearched.

The first door was locked. A thirty-inch pipe wrench was used to hyper-extend the door latch backward into the wood of the door. The action was swift, silent, and effective.

Two Marines arrived at Room 214 and beckoned the other two to the closed door. The laughter and music in the room helped cover their advance. A different tactical entrance was chosen for this room.

Jim Parker gently knocked on the door. The other three Marines crouched behind him and on either side. They could hear a man talking to the others in the room and laughing as he came to open the door.

The knob turned and the door opened.

A single shot dropped the man to the floor. With Jim in the lead, all four Marines rushed into the room. Six men lounged on the beds and chairs, drinking and sharing stories. Before any action other than surprise could register, six shots eliminated them as threats.

The third-floor sweep began as the first. Several of the rooms were occupied by small groups of two or three men. All were quickly killed. To the surprise of the Marines, none had weapons. However, guilt by association was enough.

The fourth floor showed evidence that men had been in the rooms, but the entire floor was empty. The fifth floor provided the same evidence. The men, who had been in the rooms, were now gone.

As the last room was cleared, Jim Parker heard the squeal of brakes in the parking lot. He peered out the fifth-floor window. Three large trucks came to a stop in the parking lot. He counted thirty heavily-armed men climbing slowly from the trucks. The marauding invaders were tired from a long day of killing.

It was time for a new plan.

White House – 8:05 PM EST

Alex Hodson retrieved the ALI plot from the printer. He left Mort alone at his station. Mort knew who Alex suspected, and he suffered a mixture of anger and shame. He felt anger at the man who betrayed them, and shame that he was the man to discover his betrayal. Alex simply hoped Mort had the courage to be quiet.

Alex climbed the stairs to the second basement. He wanted time to think. He wanted to be certain his intended actions were warranted. With every step, he weighed and rethought the evidence he carried in his hands.

On the second floor, Alex walked briskly through the corridor. He'd spent much of his time in the security and surveillance areas of the White House basement, and everyone knew or recognized him. He wanted to walk past one particular office before going upstairs.

As he passed that office the man hard at work, glanced up and briefly waved. Alex almost stumbled. He managed a hurried wave and walked quickly down the hall to the elevator.

Alex arrived on the ground floor of the White House West Wing and nearly sprinted toward the Oval Office. He ducked into the Roosevelt Room. Steve and Sam were standing close together, talking quietly. He motioned to them to come with him.

He rounded the corner and gently tapped on the door to the Oval Office. The voice he recognized as that of the president called him to enter the room. Mike Trapper sat on one couch; the president sat pensively on the other. They both looked at Alex. Their faces reflected the strain of the day.

"Thank you, Mr. President," Alex began. "You need to see this, and we need a decision."

Sam and Steve walked through the open door of the Oval Office as Alex spoke.

"What is it, Alex?" the president asked.

"Sir, I have the location of the person working against us here in the White House."

"Let me see it."

He looked at the image. Alex briefly explained the lines, the column of numbers and their meaning.

Mike moved to sit beside the president to see the paper Alex had brought into the room. Steve and Sam sat on the opposite couch. The location was unmistakable. Alex confirmed the man was in his office only moments before.

President Al Makin looked at Mike.

"Mike, you know what to do."

"Yes, sir," was Mike's only response.

Mike walked briskly from the Oval Office to the Roosevelt Room and picked up a single piece of paper. He motioned for six Secret Service Agents to follow him and walked directly to the elevator.

A few seconds later the door opened into the second basement. The small group of men walked down the hall toward the office in the northeast corner of the section. A few feet from the door, Mike paused.

He removed his cell phone from his pocket and dialed the number Mort had charted on the ALI plot. Just outside the door he pressed the send button. As he stepped into the room, Mike heard the soft ring of the cell phone he had called.

"When did you know?" asked the man at the desk.

"Just now," Mike said. "Barry Goldstein, you're under arrest for treason against the United States of America."

chapter 22

Roosevelt Room, White House – 8:10 PM EST

Mike Trapper felt exhausted. Steve Granger sat beside him. Both men were stunned by the revelation of Barry Goldstein's treachery. Barry had provided key information that led Mike and the team to Oak Mountain Nuclear Facility only a few days before.

It occurred to Mike and Steve simultaneously that someone from within the White House notified the terrorists of the force of Marines arriving at Oak Mountain from the north. Sixty brave Americans died as a result of that information being leaked. Barry Goldstein was the leak.

"You okay?" Steve asked Mike.

"Yeah, I'm fine," Mike answered. "It's never easy to deal with a traitor. Where's Sam?"

"I think she went with Alex to confirm locations of some suspected terrorist groups."

"I think—" Mike was interrupted by his cell phone buzzing.

"Trapper," he answered.

"Hey, Mike. This is Aaron."

"Hi, Aaron," Mike began. "Your information was helpful in finding our mole. Thanks."

"Mike, you're welcome. Who was it?"

Mike paused. "Barry Goldstein."

"Oh, no. Mike, I'm sorry."

"That makes more than two of us." Mike scanned the room thinking how many of this group had worked closely with Barry for many months. "What do you have for me, Aaron?"

"Mike, there's more." Aaron's tone almost made Mike's heart stop. *How could there be more?*

"Mike, the two calls we traced to Barry were instructions to someone to find and take out a target." Aaron drew in a long breath.

"There is a plane preparing to leave Suburban north of DC in about twenty minutes. Mike, they're headed to eastern Kentucky. We think they're going after Elli and the kids."

Mike's heart leapt to his throat.

"What? What did you say?" Mike couldn't believe his ears. That couldn't be right. It just couldn't.

"Mike, the code in the phone calls spoke of new targets in the west, and they would be no problem because they were like women and children. The plane is scheduled to leave Suburban at 8:30 p.m. and land at Seller's Field near Olive Hill around nine-forty or so."

"That's a long time for that flight isn't it?" Mike asked.

"It's a twenty-four hundred foot runway. Anything with much speed needs a longer landing strip." Aaron stopped and waited for a reply. None came.

"The plane is a Piper Seneca II, twin engine that cruises at about 170 knots. It seats seven." Again, Aaron paused. "We assume there will be others meeting them with transportation and . . . and probably weapons."

"Aaron," Mike was poised on the edge of his seat, his hand rubbed his forehead. "Can't they be stopped before they leave Suburban? Can't we send the police, a SWAT team or, I don't know . . . the National Guard?"

"I've already done that," Aaron replied. "Traffic is still heavy from people leaving town, and the police have no idea what they'll be facing. I don't think they'll get there in time."

"You have to get me there!" Mike was almost shouting into his phone. The room fell silent around him.

"I've got it, Mike. Marine One is going through flight check right now and should be ready any time." Mike began to breathe again. A plan was already underway.

"Mike," Aaron continued, "only moments ago the president gave his approval for the plan. You'll be taken to Andrews. Everything is being prepared as we speak. You need to go, now."

Mike was stunned, unable to move. He was probably in shock.

"Mike?" Aaron said over the phone. "You there, Mike?"

"Right. Yeah, Aaron," Mike stammered. "Got it. Thanks, but I have to go."

He stood to leave.

"Mike. What is it?" Steve asked.

"They're going after Elli and the kids," he replied blankly. "They're going after my kids!"

"I'm going with you. You're not going anywhere without me."

"No. No you don't need to—"

"Shut-up, Trap! Let's go!"

"Hey, where do you think you're going?" Sam had walked into the room as Mike closed his phone. All she had heard was that they were leaving.

"I'll explain later," Steve told her flatly.

"I'm coming with you. You can explain on the way."

Sam fell into stride with Mike and Steve. The threesome marched quickly down the hall to the south lawn and the waiting helicopter.

As they left the building, President Makin jogged up to them.

"Mike, you have the full power of the presidency and Unites States Marines supporting you," he said. "Don't worry about things here. Take care of your family."

"Thank you, Mr. President," Mike replied without breaking stride.

Mike, with Steve and Sam jumped quickly into Marine One. Within seconds it lifted from the lawn and banked toward Andrews Air Force Base.

Denney's Lounge, Swoope, VA – 8:12 PM EST

Throughout the trip, Rick had been annoyed by the constant rumblings from George's stomach. Tonight, dinner was later than usual, and George's system was registering complaint.

Rick brought the SUV to a stop and slid the gearshift into park. He closed his eyes and took a deep breath. *Salad, I'm going to eat a salad. That's it!*

"Finally!" George blurted out as he began to climb from the vehicle. "It's time for supper!"

"Don't forget, George, we're here for information too." He knew he didn't need to remind his partner, but Rick felt he needed to say something to counter Geroge's last dominant thought being about supper. From the parking lot Rick could feel his cholesterol rising.

The two men entered the restaurant and looked across the large room. It seemed different at night. The lighting was different, softer. The shades were drawn, blocking headlights from the highway a few yards away. A jazz trio played in the far corner.

"Is this the same place?" Rick asked aloud. The smell of bacon frying and strong coffee brewing was replaced with an aroma that he couldn't identify.

George breathed deeply, drinking in the fragrance of something that could only be elegant, enticing, and delicious.

"Well, my favorite spies are back among us!" It was Ilo Campbell. This time he had his teeth in, wore a tie, and a surprisingly expensive jacket. Rick had to look twice, but, yes, it was Ilo.

"Come on in, boys. Got a table for you right over here." Ilo walked the two men to a table close enough to the trio to enjoy the music without being overwhelmed by it.

The room was nearly full. The patrons were a much higher scale than Rick anticipated. George didn't care. He wanted to eat whatever it was he smelled.

"How's this do for ya?" Ilo asked with a sparkling grin. Rick obviously registered surprise. "Don't worry, son. I get that a lot. Some folks say I'm downright handsome with my teeth in."

Ilo grinned at his own joke and chuckled. He seated the men and handed them menus.

"Don't bother with that, Ilo," George began. "Just bring me whatever *that* is." George closed his eyes and inhaled long and deep.

"That's why everyone comes on Wednesday night. It's my special." Ilo smiled broadly and looked at Rick. "Same for you, young fella?"

"No, just give me a minute with your menu, please," Rick replied as he scanned the menu, his eyes adjusted to the soft lighting.

"Is there somthin' you'd be more a likin' than this ambrosia?" Ilo said as he fanned the aroma to his own nostrils.

"No, just something on the lighter side this time, maybe something organic," Rick said while reviewing his options.

"Oh, you're one of them," Ilo chuckled. "Don't you know eatin' all them vegetables will make your brain shrink up for lack of protein?"

"I have tried and tried to tell this boy," George shook he head, "but if you're not his mom, he just won't listen."

"Well, that's not a bad thing." Ilo turned to Rick and said, "You're not a mama's boy now, are ya?"

"Oh, brother." Rick buried his head in the menu, attempting to ignore the two men who were having a wonderful time at his expense.

"Maybe I need to have Bernice come over here and set you straight," Ilo said through a smile as George roared with laughter.

"No, gentlemen, that won't be necessary. Ilo, just bring me a salad, that's all. Keep it simple." Rick sat back in his chair.

"Don't let us be too hard on you, son," Ilo said. "I know exactly what you need. Just trust me." Ilo left the table before Rick could say another word.

Stephen T. Gerdel

"I did that at breakfast the other day and nearly died," Rick said toward Ilo as he walked away.

"Oh, don't say that! You have to admit your delicate system simply wasn't up to real food."

"Yeah, well maybe." Rick leaned forward and placed his elbow on the table. He really loved jazz and these guys were good.

"I wonder where they come from."

"I didn't realize you were into jazz."

"I played in high school and college a little."

"Piano?" George smiled and leaned back in his chair.

"No, sax." Rick smiled at his partner, realizing though they spent their days together, outside of work they knew little about each other. But the music was nice.

"Do you mind if I take a bit of your time?" Ilo was back. This time he was serious.

"Actually, we wanted to ask you some questions, if you don't mind," George said politely.

"No, I don't mind," Ilo began. "But I wanted to tell you one of them big black SUVs came roarin' through here all ninety-to-nuthin' about an hour back. They was drivin' more like bank robbers than anything I've seen in years."

"Could you see who was in it?" Rick asked.

"You know, them windows are as black as pitch. Cain't tell if anybody's even drivin' the thing. Maybe it's a robot, or somethin' driven by the devil hisself." Rick had a feeling that if there had been a place to spit, Ilo would have done so.

"But you boys will be proud of me," he continued. "I didn't know you was comin', but I was givin' thought to callin' ya'all." Ilo smiled again. This time he really did look smart and dapper. He reached into his shirt pocket and drew out a slip of paper.

"I wrote down the number on the plate." Ilo beamed as he held the paper loosely in his fingers.

"May I?" Rick asked reaching for the paper.

"Thought you'd never ask, son." Ilo was very pleased to be a part of the mystery. He leaned back in his chair.

Rick took the piece of paper and squinted in the soft lighting. Suddenly, his eyes widened.

"It's the same number, George." Rick half stood as if to leave.

Ilo placed his hand on Rick's shoulder, gently lowering him into his chair. His smile faded. His grip was much more than Rick expected from this small man.

"Young man, you are in my place and ready for a fine meal. You put your butt right back in that chair," he said firmly. "If you leave now, Bernice herself will track you down and make your life a livin' hell. You hear me, boy?"

"But—" Rick protested.

"A living *hell*," Ilo said in a deepening voice as he stared him down. George stifled a laugh and waved Rick to sit and be quiet. Rick sat.

Presently, the table in front of them was swarmed with servers. Hot rolls and honey butter heaped in a basket were set on the table. George watched as an unbelievably large plate mounded with steamed vegetables and brisket smothered in mushrooms was laid in front of him. It was the sauce. Whatever the sauce was, it made George nearly swoon.

Rick's eyes widened as his plate floated to the table top before him. A spinach salad adorned with nectarine sections and walnuts in an incredible dressing he could not identify. Neatly to the side rested two strips of brisket with mushrooms and steamed vegetables topped with a lemon and pineapple hollandaise. He was amazed.

"Gentlemen, please enjoy," Ilo said smiling again. "Bernice will be very pleased. And tonight, boys, dinner's on me."

chapter 23

Hollow Brook Lane, Dallas, TX – 7:16 PM CST

For Jim Parker and his fellow Marines, speed was of utmost importance. He watched the small army of invaders climb out of their trucks. Parker was sure the thugs were bound to enter the building, and in short order, find the bodies of their comrades on the lower floors. Jim Parker clicked his comm. device three times, calling the team together.

To avoid the potential of cross-fire, Jim dispatched five Marines to the west end stairwell. Two covered any advance up the stairs, two targeted down the hall, and one would follow, covering the rear as the team moved down the stairway.

In the main stairway, Jim and five Marines prepared a similar maneuver with three guns trained on the main hallway and the elevator doors. To their advantage the halls were well lit. The stairwells were dark.

Jim gave the command to move down the stairs.

The fifth floor was clear. Quickly and silently the Marines swept to the next floor. Fourth floor was clear.

Suddenly, several voices echoed up the main stairwell. They weren't speaking English. The echo made the words indistinguishable. The Marines could hear the shouted commands and the tramping of many feet.

Jim leaned over the handrail and peered down the stairway. There was no movement. The hallway was clear on the fourth floor. The Marines continued down the stairs.

Jim could still hear shouting and the sound of men climbing stairs. Both teams arrived at the third floor. They paused.

Immediately across from their position in the main stairway, the elevator door dinged. Slowly the doors slid open. The elevator appeared empty.

Five silenced M-16s were aimed into the elevator. The doors did not close.

Jim did not want to break radio silence. They were too close to a force three times their size for any noise. He noticed his breath was short and shallow.

The sound of men rushing up the stairwell ceased. Again, Jim peered below in the stairway. He saw nothing.

The elevator doors didn't close. Jim knew someone inside was holding the doors open.

He signaled to his men that he believed enemy troops were in the elevator. Each man nodded and held his position.

A small round object rolled into the hallway. Jim looked at it slightly puzzled. It looked familiar, but—

"Flash grenade!" one of the Marines whispered a little too loudly.

Jim's head whipped toward the Marine and back to the grenade rolling across the floor.

That split-second delay proved a mistake. The explosion caught Jim wide-eyed. He was immediately blinded by the flash.

Half-a-dozen terrorists rushed from the elevator with guns blazing. Crouched low and very close together, they shot wildly in every direction.

Two short flashes from the west stairway dropped two invaders. The four that remained standing turned their weapons down the hall and opened fire as they advanced toward the stairway.

Five of the Marines in the main stairway had avoided Jim's mistake. At the moment of the flash, their eyes were buried in their arms. Their eyesight was excellent.

Five shots rang out in the main stairwell. The four thugs in the hallway dropped to the floor, dead.

Jim realized the main group of terrorists was in the east stairway. He could hear them running down the hallway of the second floor.

"Watch below!" he said out loud. There was no more need for stealth. Radios were on.

A dozen of the invaders entered the third floor hallway from the east end. The Marines in the west stairway opened fire. Their targets charged, brightly lit and confined to the breadth of the hallway. Each target was picked and quickly dropped.

As the enemy advanced down the hallway, the Marines in the main stairway opened a new front and fired on them from the side. It was a brief fight.

"Badger West!" Jim commanded. "One to the top, one to the hall, three below!"

The redeployment prepared for a charge from the second floor.

Jim was a liability to his team. He could not see. His fear was that some of the terrorists would continue up the east stairway. They might find an advantage and come at them from above.

"One of you stay here and watch the east stairs!" he barked at the Marines. "Shoot anything that moves! The rest of you watch below. Same thing. If it moves, shoot it!"

Jim was thankful for the stairway being glass rather than cement. Ricocheted bullets would be deadly in a concrete enclosure. His eyes burned, but he was beginning to see shapes. Effect of the flash was wearing off.

A constant blast of gunfire ripped into the stairwell from the second floor. The Marines stayed close to the floor as glass shattered and fell around them. In the darkness, a Marine saw movement.

His M-16 popped two rounds and the shadow fell. It was immediately replaced by another shadow. Pop! Pop!

A small, baseball-sized object seemed to float up between the rails.

"Grenade!" One Marine swung the butt of his rifle around like a bat and swatted it through the glassless window. Fifteen feet outside the stairwell it exploded.

The small band of Marines crouched on the stairs as shrapnel ripped into the building. They were hurt, but now the Marines were really pissed.

In the next moment, five M-16s were aimed over the stair railing, and blasted on full automatic into the advancing invaders. The firing stopped only when each of the seventy-round clips were emptied. In a split-second, the clips were replaced.

The firing continued. Slowly, the Marines moved down the steps. Through the smoke they could see the bodies of their adversaries.

The Marines in the west stairway had been alerted by the attack in the center of the building. They met the invaders running toward them on the second floor. It was a brutal slaughter. Seventy rounds from each of the five weapons filled the hall in less than thirty seconds. None of the enemy survived.

The roar of the gunfire stopped as suddenly as it began. Smoke filled the stairways and halls. This fight was over.

"Will," Jim winced and leaned against the shrapnel torn wall. "I got hit."

Will reached for his fellow Marine, and holding him firmly to his side, led him down the stairs and through the tangle of bodies. The eleven men met in the main floor lobby.

They had been in the building for less than twenty minutes. The firefight lasted less than ninety seconds. Four of the Marines had slight shrapnel wounds. Jim's was the most serious.

As they made their way across the darkened parking lot, Jim could faintly make out the toes of his boots running between the two Marines on either side of him.

The team's efforts would have consequences. They all knew their success would have a psychological impact on their enemy.

Tomorrow, the Marines would develop another plan. They would strike again, and soon.

Roosevelt Room, White House – 8:20 PM EST

"If I could have your attention, please." Alex Hodson stood at the front of the room, trying to bring everyone to order. "Would you please take your seats?"

The crowd quieted and found places to sit. The decision to bring National Guard units into a coordinated effort required more cooperation than e-mails or phone calls could provide. Every effort or response resulted in more questions and less action. Everyone hoped a face-to-face meeting would make communication more effective.

"Thank you all for coming in tonight." Alex was glad to have an open meeting. His day consisted of one frustrating exercise after another. "I'm not going to go though the details of how the country got to this place. We are not going to reduce the discussion to a level of what is fair, not fair, or anything along that line. What we are facing is an invasion of a significant part of our country. Much of the Southwest and West, parts of the Northwest and Northeast are no longer under our control.

"The three topics for tonight are the resources available to us, the manpower we've lost, and how we can work together to take back our country. You've all been briefed, and many of you have been working with National Guard. Citizen groups across the Midwest are mounting courageous resistance.

"You have all been updated on the situation at Camp Pendleton. The Marines have secured the Camp and are holding over a hundred enemy combatants."

Alex continued his briefing about the conditions on the West Coast. The breakdown in communication on the civilian level left many questions about what was actually happening. From the meager reports that made it to Washington, there was little good news.

The president told Alex he didn't care how late they worked into the night. He wanted recommendations on his desk by 7:00 a.m. The Joint Chiefs would be in his office with a situation report in preparation for a coordinated counter-offensive. It was going to be a long night.

Andrews AFB – 8:25 PM EST

Marine One descended swiftly to the tarmac. When the president was on board, the approach was statelier and the landing even elegant. Tonight, the president was not on board and the chopper wheeled in like it was landing in a battlefield.

Mike, Steve, and Sam leaped from the chopper the instant it touched down. Thirty yards away an MC-130W Hercules waited. The four giant props roared in the night air, and the rear bay door stood wide open.

The MC-130W Hercules, Combat Spear, was equipped for special operations at a cost of $60 million per aircraft. The twelve aircraft, built specifically for the Air Force, contained a standard system of special forces avionics; a fully integrated Global Positioning System and Inertial Navigation System; an AN/APN-241 Low Power Color weather/navigation radar; advanced threat detection and automated countermeasures, including active infrared countermeasures and angel flares; upgraded communication suites, with dual satellite communications using data burst transmission; and ultra-secret deployment systems.

Ultra-secret deployment systems (USDS packs) are rolled on and off aircraft, matching USDS packs to particular missions. USDS packs provide technological operations that escape modern imagination. The stealth technology, developed in the early 1980s, was part of the USDS black-funded ops. Advanced mega-black studies with meta-material continued to develop efforts to manufacture a cloth that absorbs all light, while allowing certain visible rays to pass through. The ultra-light absorbing material offers hope for an invisibility cloak for troops in theater equal to the radar invisibility provided to stealth aircraft in the skies.

This MC-130W aircraft was equipped to covertly deploy more than a dozen manned jet-pack wing units based on the jet-propelled wing developed by a Swiss adventurer a few years earlier. The original flight from France to Britain across the English Channel was made at 125 miles per hour, powered by kerosene, with minimal technology.

The USDS re-designed units exchanged the original four Jet-Cat P200 engines with Rolls Royce Mini-jets that increased the speed by ten percent and provided auto-start on deployment. The kerosene was replaced with the new ionized-hydrogen gel that provided stability, higher thrust and extended range.

Mike ran up the bay door ramp and was greeted by the crew chief.

"I need to make a phone call," Mike shouted over the roar of the engines.

The crew chief looked at Mike's cell phone and shook his head.

"Sir, that won't work in here. Nothing like that will operate within a hundred feet of this bird."

Mike was bewildered. He must call Elli. They needed to get out of her parent's house and to someplace safe. The crew chief saw the look on Mike's face and motioned him to follow.

Mike and the chief jogged to the interior of the plane.

"Here, sir, put this on." The chief handed Mike a slightly bulky black helmet that seemed to have a solid, opaque face mask. Mike slipped the helmet on. The chief placed one on his head also.

"Can you hear me, sir?" The voice was unmistakably that of the chief. From inside, Mike could clearly see him through the visor.

"Yes, I can." Mike noticed he no longer heard the roar of the propellers. Other than the voice of the chief, everything was silent.

"Sir, if you look to the upper left corner of your visor . . ."

Mike hadn't noticed the icons lining the upper frame of the face mask. The icon farthest to the left was a telephone receiver. He looked at it for perhaps a second and a half. Suddenly he heard a dial tone.

"Sir, just speak the number you need to call," the chief said calmly.

Mike spoke Elli's cell phone number and heard the familiar ring heard on any phone. Then he heard Elli.

"Hello?" Her voice was tentative after seeing the calling number was unknown.

"Honey, it's Mike," he said, marveling that he was calling her from a flight helmet.

"Hi. Why aren't you using your phone?" Elli asked.

"No time to explain now," Mike began. "But you need to listen to me very carefully."

Mike told Elli of the intercepted phone calls and the information they'd discovered. He knew that while he spoke, a team of very bad people was leaving Washington with the aim of bringing harm to her and the kids.

"Elli, you all need to get away from the house as quickly and as quietly as you can,"

"Should we drive back toward home?"

"No, honey, don't drive anywhere. They're probably watching the road to the folks' house already." Mike wanted Elli to know of the danger. The last thing he wanted was for her to be afraid.

"Okay," Elli said softly. Mike could hear her smiling. "Hey! What if we took the kids on a hay-ride up into the hills behind the farm?"

"That's exactly what I was thinking," Mike replied.

"Do you remember the hay field, the one on the east side of Hawk's Hill?" Elli asked. "Remember the night Mom and Dad took the kids to the movie, and we hiked up there in the moonlight, and, well, did it?"

"That's one night I'll never forget," Mike said. "It's what, about two miles from the farm?"

"Something like that? But it will take some time to get ready and on the way."

"You just need to move as fast as you can, okay?" Mike's greatest fear was that his timing was wrong. "Oh, Elli, take your phone. I'll call you later. If you need me just return this call. The number will show as unknown, but you'll be able to call me. Got it?"

"Got it, commander!" Elli piped into her phone. "I know, no more being silly. I understand, babe."

It was her serious voice. Mike knew she was on track.

"I love you," Mike said.

"See you soon!"

Mike pulled the helmet off his head and was immediately overwhelmed by the thunderous roar of the props. Steve and Sam stood beside the chief, questioning looks on their faces.

"We're good!" Mike yelled giving a thumbs up.

"We need to brief you on this system," the chief yelled over the engine's roar. "It's gonna be fast, and you must pay attention."

He looked at each of them and motioned for them to follow. The C-130 lurched as it began to taxi for take-off. The ramp in the tail slowly closed as the plane moved ahead.

At the same moment, and unknown to those on the C-130 Hercules, another plane cleared the runway a few miles to the north, ahead of schedule. There was no time to spare.

chapter 24

Denney's Lounge, Swoope, VA – 8:30 PM EST

Rick couldn't remember eating a better meal. Subtleties of aroma and flavor continued to mystify his senses. It was a rare euphoria, and one experienced without the enhancement of a good wine.

Ilo Campbell casually walked Rick and George out the front door of Denney's Lounge. Night came quickly to the Virginia hills when the sky was overcast. Often the tips of the highest hills would catch the last rays of the setting sun, but not tonight. The cloud cover was thick and the promise of rain hung in the air.

"You boys headin' out into the hills, or are you goin' home?" Ilo liked Rick and George. He found Rick's youthfulness and naiveté a delightful challenge, like a favored toy. His little games elicited George's deep rolling laughter.

Most of the fun was at Rick's expense. He knew it and was only a little embarrassed by the fact. The three made a strange trio, not only in size and stature, but also in the diverse backgrounds each had experienced.

"What do you think, George? Should we head on out to the Makin Estate this late at night?"

"It's been a long day," George replied. "I don't know what we might turn up, but since the boss asked us to go, I think we'd better at least make an appearance."

Rick let out an audible sigh and slightly hung his head.

"Come on now, young feller," Ilo said with a lingering smile. "It cain't be all that bad."

"Oh, it's not bad," Rick replied. "I just think I could enjoy a quiet evening, without George!"

All three men laughed.

The parking lot had cleared since their arrival, but their SUV was across the highway. Ilo's overflow parking was the shoulder on the other side of the road. He felt the State of Virginia owed him some extra space anyway.

"Well, thanks for dinner, Ilo," George said shaking the old man's hand. "It was a delight."

"Well, I'm delighted to have ya." Ilo smiled a sparkling grin. It was true. Teeth helped. "And, George, next time bring someone a little better lookin' than this sorry mongrel, would ya?"

Rick groaned, covering a smile. He threw his head back and covered his eyes with his hands as he walked onto the roadway.

Ilo's head snapped up the road.

"Boys!—" Before he could finish half a sentence, the lights of a very fast moving vehicle flew over the rise in the road a few yards away.

With surprising speed George grabbed Rick by the waist and lunged to the far side of the two-lane road. The two men sprawled on the ground as seven black SUVs tore through the night.

The force of the wind made by their passing blew hard against Ilo's light frame, staggering him backward. Rick blinked and turned his head in time to see the last of the large vehicles speed by.

"You boys all right?" Ilo called from the far side of the road. He looked both ways several times as he hurried across the highway.

"Are you okay?" Ilo asked a second time.

"Yeah," Rick replied. "What the hell was that!"

"George, you okay?" Ilo asked bending over the huge man.

George groaned as he began to get up. Moving that fast was clearly not in his daily routine, and after moving fast, getting up was slow.

"I don't think I broke anything in particular," George muttered. "Feels like I broke most everything in general, though." He dusted himself off and looked down the road after the speeding group of vehicles.

"That's exactly what I was talkin' about the other mornin' when you came for breakfast," Ilo said.

"Was that people from the Makin Compound?" Rick asked as he stood and brushed the dust from his slacks.

"Sure as hell weren't the Baptists goin' for pizza." Ilo's eyes were locked on the road the cars had taken, and they burned with a white hot anger.

"Come on, Rick," George said as he moved toward their vehicle. "Let's go. Gotta see where they're headed."

George climbed into the driver's seat as Rick scrambled to get up and dust himself off. He ran toward the passenger door.

"Be careful, boys. Be real careful," Ilo said as he backed away.

George looked at Ilo. He was a friend, and George was glad to know him.

"Take care, Ilo," George shouted out the window. "See you soon!"

The engine roared to life and the rear tires spun in the gravel. The race was on.

Grey Horse Farm, New Salisbury, Kentucky – 8:35 PM EST

Elli walked from the living room and headed upstairs. Her parents understood there was a credible threat. They weren't flustered or frightened. Granddad walked out the back door and headed to the barn to hook the hay rack to the tractor. Grandma pulled out three picnic baskets from the pantry and began to load them.

"Hey, kids!" Elli called at the top of the stairs.

"What? Are we in trouble?" Robbie Trapper asked with wide-eyed anticipation. Just enough evidence remained to cause Elli to wonder what they were up to. She dropped it.

"No! No way! We're at granddad's house. What do you mean trouble?" Elli rolled onto the bed where the boys were playing with antique Match-Box cars and trucks.

The worried looks immediately melted into smiles.

"How would you like to go on a hay ride?" Elli asked with the most animated voice she could muster.

"Really?" Sara asked. "A real hay ride?"

The room burst into cheers. The boys bounced on the bed in excitement. Fourteen-month-old Riley turned to watch the activity on the bed while he continued to chew on the shoe he had pulled from his foot.

"Okay, we've got to get ready!" Elli said, jumping from the bed. "You kids get your shoes on and find a jacket. Robbie, help Jackson get ready and come downstairs."

Elli swept Riley into her arms with his shoe firmly gripped in his hands and teeth, and stuffed a handful of diapers in the knapsack. As she turned, Elli caught her reflection it the mirror. In her own eyes she saw fear and panic.

That has got to stop, right now! she told herself. She made a two-second attitude adjustment. *You choose how you're going to do this. Not in fear! You choose!* Courage was the choice.

The gang, Elli and four little people, thundered down the stairs as Elli had all her life. The flurry of feet brought grins on many occasions. This was different. The smile on Grandma's face as they crashed into her kitchen was a little forced.

"My, you look like you need a hay ride!" Grandma said, placing the last thermos of hot chocolate in the basket. "Tonight's hot chocolate will be served under a canopy of stars around a sparkling campfire!"

The bouncing band cheered and broke into a run for the barn. Granddad drove the tractor out the barn doors, and the kids exited the house. Grandma and Elli carefully negotiated the back steps, arms loaded with baskets and baby, and made their way to the hay wagon.

Granddad gleefully tossed Jackson, Sara, and Robbie into the soft pile of hay that was strewn across the wagon. Jackson stood up and spread a woolen blanket over the hay to the best of his ability. He managed to get the blanket wrapped around his legs. He was getting frustrated when Elli and Grandma arrived.

"Let me help you with that, Jackson," Grandma said as she climbed onto the wagon. Elli smiled inwardly, remembering her mom doing the same for her as a young girl. She passed Riley to Grandma and pulled herself onto the wagon. She remembered it was easier only a few years ago.

"All aboard!" Granddad shouted as he mounted the driver's seat on the tractor. He pushed the throttle forward, the tractor lurched, and the children tumbled into the pile of hay with squeals of laughter.

Elli smiled and cuddled Riley to her breast. She looked back at the home where she grew up, and wondered who was coming after them and why. As they drove into the surrounding darkness, she felt alone. Elli knew it was the uncertainty of it all. It ached in her stomach.

Hurry, Mike! she said to herself. *Please hurry!*

Mainside, Camp Pendleton, CA – 5:40 PM PST

Brigadier General Gene Westrup stood at the front of the classroom used for war games strategy training. Today, the training was real. The game cost hundreds of men and women their lives. No one was celebrating. There were no back-slaps nor atta-boys among the officers in the room.

The men and women sitting around the table had led their troops, mostly students, into fierce and violent combat. It was very real.

"The latest sit rep lists all sections of the base on alert/standby and gates are secured," the general began. "One-hundred-seventeen insurgents are in lockdown in the brig. They are being processed and identified. We will begin interrogating them in a few hours."

The general continued reporting the details of damage inflicted, troops wounded, estimated expenditure of weapons in the conflict, and as much information on the dead as could be gathered. Other officers relayed information on the performance of their platoons, where they executed their orders, and the instances communication broke down.

The day was reviewed in detail to ascertain every aspect of activity; success and failure, right and wrong, victory and defeat. Each order and response was evaluated, noted and processed into the training.

"Ladies and gentlemen," General Westrup said as he stood, "you're going to have a short night. There is a lot to finish up. The war strategy team will convene within the hour to map the next twenty-four hours.

"You need to understand what we faced today was the enemy coming at us. They were unprepared. They made foolish and costly mistakes. But in a matter of hours this mob of aliens and thugs grabbed thousands of square miles of the United States of America.

"Tomorrow, we begin taking it back. We'll meet here at oh-five-hundred hours to review the war team's recommendations. This meeting is adjourned."

The officers stood to attention as the general left the room.

12,500 Feet Above West Virginia – 8:45 PM EST

The armory room in the MC-130W Hercules was amazingly quiet. As Mike, Steve and Sam entered and closed the door, the roar of the four turbo-props reduced to a faint buzz. The movement of the plane as it taxied to takeoff was the only indication they were in an airplane.

After takeoff, the plane slipped smoothly through the cool night. Occasional bumps rattled the equipment in the room as the aircraft moved through pockets and currents in the air.

"This aircraft is equipped with the latest in covert technology." The crew chief sounded like he was opening a morning class. The visitors on this flight were about to be schooled in something they dreamed of as children.

"In a few minutes you will be fitted with a jet-pack wing." The chief was very matter-of-fact. "We're gonna tell you how it works and have you jump out the back of the plane."

Steve felt Sam grab his shirt sleeve. He knew she wasn't at her best when it came to heights. Sam had successfully completed paratroop training, but the idea of jumping out of a plane, twelve thousand feet up in the black of night, would be unsettling to her.

"The helmet you'll be wearing is a fully integrated command and communication unit. You will be in constant contact with your navigator on this plane. Each unit has a navigator who monitors how well you are approaching the target. They'll guide you through it. Your job is to listen to us, do what we say, and jump out of the plane. Are there any questions?" The chief looked at them like he was expecting a real response.

Hundreds! Mike thought. He could feel the tingle of tension in his neck. No, it was fear. *Suck it up, Trapper!*

"You will be armed and accompanied by nine snipers," the chief continued. "They are our best and normally assigned to the White House. The president sent these men for your protection and safety. Now, let's get you suited up and ready."

chapter 25

Interstate 66, West of Washington DC – 8:50 PM EST

"We're in pursuit now!" Rick said into the truck's sat-phone. The communication pack on the SUV was linked through the satellite provided by the State Department that Sam arranged. The system was more reliable than private cell phones, and for what it was worth, it would work after a nuclear explosion.

"We have a visual on you," Alex replied. Alex Hodson and Mort, the technician, spent several minutes finagling permissions to command two more satellites for tracking. The two had been busy.

"You see us?" Rick asked.

"Right here on the screen from two hundred miles out in space," Mort replied. "You didn't think Hubble only looked at stars did you?" There was chiding and sarcasm in his tone.

"Never thought about it. Do you have visual on the guys we're chasing?"

"We do, Rick. They're about a mile and a half ahead of you." Alex did his best to be calm. He knew Rick and George were drawing close to a potentially dangerous situation. Everyone needed to keep their cool.

"What's in the plan to stop these guys?" Rick asked as George drove furiously, exceeding one hundred miles per hour.

"You're going to get some company as you go past the Crest Hill Road and West Main exit about a mile west of the Highway 17 exchange in The Plains," Alex said. "By the time you get to the exit for 17, they're going to be shut down."

"Can you do it that quick?" Rick asked.

"We have to," Alex replied. "We have to stop them before they get to Haymarket or Gainesville. Too much traffic and too many exits."

"Makes sense. What's your time expectation on all this?" Rick held serious reservations about stopping seven massive SUVs driving nearly one hundred miles per hour.

"You're about forty-five miles out, so you tell me. What's your best guess?"

"Forty-five miles? We'll be there in twenty minutes at this rate." Rick looked at George who smiled back at him and shook his head.

"Young man, you got a lot of learning ahead of you." George chuckled softly.

Rick wasn't sure what George meant, but decided this wasn't the time for a discussion. Alex's voice broke his thought.

"That's what I expected," Alex said to Rick. "We'll be ready for you."

Rick hung up the sat-phone. He sat back and sighed. He had a few minutes to focus and prepare himself. It frustrated him that he had no idea what to get ready for.

LAPD, Los Angeles, CA - 5:55 PM PST

Colonel Herrera stumbled as he entered his office. He staggered and fell into his desk chair. He could not believe what his own eyes had witnessed. It was not possible. He had never seen a small military unit, greatly outnumbered, master a ferocious mob so quickly.

All of his studies of the American commitment to military conflict led him to conclude they were cowards. Historically, he rationalized, their victories stemmed from dumb luck or the blundering, hapless stupidity of their opponents. What he witnesses at Camp Pendleton had stunned him.

Three of Herrera's closest advisors walked into his office with long faces. They, too, were surprised at the strength and battle readiness displayed by the American Marines. The small group of men witnessed, from separate vantage points, overwhelming military might unleashed by a comparatively small army.

"What is next for us?" Johor was known as The Algerian. He was ruthless and would execute the harshest order without flinching.

"For us!" Herrera roared. "You say for us! Do you not think?"

Colonel Herrera could not contain himself. He knew much of their plan must be restructured. He must calm down before beginning that analysis. He knew the decisions must be made with a clear mind. No emotion. No feelings.

"We did not expect the Americans to actually fight," Cero said. Cero grew up in Belize hearing stories filled with hate for Americans. Not one of the stories he heard as a boy spoke of Americans with strength.

"But they did fight!" the colonel bellowed. "We saw weapons we never imagined! Who could prepare an army for a . . . for a big . . . sound! How do you do that?"

"Obviously, we—" Cero began.

"And where do you find men who never stop firing like that? Where? I watched hundreds fall in mere minutes!" Herrera's ravings echoed from the office walls. "I have never known Americans to fight a battle in such a manner."

Had Herrera been truthful, he would admit he never faced an American in battle. The stories they all heard as young men were proven false in a single afternoon. The tales were no more than fables.

"Certainly not in the manner we witnessed today." Estefan was a man who was not easily flustered. He did not react emotionally like the colonel. He was like sharp, cold steel.

"Perhaps today," Estefan continued, "perhaps what we saw was a battle with the American generals, not the American politicians."

Herrera stopped mid-stride. He turned to Estefan. His face blanched in rage. But the rage was not for Estefan. His rage centered on the truth of his words.

"Today," Herrera said slowly, "yes, today we fought generals, not politicians."

How could I have been so blind? Herrera thought. The stories did tell of ruthless American businessmen, harsh men who enslaved common people with brutish cruelty. That was the ferocity his army met in battle.

"Yes, you are right, Estefan." The revelation came to Colonel Herrera slowly. It was the politicians that controlled the military in America. It was the weakness in the politicians that kept the borders open and easy to pass through. Their lack of political will enabled tens upon tens of thousands to stay in the country unregistered.

The weakness was believed to be in the military, but that was not so. *The weakness is in the leaders!* Herrera thought.

The thought sent a chill through his body. He had not considered the strength of the people. The realization numbed him. But his mind was suddenly clear. He knew his cause would lose. They would be defeated by the Americans.

"We must begin." The colonel swept his desk clean and spread a fresh map over the surface. He had a plan.

Grey Horse Farm, New Salisbury, Kentucky – 9:00 PM EST

Elli managed to mask her fear by singing with the kids, playing games and listening to Grandma's stories. The favorite was the tale of Elli's foot being caught in the fork of a tree she climbed. She was late for supper. Her dad found her in the hedgerow along the logging road.

"It was that tree right there where your granddad found her just as it was getting dark," she said as they passed a particularly sinister looking tree.

The children drew close to their grandmother, fearing the tree might reach out and grab them. Elli smiled, wondering what was racing through their young imaginations.

The old tractor lugged the wagon up the logging road. The road wasn't fit for a vehicle any less stout than a tractor. The small party could have walked as fast, but the magic of rolling through the evening countryside would have been lost.

The past twenty minutes had taken them almost a mile up the mountain. The hillside was long, not terribly steep, but heavily washed from the snowmelt and early spring rains. The tractor and wagon lurched and slipped from rut to wash, bouncing the passengers, who squealed with glee as they tumbled on the hay.

Elli thought about the climb she made with Mike after his first tour in Iraq. He had marveled at the lush green hills and the hay fields gently swaying in soft breezes. She was pretty sure Sara was conceived that day in the hay field. Elli smiled.

She watched her children's bright faces singing with their grandmother. They sang along without knowing the words, mimicking the expressions on grandma's smiling face.

The flash lit their faces before the noise of the explosion thundered up the mountainside. The house, Elli's childhood home, burst into flames with a distant roar.

Elli gasped. The thought of her children asleep in the house ripped deeply into her heart. *What if they hadn't warned us! We'd all be there! We'd all be . . .*

She couldn't finish the thought.

"Mommy! Is that grandma's house?" Robbie asked.

"Yes, Robbie. I think it is," Elli replied softly. She couldn't take her eyes off the blaze. Whoever they were, they were that close, and it was too close. Elli fought the panic rising in her.

"Daddy?" she called to Granddad on the tractor. "How's that tractor doing?" she said without turning from the blaze.

"We're almost to the ridge," he replied. "Once we get up there, I can open her up a bit. We can make a little more speed."

Elli looked at her mom. She could see tears pooling in her eyes. Grandma smiled and shrugged, then brought her hand to her mouth and pressed it against her lips. She looked down at Riley as he climbed into her lap.

"Mommy, why did grandma's house blow up?" Sara asked. Her voice was soft and laced with fear.

"I don't know, honey. We'll be fine," Elli said and smiled her best reassuring smile. "Hey, I forgot to tell you! Daddy is going to meet us at the top of the mountain!"

Three sets of young eyes whipped around from the fire below.

"Daddy's coming?" Robbie's eyes were wide with excitement.

"How's he going to get here, Mommy?" Sara asked.

"I really don't know, Sara. He just told me he was on his way."

Elli smiled as her three older kids flung themselves toward her through the hay. She was smothered in their hugs. Elli held all three of them close to her. Finally, Riley crawled into the huddle and grinned. They all laughed.

The wagon lurched, causing them to tumble into a heap with giggles and tiny squeals. They were together and safe, but the spell was broken. Something evil had spun a dangerous web down the mountainside. How long would that evil stay down the mountain? When would they discover the house was empty? When would they begin their pursuit up the logging road?

Elli looked toward the house. Through the trees she could see the glowing flames. Nothing else was recognizable. It was too far away.

Not quite far enough away, Elli said to herself. *Hurry up, Mike!*

National Guard Armory, Frisco, TX - 8:07 PM CST

The ride north to Frisco was hard on Jim. His wounds from the grenade were not serious, but they were painful. The explosion caught him turning away and bending to duck behind a half-wall in the staircase. His turning and bending had left Jim with his backside exposed, and a victim of the grenade's shrapnel.

Once the men knew Jim's injuries were minor, the ribbing began. It was endless. Although he outranked every man with him, having an ass shot up with grenade fragments overrode rank.

"Hey, Jim, maybe you'll get a medal! Oh, never mind, you already got four!"

"Hey, Jim, didn't they teach you in OCS to wear your medals on your dress uniform?"

"Hey, Jim, can I get you a pillow?"

"Hey, Jim, we can soak your butt in beer!"

"Okay, guys, come on. Make an end of it!"

"Sorry, Jim, didn't mean to make you the butt of our jokes."

After each sophomoric quip the men choked with laughter. Tears streaked their faces. Jim nodded his head and smiled. *Cute*, he thought. *Damn this hurts!*

He took it in stride, though. These men had just killed over one hundred enemy soldiers. They faced three times their number in heavily armed, seasoned fighters. They killed every one of them. Coping with the internal conflict of destroying life to preserve the lives of others is never an easy task. Laughter was the best and most readily available release. Jim was fine with it.

Finally, the truck stopped in the parking lot. The joking stopped, and a small group of brave warriors gently helped their young wounded officer from the truck. Jim was struck by the contrast he saw in the men. One moment ribald with course laughter at his expense, the next, carefully lifting him with strong, stable hands.

Jerry "Doc" Smith ran from the Armory as they dismounted the trucks. Jerry was a captain in the unit and a surgeon at Baylor Medical Center. He was never a fan of rank or titles awarded or imposed on him. He refused to be called "captain." Doc would do just fine.

"What the hell have you guys been up to?" Doc stopped dead in his tracks as ten Marines carried Jim Parker shoulder high with his backside poking high in the air. "What the . . ."

"Evening, Doc."

"Hey, Doc."

"How ya been, Doc?"

"Good to see ya, Doc."

"Thanks for comin' over, Doc."

The short greetings jumbled together as the scrum of soldiers packed their lieutenant inside the building.

Doc followed with a look of disbelief on his face.

Once inside, everyone was serious. Jim lay on his stomach on the aluminum-topped table in the kitchen. The Marines stepped back as Doc walked up to him.

This was the part they all knew had to happen. It was time to take Jim's pants off. Doc stood beside the table and looked at the ring of warriors around him.

"Who's gonna do it?" he asked. He looked around again. No volunteers.

"Are you guys just going to stand there and let this officer bleed to death?" Doc asked. There was no way that was going to happen, but it added to the moment.

"A little help would be nice, but what the heck!" Jim said. "I'll do it myself!"

He raised his midsection from the table and held himself up on his knees and the right side of his face. With his hands he unbuckled his pants, popped the button, and pulled his khakis down, exposing his glistening white rear-end.

A collective groan rose from the ranks of the ring of warriors.

"Hey!" Jim shouted.

"Okay, guys." Doc helped Jim lower his trousers to his knees.

"Hey, Doc," Jim began. "One thing. Would you put a towel under me? This table is really cold."

Quickly surveying the extent of Jim's exposure, Doc grabbed two of the large towels on the counter and gently spread them beneath his suspended torso. Jim slowly lowered himself to the table.

"Ah. Thanks, Doc."

"Jim, this might hurt a bit. Do you want something?" Doc asked.

"Just get it done," he replied.

"Man." Doc began a close examination of the wounds. "It looks like they really tried to rip you a new one. Fortunately, they missed!"

The laughter broke out once again.

This is never going to be over, Jim thought. *Never!*

chapter 26

West Main Exit, I-66 West of Washington DC – 8:12 PM EST

"George, you're gonna run right up on top of them!" Rick's voice sounded almost out of control with panic. George's one-hundred miles-per-hour chase brought them directly behind the last of the seven SUVs that almost ran them down half an hour before.

"Look and learn, young agent. Look and learn." George gunned the engine and came within inches of the rear bumper of the SUV in front of them. "Oh, and hold on, while you're lookin'."

George's smile was mostly on the inside. This was part of the game of pursuit. Once counter measures were in place, his objective was to keep the target distracted. Nearly ramming them from the rear at eighty miles per hour was distraction enough.

"How far to the overpass, Rick?" George knew his obligation to distract would come to a very abrupt end once the counter measures came into play. He didn't want any surprises on his end.

"About a mile and a half." Rick gripped the door handle and the console between them, staring straight ahead. He half expected someone to shoot at them from the SUV only inches away.

"Rick! This is Carter. Do you read me?" Carter's voice caused Rick to jump. George noted the stress beginning to wear on his young partner.

"Yeah! I mean, I read you loud and clear!" Rick blurted into the sat-phone.

"Okay, guys," Carter began. "This is going to come down very quickly. As soon as you go under the overpass you will be joined by six vehicles. The largest one will pull in front of you. That's when you're going to need to stop fast, and I mean very fast. Got it?"

Rick looked at George. Rick's eyes said, *Do we? Do we got it? What's* it? George nodded.

"Yeah, we got it." Rick slumped a bit. He didn't know if it was bewilderment or his being clueless.

"Just hang on, son." George's deep, calm tone soothed Rick just enough. Rick focused on the road ahead. Suddenly, George slowed by twenty miles per hour.

With blinding speed five SUVs, all black, flew down the ramp as Rick and George passed under the overpass. In the darkness one vehicle, the sixth of the group, roared in front of them. It was huge and a shape Rick didn't recognize.

"What in the world . . ." But before the sentence formed in his mind the vehicles swarmed around Rick and George. The sixth one, the huge one, leaped ahead of them all. The distance George left between them and the seven SUVs they pursued was quickly filled by the behemoth.

Bright orange lights flashed rapidly on the back of the huge truck. George slammed on the breaks, locking them and screeched to a sliding stop with the other government vehicles.

The flash was accompanied by a loud pop. The large black truck that pulled to the front was silhouetted for an instant, and screeched to a stop, smoking its tires in the process.

The seven vehicles they had pursued sat still on the Interstate with smoke rising from the hoods, the wheels and every window allowing its escape. The cabins of the vehicles were filled with smoke.

Rick looked at George to ask what had just happened.

"Sit still. Don't get out," George demanded.

"Okay, I can do that." Rick nodded, looking from George to the odd scene that lay before them, and back to George.

"What you saw was a focused electro-magnetic pulse weapon discharge." George rested his left elbow on the steering wheel and leaned toward Rick.

"A *what*? I mean, that's like science fiction, it's just . . ."

"The discharge simply melts every circuit and chip, as well as neutralizes polarity in a limited area. Within the range of the pulse, say an area fifty by seventy feet, there is suddenly no more positive or negative electrical charge. Everything that makes an electrical connection is instantly disconnected. Nothing that is electric works.

"That's why we stopped this far back. They shape the pulse to cover the target. And on these newer vehicles, when the electrical systems fail, the brakes lock up." George smiled. "Sort of a little extra that Detroit engineered for us as part of the bail-outs a few years back."

"Damn," was all Rick could say.

"And you can't say anything about this," George said, his eyes were locked on Rick's. "Ever."

The doors on the seven melted SUVs popped open and four men emerged from each vehicle. They opened fire on the large black truck that had stopped their escape.

Rick reached for his handgun and started to open the passenger door.

"Don't do that, Rick. Stay put. Look and learn, son." George's hand touched Rick's elbow as he spoke to him.

The Uzis sprayed ordnance on the large truck without damage. Bullets bounced and ricocheted in every direction.

Slowly two suitcase size hatches opened on the top of the large black truck. Two strange looking tubular objects emerged.

"Those are called infrared scan, multi-launch, precision ordnance. They are scanning the position of each of the men firing a weapon. Once that's done—"

A sudden loud zipping sound like a roman candle on the Fourth of July, and a flash from each of the tubular objects interrupted George.

". . . then, that happens."

The air was filled with contrail tracings of the projectiles. Each projectile functioned like a mini-cruise missile, with the ability to fly a path over or around any object and strike a target from any side. It happened in an instant. Twenty-four of the twenty-eight men firing at the large truck dropped to the ground.

"Each one only shoots twelve at a time." George looked at Rick and shrugged. Rick was slack-jawed.

The four remaining gunmen dropped their weapons and raised their hands in surrender.

"Okay, Rick," George said smiling. "Let's go get the bad guys."

North Waco Street, Wichita, KS – 8:15 PM CST

Robert and Yolanda strolled back toward her uncle's home hand-in-hand. The evening was like none either of them could remember. They had no idea what the weather was like; they only knew the evening was remarkable.

"Is this how you imagined it might happen?" Yolanda asked looking deeply into Robert's eyes.

He looked at her, blushed and then turned his gaze to his feet, and back to her. "I didn't have any idea. I mean," Robert said a little flustered, "I had no idea it should, could or ever would happen. Then, all of a sudden, wham!"

"I know. That's what happened," Yolanda replied with a smile that melted him. "I wasn't expecting to find you at all! I only hoped." Yolanda's face suddenly darkened as the memories of the morning flooded her mind. The pictures of horror had vanished from her thinking until that instant.

Robert saw the change immediately. "What is it? Are you all right?" He held Yolanda by the shoulders and looked into her terror-filled eyes.

"Oh, my! Everything from this morning just came back to me!" Her emotions swung to the other side, far from the safety she felt with Robert. The images of those murdered at the police station; the evil looking men in the pick-up truck; the face of the man who ordered her out of the police station.

"You're safe here, Yolanda. It's okay!" Robert bent lower, seeking her gaze now buried in her hands. "Yolanda!"

She looked up revealing her tear-stained cheeks. "Let's go back to the house. Please?"

"Sure." Robert put his arm around Yolanda's shoulders. She shivered, even though the night was warm. Robert was alarmed at the sudden turn, but he was not surprised. Trauma and terror could suddenly return with a vengeance.

Their walk was short, and they huddled closely together. Yolanda continued shivering. He spoke softly to her of how far she had come. He told her the evil she had left behind had not followed her. Twice she stopped and buried her face in his chest, sobbing silently. Robert could not comfort her.

As they entered the house the conversation abruptly stopped. Yolanda's mother rose from her chair and rushed to her daughter.

"What is it? What happened?" Bea looked from her daughter to Robert.

"She remembered this morning," Robert said flatly.

Bea embraced her lovely daughter, pulling her close. Robert stepped back but remained focused on Yolanda. The phone in his pocket vibrated. He turned away to answer it.

"This is Robert."

"And boy, this is your daddy." Perry Hitchens always responded to his son's greeting the same way. Every time. Perry's response made Robert smile.

"Hey, Dad," Robert replied. "How's Norman, Oklahoma this evening?"

"Safe and sound, son. Safe and sound."

"Good. I'm glad to hear it." And he was. Robert's boyhood home was special to him, and knowing that things were settling down brought him comfort.

"And how are your charges doing?" Perry asked. He suspected something may have sparked between his handsome son and the lovely young woman. He was looking at her face when Robert walked up to them under the overpass.

"Well, Yolanda just had some reaction to the events of her day," Robert said as he walked onto the porch. "Dad, she saw a lot of people get killed this morning. I think she was so busy runnin' away she didn't take time to process it all. Kinda hit her quick."

"From what you're saying, it sounds to me like a soldier's reaction to first time hand-to-hand combat." Perry had seen that fear. "I remember your stories you told me when I was a kid. It was only a story too until the day I looked into the eyes of a man as he died. Watching the life fade away is the strangest part."

Both father and son had shared the experience of taking the life of another man in combat.

"Just give her some room, son. She needs to let things fall into place."

"You're right, Dad," Robert said looking back at Yolanda, sobbing in her mother's arms. "I think she needs some time."

"Well, time is one of the things I called about," the sheriff said slowly. "A lot of folks down here don't want to waste any more of it. Son, they're ready to mobilize and start goin' after the rascals that started this mess."

"I thought that's what happened this afternoon out by the airport," Robert said. "I'm a little surprised people want to go looking for a fight."

"More like it *started* out by the airport," the sheriff replied. "Robert, we stopped a small army of very bad men comin' up from Dallas. But there's a bigger bunch of bad guys already in Oklahoma City. We gotta rout them out."

"Dad, shouldn't the army or Marines come in and do that?" Robert asked with the slightest tinge of fear in his voice. "Isn't that their job?"

"Son," Perry began, "at this point the army and Marines are us regular folks who have served, who have been in the fight, and now find it chompin' at our heels. We fought these bastards in the Middle East to kill 'em off over there. Now the damn politicians opened the door, and, well, here we are."

Robert knew his dad and his politics. Perry Hitchens had no use for a politician who would sell his principles for a new highway in his home county. Many had fought in the long war in Iraq only to see their victory fade under feeble oversight. The lackluster effort in Afghanistan showed no more promise. The enemy was emboldened by weak American leadership. Now the country pursued a vision of strength that was lost. And one that was lost in only a day.

"What do you want me to do?" Robert asked. In his heart he was willing to do anything. Since his mother had died, his dad did everything possible for Robert. Not to the point of spoiling him, but Robert's dad had never let him down. He was willing to return the favor, whatever it might be.

"Robert, we're gonna need you back down here," Perry said in a matter-of-fact tone. "We need you to help manage and control the assets we've got, and make sure we don't mess things up."

"But surely you have guys there for that." Robert was upset. "I'm not very comfortable thinking about you putting yourself in harm's way again. At the same time a little insulted you want me to run a weapons warehouse. Wouldn't I be more useful with a rifle helpin' you?"

"Robert, you're one of the finest shots in this state. But I know you, and that I can trust you. We're gonna be dealing with a lot of property and armament. I need you to cover my back, okay?"

"Sure. Absolutely. When do you want me back?"

"Things are moving very rapidly. The sooner the better."

"Fine. I'm on my way." If his dad needed him, he was ready.

"Thank you, son. See you soon."

Robert pushed the button on his phone that broke the connection. As he slid the small phone into his pocket, he looked through the screen door at Yolanda. He opened the door.

Yolanda looked up at him. Immediately she stood, walked to him and embraced him. He held her firmly in his arms.

"Hey, are you okay?" He looked over her to her mother. Bea's cheeks were wet with tears.

"Now I am," Yolanda replied with her face buried in his chest. Robert was glad to hear her speak calmly. The panic was gone. Her words were soft again. The shivering stopped.

"Listen, that was my dad, and they need me back in Norman."

Robert held Yolanda at arm's length so he could look into her eyes.

"I want you to stay here with your family. That way, I'll know you're safe and you can get some rest."

"No." Yolanda nearly spat her answer. "I will go with you!"

"Yolanda!" Bea said rising from the couch. "You need to rest! You cannot just take off like this. You must stay here with us!"

"No, Mama." Yolanda snapped. "You are here. You are safe here. That's why we came. I want *you* safe here. You stay. You have worked all your life for me. You need to stay."

"Yolanda," Robert said, "I don't know what I'm heading into. I'd prefer it if you would stay."

"No. You listen to me! I have worked hard. I have looked and waited for you. I have prayed for a man like you. I will *not* let you just slip out of my life. I am going with you!"

Robert was stunned. He was also thrilled. No one, man or woman, had ever spoken to him like that. He was put off by her bluntness and at the same time flattered that she wanted to be with him. He looked at her without words to reply.

Robert looked at Bea. She half smiled and waved her hand. "She's always been like that. I could never talk her out of anything!" Suddenly Bea burst into laughter. "There was this one time she brought home a dog . . ."

Whatever the story was, it instantly carried Bea, her brother and his wife into hilarious laughter. They laughed unable to speak.

"Mama!" Yolanda stomped her foot on the floor. "Don't bring that up now! He was a cute puppy!" And just as suddenly she burst into laughter.

"It was a rat!" Bea screeched. The story of young Yolanda befriending a small "puppy" on the beach in Mexico only to learn a few days later it was a South American rat, was a family treasure.

By now, everyone but Robert was collapsing on the sofa, a chair, anything that would keep them from falling on the floor. Tears rolled down their cheeks as they gasped for breath, only to be swept into laughter again, unable to speak.

Robert took his time. He knew there would opportunity to gather all the details. He also knew in the last few hours his life had changed. He met a woman who was beautiful, easy to talk with, wonderful to hold and had a backbone to boot. He looked at her and marveled.

There she was, the woman of his dreams. All he had to do was to wait for her to compose herself. Then, it would be time to head back to Norman.

chapter 27

West Main Exit, I-66 West of Washington DC – 9:22 PM EST

After George gave the go ahead, Rick exited the SUV and joined two dozen Secret Service agents approaching the smoking vehicles. An acrid stench hung in the air. A mixture of gunpowder, melted plastic, and something he couldn't quite sort out. The combination of odors brought a slight burning to his nostrils.

"Get out of the vehicle!" George shouted, raising his Glock .40 to firing position. Even with his large hands, the Glock was the perfect handgun for George. The magazine extender fit the weapon to his hand. The design and durability of the gun fit the task. And George was an excellent shot.

"Get out and lie on the ground!" George's orders were immediately obeyed. His booming voice left no question. To not surrender would be a choice for certain death. Or so it seemed to the one on the business end of his handgun.

Three more men exited the smoking SUV. The last man to exit wore traditional Egyptian attire and moved like a very old man.

"On the ground!" George could command like no one Rick had ever seen. His booming voice was enough to enforce his will. In Rick's estimation, he could have shouted ten times as many men into complete submission.

The old man slowly lowered himself to the pavement. He looked up at George with the slightest challenge. George bore in on him with the barrel of a very powerful handgun. The older man laid himself on the pavement.

"This is an outrage!" the old man sneered. "I have diplomatic immunity!"

"*Had* diplomatic immunity," George growled. "Cuffs!" Rick swept into action, handcuffing the three men laying prostrate before him. The click of the restraints brought each man into the complete control of the Secret Service.

Twenty-four men lay wounded or dead from the multi-launch ordnance. Another ten were cuffed and prepared for transfer, including an older man in traditional Egyptian attire. There were many questions being prepared for him alone. The others would be questioned, but the older man was the focus. He held the key, and everyone in the Secret Service wanted that key.

12,500 Feet Above West Virginia – 9:25 PM EST

The back ramp of the MC-130W Hercules slowly opened onto a black sky. The roar of the props washed into the interior with a rush of cold air. Twelve black-suited warriors stood silently. The cold rush pressed against them, even with the reduced air speed. The ramp was almost fully open.

"This is Crew Chief Schwartz. The mission is *Go*. Communication is *Go*. Departure is imminent. All hands standby."

Samantha Long stood as the only woman with eleven men. She never let her feminine nature get in the way before. But suddenly, she didn't feel very brave.

What am I doing? I'm about to jump out of a plane, twelve thousand feet above solid ground, at night, wearing God-knows-what, and I don't even know if it works!

"How are you doing, Sam?" It was Tony, her navigator.

"Great!" Sam snapped. "Why?"

"Oh, nothing," Tony answered. "You're just the only one bouncing back and forth from one foot to the other. Thought you might be a little nervous, that's all."

A little nervous! Sam thought. Then she realized she really was bouncing back and forth. She was hopping from one foot to the other like a runner before a race.

"Well Tony," Sam began, afraid of being perfectly honest. "Let me say, I wish I had to pee so I could call this whole thing off!"

She heard Tony laugh softly.

"Sam, I'm the one in control," he said through a smile. "All you need to do is dive into the pool."

Their instructions in leaving the plane were to simply run off the end of the ramp, diving head first into the dark night. Just like diving into a swimming pool. It was that simple.

"But I can normally see the pool I'm diving into, Tony," Sam protested. "This is a bit different."

"I know. Trust me, Sam. I've done this a hundred times. You'll do fine." Tony's words were received as little more than sarcasm.

I'll do fine! Right, I'll do just— Sam's thoughts fell silent.

"Execute launch! In five . . . four . . . three . . ." Chief Schwartz's voice boomed in her headset.

Wait! Wait! Wait! I can't breathe. Can we talk about this? No! Wait! NO!

"Two . . . one. Launch! Launch! Launch!"

Sam watched the first three team members run out the end of the plane. Everything seemed to be in slow motion to her. Then the second set ran to the end of the ramp and dove into the darkness.

Her legs felt like rubber. Sam leaned forward and ran with all her might. It felt like she was running in hip-deep water. Everything in her cried for her to stop. *Don't do it! Don't jump! Stop! Go back!*

One foot then another slammed into the deck of the ramp. Each foot weighed two-hundred pounds. One more step.

Sam dove headlong into the sea of black. She braced her arms to her side, gripping the hand controls in white-knuckled fear. She didn't know if her eyes were open or closed. She felt she was spinning and rolling through unseen turbulence. *Lost!*

"There ya go!" It was Tony. She almost forgot about him. "Gyros comin' up."

Sam felt herself suddenly stable. She looked around. Thousands of feet below, she could faintly distinguish pinpoints of light.

"Engaging engines." Tony's voice was so matter-of-fact it seemed out of place.

The four engines popped and roared to life. Sam was thrust forward in controlled flight.

She was flying!

"Okay, Sam. Can you hear me well enough?" Tony seemed to be inside Sam's helmet.

"Yes . . . yes, I hear you fine." Her voice sounded strangely calm. She was not calm. But she was flying! Flying!

"Good," Tony replied. "Be sure to keep your back straight and your head up."

The position felt completely natural. It was exactly what she expected from flying in her dreams. *Doesn't Superman fly with his head up?*

"Sam, if you move your head to the right or left it will change your course slightly, so be aware of that, okay?" Tony had this procedure down. Sam felt total confidence in his voice.

"Got it," Sam said. "Yeah, this is all right."

"Excellent." Tony answered. "You're gonna have a twelve-minute burn before you begin your descent. I'll make a couple of corrections as we go. You just hold your head up and enjoy the ride."

Enjoy the ride? Oh, dear God in heaven, I'm flying! "Sure thing, Tony, sure thing."

There was no sound inside Sam's helmet. She faintly heard the rocket engines strapped to the bottom of the wing on her back. Though the engines were no more than ten inches from each elbow, her flight soared ahead of the sound.

The wind rushed over her helmet with enough pressure she could easily hold her head in place. Sam quickly learned she could roll her head to the left or right without changing the angle.

Sam felt the material of the suit pressed firmly against her body. She seemed to be laying on the suit, as if the suit was holding her above the earth. She had to remind herself she was moving very rapidly through the air. She wasn't suspended, she was flying!

Ten yards to either side she could see the men who dove from the ramp with her. Her first glance to the right nearly took her breath away. From the side, her companion appeared as a superhero rocketing through space, light blue flames illuminating the underside of the wing. The backdrop of stars completed the effect.

Fifty yards ahead, Sam could clearly see the four rockets burning on the wings of three other men. She knew the middle set of rockets carried Steve. The first group held Mike in the middle of the trio. Everything was okay. It was working.

"Okay Sam. You're flying at 147 knots with four minutes of fuel remaining. Do you have any questions?"

"Tony, everything is fine," Sam said, surprised at her confidence. "How is everyone else doing?"

"Everything's A-OK, if you'll forgive a slightly over-used term of communication," he replied.

"It fits, Tony," Sam said. "Everything *is* A-OK! Absolutely!"

"Enjoy your flight." Tony sounded like a flight attendant and made Sam smile.

She could see the horizon, as well as street lights below, headlights of cars driving down country roads were visible. Stunning. Sam was awestruck. She was flying!

Grey Horse Farm, New Salisbury, Kentucky – 9:29 PM EST

The team of assassins stood more than a hundred yards from the burning farmhouse. The youngest of the group turned and looked into the night sky, hearing the distant propellers of a lone aircraft. He dismissed it as a passing commercial flight.

"You should have waited," the older man growled. "They will be here any moment, and all we have is a burning farmhouse. You don't even know if anyone was home!"

The leader of the group stared blankly into the flames. His face was angry. He was angry.

The surface-to-air launcher lay at his feet. He knew he should have waited. He knew he should have checked the house before firing the missile. He knew the mission was either a success or a complete failure, and that he would pay with his life if the latter was true.

His eyes betrayed his fear, and the others saw it.

"We will go check the house when the flames die down a bit," the impulsive leader said to his team. "It is too hot for now. We can count the bodies later."

He turned his back to the flaming farmhouse and walked up the road. He needed a cigarette. *Don't heroes always get a last cigarette in the movies?*

OCT, Little Rock, AK – 8:31 PM CST

"Mort, this is Aaron Stevens in Little Rock." The restoration of the internet created a much more effective tool for combating groups of terrorists across the Mid-West. The virus released into the White House network, and ultimately the World Wide Web, cast a cloud of confusion over a significant portion of the United States government communications, as well as the military's ability to communicate.

The repair and reconstruction moved much more rapidly after the arrest of Barry Goldstein. His treachery was responsible for the loss of hundreds of man hours in making the repairs, as well as the lives of thousands of American citizens who died without warning.

The coordinated efforts of the Office of Counter Terrorism in Little Rock and the top secret Automatic Location Identification map, or ALI maps in the White House basement, enabled United States forces to locate the positions of sleeper cells. Teams of Special Forces invaded the cells as military commanders monitored in real time.

"Hi, Aaron," Mort replied. "We're coming up to generate more locations on the numbers you gave me."

OCT monitored phone calls across the United States. Since the assassination on Sunday, a growing list of key words opened a new world of surveillance. Words that carried no meaning a week ago were popping up across the country when matched with other key words and phrases by the two Cray computers.

The invading terrorists were delighted to use the infidel's technology to defeat and destroy the Great Satan. What they didn't know was the technology was able to be used against them.

"Great," Aaron Stevens replied. "We're still getting IDs on about fifty new numbers every half-hour."

"We have top priority for this," Mort replied. "We'll get 'em all."

National and Air Guard units in the Dakotas, Nebraska, Montana, Kansas, Missouri, Iowa, Illinois, Ohio and Indiana were a few hours away from full deployment. Normal alerts were required to be fully staffed within twenty-four hours. On this alert, the response was nearing seventy-five percent after five hours.

Mort's keyboard was now the command center for the country. Soon his normally quiet work area would be bustling with the Joint Chiefs of Staff and their subordinates. Mort would run the show based on the data from the team in Little Rock.

This unassuming technician, Mort, with balding head, horn-rimmed glasses and bow tie, was the center of attention. He would be telling the generals where and when to send attack aircraft, drones, or troops. He would be instrumental in repelling the attacks on his nation. He felt like a real American.

chapter 28

12,000 Feet Above Eastern Kentucky – 9:37 PM EST

"Okay, Mike. Your twelve-minute burn is just about up." Mike's navigator Curt prepared him for the next event. "You'll hear a pop when the engines cut out. After that your air-speed and altitude will degrade rapidly. You won't be out of control, but you will feel yourself begin to drop."

"Roger, Curt." The familiar communication seemed out of place. Mike had never been on a mission where communication protocol was not used. It was weird for him to simply talk to this other person.

No sooner than he replied, Mike heard the pop and felt his body weight begin to pull against the wing. Rather than feeling pinned against the wing by the force of the engines, he felt he was dangling.

"Hold on there. Relax." Curt's voice was calming. Mike felt the controls in his hands move slightly as Curt adjusted his flight. His reaction to the change he experienced was more violent than he intended.

"Sorry about that," Mike replied.

"That's okay, perfectly normal reaction. Almost everybody does it."

Almost everybody! Mike thought. *Right. Like everybody gets to fly on one of these.*

"Mike, keep your head up and look directly ahead." It sounded like Curt was sitting right behind him. The fact was that he was nearly one hundred miles away. The air-speed of the MC-130W Hercules at 345 knots flying east, and the 147 knots of Mike and the team moving west, had separated them rapidly.

Mike looked straight ahead. He noticed a small, orange square that appeared to be on the ground several miles ahead.

"What's that?" he asked.

"That's your target. The field you'll be landing in," Curt replied.

"Does everyone else see it?" Mike asked.

"They do now, sir." It was the first indication of military bearing. To this point he had been called Mike, suddenly he was *sir*.

"But the orange box really isn't there, is it?"

"No, sir," Curt replied. "It's very much like the lines the networks project on the football field. It's a simple projection on your facemask, sir. Does it help?"

"Absolutely," Mike replied. "Absolutely, it does."

Mike knew that Elli and his children would be near that mark. His sense of euphoria moved to one of purpose. A handful of the most precious people on earth were waiting for him to protect them and bring them to safety. Mike's mind honed like an arrow on the small orange square.

I'm coming, Elli! I'm coming!

Grey Horse Farm, New Salisbury, Kentucky – 9:41 PM EST

"Mommy, I'm getting tired." Sara rubbed her eyes and cuddled closer to Elli. The excitement of the hay wagon ride was wearing off. Sleepiness was settling in.

"I know, sweetie. Just a little longer, okay?" Elli stroked her little girl's head and pulled her closer. Elli glanced back toward the house. She could still see the flames although they were mere flickers of light coming through the trees.

"Me too, Mommy." Robbie and Jackson climbed through the hay on their hands and knees to reach the safety, warmth and comfort of Mommy's lap. Elli was buried in kids. She held them as tightly as she could in her arms.

Baby Riley slept soundly in grandma's arms. When sleep came to Riley, he rarely complained or hesitated. He was out like a light.

*   *   *   *   *

Elli's dad looked over his shoulder. He suspected the children would be exhausted. Their destination was a couple hundred feet ahead. He knew it well.

The escape up the mountain was made in total darkness. No lights. Granddad's eyes had adjusted well to darkness. Even in starlight he could distinguish the features of the mountain. He knew the road, where the ruts were difficult, where rocks jutted from the hillside. He knew which gate would give them the best protection and the softest grasses for the children to rest on.

And he saw the flames consuming his home. A lifetime of memories had literally gone up in smoke. He chuckled inwardly. *Another lifetime of repairs and fixing is also going up in smoke!* he said to himself.

Suddenly, a helicopter streaked over the treetops.

"Dad! That's Mike! Turn on the lights! Quick!" Elli cried, stirring the children.

"Wait just a bit there, girl." Granddad's wary eye followed the small chopper. The pilot didn't swing around and land in the field ahead. The helicopter didn't move slowly as if searching for a small band of fleeing grandparents and children.

The helicopter flew straight toward the burning home. It circled and landed in the pasture close to the road.

"No, honey," Granddad said. "That wasn't Mike. That was more of *them*."

*   *   *   *   *

Elli gasped as she watched the chopper land on the far side of the house. If it had been up to her, she would have screamed and yelled, flashed lights, set off rockets, flares or bonfires to get the chopper's attention. She suddenly realized how wrong her impulse was. She felt a cold shudder deep inside.

"We're almost there," Granddad said. "Don't worry. We're almost there."

North Waco Street, Wichita, KS – 8:43 PM CST

Robert and Yolanda climbed into the truck. Her mother Bea stood on the curb and spoke to her through the window.

"You do your best to sleep on the trip, all right?"

"Yes, Mama," Yolanda replied as she rolled her eyes and smiled at Robert.

"She's just lookin' out for you, you know," Robert said with a smile.

"I know." Then she spoke to her mother. "Mama, I have my pillow right here. When I get sleepy I will sleep, okay?"

"You have had a very long day, and I just don't want you to make yourself sick or something."

"Yes, Mama. I love you!" Yolanda waved as the truck pulled from the curb.

"Hey, girl. It's a mother's job," Robert teased. "Moms always need to fuss and worry about something."

"Then that woman is a great mom." She laughed and suddenly saw that it was true. Her mother was a great mom.

The drive ahead of them wasn't too long, but this time it was at night. Yolanda felt safe and protected when she was with Robert. Everything felt right to her when she was with him. She had no idea what might happen in the next day, week or month. What happened around her no longer mattered, though. What happened in her work or the circumstances she may face didn't matter. She was with Robert. That mattered. That was enough.

Grey Horse Farm, New Salisbury, Kentucky – 9:45 PM EST

Five men stepped from the small helicopter in the pasture. The blades swirled over their heads as they surveyed the blazing farmhouse. The fifteen thugs waiting for them stood aimlessly on the road leading to the farm. They drew together as the men from the chopper walked across the pasture.

"So, everyone was in the house when you blew it up?" Yusef was clearly in charge. He was short, his black hair and beard were trimmed close to the skin. But even in the dark, his eyes sparked an evil, icy stare.

"We didn't go up to the house to see. All the lights were on and it looked like they were home." He tamped out his cigarette on the sole of his boot.

"And you didn't wait for us to get here first, did you?" Yusef challenged.

"No, no. I made a judgment call. We had the element of surprise. They didn't know we were here. Your helicopter announced your coming from miles away," the man with the cigarette complained.

"What were your orders?" Yusef demanded, walking directly up to him and staring face to face. "Tell me your orders!"

"We were told to meet you here, blow up the house, and kill the family!"

"Well, you did part of it. The house has been blown up!" Yusef yelled.

"You were late. We had the advantage of surprise." the man yelled back at him.

"But you didn't wait," Yusef said spitting in the man's face. "You didn't wait. You didn't meet me here. You probably didn't kill the family, either."

Yusef stepped back, glaring at the man. Swiftly he raised his pistol and fired a single shot into his forehead. Yusef turned to the others.

"There is no room for insubordination!" he snarled at them. "No room!"

Yusef faced the burning house. It was too hot to attempt an entry, but it had to be checked out. "Come!" he ordered and began marching toward the house.

North Meadow, Grey Horse Farm – 9:48 PM EST

The crack of the pistol shot echoed through the valley. Elli jumped at the sharp report. She looked at her mother holding Riley in her arms. Elli's mom looked back at her. Elli knew the expression on her face. It said, *We'll get through this, we will!*

Elli had seen that confidence all her life. Her mom was tough and confident that nothing would come their way they weren't able to bear or handle. If escape was needed, a way would be made. If they needed to stand and fight, they would do so valiantly. Elli needed her mom's strength. It wouldn't fail her.

The tractor lurched as it pulled into the meadow. Granddad drove the tractor and hay wagon under the hedge row that bordered the field. The motor stopped.

Elli sat on the hay, holding three of her children. Mike was to meet them here soon. She knew he would come. How soon he would arrive was an open question. That bothered Elli. Confidence and fear battled within her. She knew Mike was coming, but what if—

No, she said to herself. *There are no what ifs! Mike is coming.*

Elli could still see the flames flickering through the trees. She knew an unseen enemy had destroyed her childhood home. She knew they were there. How soon would they begin looking for her and the children?

4,000 Feet Above Eastern Kentucky – 9:50 PM EST

"Hey, Mike. It's Curt." Curt was familiar and laid-back again. Mike's intuition perked up a bit. "How's the flight?"

"Smooth as silk, Curt," Mike answered.

"Two things I need to tell you," Curt began. "First, you're about sixty seconds from chute deployment. Your wing will flare, sorta stand you up, then the chute will pop. The rest is like any other jump."

"Okay. What else?" Mike prepared himself.

"About six minutes ago," Curt began, "a small helicopter landed in the pasture south of the farmhouse. We believe it's the guys from Washington that were sent to . . . well, get your family."

The thought angered Mike. The very idea that Barry Goldstein would send an army of thugs to kill his wife and children made his eyes burn.

"Yeah, Curt. I get the picture." Mike knew danger was waiting.

The orange square projected on Mike's faceplate looked about the size of a playing card. He estimated he was still three or four miles out.

Suddenly, to the left of his flight path, the burning farmhouse emerged from behind a hill. Mike felt panic grip him. *Were the terrorists already at the house? Where are Elli and the kids?*

"Hey, Curt! Need your help here."

"Sure, Mike," Curt said calmly. "What do you need?"

"I just saw Elli's folks' farmhouse. It's engulfed in flames." Mike choked back the fear and rage that was rising in this throat. "Can you give me any status on that?"

"Just a minute." Curt was clipped and short. The silence pounded in Mike's ears. Though it was only seconds he waited, to Mike felt as if it was an hour.

"Okay, Mike. The deployment directive shows more than a dozen men on the ground," Curt began. "They pinged your wife's cell phone and it shows up nearly a mile north."

"Can I call her from here?" Mike forgot about speaking with her nearly an hour ago.

"Not a problem."

Instantly, Mike heard the dial tone and the high-speed chirping, and Elli's number was dialed.

"Hello?" It was Elli.

"Hey, babe. It's me." Mike didn't know if he could talk, the relief was so great.

"Mike! Where are you?" Elli exclaimed, doing a poor job of masking her apprehension. z

"We're coming toward you from the east. Look to the east, baby."

Suddenly the wing flared. Mike was almost upright when the chute popped from the back of the wing. The flare of the wing slowed his speed, the drag chute put on the brakes. The main chute deployed about eight hundred feet above ground. They were almost down.

Elli searched the sky. The black chutes opened against the dark sky. From her perspective, they seemed to appear from nothing. All twelve chutes opened and slowly drifted toward the landing point.

"Look kids! Up in the sky. It's Daddy!" Elli's eyes filled with tears of relief.

Three small sets of sleepy eyes squinted into the dark night sky.

"Wow," Robbie said breathlessly. "That's awesome. Which one's Daddy?"

"Are you still there, Mike?" Elli asked into her phone.

"Whew! Yeah, I'm still here," he replied.

"Robbie wants to know which one are you?"

Immediately, the middle chute in the second line began weaving and rocking from one side to the other. Robbie laughed out loud.

"There he is! There he is!" he shouted, jumping to his feet.

"I heard that loud and clear!" Mike said with a chuckle. "Be there in a minute, sweetheart."

chapter 29

Colonel Herrera was convinced he was fighting a losing war. The stories he'd believed since childhood were simply untrue. The dream of chasing greedy Gringos from California and reuniting it with Mexico was based on false hopes and would never happen.

"If we do not fight," he began, "we will be captured and put in prison. And we will be there for a very long time."

"But if we fight, we might be killed!" Cero didn't mind killing but was keenly sensitive regarding his own death.

"My friend," Colonel Herrera said smiling, "you forget I am speaking of the bigger *WE,* not just the four of us."

"Cero, he means if *WE* don't fight . . ." Estefan added broadly waving his arms with a menacing smile on his face.

"Yes," replied Herrera, "we must inspire our warriors! We must tell of the great victories we saw today. We must encourage the people to continue to rise up and stand against the Gringo army!'

"And they must gather wealth for the new government." Johor stood, raising his index finger over his head.

"Yes, you are right!" Herrera appreciated the brilliance of his team. They would need gold and silver. American dollars may not help them, but jewels, gold, and silver would.

The plan designed itself. It was very simple. Enlist the efforts of tens of thousands of believers to collect gold, silver and precious stones, and bring the wealth to these four men for the new government.

The second phase would send the same tens of thousands to destroy the Gringo army. Gringos would not violate their civil rights of assembly or protest. Gringos would not call them revolutionaries or terrorists. It would not be politically correct. The Gringos would bow to their wishes and attempt to negotiate a peace.

The four men found their plan hilarious. As they peeled off layer upon layer of their farcical plan, they roared with laughter. All they needed to do was convince their loyal followers the momentum was on their side. The land was theirs. Bring all the wealth to a single place. If the Gringo army came back, the people would face them and scare the gringos away.

They felt brilliant. The faithful who really believed California could be taken back to Mexico would buy it. They would proudly lay down their lives to redeem their homeland. They would fight until the final victory.

That should give the four of them enough time to load the gold on four trucks and flee to South America and points beyond. They would be rich. They would live like kings.

All that was left to do was convince the faithful. Idiots. People who foolishly believed what they were told. People filled with fanciful visions and words of hope for the future. They were perfect for the work Colonel Herrera and his team required. They would be useful. Useful idiots.

White House, Washington DC – 9:58 PM EST

Rick and George, each holding an arm, escorted Jalal Uddin bin Kahmir al-Ahmad into the second level of the White House basement. The area is considered secure and access granted only to those with the proper clearance, or to those considered a high-value political target.

Jalal Uddin was a high-value political target. The plane scheduled to fly him home to Egypt was preparing to leave the tarmac at Reagan International Airport right on time. The men accompanying the "ambassador" on the plane were Secret Service. The contracted private jet was paid a handsome fee by the United States of America to play along with the ruse.

To anyone watching, the small convoy of black SUVs arrived at the waiting private jet only slightly behind schedule, and was about to depart on time. The "ambassador's" entourage of two dozen body guards and personal assistants protected and helped the elderly statesman onto the plane. It all looked perfectly normal.

The only differences were the plane's destination and flight time. Instead of a ten-hour flight across the Atlantic, there would be a thirty-minute flight over the Delaware peninsula. Rather than landing in Cairo, the plane would land in New Jersey.

Jalal Uddin proved to be a wiry, combative detainee. His piercing eyes revealed his contempt. His sharp tongue articulated his arrogance. But he was in custody. And he knew the government in Egypt would not stand behind him when they reviewed the evidence of his betrayal and false allegiance to his own country.

The heart of a warrior is to never surrender. Jalal Uddin was determined to remain defiant in his faithful service to his interpretation of Allah. It was an interpretation that was not embraced by most Muslims. The cult of Uddin's faith was small. And it was vicious.

"Put him in Holding Room 5. Cuff him to the chair and leave him there. We'll get to him soon enough," the security officer told Rick and George.

"Will do," Rick replied.

Holding Room 5 was the third door on the right. The door slammed against the wall as the old man resisted entering. A single chair sat in the middle of the room, bolted to the floor. Once he was seated and cuffed, he would remain there for a while.

Jalal Uddin was forced to sit. The cuffs clicked behind him, securing him to the chair.

"May you and all your dog friends rot in hell!" the old man spat at his captors.

"Sir, and addressing you as *sir* is the limit of my respect," George said, "if I have *any* friends in hell, I'd wager you'll see them a long time before I will." George walked briskly out the door.

"Have a nice day," Rick said softly as he exited and closed the door behind him.

East End of the North Meadow, Grey Horse Farm
10:02 PM EST

Mike flared his chute and literally stepped down to earth. It was the easiest landing he had ever experienced. No tumble and roll. No need to make running steps to catch himself. The weight of the wing on his back and the special chute made it a perfect landing.

The hay field provided an excellent landing spot. It was open and the dried grass was soft. Mike quickly unbuckled the chute and wing, sliding it to the ground behind him.

"Don't forget to collect your weapons from the wing and trip the beacon." It was Curt, his navigator. Mike forgot he might be listening.

"Oh, I didn't realize you were still there," Mike replied with a bit of surprise.

"Well, my job is about finished with you for today," Curt replied through the headset in the helmet. "Just a couple more things."

As Curt spoke, Mike gathered the chute and tracings, and stacked it all beside the wing.

"Okay, Curt, where's the beacon switch?"

"First, you need to open the back of the wing," Curt answered. On the left side of the inboard jet housing, on the right of the wing there is a panel. Press on it."

Mike pressed and heard a click. The panel door opened across the bottom of the wing, below the parachute pack. Inside the wing he found a small arsenal and a respectable amount of ammunition.

"First get the rifle," Curt told him. Mike lifted the AI-L115A4 from the housing. The L115A3 was the preferred sniper rifle used by British and American troops in Afghanistan. It fired a heavier ordnance promising deadly accuracy up to 1500 meters. The American version, the A4, added infrared sighting that automatically linked to the helmets Mike and the others were wearing.

Besides the rifle, Mike found four 9mm pistols with four clips for each.

"Mike, you'll find a holster built into your suit on each thigh, and on each side of the ribbing of your suit. The additional clips for your L115 fit in the long pockets on the side of each calf. The clips for the 9mm fit in the pockets on your chest and around your waist."

"Damn! Is there anything you didn't think up?" Mike asked as he stuffed the clips into their respective pockets.

"Yeah, you still have to unzip your fly to pee. But we're working on it." Curt's humor didn't fall on deaf ears. Mike chuckled as he loaded his suit. But his concern was up the hill from his current position.

"Okay, I'm all set. Where's the beacon switch?" Mike asked a second time.

"Look in the far right end of the rifle housing. You'll see a green button. It should be glowing a bit," Curt replied.

Mike saw it and pressed it firmly.

"Thanks, Mike," Curt said, "I have the beacon loud and clear."

Mike turned to run up the hill to find Elli and the kids.

"Mike, before you go," Curt interrupted, "we have two more things to do."

Mike stopped in his tracks. "What are they?" he asked.

"First, I'm turning on your infrared vision in the face mask. Then, I'll open the comm. device so you can talk to your team members."

Mike heard a soft click and a brief buzz. Suddenly, the face mask seemed transparent and the night vanished. It wasn't quite daylight, but he could see everything clearly. *Like three full moons!* he thought.

"Is everybody on?" was the first thing Mike heard other than Curt's voice. It was the voice of the sniper team leader. Eleven voices answered him in the affirmative, including Mike. Sam's distinctively feminine voice stood out in contrast to the heavy voices of the men.

"All right, regular team members, we will use our customary tags. Our visitors will be addressed by their first names. Any objections?" Silence confirmed everyone's approval.

"Our objective is at the top of the hill, almost directly to the west." The team leader raised his hand and pointed to the position he described.

Mike turned to follow his point and saw the images he knew should be Elli, the four children and Elli's parents. The infrared imaging would not distinguish facial features at one-hundred thirty-five yards. But the white, nearly glowing images were definitely three adults and four small children. One image was decidedly female, and Mike knew that had to be Elli.

"Let's roll!" the team leader said.

The twelve figures began to jog uphill toward the family. Mike felt he was bounding through the grass at a brisk pace almost effortlessly. Then he remembered the suit. When he put it on, the crew chief explained the tubes extending down the back, arms, and legs were connected to a small computer in the back-pack, equipped to assist their movement and enhance their strength.

It was an electronic exoskeleton that contracted and expanded, mimicking the muscle movement of the person wearing the suit. Mike was impressed. He felt he could run like this all day. Then he realized that was the primary purpose of the suit. It enabled a well-trained athlete soldier to perform far beyond the limits of normal human endurance.

West End of the North Meadow, Grey Horse Farm
10:07 PM EST

Elli watched the twelve ghost-like parachutes disappear into the tall grass of the North Meadow. She sat patiently, straining to hear any sound of Mike coming up the hill. Everything was quiet.

"Mommy? Where's Daddy? Isn't he coming here?" Robbie nearly whined his complaint. Elli didn't want to correct him. Whining was not acceptable speech in the Trapper household. Then again, they were in a hay field. She decided to worry about whining later.

"He's coming, Robbie. He'll be here in a minute," Elli said with a confidence that she hoped didn't betray her concern.

Elli looked back toward the farmhouse. The flames were nearly out, but flickers of orange skipped between the trees in the woods. Whoever was down there would be coming toward her family soon.

The images that sprang up the hill toward them didn't seem human. The black egg-shaped heads of the figures glistened under a moonless sky. Their strides carried them higher from the ground and the strides were longer than one might expect. They were coming very fast.

The children saw the approaching figures and climbed as quickly as possible into their mother's protective lap. Elli sensed the fear rising in her heart. It was intensified by the children gripping and clinging to her.

The lead figure charged toward the small group huddled together on the hay wagon. It stopped only a few feet away. To Elli and the children, the figure before them was unearthly and frightening. It reached up under its chin with one hand. There was an audible click and the slight sound of a pressure release. The facemask lifted.

It was Mike.

Elli didn't fight back the tears of relief. She gently rolled her children into the soft hay, leaped off the wagon, and ran to Mike.

"Dang you, Mike Trapper!" she yelled as she ran, "you scared us half to death!" Elli leaped into Mike's arms. He threw his arms around her, forgetting the amplified strength the suit gave him.

"Ouch!" Elli exclaimed. Then, she laughed. She realized her leap into Mike's arms was not much different than a headlong leap into a refrigerator. She had thrown herself on her husband, not knowing about the metal clips for the pistols, the pistols themselves, or the exoskeleton suit Mike wore.

"Honey, are you okay?"

"You feel like a man of steel!" she said smiling and pulling his face toward hers. She kissed him with every shred of passion she held in her small body. Mike gasped and steadied himself.

"Daddy!" the chorus erupted as three children bailed from the hay wagon. Riley stood at the edge of the wagon clapping his small hands together, demanding someone carry him to his daddy. Elli's mom whisked him from the wagon's edge and took him to Mike.

"Daddy!" Sara exclaimed. "How did your muscles get so hard?"

"How did you get here, Daddy?"

"Why were you running so fast, Daddy?"

"Why do you have that helmet on your head, Daddy?"

The questions were non-stop. Before Mike could answer one, three more were asked.

Two more of the figures removed their helmets. Sam and Steve walked up to the turbulent scene of the small family.

"Sam!" Elli cried and ran to her friend and embraced her.

The small group of family and friends gathered together. Introductions were made to Elli's parents. The two older children remembered Steve and Sam. Robbie and Riley were bashfully introduced to Sam, the pretty one, and Steve, the soldier.

Mike noticed the nine soldiers who jumped from the plane only a few minutes earlier, were gathered a few yards away. They were obviously in a tactical discussion. The team leader pointed toward the farmhouse.

Mike couldn't hear what was being said. They were intentionally excluding him, as well as Sam and Steve, from their discussion. None of their facemasks were raised. Mike suddenly understood Elli's fear as he approached. The nine men looked nothing like human beings. Even their weapons appeared unearthly.

Suddenly, eight of the men sprang off in eight different directions. They were gone in an instant. The team leader walked toward Mike, raising his facemask.

"Mike," he began, "I've sent the men to see what's at the farmhouse. They'll get back to me shortly with numbers and weapons count. I want you, Sam, and Steve to stay here with your family. Do not take your suits off. If for some reason they get past us or overcome us you may need to make a run for it."

"Make a run for it?" Mike said. "What do you mean?"

"Mike, we have technology and superior weaponry on our side, but we don't know what they have, or how many they are," the team leader said. "If you need to, the suit will enable each of you to carry two adults and run at full speed for a mile or two. They're built for that. If retreat is necessary to protect your family, that's what you do. And Mike, that's an order."

"Of course it is." Mike knew the objective was the safety of his family. He knew he wasn't going to be the frontline on this operation. These brave and very well-equipped soldiers were the frontline, and a formidable one to boot.

The team leader closed his face mask and bounded into the darkness. Mike looked after him and marveled at the speed of his movement.

He turned back toward his family. Jackson was wearing Sam's helmet and chattering nonstop. Sara was standing absolutely still, with Steve's helmet swallowing her down to her shoulders. Mike turned and saw her looking toward him. She waved her hand fiercely at him.

Mike smiled and waved back. He loosened the straps on his gloves. He was at least going to take those off. *I'm going to touch and hold that lovely lady over there*, he thought with determination as he walked toward Elli. That would be enough for now. But just for now. He had plans for later.

chapter 30

General Gene Westrup paced in the outer office of the containment area. In fifteen minutes, they would initiate the plan for those captured after the fight at the gates. One hundred seventeen men were isolated in one hundred seventeen cells. Their lives were about to change forever.

The door opened slowly, accompanied by the soft but deep tones of a very familiar voice. Sergeant Major John Michaels made his way into the room and closed the door. Michaels leaned heavily against the door frame and let out a long breath. He looked at his friend and shook his head from side to side.

"When you get a *hunch*, you can really mess up a day!" His weary face burst into a broad grin. John laughed and moved to the table in the center of the room.

"I'm glad I had that hunch, John," General Gene began. "Otherwise we might still be fighting those mobs all over the Camp. Good thing we could contain them."

"No question about that." John looked around the room and spied the coffee pot. "How old is that?"

"Not what you're used to, my friend. It was old when I got here."

John walked to the coffee pot and poured a cup. He sipped the steaming brew and winced.

"Holy mother of—" John caught himself. He was working on that aspect of his character.

"I know. I classified my first cup as purely medicinal." General Gene began looking for the coffee can and filters to make a fresh pot.

"John, what do you have planned for our guests this evening?" he asked as he discovered the stash of some pretty decent coffee. He examined the container and decided it was a private stash and not government-issue coffee. Gene made a mental note to have some of his personal stock delivered in replacement in the morning.

"The men are working on it right now," John replied.

"You're not up to something I'm gonna have to testify before Congress about, are you?" Gene asked.

"They haven't briefed me on their plans yet. But they're cooking up something special for these fellows." John paused and looked at Gene preparing the coffee. "And, no, we aren't going to water-board them."

"Oh, no, no, I wasn't thinking you were." Gene gently poured fresh water into the coffee maker and glanced at his Chief Security Officer. "Just didn't know if you had those bamboo shoots left over from World War II."

Both men smiled and chuckled softly, knowing it was not a funny matter. Extreme measures, as they were now called, were discontinued a few years earlier. The field manuals were written in such a way that interrogations with a raised voice could be interpreted as too coercive. If a detainee was marked, cut, or bruised in any way, the interrogators could face charges and even prison.

"No, Gene, we can't do that stuff anymore." John grinned. "But we got new stuff." His smile broadened.

"Are you going to let me in on your little secret, or just stand there smiling at me?" Gene asked with feigned irritation.

"I told you, Gene, I haven't been briefed on what they're planning."

"But you've got an idea, right?"

"Well, yes I do. I think you will enjoy watching it more than listening to me trying to explain it to you."

"Oh, all right." Gene was a little miffed, but just a little. "When's it gonna start?"

John glanced at his wrist watch.

"We've got about ten minutes, general," John answered with a grin and a sparkle in his eye. "We just need to go down the hall a ways."

"That's just enough time for a cup of good coffee, sergeant major." Gene Westrup grabbed two mugs from the shelf and filled them with the fresh steaming black brew.

Frisco Armory, Dallas, TX – 9:16 PM CST

Jim Parker stretched himself across the long stainless steel table in the armory kitchen. His rump throbbed. Doc did a good job, but the local anesthetic was beginning to wear off.

"Oh, man!" Jim complained. "What did you use to dig the shrapnel out, a fork-lift?"

"Nope," Doc replied, "just a regular fork." Doc smiled as he walked across the room to his friend. "How's your pain?"

"Which one? The one in my head or in my butt?" Jim retorted rubbing his forehead.

"I tried to tell the guys that Jack Daniels was not the preferred sedative for a wound like yours. But who am I? I'm just the doctor. What do I know? I'm most concerned about your butt, not your head."

"It feels like somebody drove about a dozen number-ten nails into my backside," Jim said with a strained voice.

"Actually, it was fourteen. But none of them were as big as nails. More like thumb-tacks." Doc gently removed the dressing to check the wounds. The stitches were neat and firm, swelling at a minimum, and the oozing and bleeding had stopped. "You're looking good from this end. So, how's the pain?"

"Irritating. Very irritating." Jim never understood the pain-number system used in medical circles. It either hurt or it didn't. Jim's butt hurt.

"Well, then," Doc replied holding a syringe up to the light, "let's make a little introduction. Jim, meet Mr. Morphine."

The prick of the needle was nothing. And just as quick, everything else was *nothing*. No pain. No ache. No remnants of Jack Daniels. Nothing. Jim felt like he was floating.

"Wow, Doc," he finally said, interrupting his sweet, soft, soaring high. "Can I get that in a six pack, to go?"

"No, we keep that stuff for special occasions. Like this one." Doc finished disposing the unnecessary utensils and papers. "You're going to need to stay off your rear-end for the night, at least. No more commando raids this week. Okay?"

"If you insist," Jim replied. His cell phone chirped in his pants pocket on the counter. "Doc? Would you hand me my pants?"

Doc retrieved the blood-soaked pants and pulled the phone from the right front pocket.

"This is Jim Parker," he said, suddenly feeling quite chipper.

"Jim, this is Bill Jenkins up in Norman," Lieutenant colonel Bill Jenkins was Jim's commanding officer and friend. Bill considered each of the young veterans serving under him more than a friend, more like a son.

"Oh, hi, Bill!" Mr. Morphine was helping Jim relax just a little too much. "I feel great! How was your trip, Bill?"

"Just fine, son. Is everything all right?"

"It's just fine, Bill. Really fine, I mean *really* fine." Jim's speech began to slur.

"Let me speak with the colonel, okay?" Doc gently took the phone as Jim became entranced with his fingers, and how much they resembled a bird's wing.

"Colonel, I'm sorry. This is Captain Smith," Doc said. "I just gave Jim a shot of morphine, and he's taking it very, very well, if you know what I mean, sir."

"Doc. I'm surprised you're there. What's up?" Bill hadn't received a report from the raid at the hotel.

Doc quickly filled him in on the success and damage caused by the raid. Three other Marines were treated for shrapnel injuries. Jim's were the most extensive. Bill chuckled as Doc gave him all the details.

"Doc, I'm glad you're there," Bill said. "Those boys need at least one adult in the room at all times. So I'm relieved you are there, and at the same time very proud of those boys."

"Yes, sir. They are a unique bunch."

"Listen," Bill continued. "Before anyone goes out on any more patrols, I need to hook you up with some fellas in Washington. They're helping us see where the enemy is congregated so we can focus on them."

Colonel Jenkins went on to describe the ALI maps system and how it could be used in the Dallas area. It would let the small group of Marines know exactly where to engage the enemy and avoid surprises and hopefully limit further injuries.

'That's excellent, colonel. I'll get the men together and we'll see what Washington can give us."

"They're waiting to hear from you, son. They know you're on the front line and will give you any help you need."

"Thanks, general," Doc said turning back toward Jim. "We'll stay in touch."

"Very good, young man. And take good care of Jim's back-side, will ya?"

"Absolutely!" Doc smiled and said goodbye to his CO.

Jim lay on his side, playing with his fingers. *Just a little too much Mr. Morphine*, Doc thought. *Gonna have to watch that.*

North Meadow, Grey Horse Farm – 10:25 PM EST

The excitement of the evening was wearing down. The children were very tired and eager to find sleep. Blankets were spread on the soft ground in a low spot fifteen feet from the tractor and wagon.

Mike and Elli spoke to their children in soft voices, gently stroking their foreheads, and lightly tickling their cheeks.

Giggles and laughter floated across the meadow. They were quickly swallowed in the sound of the breeze rustling the grass and humming through the evergreen branches. Elli's parents stood by the tractor, leaning together and taking in the view of the magic of family life.

Steve and Sam, still wearing the exoskeleton suits, sat on the side of the hay wagon. The bulk and the mechanics of the suits felt anything but soft and gentle. But Sam and Steve were together. That counted for something.

"Someday," Steve said, reaching for Sam's hand and turning to Mike and Elli.

"For the second time in history, I agree." Sam smiled as Steve turned toward her.

"You really mean that, don't you?" he said.

"Most definitely," she replied as she leaned forward to kiss him.

As they embraced they both began to laugh. Between them, the real *them*, were their slightly cumbersome flight suits, eight handguns, fifteen pounds of ammunition, sniper rifles, and two egg-shaped helmets.

"Not the most romantic conditions!" Steve commented with a laugh.

"Then, this will have to do." Sam took Steve's face in her bare hands and kissed him. For now, that would have to do. And it did.

The crack of a rifle echoed from the valley below. The sound was muted by the dense woods along the mountainside, but it caught everyone's attention. The snipers had engaged the men at the farmhouse. The response to the single shot was a thunderous blast of automatic weapons firing from the farm.

"Everybody get down!" Mike commanded, as he moved toward the wagon. Elli's parents crouched and moved quickly to the low spot with the children. Steve and Sam slid from the wagon bed and met Mike by the large tractor wheel.

"The last thing we want is someone hit by a stray bullet," Mike said peering around the tire. "What do you think, Steve?"

"We need to establish an inside perimeter with the three of us," Steve replied without blinking an eye. "Mike, you take point, right over there. Sam, you take the right flank over in the trees, I'll take the left."

"Fine," Mike said. "Helmets on, systems hot, and guns up." The three pulled on their helmets and moved to their assigned positions. If the bad guys got past the experts, they would be ready.

chapter 31

Mainside Brig, Camp Pendleton, CA – 7:27 PM PST

It was time for evening prayers, the *al'isha*. Each detainee was provided a basin and water for the *wudhu*, or ceremonial washing before prayer, as well as a prayer mat, fresh clothing and a copy of the Qur'an. A great deal had been learned at Guantanamo Bay about respecting faith, at least by the American Marines.

The detainee in cell #64 was washed, dressed and ready for *al'isha*. He could only guess the proper direction of the Ka'ba shrine in Mecca. He prayed Allah would understand and have mercy. His heart was pure. He was a soldier of Jihad. He thought intently on the prayer he prepared to offer.

"Allahu Akbar!" he said in a loud voice. *"Assalamu alaikum wa rahma-tullah!"* he said to his right. Then to his left, *"Assalamu alaikum wa rahma-tullah!"*

"Subhana kallah huma wa bee hum deeka wa ta bara kusmuka . . ." The young man continued reciting the prayer he had learned as

a youth. He was preparing. *"A'oodhu Billaahi minash-shaitaanir-rajeem."*

He took a deep breath. He was ready for Surah Fatiha. He began.

"Bismillah hir rahman nir raheem." The first verse of the First Rakah.

"Alhamdu lillahi rabbil a lameen." He spoke the second verse in a full loud voice. His recitation continued through the seven verses of the prayer praising Allah, the Most Merciful, thanking and worshipping Allah for his beneficence and pleading to be led on a straight path, not like those who earned anger or those that went astray.

"Ameen." The young man stood alone, but in his heart, he knew he was surrounded by his brothers. *I am not alone*, he thought. *We are together in prayer!* He began the second Surah.

"Alhamdu lillahi rabbil a lameen." It was almost as if he could hear his brothers. He loved evening prayers. He prayed on.

"Qul Huwal lahu—"

Suddenly, he stopped in mid-sentence. What did he hear? He continued.

"Qul Huwal lahu Ahad." As he spoke, he listened. *There is something!* He heard the words echoing in his mind.

"Allaahus-Samad. Lam yalid walam yoolad." Was it in his memory? Was there another voice praying with him?

"Wa lam yakul-lahuu kufuwan ahad." He listened intently as the familiar words rolled off his lips. What did he hear?

He paused. *"Allahu Akbar!"*

The young man raised his hands to either side of his head, palms forward. He bowed in Ruku, making his back straight and level, and placed his hands firmly on his knees.

"Subhana rab-bi yal adheem!"

"Subhana rab-bi yal adheem!"

"Subhana rab-bi yal—"

He stopped suddenly. *Yes! There it was!*

Another voice finished his sentence, *"—adheem!"* But he heard it in his *head* not his ears!

What is this? Panic and elation surged through him. *Who am I hearing?* He stood erect and raised his hands beside his head.

"Sami Allaahu liman hamidah," he prayed listening. *"Rabbanaa wa lak al-hamd."* He heard it! The voice was praying with him! But it was praying *in* him!

"Allahu Akbar!" Yes, the voice was within him. It was praying within him! With new energy in his prayer, he knelt in sajdah, a position of humility before Allah. The young man bent forward placing his hands and forehead on the mat.

"Subhana rubbiyal a'ala!" he prayed with fervor. *"Subhana rubbiyal a'ala!"*

"Subhana rubbiyal a'ala!" They were together! The voice prayed with him! He raised his head and sat back placing his hands on his knees.

"Allahu Akbar!" Together he prayed with the voice.

"Rabb ighfirlee wa irhamnee." The phrase means 'O my Lord, Forgive me and have Mercy upon me.' But there was no voice. *Perhaps I didn't hear it*, he thought. Again, he bowed in sajdah.

"Allahu Akbar!" The voice was back! He heard it clearly.

"Subhana rubbiyal a'ala!"

"Subhana rubbiyal a'ala!" The voice prayed with him!

"Subhana rubbiyal a'ala!" Yes! He exclaimed inwardly as they prayed.

"Allahu Akbar!" The young man sat back. He was shaking. He finished the first Rakah and stood.

The young warrior felt lightheaded. He staggered slightly, but quickly caught himself so he would not offend Allah. He quieted himself and began the Second Rakah.

The voice was with him. Their prayer soared beyond the walls of the prison surrounding him. Time no longer mattered. There was no effort or care. The young man worshipped with the voice.

It is Allah! the young man gasped. *It is Allah praying with me!*

He could scarcely breathe. He forced his voice to be strong. The words flowed with ease, but the young man nearly swooned. The voice was leading him through the Rakah. They were together in his mind, ecstatically reciting ancient texts and holy prayers.

Together they flew through the Surah Fatiha with great boldness. Then they recited the Surah An-Nas. It was almost magical.

He bowed in ruku, repeating the ancient verses. Then, again he knelt in sajdah declaring the perfection of the Most High.

"Allahu Akbar!" sang from his lips. The young man sat back placing his hands on his knees.

"Rabb ighfirlee wa irhamnee," he said again asking for forgiveness and mercy.

"I cannot." The voice spoke in perfect Arabic.

"W—what?" the young man stumbled backward.

"I cannot forgive you."

The young man couldn't believe what he heard. He couldn't believe the voice spoke to him.

"What?" he said again astonished.

"I cannot forgive you. You are a killer of innocents. You have shed innocent blood. You have profaned Jihad and are cursed."

The young man spun drunkenly around the room and collapsed.

Mainside Brig Observation Room, Camp Pendleton, CA
7:35 PM PST

"Fascinating demonstration, captain," said Colonel Westrup. Gene and John watched the young man saying his prayers while they listened to the second lieutenant in the booth next to them speak with the prisoner in perfect Arabic.

"Thank you, sir," the captain replied. "The acoustic phased array is a very versatile tool. We have the ability to address a large number of people, as we did this afternoon at the Main Gate, as well as a single individual. The array can be focused on a single person in a large crowd, or a person in a cell."

The captain paused and looked at the young man slumped on the floor of the cell. He turned back to the colonel and master sergeant.

"It puts the sound inside a person's head. Not in their hearing. To the person, it's as if their mind has another person inside talking to them."

The men turned back to the cell as the medics entered, sedated the young man, and moved him to his bed.

"He'll rest very well tonight," the captain added. "When he wakes in the morning he's going to want to talk to someone. We'll be ready for him."

I-35 South of Wichita, KS – 9:42 PM CST

Yolanda and Robert drove through the night in silence. Yolanda's experience from the morning found a point of resolution. She was not the cause, nor was she a victim. She had escaped the madness. The fact that she survived convinced her of God's protection. The fact that she met Robert revealed it as part of His plan.

Robert discovered fullness in his heart that was new. He never realized the emptiness existed, but he could tell the difference since meeting Yolanda. It felt right. Every aspect of life felt on course. He was happy.

"What are you thinking about?" Robert asked, risking interrupting her thoughts.

Yolanda looked at him and smiled. "I was thinking how wonderful it feels to be happy."

Robert's heart leaped in his chest. His mind raced with thoughts of being with Yolanda for the rest of his life. He marveled at how easy it was to talk to her. Would they marry? What would their children look like? What would it be like to sleep—

Wait! Don't go there! he commanded himself.

"Yeah, me too," Robert said glancing at her. Even in the reflection from the headlights, she was beautiful. He noted how the light danced in her eyes. Her entire face glowed with tenderness. He suddenly ached to hold her.

Eyes on the road, bucko! Robert said to himself, turning his attention back to the interstate. Robert felt a new tension. He was with her, but she was on the other side of the truck.

Yolanda reached across and touched his arm. Her warm hand on his forearm felt amazing. Tension melted from his muscles. Goose bumps ran up his neck. He knew he was blushing.

How did she do that? he thought experiencing a new sense of wonder.

Ahead, Robert saw the flashing emergency lights of a parked vehicle. He began to slow. As they approached, he saw a man standing in the lane, waving his arms over his head.

"I wonder if they need help," Robert said out loud. "Do you mind if we stop and check?"

"No," she replied. "If they need help, we should give it to them."

Robert eased off the accelerator and the truck slowed. The flashing lights were on an older truck. The hood was up. The man standing on the road increased the fervor of his waving as Robert pulled alongside and stopped.

"I'll be right back," he said to Yolanda. "Lock your door."

She immediately pushed the lock button on the armrest and heard the click. Robert did the same as he climbed from the truck. If anything was going to happen, it was going to remain outside.

As Robert rounded the front of his vehicle, three men appeared from behind the old truck. Two of them carried wooden clubs, the third carried a shotgun. The man who stood in the road waving at them reached in front of the truck and picked up an axe.

"So, it would be my guess you aren't having car trouble," Robert said as the four men approached.

"You are very good at guessing, gringo." The man with the axe casually walked toward Robert. "What are you doing on our road tonight?"

"We're just driving to Norman to see my dad," Robert replied with a friendly smile.

"Did you ask me if you could drive to Norman?" the man with the axe asked.

"Didn't know you were the man in charge," Robert answered, still smiling.

"Well, now you know," said the man with the axe. "And there is a price you must pay!"

Suddenly he raised the axe and swung it at Robert's head. Robert rushed forward, catching the axe handle in his left hand, and smashing his fist into the man's stomach. The man groaned and released the axe.

Robert spun with the axe and buried the cutting end in the chest of a man with a club. The second man carrying a club swung at Robert and missed. Robert recoiled and crushed the man's shoulder with the blunt end of the axe.

Bang! The explosion caused Robert to spin toward the truck.

The fourth man, the one with the shotgun, staggered, slumped and dropped to the ground. A puff of smoke lingered beside the truck's passenger side window.

The small pistol glistened in the dark night. The hand holding it trembled. Yolanda began to sob.

Robert rushed to her, gently removed the pistol from her grasp, and reached through the window for her. Yolanda grabbed his arm in desperation.

"Robert! Robert!" she cried. "He was going to shoot you! I am so sorry. Is he dead? What have I done, Robert?"

"Hey, shh! You're fine. I'm fine. You're okay!"

With tears streaming down her face, Yolanda looked at Robert. She shuddered and tried to compose herself.

"Robert, get back in the truck this instant!"

"Okay, baby. Okay." Robert withdrew his arm from the truck. As he walked in front of his vehicle, he checked the men on the ground. The one with the shotgun was finished. One was out cold, and another wasn't long for this world. His chest bled profusely. The first man, who attacked Robert with the axe, groaned on the ground.

Robert stopped over him. *Should I kick him once for good measure?*

"Robert, get in the truck!"

The adrenalin was raging through his veins. Her voice cleared his mind for an instant, and he knew she was right. They needed to leave.

Robert climbed into the cab and started the engine. He looked at Yolanda. She was gathering her composure. She looked back at him with tear stained cheeks.

"No more stopping to help people," she said flatly. "No more."

"Fine," Robert said. *No more Mr. Nice Guy for me.* The engine roared to life. They sped off into the night.

Robert and Yolanda rode quietly. The encounter had lasted only seconds, and left them both shaken. Robert heard a muffled sob and sniffle from the other side of the cab.

"So, where did you learn to fight like that?" Yolanda asked after a long stretch of silence.

"I was in the Navy. The SEALs." Robert wasn't sure what to expect. Would she understand? Would she be frightened of him?

"A Navy SEAL?" she asked.

"Kind of a soldier that swims a lot." Robert glanced at her and smiled slightly.

"You mean, like Rambo?" her voice carried wonder and curiosity.

"Sorta, just no swamps," he chuckled.

"Oh," Yolanda's reply was drawn out.

"And what about the pistol?" Robert asked. "Where did that come from?"

"Mama," Yolanda said and smiled. "She gave it to me before we left . . . for good luck."

"Does your mama always carry a pistol?" he asked.

"Always."

She unbuckled her seatbelt and slid to the middle of the seat. She clicked the center belt around her waist and wrapped her arms around his. She touched her face to his arm and pulled close to him.

"It's going to be all right, isn't it?" she asked softly.

"Yes, baby. It's gonna be just fine." He kissed the top of her head.

It was already just fine.

chapter 32

North Meadow, Grey Horse Farm – 10:52 PM EST

The initial burst of gunfire from the farm lasted only a few seconds. It seemed forever to Elli, huddled with her children. She looked over the embankment and could see Mike a few yards away. She told herself she could see him. There was a large, dark object that moved very little, sitting where she last saw him.

After the firing stopped, Elli's parents ran from the tractor to the small depression where Elli and the children hid. Granddad actually made the two boys giggle with some silly joke. Sara clung to Grandma with an iron grip, staring off into the darkness. Riley slept in Elli's arms as if nothing unusual was happening.

Elli heard more laughter from the boys. "What are you boys doing over there?" she whispered loud enough for them to hear.

The response was more muffled giggles. "Jackson! Robbie! Dad! What are you doing? All *three* of you are acting like little boys."

Suddenly three heads popped up looking directly at Elli. Their cheeks bulged like chipmunks, mouths stuffed with marshmallows that were denied a long roast over a campfire.

Jackson threw his head back and laughed out loud. Bits of marshmallow rolled down his chin onto his shirt. Granddad snickered almost choking on his mouthful.

"Grandma, can I have a marshmallow?" Sara asked, sitting up.

The rifle shot cracked the night and shattered the moment. Everyone clung to the ground. They hadn't been seen, but only faintly heard.

Immediately, two sounds came from opposite sides of the hill. They didn't pop like a rifle being fired. The sound was slightly muffled, more of a *tuft* than a *bang*.

Elli could hear shouting from far away. The words weren't English. But it was definitely shouting.

Suddenly, Mike leaped out of the darkness. "Okay, how's everybody doing here?" he asked, sliding into the depression.

"I think Dad and the boys are making pigs of themselves with the marshmallows," Elli said with a slight edge in her voice.

"Jealous, are we?" Mike replied smiling.

Elli snorted in disgust. This was no time to be wolfing down marshmallows. People were at the farm, and they had guns.

"Listen, honey," Mike said sliding close to Elli. "A truck just arrived at the house. Our snipers watched another twenty men unload. We think they're getting ready to come up the mountain. They've discovered that nobody was in the house when it blew."

Elli was very practical. She knew how the odds could play out. More bad guys than good guys meant the plan was about to change. She was ready.

"So, what's next?"

"We're going to move toward the extraction point on the Miller farm, over the mountain," Mike answered. "But we're going to need to move quickly."

Just then, Sam and Steve slid into opposite sides of the depression. It was obvious to Elli they were aware what was happening. *Probably those magic helmets,* she thought.

Suddenly, a burst of gunfire exploded from the farm, sending bullets flying high over their heads. Elli heard several of the softer *tuft* sounds she assumed to be the snipers returning fire. Not a shot was wasted. Each report of the sniper's fire was echoed by a distant groan or yelp.

"Okay," Mike said drawing everyone together. "Our guys are going to come back up the hill very slowly. They can hold the enemy off while we make some headway. Here's how it's gonna work:

"Elli, you're on my back, holding Riley. Sara, I'll strap you on in front. Dad, you'll ride on Steve's back, and we can strap Jackson in front. Mom, you're going with Sam, and Robbie will be in front. Got it?"

Everyone heard it, but no one *got* it.

"We have to get out of here now and fast," Mike replied to the blank stares from his family. "We're doing it piggy back. Any questions?"

Mike, Steve, and Sam stood and began unhooking straps, buckles, and slings from the front, back and sides of their exoskeleton suits. Each strapped a small child in the front sling, then knelt so an adult was able to climb into the sling on their backs.

The suits were built to remove wounded soldiers from a battle zone. The exoskeleton suits allowed him to carry two full-grown soldiers at a jog. Balance was maintained by the same gyroscopes used to stabilize the flight earlier.

When everyone was in place, three larger-than-life shadows rose from the earth. Mike, Sam, and Steve could see clearly through the facemasks. Mike motioned for them to follow him up the logging trail toward the Miller farm.

Grey Horse Farm, New Salisbury, Kentucky – 10:55 PM EST

The arrival of a second truck filled with armed men gave the advantage to the insurgents. As the flames died in the farmhouse, they discovered the inhabitants had escaped.

Yusef, the man in charge, was displeased. He and the four who had arrived in the chopper with him were kept behind the barn by the sniper fire. The "warriors," who had been sent to murder everyone at the farm huddled behind the large truck that had brought them. They were pinned down but they could still devise a plan of attack.

"We cannot just sit here all night until the soldiers in the woods grow tired of shooting us," Yusef complained. He had killed one man when he arrived, and now the bodies of seven additional insurgents lay dead and dying shot by the American snipers in the woods.

"But neither can we rush across the open area. It's suicide!"

"And look at you cowering behind a milk barn like a woman." Yusef felt like shooting his companion for stating the obvious. He was angry and frustrated with himself. Making a rash decision would only make him look foolish.

"All right! We must move into the woods and around the field, rather than through it," Yusef said. He could see the plan in his mind. "We will leave eight men at the truck. You two will take five men into the woods on the far side of the truck. The rest will come with me."

Yusef yelled across the distance between the barn and the large truck. On his orders, eight men began firing automatic weapons into the woods. One insurgent climbed into the truck, started the engine, and, staying low and out of sight, he backed the truck far enough to allow five men to slip into the woods.

He ground the gears getting into first, and shielding the other men, slowly drove the truck across to the barn. Another group dove behind the barn while two leaders moved behind the truck for the return trip to the woods. The random firing continued as the truck backed from the barn.

A sudden thump in the cab of the truck, and the lurch that killed the engine was the clear indication the driver was dead. They were five feet from the woods. The two from beside the barn raced from behind the truck and dove into the bushes. Another thump was heard. Only one man crawled from the bushes into the safety of the woods.

*   *   *   *   *

The sniper team leader was the center of the measured retreat. Three three-man teams were spread across the side of the mountain, between the farm and Mike's family. Two men on each team held their scopes on the enemy combatants, while the third relocated ten yards farther up the slope. As they rotated their positions, the teams made their way toward the old tractor and hay wagon.

"Team leader, this is shooter-left two, over!"

"Bring it, shooter-left two, over," came the reply.

"Sir, we've got seven ECs in the woods moving toward our left flank, over."

"Roger that, shooter-left two. Can you mark them? Over."

"Negative, sir. They're moving fast and low in the brush. Over."

"Shooters-left one, two and three, engage automatic fire to their lead. Strafe to the rear. Do you copy? Over." Simultaneous targeting was dedicated by the shooter's number. One aimed head-high, shooter two chest-high and the third, knee-high.

Three voices affirmed the order. A sniper's greatest advantage was in remaining undetected. Bursts of automatic machine gun fire create a significant amount of muzzle blast, easily seen at night. Even with the reduced muzzle flash of the L115A4, their positions would be known quickly.

"Engage," the team leader commanded.

The noise was that of a sand-blaster on a stone building. The bushes concealing the enemy combatants were shredded. So were the combatants. But the two-second blast from the left flank snipers was enough to expose them.

A single rifle shot from behind the barn followed almost immediately.

"Team leader, this is shooter-left three. I'm hit. Over."

"Shooter-left two, evacuate. Shooter-left one, lay covering fire. Shooter-core two and three, lay covering fire. Engage."

The team leader peered through the darkness. The infrared enhanced vision helped him locate his men. He watched as the wounded sniper climbed onto the back of shooter-left two. The exercise was well rehearsed and executed flawlessly.

"Team leader, this is shooter-right one. We've got another bunch of ECs on our right flank. Over."

"Copy, shooter-right one. On my mark, shooter-right one target ECs behind the truck. Shooters-right two and three select targets on the right flank. Shooter-core one, two and three engage, ECs at the truck. Shooter-left one, engage the truck. Continue rotation and withdrawal. Engage!"

* * * * *

Yusef ran through the dark woods. His heart pounded in his chest more rapidly than his feet pounded the forest floor. He knew they could be seen by the evil magic of the Americans. His bravery and courage were his greatest weapons. He was determined he would not fail.

He heard the familiar *tuft* sound made by the American guns, and felt the bullet pass inches from his head. Yusef dove to the ground. The men behind him fell flat in the weeds and brush.

Yusef madly crawled on his belly to the base of a large tree. Behind the tree he felt safe. He was out of sight. He stood and motioned to his men to lie still.

The gunfire from behind the truck was no longer coming from the eight men Yusef left to provide cover. He listened. Only five remained. He could tell by the sound each rifle made. Each gun made a different sound when fired. There were only five rifles.

Yusef motioned his men forward. The first one arrived at the large tree and stood beside him. "You must run to the next tree. That one!" Yusef commanded, indicating a large oak ten yards away.

The soldier looked at him. His gaze was uncertain and fearful.

"We will give you cover!" Yusef assured him. He ordered the others in the brush to open fire on the hillside. "Now, go!"

The soldier raced from the cover of the tree. He took four strides. *Tuft!* The impact threw the man sideways into the bushes. He didn't get up.

Yusef called his men to the tree that sheltered him. They stood and continued firing while they ran to the tree.

Tuft! Tuft! Two men were slammed to the ground.

Three men joined Yusef in the shelter of the large tree. Each face reflected terror. Their eyes were wide and their faces covered in sweat. It was the body heat that made each man glow in the infrared sights of the American snipers.

The four men sat together, breathing hard, and not knowing what to do next.

"Sir," one of the men cautiously offered an idea. "Sir, if we cover our faces with mud, they won't see us in the cool grass."

"Excellent idea," Yusef replied. "Yes, pull up the grass and spread the soil in the roots on your faces!"

The men dug in the soft soil with their hands, uprooting clumps of grass. The dirt was moist and cold on their faces and necks. They shuddered under the chill the mud brought to them.

Slowly, Yusef began crawling on his belly from behind the tree, through the tall grass and brush. He was followed by the other three men, now covered with mud and clinging to the earth.

*   *   *   *   *

"Shooter-right two, right flank sit rep. Send it! Over," the team leader asked.

"Team leader, this is shooter-right two. Four ECs are down, but the grass is too tall to confirm the kills. We believe three more are pinned down behind a large tree. Over."

"Roger, shooter-left one. Give me a sit rep on the left flank. Over." The team leader, known as shooter-core one, was focused on the truck.

"Team leader, this is shooter-left one. There's no movement on our left flank, sir. Over."

"Affirmative, shooter-left one. Shooter-left two, give me your grid."

"Team leader, this is shooter-left two. We're a hundred yards to your rear. I'm applying first aid. Everything's clear. Over."

"Copy, shooter-left two," the team leader replied. "Everybody remain on target, and let's keep movin' up the hill. Team leader out."

The well-practiced withdrawal continued in rotation, while sights were trained on the truck and the bushes on the right flank. Sporadic fire came at them from the truck at the farm. Each was answered by the familiar *tuft* from an American sniper's rifle, followed by a groan or cry of an enemy in defeat.

chapter 33

Holding Room 5, White House Basement – 11:00 PM EST

Julal Uddin sat stiff and defiant in the straight-back metal chair. He was alone. The room was stark, the walls were painted grey, and the one-way mirror on the wall he faced convinced him he was being watched.

In addition to the chair he sat on, there was a small table and another chair with padding. He stared directly ahead. There was nothing to distract him. Julal Uddin was confident he could maintain his focus and defeat the imbecile who would attempt to interrogate him. He knew the routine. He could win their little game.

The door opened swiftly and a young man entered carrying a clipboard. He sat in the padded chair, leaned on his elbows on the table, and looked directly into the face of Jalal Uddin.

"Sir, my name is Rick Johnston. I am an agent with the United States Secret Service." Rick sat upright, his shoulders squared, and his eyes firmly fixed on his subject. "You are Jalal Uddin bin Kahmir al-Ahmad, correct?"

Jalal Uddin sat stone-faced in the metal chair, staring at his reflection in the mirror. He did not answer.

"Sir, it is my duty to inform you that our ambassador in Cairo is speaking with President Nazif, Prime Minister Suwayf, the leaders of the Shura Council, as well as the Maglis El-Sha'ab," Rick leaned toward him and lowered his voice. "Our agents and ambassador are presenting the evidence we have gathered in the last few days regarding your involvement in the assassination of President Harriet Marshall. You should know you no longer enjoy the privilege of diplomatic immunity." Rick paused.

"So, again, are you Jalal Uddin bin Kahmir al-Ahmad?" Rick sat silently awaiting the reply. Jalal Uddin stared directly ahead.

"Have you served as ambassador to the United States for three years for your nation, Mr. Uddin?" Again Rick paused. There was no response.

"Okay, Rick, let's take him through the first list of evidence." Alex Hodson's voice was quiet in Rick's earpiece. Rick flipped to the second page on his clipboard.

"Mr. Uddin, are you familiar with the Kafir documents and the immigration program they outlined?" Rick asked calmly. Jalal Uddin stared straight ahead.

"We'll take that as a *yes*," Alex said through the earpiece. The lack of any reaction helped establish a baseline for truth. Even the slightest response was noted.

As he suspected, Jalal Uddin was being watched very closely. Scanners, focused on the eyes, measured contractions of the pupil. High-definition cameras detailed the corners of his mouth and eyes, as well as the nape of the neck. Infrared sensors detected perspiration on the hands, forehead, and upper lip, indicating stress.

Jalal Uddin sat on a metal chair bolted to the floor. But it was also connected to some very sensitive equipment. Sensors in the chair measured his heart rate, minute muscle reflexes, and body temperature. The equipment was designed to analyze and chronicle responses interpreted as *kinesic behavior*. Kinesic behavior consists largely of the unspoken *words*, or involuntary physiological and emotional responses made by the one being interrogated.

Rick continued with the questions on the page before him. All were well-known facts, and none elicited a visible response. Not until the second to the last question on that page was asked.

"Your granddaughter is a senior at Cornell. Correct?" Rick asked leaning back in his chair.

"Wow," Alex spoke in the earpiece. "That hit a nerve!" His granddaughter was a senior in college, but not at Cornell. She attended Rutgers. The emotional trigger and the intentional error were the combined factors initiating the response.

Rick saw it also. The "tell" was no more than a twitch in Jalal Uddin's eyelid. One emotion, one single reaction gave them the base upon which they could build. The interrogation of Jalal Uddin continued with questions designed to evoke such reactions. Over the next two hours the interrogators would learn exactly what they needed to know, even if the subject never spoke a word.

I-35 Near Kansas/Oklahoma Stateline – 10:12 PM CST

Robert and Yolanda drove through the surrounding darkness, again in silence. The tension brought by the roadside encounter with the four men was evident. It had been a close call. They were both aware it could have ended differently.

Yolanda's head rested heavily on Robert's shoulder. He wondered if she was asleep. Her grip on his arm was firm, though. He didn't believe she was sleeping.

His thoughts drifted from his dad with the band of civilians preparing to engage in real warfare, to his hopes for a life with Yolanda. But to be perfectly honest, he didn't want to arrive anywhere. Spending the rest of his life in this truck with this woman seemed a good option for the moment.

Yolanda was not asleep. He was pretty sure she wasn't. From his experience in battle he knew how evasive sleep could be. He remembered the night after his first kill in battle. It had been hand-to-hand combat and Robert did not sleep for the following two days.

The threat posed by the four men on the side of the Interstate was over and done. She had shot and maybe even killed a man. It was finished, but Yolanda was probably not sleeping.

"Are you asleep?" Robert asked softly, not wanting to wake her.

"No," Yolanda replied without opening her eyes. "Well, maybe. I'm not sure."

They both smiled.

"Are you hungry or need something to drink?" Robert inquired.

"No!" Yolanda sat up suddenly. "We are not going to stop! Do not stop anywhere tonight!" She blushed at the urgency of her demand. "I'm sorry, Robert. I didn't mean to snap at you."

"No, that's fine," he replied. He was surprised at her reaction, but understood why she had snapped. "There's a very nice station up here a bit, and I need to visit the Men's room. I just wondered if you might need something."

"Oh, I guess it will be all right," Yolanda said. "We must be careful. Will you please be very careful, Robert?"

"Of course," he answered. "We'll drive around the store before we stop. If we see anything we don't like, we'll keep going, all right?"

Yolanda agreed and Robert steered the truck to the off ramp and turned into the parking lot at the station. The lights were bright on the store and surrounding area. A single highway patrolman holding a shotgun stood beside the front entrance.

Robert slowly pulled into a parking stall to the right of the entrance. He looked at the patrolman, and after turning off the truck he raised both hands. The officer was clearly nervous. He looked at Robert and Yolanda and nodded.

Robert cautiously exited the truck and smiled. "Rough night?" he asked.

"If that was all. It's been the whole damn day!" the young officer replied. "Where are you coming from?"

"Wichita," Robert said. "We're headed to Norman to meet my dad."

"Norman? Isn't that where they had that big fight this afternoon?"

"I believe it was. My dad was right in the middle of it." Robert walked toward him casually.

"No kiddin'. Lot of bad stuff goin' down today, did you know that?" The patrolman's eyes were red, probably from stress. His gaze shifted from Robert to the inside of the store, and then back to the interstate. His hands trembled gripping the shotgun. It seemed odd to Robert that one officer, normally in a cruiser was guarding a gas station in the middle of the night.

"Saw it with my own eyes just this morning," Robert answered. "A few of us went dove hunting north of Norman. We got back to the sheriff's office just after a gang of hoods killed several of our friends."

"You know Sheriff Hitchens?" the patrolman asked.

"Yeah, he's my dad. How do you know him?" Robert stepped onto the curb of the walkway in front of the store.

"Met him once on a prisoner exchange." As Robert approached he noticed the terror in the eyes of the young man. "Damn bastards killed everybody! They didn't give 'em a chance! The ladies, even two kids that were there selling candy or something. Everybody."

The officer broke down and collapsed against the glass store front. Robert stepped toward him and took the shotgun from his shaking hands. He eased the trembling man to the ground.

Yolanda climbed from the truck and rushed to Robert's side. The young officer sobbed heavily, deep in shock.

The three had shared the experience. All three survived the same event with decidedly different stories. Yolanda had hidden under a desk as the hellish slaughter raged. Robert had fought the enemy face-to-face. And the young unarmed officer returned to the building, carrying fresh donuts, and barely escaped the fate shared by his friends and fellow officers.

The man who had been behind the counter in the convenience store ran out the door when the officer collapsed.

"I called him," he said. "He came to help me out."

"I'm sure he did. My name is Robert Hitchens," he said as he held out his hand.

"Walter Shanks. Glad to meet you." Walter was in his late fifties and had owned the convenience store for years. "He's my nephew, Bobby Shanks, my brother's oldest boy."

"Pleased to meet you, Bobby," Robert said as he knelt. "You're not alone. Both Yolanda and I shared the same thing this morning."

Robert and Yolanda briefly related their stories to Walter and Bobby. It seemed to help. The terror of the day had been shared by many.

"I called Bobby after four men came by here a couple of hours ago," Walter added. "They come in here, filled up on gas and then didn't want to pay. They walked right into my store and took food off the shelves. Two of them was carryin' clubs and one had an axe."

Yolanda looked quickly at Robert. He saw her glance and nodded at her. His look was intended to tell her everything was fine.

"I thought they was gonna kill me." Walter buried his face in his hands and sobbed. "They just took the fifty-dollars I had in the register and headed north. I felt lucky when they left."

"I think we met them," Robert said looking back at Yolanda.

"And they weren't so lucky," Yolanda added. "This big, strong man I'm with beat-up three of them, and I shot the other one." She was embarrassed. "What must I sound like to you, bragging about shooting a man?

"Well," Walter said with a crooked grin and wiping his eyes. "You're quite the pair!"

Bobby pulled himself together. Their brief stories reminded him he was with comrades, no longer alone. They stood and entered the store.

"Is there anything you need?" Walter asked. "Can I get you something?"

"No, thank you. We're good," Robert replied. "I just need to use your john."

"You're welcome to it, son," Walter said, opening the door.

Grey Horse Farm North Logging Road – 11:15 PM EST

The three larger-than-life forms ran up the logging trail with remarkable grace and speed. Mike was breathing hard inside his helmet. He marveled that the facemask didn't fog over. Whoever designed the outfit had thought of everything, except one.

During the run, the three wearing the exoskeleton suits were able to communicate with each other, but not with their passengers.

"Mike," Sam asked over the intercom, "how much farther is the extraction point?"

"Just a couple hundred yards," he replied. "The trail ends at the gate to the Miller farm. We can't miss it."

Suddenly, Mike felt a soft pounding on his shoulder. He stopped and motioned for Steve and Sam to halt as well.

"Mike, I think Elli wants to talk to you," Steve said.

Mike reached up, released his helmet and took it off. That was when he heard her.

"Mike! Will you stop! Can't you hear me!" she screamed. "The strap I'm sitting on is broken! I'm about to drop Riley! What's the matter with you?"

Elli was frantic. Her screams for help were blocked by the helmet Mike wore. As she held on for dear life with one hand, she had pounded on his back with the other trying, to get his attention.

Sam and Steve removed their helmets and came to help. Mike couldn't see his back or the strap that had broken. He would need them both. Steve lifted Elli slightly to relieve the strain on the broken strap, while Sam worked to repair it.

"Honey, couldn't you hear me yelling at you?" Elli said through her tears. "I was falling! I couldn't hold Riley. And you wouldn't stop! Couldn't you hear me?"

"No, Elli, I'm sorry, but I couldn't hear you," Mike answered over his shoulder to her. "I'm sorry!"

"I think that will hold for the rest of the way," Sam said, pulling firmly on the strap she'd tied. "It just tore away from the suit. I tied it to the magazine strap. It should hold." Sam's confidence calmed Elli.

"Thanks, Sam," Elli said. "How much farther do we have to go like this? I mean, we're making great time, but being carried like a sack of grain is humiliating and uncomfortable."

The exoskeleton suits were rough on the outside. Their design didn't account for carrying mothers and children.

"Babe, we're almost there," Mike said over his shoulder to her. "Maybe another hundred yards or so. It's not far."

"Okay. Just get us there." Elli was resigned to being carried like a sack of grain. Making the trip of even a hundred yards with small children on foot would take three times as long.

"We'll take it slower," Mike offered as he slipped his helmet back on his head.

The three figures moved at a brisk pace through the darkness and up the logging trail. As they walked, a small voice echoed through the woods saying, "Hey, Mommy! Isn't this fun?"

Grey Horse Farm Woods – 11:19 PM EST

Yusef crawled into the creek bed. The water was ice cold. It washed into his clothing, down his pant legs, and into his boots. He was alone. Somehow, perhaps by the grace of Allah, he had evaded the sights of the American snipers. But he was the only one.

Slowly, he lifted himself from the water.

What was that? A woman screaming! She is yelling at someone! He followed the voice. As a boy, Yusef learned to run up the craggy mountainsides in Afghanistan, teasing the Russian soldiers. They could run all day. The training and conditioning benefited him even after many years. Yusef moved with great speed through the underbrush and up the side of the hill. He paused to listen.

It is a child's voice! He was headed in the right direction.

chapter 34

Frisco Armory, Dallas, TX – 10:20 PM CST

An hour had passed since Doc had gathered the men and made contact with Alex Hodson in Washington. Jim Parker had come down from a very respectable morphine high and, seemed almost normal, a little embarrassed, but normal.

Doc, Captain Jerry Smith, assumed command of the unit while providing care for his primary patient Jim and his perforated posterior. In spite of the discomfort of the wounded, and the serious nature of their efforts, the men were in very high spirits.

Vigilance was the task at hand. Sentries were posted, watching for a second attempt to attack the armory. The Marines knew they had inflicted serious damage on the invaders, and a counter attack from the bad guys was expected. It simply hadn't happened yet.

Doc's cell phone buzzed on the countertop. "Captain Smith," he answered.

"Captain, this is Alex Hodson in DC. How are your men holding up?"

"Mr. Hodson, these are a tough bunch of good fighters. Now that they're defending their own neighborhoods they are something to behold."

"I'm not surprised. Captain, we were finally able to access the ALI mapping device and make the information available to units across the Midwest. Like you, they've been planning attacks on strongholds in every state east of the Rockies. I think this will help you in Dallas."

"Mr. Hodson, we appreciate all the help we can get."

"Sorry it took so long to get back to you. It's been a hectic day."

"Not a problem, sir," Doc replied, "I understand completely."

"Do you have an internet connection at your location, captain?" Alex asked.

"No sir, it hasn't come back yet."

"Do you have cable or dish?"

"It's hooked up through a dish on the roof. Why?" Doc asked.

"That's good!" Alex responded. "I'm going to have you re-aim that dish to a state department satellite. Then we can send you the data directly. Do you have someone who knows how to do that?"

"Yes sir. I'm looking at a jar-head right this moment that does it for a living." Doc smiled at Bob Meeks. Corporal Meeks had caught three small pieces of shrapnel in his right shoulder at the hotel raid. "I think he's up to the task"

Alex relayed the new coordinates to Doc. They would provide ALI map updates for the Dallas area every fifteen minutes. The men in the armory could rest. Only one man was required to watch the updates as they downloaded from the satellite. He would be the one to see the groupings of orange dots, and if they were coming toward the armory.

Holding Room 5, White House Basement – 11:30 PM EST

Rick's line of questioning pursued the truth by inserting known facts and events, confirmed associations, and assumed intentions. The team of observers behind the glass monitored every inflection and response made by Jalal Uddin. When they saw opportunity, a question was re-phrased or restated to probe deeper.

Advances in functional Magnetic-Resonance Imaging (fMRI) in recent years opened new avenues in criminal interrogation. Initially, teams of students and scientists learned the brain reacted dramatically different when confronted with a truth versus a lie. Blood flow and cranial temperatures varied in specific patterns between falsehoods and truth. Designated as separate patterns, they were able to determine when a suspect was being evasive.

All that was required for measurement was for the suspect to remain still. In the majority of cases, an enemy combatant under examination was trained to focus on a single spot in the room and remain expressionless. They would sit perfectly still.

The examiners were able to scan, from as many as seven vantage points, an area of approximately one cubic-foot. The obvious cubic-foot selected was the area that contained the suspect's head. In as few as twenty-five questions, the responses of any suspect could be quantified.

As Jalal Uddin sat rigidly in the chair, every thought and response was monitored. Every time a question relayed a true fact, the scan pattern was noted. The same notation was made with every falsehood. As they moved past the first thirty minutes of questioning, the tactics would change subtly.

Donald Stewart, retired Director of Secret Service, was among the team of interrogation experts and psychologists. The records Don had stored in his basement proved invaluable in reconstructing the events surrounding the Kahmir Arrangement and the immigration program established in the early 1970s.

Don's time in Washington had come to an end. In the morning, he would fly to Chicago for the funeral of his life-long friend, Ansel 'Bud' Wainright. Bud had been murdered while sitting at his desk, working to unravel the mystery behind the assassination of President Harriet Marshall. After the funeral, Don would disappear forever to a new life he'd planned for years.

LAPD, Los Angeles, CA – 8:40 PM PST

The looting of Los Angeles had continued through the afternoon and evening. Yesterday's civil order had been exterminated by marauding bands of angry blacks and Mexicans. They were taking the land and everything else they could get their hands on.

The gangs of Los Angeles banded together under the insurgent leadership. Local thugs became the enforcers of the invaders' wishes and held absolute power in their own turf. They immediately responded with violence to any question or act of resistance. Even hesitation was considered insubordination.

Colonel Alvaro Herrera stood on the steps of the former police station with his arms folded across his chest. Dozens of cars and trucks packed the parking lot. More than one hundred men and women unloaded the wealth gathered for the new emerging nation. Everyone knew it took money to run a government.

The wealth of Los Angeles, including cash, jewels, gold and silver, had been harvested. They all expected their lives would be rich and bountiful once the redistribution was made. All had taken part. All would be rewarded. It was a new world.

Colonel Herrera raised his hands and spoke. "My fellow liberators! Listen to me!" he shouted over the excited mob. "Listen to me!"

The crowd hushed and turned to hear their new dynamic leader. The colonel stood tall and strong before the crowd.

"What began this morning as the liberation of an oppressed people has brought retribution to the guilty and freedom to millions of African and Latino brothers and sisters!"

The mob burst into a thunderous roar, applauding and cheering. Their faces glistened with perspiration, but each one glowed with a new found hope and excitement. The change they longed for was finally in view.

"You have fought and labored today for the new People's Republic of California! Your victory is assured! Your time has come to possess this rich and bountiful land! You have earned it!"

Cheers again erupted from the throng. The colonel let them celebrate. He was pleased to let the illusion continue a while longer.

"Thank you, thank you for your devotion and hard work! My chief officers are here with me. These brave men have sacrificed their homes and families to bring you this great liberation!"

The celebration roared to life once more in tribute to the officers. Cero, Estefan, and Jahor stood on the steps in front of the colonel, their hands clasped behind their backs. They smiled at the cheering crowd. The plan was working perfectly.

"These brave and trusted men are here to assist me in protecting this great wealth, and assure it is distributed to you who are worthy to receive it!" Alvaro Herrera smiled broadly as he spread his arms toward the crowd. The people cheered and danced together.

"Tonight! This very night, my officers and I will protect what you have brought to us. Tomorrow, we will discuss how we will provide for each of you that have done this great service! Bring your collections forward now!"

The cheering raged on as boxes and bags of cash, jewels, gold, and silver were carried forward. Cases of beer, wine and whisky were brought from one of the trucks and given to the celebrants. Music suddenly blared from the radio in one of the cars. Immediately, the radios in all the vehicles were tuned to the same popular station, turned to full volume, and filled the parking lot with music.

Alvaro Herrera bent forward and spoke privately to his officers. "Gather all the collection and place it in the four large yellow trucks. Then lock them, and place six armed guards around each one. I'll be in my office."

He stood, smiled and waved both arms to the scores of men and women celebrating in the parking lot. The smile disappeared as he turned and entered the station.

Frisco Armory, Dallas, TX – 10:20 PM CST

Jim Parker rested on his side. He was prevented from sleeping on his back by the shrapnel wounds in his rear end. He was prevented from sleeping altogether by the wounds. The other Marines prepared to get some sleep. Tomorrow would come soon enough. They all needed rest.

Parker volunteered for the first shift monitoring the ALI map downloads from Washington. He was fascinated by the congregating of the orange dots, interspersed with red, green, and purple dots.

The second download showed a separation of the orange dots from the others. The download also included a legend assigning nationalities to the different colors. The orange dots, those from Latin America, were housed separately from the men represented by the red, green, and purple dots.

Jim's thoughts focused on the separated dots. He decided they must go after the non-Latino invaders. War had been declared on the United States by terrorists in the Middle East in 1996. These were men from Iran, Saudi Arabia, and Egypt. They were the kingpins. Now, they would become the targets.

He marked the locations shown on the ALI maps. There were thirty-five groupings across the Dallas Metropolitan area. Jim Parker plotted a pre-dawn plan of attack. He wished he had another hundred soldiers to take into the fight.

chapter 35

Miller Farm Pasture, New Salisbury, KY - 11:50 PM EST

The group of snipers was the last to arrive at the extraction point. They huddled together comparing notes and confirming kills. They were confident they had eliminated the band of terrorists that burned the farmhouse. A reconnaissance team would return in the morning to confirm the events of the battle.

Now it was time to evacuate and return the Trapper family and Elli's parents to safety. However, the term *safety* had taken on a new meaning. In the minds of every man and woman in the pasture, *safe* was a relative term. A feeling of safety no longer applied to them.

Their land had been invaded. Their home destroyed. Their very lives threatened by an unknown force, for the most ridiculous of reasons. No one could put reason to the circumstance they had faced on this night. It was all too absurd.

Steve and Sam stood by and watched Mike and Elli tuck in their exhausted children. Grandma's blankets and comforters were nicely suited to the soft ground and tall grasses in the field. The children would wake up in the morning in their own beds. It would all seem like a dream. Perhaps more like a nightmare.

Steve helped Sam by unbuckling the exoskeleton suit where she couldn't reach. Sam would return the favor for him. But they both closely watched Mike and Elli. Children had been of little interest to either of them, until tonight. Something had changed. Without choosing or planning it, they both viewed the world around them differently than they had only a few days ago.

Words were not needed between them. Sam glanced at Steve. She caught his eye and smiled at his returned gaze. She blushed. This time, it didn't anger her. She wanted a family. She wanted Steve. And she was willing to take the risk.

The team leader of the snipers approached Steve and Sam. He spoke as he walked up to them. "You can stow those suits in the duffle bag over by the guys. Hang on to your weapons. We'll collect them when the chopper arrives." He looked at them both, nodded, glanced at Mike and Elli, and walked away. He could tell there was something distracting them. He knew exactly what it was.

Mike stood and walked to Sam and Steve. He loosened the strap around his collar and looked back at his wife and children on the comforters.

"Pretty cool, huh," Mike smiled, obviously pleased.

"Very cool, my friend," Steve responded. "Very cool."

Both men looked at Sam. Again, she blushed. Without a word she looked toward the group of snipers. She knew if she looked at Mike or Steve, she would cry. Her emotions were frayed and exhausted, and she didn't feel it would be cool for her to get all teary.

Sheriff's Office, Norman, OK - 10:55 PM CST

Robert pulled the truck into the space by his dad's cruiser. Yolanda awakened with the stop. She felt disoriented and groggy.

"Are we there?" she asked sleepily.

"Sure are," Robert answered. "Are you awake enough to get out of the truck?"

Yolanda stretched and groaned softly. Robert thought she was very cute, and chuckled at her.

"What are you laughing at?" she said whimsically. She tried to act offended, but her smile gave her away and she laughed.

They climbed out of the truck and walked arm-in-arm toward the front door. As they approached the door, Yolanda stiffened. Her last experience at a police station haunted her.

"It's okay. This is my dad's place," Robert said comfortingly.

She nodded, strengthened her hold around Robert's waist, and moved through the doorway.

"Robert! Good to see you again, son." Perry Hitchens stood from behind the reception desk with a broad grin on his face. He walked around front to greet Robert and his guest.

"Hey, dad." The two men embraced. "You remember Yolanda, don't you?"

"I surely do, I surely do," the sheriff replied. "How are you feeling, Ms. Vasquez?"

"I'm fine, thank you. But please, sheriff, call me Yolanda," she asked with a slight blush.

"That will never be a problem, Yolanda." Perry Hitchens never had a problem talking to a pretty girl. And since it seemed his son was interested in this particular pretty girl, he could see no problems whatsoever.

"Dad, there's something I'd like to talk to you about," Robert began glancing at Yolanda.

"I'm sure there is," Perry said. "Can it wait 'til we get to the house and find this lady a comfortable place to rest?"

"Sure, no reason to rush." Robert smiled and looked at the floor.

OCT, Little Rock, AK – 10:58 PM CST

Colonel Aaron Stevens tossed his clipboard onto his desk. Keith Dillon sat slouched in the chair across from him. Neither man realized how tired he was, at least not until they stopped a few minutes ago.

"Are the choppers there yet?" Keith asked.

"They will be in a couple of minutes," Aaron replied.

"Do you mind if I stay until we get the kids out of there?" Keith had been the one to discover the plot to bring harm to Mike Trapper's family. He discovered the terrorists' flight plan. He had organized the evacuation, and with a little help from the president, pulled it off with some pretty exciting technology.

Aaron and Keith had monitored the entire ordeal. They took pride in their watchful oversight, making sure everything was identified and accounted for.

"It's your life. Spend it as you will," Aaron replied nonchalantly. He scanned the report detailing the evening's action. His glasses were perched on the end of his nose, and he dangled a pencil as he perused the page. "So we got everybody to the extraction point, one wounded, not seriously, all civilians accounted for, and twenty-one KIAs."

"Twenty-two KIAs," Keith corrected.

"Says here we got twenty-one." Aaron looked at Keith. "I watched it on the infrared feed from the satellite. They died and cooled off. We counted and marked twenty-one."

"Yeah, but we counted twenty-two at the farm before the shooting." Keith sat up straight. "Aaron, there were twenty-two of them!"

The sense of victory vanished in an instant. Keith bolted from the office toward his workstation. The screen on his computer was black. He punched the keys to bring it to life.

"Come on, come on, come on!" The screen flashed as his desktop came up. Keith flipped through files until he found the infrared video of the terrorists unloading from the truck. The video seemed to drag in slow motion.

"There! They're all in the open." Keith paused the frame and counted each man, marking them with a pen on his screen.

"Aaron, there are twenty-two of them!" he yelled. "Definitely, twenty-two!"

Aaron was busy calling the number linked to Mike's helmet. There was no response.

"Did you get them?" Keith asked, running into Aaron's office.

"They all must have their helmets off. No one answers," he felt himself near panic. *How could we have missed that!*

"Call Elli's phone! She has her phone, right?" The sound in Keith's voice reflected Aaron's frantic sense something was going wrong.

"Yeah, right!" Aaron fumbled through the notes on his desk. *Seconds wasted!* he thought. "Here it is!"

Aaron grabbed his desk phone and dialed Elli's number. It rang. It rang a second time.

"Damn! What if she's too far out for any reception?" Aaron said, looking blankly at Keith.

* * * * *

Elli's phone ringing at almost midnight surprised her. *Who in the world would be calling me this time of night?* she thought. Her jeans were tight, too tight to pull her phone from her pocket while kneeling. She stood and forced her hand into the tight pocket.

"Hello?"

Suddenly, the shadows exploded with a dark shape of a man charging her. Elli screamed just as Yusef smashed into her at a full run, knocking her backward to the ground. He raised his knife and plunged it into her chest.

Mike spun, hearing Elli's scream. His reaction was instant. He watched Elli crash to the ground as the attacker stabbed her with his knife. Mike bolted. The exoskeleton suit he had just started to take off enhanced his every move.

He covered the twelve yards to Elli in three steps. The man straddling her raised his knife for a second blow. Mike got there first. The impact of his running as hard as he could, amplified by the suit, was similar to that of a small pickup truck on Yusef's body.

The crunch of the impact broke Yusef's ribs and forced jagged edges of bone into his lungs. The two men rolled in the grass, both regained their feet. Yusef struck at Mike with his knife, hitting him on the chest of his exoskeleton suit. The blade ricocheted off the hardened coils of the suit. Yusef was stunned. That pause of a fraction of a second was all Mike needed.

He grabbed Yusef's right arm, the hand with the knife, and forced it over his head. Turning sideways, Mike kicked down with his right foot on the outside of Yusef's right knee. Again, his fortified strength resulted in a bone crunching blow, shattering Yusef's knee, breaking the femur and sending the bone through the skin on his leg.

Mike spun the attacker by the arm, flipping him to crash on his back. The force of the spin wrenched Yusef's arm from its socket, tore the muscles from the bone and left his right arm useless, dangling by severely stretched tendons. Mike dropped on Yusef and crushed his face with a blow from his fist. The second impact of Mike's fist separated Yusef's jaw from his skull.

Elli! Mike spun to the still figure of his wife. Her shirt bore a dark stain on her chest. It was blood. He ran to her.

"Elli! Elli! Elli! Sweetheart, wake up!" Mike cried as he gently slid his arms beneath her limp body. *This can't be! This cannot happen! Wake up girl! Wake up!* Elli hung lifeless in Mike's arms. His mind was blank. He was numb. This could not happen.

Steve and Sam ran to Mike's side in stunned disbelief. Elli's parents knelt in shock, staring at the sight of their daughter's lifeless body.

Suddenly the cry of a small boy echoed across the field.

"Mommy!" Robbie shrieked in terror.

Elli jerked and gasped for breath. Her eyes fluttered as she regained consciousness. Yusef's tackle had knocked her out. His impact drove the wind from her lungs.

"Was that Robbie? Did I hear Robbie call me?" Her voice was raspy. She coughed. It was then she felt the knife wound in her shoulder. Yusef's blade entered her chest too high to hit her heart.

Mike was surrounded by medics begging him to let go of Elli. Finally, he could bring himself to lay her on the grass. He fell back, weak and exhausted. It was too much. Way too much.

He glanced at the man who attacked Elli. Yusef's body lay broken and twisted. Mike had nearly torn him apart. Their eyes met. Yusef's eyes glazed as life drained from him.

In the distance, four choppers made their approach to the extraction point. It was time for everyone to go home.

chapter 36

Miller Farm Pasture, New Salisbury, KY
Thursday, 12:00 AM EST

The wash of the props swirled the tall grass around the legs of the sniper team. The men stood separated from the family and the medics. Although the mission was a success, each man felt the failure to protect Elli Trapper from injury. They took it personally.

The large choppers settled into the grass and the pilots cut the engines. What was planned to be a quick extraction was now a medical evacuation. Two additional medics hopped from the first chopper and ran to where Elli lay. Their equipment and resources were more extensive than the fieldpacks carried by the sniper team medics.

Mike forced himself to stay away from the medics helping Elli. She was in good hands. He knelt with his children and Elli's parents. Baby Riley slept through the entire series of events. Jackson, Sara, and Robbie clung to their daddy as they watched the medics prepare Elli for transport.

Steve and Sam stood nearby. Sam leaned against Steve, unable to voice her feelings, unable to collect her thoughts, and certainly unable to make any sense of it all. She had always considered herself a tough woman. The toughness was gone. She felt drained.

Steve felt frustration in his inability to comfort or encourage his friend. He and Mike had lost men in battle, holding them in their arms as they died. Friends, brothers in arms, had suffered injury and loss and faced it with laughter and tears. That was expected in war. It is never expected at home.

Three members of the evacuation team jogged to Yusef's broken form. They quickly loaded the body into the large plastic bag and transferred the remains to the farthest chopper.

The medics slowly lifted Elli onto a stretcher, and carried her to the nearest helicopter. Mike stood as they passed. The team leader walked to his side.

"Mike, I am very sorry we missed that guy." Soldiers can cope with the risk they face, but find it painful when injury comes to those they seek to protect.

"No, hey, don't do that," Mike responded. "He beat us. He got here without being detected, but he didn't win. I was glad I could stop him."

"Still, man, we shouldn't have missed him. I'm very sorry." The team leader looked to the ground.

"Thanks." Marines don't often embrace. These two men did.

Mainside, Camp Pendleton, CA – 9:10 PM PST

Brigadier General Gene Westrup sat in his office behind his desk. The day had begun with an unsettled feeling in his gut. That feeling was gone, but an entirely new list of concerns flooded his mind.

After witnessing the event in the cell of the detainee, he was confident his team would acquire the necessary information. He was happy to let them. Whatever games needed to be played in the conscious and subconscious minds to the invaders was fine with him. The insurgents were responsible for the deaths of thousands.

They were animals that required extinction. He was pleased to assist in any way possible.

The general leaned back in his chair as he scanned the list of officers assigned to conduct the interrogations. He slowly turned to the window behind his desk overlooking the Camp. He was proud of the men and women in his command. He also understood that he was well behind the curve in understanding the procedures and techniques they would employ with the detainees. His time of service was coming to an end. Maybe when this was over he would have that talk with Marge.

Not only did Marge make great chili, she made a lot of sense. It was time he had a discussion with her. Gene stretched and stood. The Camp was quiet, but it was not at peace. The threat that brought bloodshed to the gates of Camp Pendleton was lurking somewhere in the night. He'd deal with that tomorrow.

Now, it was time for dinner and an evening with his oldest and best friend, his wife Marge. He put on his hat, walked out of the office, and headed home.

Holding Room 5, White House Basement – 12:15 PM EST

Rick continued the questioning of the old Egyptian. Each statement and question was designed to illicit a twitch of the eye, the corner of the mouth, or a mental response from Jalal Uddin. As hard as he tried to avoid it, reactions to the questions were inevitable.

Jalal Uddin remained speechless, yet a great deal was learned from him. The plan to assassinate the president of the United States had been initiated more than forty years before the actual event. Those who had devised the concept of placing entire armies within the borders of the country were long dead.

Children in the Middle East were hand selected by the designers. Jalal Uddin's father had been instrumental in arranging student exchange programs with the United States. American politicians were more than eager to welcome students and their families in exchange for a promise to continue oil exploration.

After World War II, many Arab and Persian families immigrated to the United States after the British established the nation of Israel and displaced thousands. Some immigrated for the opportunity they saw in America, others as part of a plan for revenge. They were patient and observant men. The grandfather of Al Makin was one of those patient men.

"Sir, does the name Abu Mahkin Mohammad bin Kareem bin Nidh'aal al Kahn mean anything to you?" Rick was very patient in his questioning. He maintained an even tone in his voice, kept direct eye contact, and remained stone-faced. The name of President Makin's grandfather, and Jalal Uddin's mentor caused a stir that registered on the monitoring instruments.

"This guy is a rock," Alex said through Rick's earpiece. "Not a single sign on the outside, but inside, man, he loved old Mohammad."

Rick repeated the name. It did the trick.

"Okay, Rick. Talk to him now." It was the voice of Don Stewart. The line of questioning had finally taken the former ambassador to the brink.

"Nahnu n'alamoo alkhatdah. Nahnu na'arifu kula shay," Rick bluffed in perfect Arabic. He repeated in English, "We know the plan. We know everything."

The old man's eyes welled up with tears. His head dropped to his chest, and his shoulders shook with silent sobs. For the first time, Rick felt compassion for the elderly man. The old warrior broke for he realized the work of three lifetimes, the entire plan, was exposed.

Miller Farm Pasture, New Salisbury, KY - 12:20 AM EST

Mike sat in the chopper with Elli. She was awake and sore. What hurt her the most was that she wouldn't tuck her children into their beds this night. Elli felt that the interruption of the routine was a greater injury than her wound.

The children sat with their grandparents a few feet away, strapped in and ready for take-off, too sleepy to make any sense of it all. The adventure-turned-terror left them confused and exhausted.

But they could see their mother smiling and talking to their dad. It was going to be okay.

The pilot poked his head into the cabin area and motioned to Mike. "Sir, we have Marine One inbound. You're probably gonna want to step out here."

Mike kissed Elli gently and climbed out of the chopper. Marine One was just settling into the tall grass a few yards away. He stood, his eyes squinting against the wind made by the spinning props. The door on the side of the chopper opened.

Breaking protocol, President Al Makin was the first man down the steps. He immediately saw Mike and jogged toward him.

"Mike, I just heard about Elli. How is she?" he yelled over the thunderous wash of the chopper's rotor.

"She's going to be fine. She's right in here." Mike indicated the chopper Elli was resting in. The president walked right past him and climbed into the helicopter. Mike followed him.

"Elli? Mrs. Trapper?" the president said as he knelt by the stretcher that held her. "Hi, I'm Al Makin."

Elli's face flushed with the surprise. "Mr. President, I—"

"I couldn't sleep, and I just couldn't sit around the White House waiting to hear the outcome on this one. Mike's too important to me. And you're obviously very important to him. How are you feeling, Elli?"

His concern was real.

"It only hurts when I laugh," Elli said smiling. "I guess I bounce back pretty quick." She paused. "I mean, well, Mr. President."

"I would suspect as much," he smiled at her and rose enough to seat himself on the bench opposite her. He placed his hand on Mike's shoulder to draw him closer. "Listen, I have something I want to discuss with the two of you. There is an opening in my personal staff that needs to be filled. I need someone I can count on, and someone who will speak honestly and directly to me. Mike, would you be willing to fill that role?"

"Uh . . . Mr. President, well . . ." Mike looked at Elli. She smiled at him with approval. "Does this mean I can go home at night?"

"Most of them," Al Makin answered grinning.

"Then, sir, I accept." The president grabbed his hand and shook it. "Thank you, Mr. President."

Al Makin felt a tugging on his jacket sleeve and turned. It was Jackson.

"Are you the real president?" he asked.

"Yes, son, I am," Al Makin replied.

Jackson stood at attention and saluted as best as an exhausted six-year-old could. The salute was returned by a man who was greatly humbled and very proud to serve his nation.

DRAGON'S BREATH

Book Three
The Oak Mountain Trilogy

Chapter 1

Clear Air Force Station, Alaska – Friday, 3:10 AM AST
64°17′19″N, 149°11′22″W

Marty Connors needed a smoke. His eyes were tired from staring at the monitors at his workstation, and scanning a distant horizon would ease the strain. He stepped out of the building and closed the door, leaving the noise and activity behind him. He lit a cigarette and inhaled deeply.

Outside it was still cold. Marty loved the cold. As a kid, he would run and play in the snow wearing only a light jacket. His mother scolded him that he would catch his death of pneumonia. But he never did. He was simply built for the cold.

Then, there was darkness. He was a night person. Marty found himself the most productive and active during the night. When all around him was quiet, he was amazed at what he accomplished. His mind was focused and creative when there was little to distract him. Sleeping all day created problems only for the people at the school he was supposed to attend. It had never bothered Marty.

The job at Clear AFS, Alaska, sounded to him like a dream come true. Alaska was cold most of the time, and never hot. It was also dark for a good part of the year. When the sun came up and stayed up for five months, he could pull the curtains. It would be great.

This particular night was both cold and dark. The frigid night air made his skin tingle. He felt refreshed, like jumping into a glacier-fed spring. It was exhilarating!

Marty took another drag on his cigarette and gazed across the tundra. The land stretched before him flat and desolate. It was a wilderness. He knew if he stood on that porch all night he would see very little wildlife, and not a single person. Perfection.

The buzzing was faint at first. He thought of the sound of lawnmowers on the next block when he was a kid in Illinois. But the buzzing grew louder . . . much louder. Something was coming at him, and it was coming fast. Marty turned around to look to the northwest wondering if he could see it.

The plane was the biggest he'd ever seen. It roared straight at him, barely one hundred feet from the ground. Marty stood transfixed, slack-jawed and awestruck. The giant black plane swooshed past him with a thunderous roar. The concussion of air and sound almost knocked him over.

He clung to the handrail with a white-knuckle grip as the giant apparition fled southward from his sight. To the east where the sky was slightly brighter he saw the silhouettes of at least a dozen more aircraft. Marty quickly spun to the west and could make out the same black shapes moving through the darkness.

What the hell! he thought. *What the blinkin' hell!* Marty tossed his half-smoked cigarette to the ground and threw the door open. He rushed inside to a room filled with radar technicians who seemed oblivious to what he had just observed.

"Hey!" he yelled into the room. "Did you guys see that?" Conversation came to a sudden halt and everyone looked at Marty. "Did you see that?" he asked again.

"Well, Marty, what is it that we were supposed to see?" Tim, his supervisor asked. Marty was white as a sheet, bug-eyed, and looked totally spooked.

"You didn't see it?" he was incredulous. "You didn't *hear* it?"

"No, Marty. You know that between the heating system, the insulation and the noise of the computers that we never hear outside noise."

"Guys, I just watched the biggest plane I have ever seen fly not more than one hundred feet directly over this station, going what had to be nearly three-hundred miles an hour, and you didn't pick it up on anything?"

"Marty, nothing has showed up on any of the radars." As supervisor, Tim had seen it before. The isolation, the extended darkness, the bitter cold, took a toll on a man. Sometimes they cracked. He feared Marty was falling apart.

"Wait!" Marty said putting his hands up as if to ward off the doubts of the people in the room. "Just wait! I just saw, and *heard*, a huge plane fly over, and all this fancy radar stuff didn't register a thing?"

"We did have that glitch a minute ago, chief." Penny stood and her workstation and came toward Tim and Marty.

"What do you mean 'glitch'?" Marty asked.

"Probably a sunrise anomaly we get now and then," Tim responded calmly. "You know about them, Marty. It looks like a crow flying a couple hundred miles-per-hour, and it turns out to be an echo from a satellite or the moon coming up."

"Okay, okay. Tell me then, was there more than one 'crow' flying over?" Marty asked looking a bit more wild-eyed.

"Yeah," Penny shrugged. "There were dozens. Why?"

"I'm telling you, they weren't *crows!*" Marty suddenly realized he sounded like a raving lunatic.

"Marty, just what are you telling us?" Tim asked putting his hand on Marty's shoulder.

"Tim, I'd take you outside and show you but they're too far away by now." Marty shook his head and swallowed hard. He turned and faced Tim square on. "Tim, an airplane just flew right over this building at close to three hundred miles per hour, not one hundred feet up. It was black, the wings had to stretch close to five hundred feet across, and the fuselage was like a long, square box. And on the underside of the wing—" Marty stopped and gasped. "Under the wing was a big gold star!"

Tim suddenly felt as crazy as Marty looked. He stumbled backward toward his desk and grabbed his phone. The numbers he punched in meant only one thing. DEFCON 2.

Lakeside, OR – 4:35 AM PST

His eyes simply refused to open. He wasn't sure if they were taped closed or if he had been drugged. The sounds around him were familiar but different from what he remembered before everything went black. His head felt horrible.

The first thing I need to do, he told himself, *is wake up.* But he didn't know where he was. He needed to know what had happened and why he couldn't remember anything. The pain in his head was blinding.

Maybe that's why my eyes won't open, he thought. *Maybe they've just given up on me, too.* But he still wasn't sure. He moved just a bit. His back disapproved. *What the he—*he thought. Everything hurt. *If I move again I'm gonna throw-up and die!*

He knew he couldn't stay, but wasn't sure why. He just knew he couldn't stay. They would be looking for him. He would have to be very careful because he knew they wouldn't approve. They would be on him like a duck on a June bug, and he was in no shape to deal with that.

Okay, just one eye. It was all he could manage. Through an excruciating process of incoherent thought, he selected his left eye. *Just a crack,* he thought. *Just enough to let a little light in.*

Then, he would know. It took all his effort and the small amount of concentration that was available. He forced it, and his left eyelid moved. The pain stabbed into his eye. The light was too bright.

Oh, don't do that again! He couldn't move enough to get away from the pain. His breath was shallow and labored. He clinched his teeth and the pain lessened. *Okay, I'll try it again,* he thought. *Just a little slower this time.*

Very slowly, he opened his left eye, just a little bit. Between his eyelids and lashes he could make out the pinewood slats on the ceiling. The blades of the ceiling fan turned slowly overhead.

Oh, good. I'm not dead. He let out a long breath and felt relief. He decided he would try both eyes, but very slowly. First, he had to make a decision. It was one he knew he put off too many times. And with the new laws, it was a risk. This time, he had to mean it. Reggie

Porter made up his mind. He would never drink that much rum in such a brief time ever again.

The new laws came with the invasion. All the bars were closed and their owners shot. Anyone caught drinking, or with alcoholic beverages was immediately shot. There were no questions asked. Drinking alcohol was no longer tolerated.

The churches were closed. No public assembly was allowed. Radio and television broadcasting was strictly controlled and only allowed during certain hours of the day. There was nothing on the broadcast that interested Americans, but TV sets were required to be on during broadcast hours. No exceptions.

Everyone worked their jobs, unless they were told to go home. No reason was given; people were simply told to stop working and leave. The few incidents that had occurred were convincing enough. Everyone learned quickly to go home.

Curfews were established. No one was allowed outside after dark or before dawn. Anyone caught out during curfew was shot. Several made the attempt and paid the price.

The world had changed, and no one in Lakeside, Oregon understood why. When the invaders had arrived and killed everyone in the sheriff and police departments, the television and radio broadcasts stopped. Phones stopped working, and cell phones and internet communications were a thing of the past.

The new local officials encouraged cooperation. There was no reason for anyone to be hurt or killed. Just mind your own business, they said. Leave well enough alone. In essence, shut-up and submit.

That was fine for the city officials, but several people around town resented the bars' being closed. A handful of homes held secret stashes of booze. Those who knew were the ones who cared, and they could keep a secret.

Reggie Porter found himself at risk of being caught. Not only was he too drunk to walk, he could barely open his eyes. Racked with pain, he considered staying right where he was and sleeping it off. He knew that wouldn't work. He'd stayed too late and drank too much. He needed to be home by sunrise.

With considerable effort and significant assistance from his partner in this drunken crime, Reggie made it out the side door of John Nelson's house. Now he was on his own.

His own home wasn't far, but Reggie felt he was taking two steps backward, or sideways for every three he went forward. He knew he was pathetic. He also knew if a patrol came by he would be finished.

He only had to make it through the town square, past the courthouse, and two blocks down North Lake Avenue to Sixth Street. Then he would be home free. He didn't remember walking ever being this difficult.

As he approached the courthouse, everything looked different. Of course, the lights were out. Street lights were no longer needed or allowed. Other than moonlight, it was dark. But it didn't look right.

As he walked, Reggie did his best to figure it out. The courthouse was there all right, but it was wavy. Then he saw the lines. He couldn't tell what they were. He got curious. Drunk and curious was a bad combination for Reggie Porter.

What the hell is that? The light was bad, he was drunk, and nothing made sense. As he looked at the line of objects, they seemed to be suspended in thin air. Every one of them hovered about head high. They didn't move. He could see beneath them, behind them, over and between each of them. But what the hell were they?

Reggie placed each of his feet firmly and deliberately on the ground, and set a course as straight as he could toward the floating objects. He didn't take his eyes off them.

"There," Reggie said out loud. "Shhhh!" he said holding his index finger to his pursed lips and quieting everything around him with his other hand.

"There. That one," he whispered. He selected one of the objects and pointed his finger so he would not lose it. He focused and plunged ahead.

He drew closer to the objects. They didn't move. They hung in the air motionless. Then suddenly he was close enough to see it.

"Oh, my God!" Reggie said in a full voice. "Oh, my *God!*" He walked directly up to the object. Reggie was no more than three inches from it.

Floating in midair, with nothing holding it up, just hanging there was the face of a man!

"Oh, my God!" he exclaimed a third time.

Suddenly the face looked back at him and spoke. "Good morning!" The face broke into a broad smile.

Reggie Porter's knees buckled and he collapsed, passing out and crumpling into a drunken heap.

Glossary of Terms

DHS First Response   An imaginary nationwide system that provides notification to the DHS that all systems and departments are operating at normally.

Automatic Location Identification -(ALI maps) Originally called *Enhanced 911*(E911), the system was designed to assist in processing 911 emergency calls. With the rapid expansion of cell pone usage, the FCC required in 1998 that all cell phones carry a unique identifier number that provided the phone's location to within one mile. The second phase of the program further enhanced the system's ability to pin a location within 100 meters. This system is referred to as the Automatic Location Identification, or ALI. The ability of the system to identify the precise location of all cell phones in a given region (the United States of America) is fictitious.

Junaid   Arabic word for young warrior.

Acoustic Phased Array-(APA) This is a real weapon that produces a massive shock wave of sound that temporarily renders a person unconscious. The system has never been used in the United States so as to not violate citizens' right of assembly.

Abrams tank   The M1A2 Abrams Main Battle Tank is the latest upgrade of the M1A1 deployed in 1988. It is armed with the M256 120-mm smooth-bore gun, two 7.62-mm machine guns, and a 12.7-mm machine gun mounted over the commander's hatch. There is nothing fictitious about this sixty-two ton behemoth.

F-22A Raptor   Single-seat, twin-engine stealth tactical fighter developed by Lockheed Martin for the US Air Force. Deployment was halted due to cost over-runs in 2009, but reinstated in 2014 to assist operations in Syria.

JDAM   Joint Direct Attack Munitions are unguided bombs with add-on all-weather avionics kits that allow them to fly to a specific target with great accuracy. The integrated inertial guidance system is coupled with a Global Positioning System (GPS) giving the bomb a fifteen mile range of precise strike capabilities.

MC-130W Hercules These planes have served more than sixty countries around the world as a military transport aircraft. The plane has been adapted in more that forty configurations providing a great diversity of support. The version used in the story, Combat Spear, is real. Several "kits" can be rolled into the rear of the plane to provide cargo and troop transport, medivac, airborne assault gunship, search and rescue, weather reconnaissance and many other tactical roles and special operations.

Ultra-Secret Deployment Systems (USDS) These deployment packs are very real and top secret. The unit described in the story is fictitious, although it may be assumed similar units exist. The jet pack wings are based on the carbon fiber wing developed by the Swiss pilot Yves Rossy in 2013.

Focuses Electro-magnetic Pulse Weapon This is a totally made-up weapon. It does not exist . . . I hope.

Infrared scan, Multi-launch, Precision Ordnance This is a mostly made-up weapons system. The only part that is real is the individually guided ordnance that performs like a mini-cruise missile.

Exoskeleton Suit and Helmet The helmet Mike wears in the story is based on the most advanced fighter pilot helmets used by the Air Force. Exoskeleton suits used in the story are fictitious but currently being considered for deployment by the military.